ALSO BY ALEXANDER H. ROSENBERG

THE FIRST RIDE, A MEMOIR

FAT KILLER
AND
THE POMERANIANS

A NOVEL
ALEXANDER H. ROSENBERG

SWITCHMAN PRESS
Los Angeles

FAT KILLER
AND
THE POMERANIANS

"Give a man a mask, and he will show you his true face."
- Oscar Wilde

1

Moscow, Russia

Nobody **expects their** plumber to carry revolvers in his toolbox.

Ivan rang the doorbell and stared into the glass eye of the surveillance camera: The guards should recognize the old coat covered in oily spots, the well-worn Ascot cap, and the thick glasses. But no one else will.

A click, and then the steel door opened. Vasya, a tall bodyguard with a buzz cut, waited on the other side.

"What took you so long?" Vasya said. "You were supposed to be here at noon." He moved aside.

Ivan stepped into a long hall. "Clogged toilet. Same building as this one, seventy year old plumbing."

The guard crinkled his nose and sniffed the air. "I don't smell anything."

Ivan brushed the front of his soiled coat. "I cleaned up. I know your boss is a sensitive man."

The guard let out a chuckle. "That he is. He's here, by the way. So try not to make any noise." He looked at Ivan's toolbox without interest and nodded toward the end of the hall. "You know where the bathroom is."

"Vasya, wait. I need to see your boss before I install it."

"Why?" The guard's smile faded. "You brought the same faucet, yes?"

Ivan held up his toolbox and pointed at it in an apologetic gesture. "They don't make the same one anymore. I brought what they sell as the replacement. Same gold plating on the spout. But they make the handles out of porcelain now."

The guard scratched the back of his head. "Blyat. He has to see it before you put it in." He waved. "Come with me. Don't touch anything." He led Ivan past the kitchen and bathroom doors decorated with frosted glass.

1

Ivan scanned the apartment as he followed. Should be three people: two guards and the boss. No one else on the feed from the camera. The bodyguards—it would be nice to have them grouped.

Vasya, wearing socks, walked without noise. Ivan let his boots make a heavy thud on the parquet with every step.

"You are big for a plumber," Vasya said. "You should play center-back for Spartak."

"Did you watch the game on Sunday? I can't believe it came down to penalties."

"There was snow on that pitch. How can anyone play football well in the snow?"

Ivan grunted in agreement.

They entered the bedroom and approached a doorway into an office added during renovations. Vasya stopped and raised his hand. "Wait here." He slipped into the office, leaving the door ajar.

Ivan surveyed the room around him through his thick-rimmed glasses. Tall mirrors on each wall reflected the bed from different angles. Gray daylight filtered in through the curtained windows and fell on the floor in a large square.

He put the toolbox down, kneeled in front of it, and snapped off the clasps. Good setup here. Easy access to revolvers. Stechkin—what a great weapons designer. No need for suppressors with these guns. Pleasure to shoot with the customized triggers—and almost no muzzle jump with the specialty rounds fired from the bottom chambers of the cylinder.

From the office came Popov's shrill voice. The longtime member of Russian parliament sounded aggravated while his guard offered apologies. A phone rang, and a second later Popov barked, "What?" but went on to speak in a softer voice.

The door swung out wide, and Vasya emerged from the office followed by his counterpart—Alexey, was it?—who wore a leather jacket.

"Listen, master," Vasya said as he stepped into the bedroom, "he says if the plating on the faucet is different—"

Here they are. Two guards and the boss on the phone, distracted. Everyone here together.

Ivan flipped the toolbox open, put both hands inside, and produced the OTS-38 revolvers. A pair of red dots danced on the men's chests as he took aim.

Vasya's eyes grew large with astonishment.

Ivan fired both guns, their trigger actions quick and smooth

2

despite his thick gloves. The shots made as much noise as a book falling flat on the floor.

Vasya's head jerked back when a bullet made its entry just below his hairline. Blood spray hit Alexey's face, but that was the least of the man's problems; Alexey's wide torso made for a perfect target.

The recoil pushed into Ivan's wrists as he fired two shots at the second guard's chest.

Just outside the aorta. Quick succession. Good execution—the body falling backward, behind the bed. No, wait—scrambling? Why was he still moving?

Ivan stepped forward to gain a line of sight on the remaining guard, whom he found crab-crawling toward the office door, way too quick for someone who just took two to the chest.

Small caliber not getting through. Armored vest under the jacket?

The guard whipped out a pistol of his own and fired without taking time to aim.

Ivan lunged left. A mirror on his right shattered, covering the floor in shards of glass. He advanced in a zigzag pattern, shooting, aiming for the head.

But Alexey wasn't waiting for more bullets to arrive. He fired another wild shot from the supine position and kicked something on the wall near the doorway. The doorjamb exploded off the frame. A sliding door emerged from its hidden compartment and slammed into the opposite side with a thud. The new barrier caught the last shot meant for the guard's forehead.

Ivan came closer. The bullet barely dented the thick steel. He put his ear to the door: voices on the other side—Popov and his guard in panicked conversation. Will they call the police or run? If they run, they'll have multiple routes of escape through the balcony connecting to the other apartments.

Ivan inspected the doorframe. Flush with the wall. Strong. Zero chance of direct pursuit. Better find a new approach. Go to contingency.

Irritation tightened his chest; contingency plans often invited chaos.

He ran his fingers over the steel frame. No way to breach this without explosives. No SEMTEX putty in the kit. The job was supposed to be fairly straightforward, no fireworks. The blueprints from the renovation had shown no signs of a panic room.

He shook his head at the oversight and noted the time on his wristwatch: an armed response team from the local station would be on their way if Popov had triggered the alarm. Last time the alarm went off 'by mistake', the response took seventeen minutes.

Their muted voices barely came through the thick door. Still arguing. Were they deciding to stay?

Ivan picked an empty glass from the bedside table, returned to the door, and put the glass against the surface, his ear on the bottom. A couple of exclamations, receding in volume. So, they chose to run instead of waiting for the cops. Bad choice but understandable. When faced with armed assault, most people either freeze up or flee.

He put the glass back on the bedside table. A bit of luck, with Popov running. Would have been hard to reach him inside the panic room without SEMTEX.

Ivan snapped two clips off the holder on his belt and reloaded the revolvers. The younger guard, Alexey—he did well, the way he retreated into the safe room under fire. Calm man. Good judgment. Means he wouldn't return to the Mercedes—he would judge it compromised. They would either stay in the building or use some other vehicle.

Ivan stood still and listened. No more sounds from the panic room. Probably climbing from one balcony to another. The building wrapped around a square yard with exits on all sides. No way of telling which apartment they would use to reenter. No way of telling from which side of the building they would exit.

He turned from the door, bitterness seeping into his thoughts. First the guard's vest. Then the panic room. Too many surprises. And now the indoor job escalated to street scenarios.

Street—it was important to cover all sides of the building.

He picked up his toolbox and left the apartment, locking the front door on his way out to give the response team a pause.

A sprint up two flights of stairs brought him to the top floor. In under half a minute, he'd climbed an access ladder to the building's attic, squeezed his large frame through a dormer window, and walked up to the ridge of the roof, careful to avoid melting snow. There he squatted, closed his eyes, and listened to the sounds of the big city.

The wait didn't last. From amidst the hum of distant traffic came the bang of the hallway door down in the yard, and a minute later the sound of an engine starting in the street. The engine sound grew louder and entered the yard.

With small, sure steps, Ivan descended to the ledge and looked down. For an obese man, Popov was making an impressive dash for a dark blue Lada. The car took off before Popov could close his door.

4

Ivan clenched his teeth. Target out in the open—a complication Partorg wouldn't like, guaranteed. But no other option now, short of waiting. And the boss had said, 'no more waiting.'

Back in the attic, the doves burst off the rafters, spooked by movement. Ivan stopped to take a slow breath.

Do not rush. Be deliberate. Calculate.

He shoved the revolvers deep into his coat pockets and pushed his toolbox under the pile of old floorboards—no prints on the tools. On the way down, he took a few seconds to lock the padlock guarding the attic access. There was plenty of time left to ride the slow elevator downstairs.

From the landing, he jogged across the yard to a rusty sedan parked a block away. But he didn't launch a car chase; the contingency plan didn't require it. Instead, he drove at a moderate speed for several blocks, until a narrow alley brought him near the circular avenue of Sadovoe Koltso.

He parked the junker, stepped out, and raised the collar of his coat before heading for Sadovoe at a brisk pace. Reaching the avenue, he made a right turn along the building to follow the flow of traffic. There were multiple lanes going in both directions, the old city's artery swollen with vehicles. Popov's guard would go clockwise here. No other choice.

Biting wind cut through wide sidewalk, through pedestrians in winter coats who turned their faces sideways. More wet than cold.

Ivan eyed the span of ten traffic lanes to his left with mild satisfaction. Nice to see the earlier calculation proven correct—perfect time of the day for the job, with cars in every lane crawling at pedestrian speeds.

Scanning the cars, he weaved his way through pedestrians until he spotted the dark blue Lada wedged in a middle lane between a bus and three other cars.

Without making any attempt to approach, Ivan walked in pace with the car until an 'M' sign for a subway station caught his eye. Only then, hands in his coat pockets, did he dive into the spasmodic traffic to catch up with the Lada. He bowed toward other car windows as he walked; to the drivers, he would appear as a beggar, panhandling.

Coming closer, he didn't crouch or otherwise try to hide his approach—the sedan was wedged so tightly between two other vehicles that its doors wouldn't open wide enough to let them out.

No dash cam in the car behind.

Ivan came in from the driver's side and leaned against the Lada's window.

No need to pull the revolver out. Close enough to fire through the coat.

He shot the guard in the head through the glass. This time, the blood spray painted the lawmaker's face; Popov's little eyes bulged in horror, his mouth moving.

Begging for his life?

A shot to the chest jerked Popov's rotund body and pinned him to the seat. Ivan came around the car and leaned against the window a second time, looking inside for better aim. A control shot ripped through Popov's temple and jerked his bald head sideways. Pieces of bone and brain matter sprayed the tan interior with clots of crimson.

A fresh coat of paint. An assurance the Russian parliament would have a new serving member.

Before walking away, Ivan gave the dead guard a quick nod of respect—the man did a better job than most, his hand on the handle of a Makarov in its armpit holster. Probably another veteran. Too bad his pig of a boss wasn't worth dying for.

The car behind honked. Ivan slouched and walked to the right, to the sidewalk. Unaware of the shooting, the Muscovites trudged through slush and sleet. Nobody looked or shouted or pointed at the Lada in the middle lane. The engine roar of the nearby bus had drowned out the already quiet shots.

Ivan hurried past a few people and slowed behind a young couple, the girl's golden hair spilling over her shoulders. He pulled his hat lower over his glasses. A clean getaway would be nice. A shootout with a random police patrol would turn this already messy job into a disaster.

The sidewalk crowd thickened, streaming toward the subway entrance. Easy to blend in if you keep your gaze low. Ivan looked up to search for uniforms, for one or two patrolmen always posted near the station doors.

A young one stood with his hands inside his coat pockets, looking bored. Ivan hunched behind the pretty girl in front of him, her perfume filling his nostrils with jasmine.

Look at the girl, tovarish. The girl.

The patrolman ogled the girl's long legs. Ivan pushed through the doors, unnoticed.

The escalator descended into the tunnel. On his way down, Ivan licked his lips. Years of work and the mouth still dry from adrenaline. A lot like skydiving—you get used to it, but your pulse still goes up before you step out of the plane.

He took off his hat and glasses and shoved them into his pocket before hopping off the folding steps. Nowhere to dispose of the disguise here. No trash bins inside the subway. Should thank the Chechens for that—they're still looking to even the score after the war by blowing things up.

Another patrolman at the opposite side of the platform was saying something into his radio, his face tense—the alert must have gone out. But the next train was already roaring into the station, a push of wind preceding its arrival.

The crowd pushed in, jostling for available seats. Ivan slipped inside, and the doors closed behind him with a bang. By the time the patrolman crossed the platform lengthwise to the escalator, the train was already rolling into a tunnel. The patrolman's figure, his radio at the mouth, flew by as the train sped away.

Ivan relaxed his grip on the handrail. Rush hour train to the rescue, as expected. Time to review every step of the proceedings.

He peered past the glass, into the darkness, and visualized the moment the guard opened the door to Popov's hallway. Trusty plumber, so nobody cared to check the toolbox. No shooting at the door. Smooth entrance. Bodyguards emerging from the office. The first shooting. The cleanup. The chase. The second shooting. The sidewalk. The station entrance. The jasmine perfume on the pretty girl. A nervous patrolman running toward the escalator with a radio at his mouth.

The playback showed no major mistakes in any of the snapshots no matter how many times Ivan rolled the record back and forth in his mind. The target was no more, but that offered little satisfaction. This job didn't even come close to well-executed.

He blinked as apprehension stirred in his gut like indigestion from undercooked food. Remorse? No, this wasn't remorse—the fat pedophile deserved a bullet, and his guards knew what they were signing up for when they took the job. There was something else.

Brightly lit stations alternated with pitch-black tunnel as the train moved further away from the city center. Ivan's mouth stayed dry. His old survival instinct, sharpened by years of risk, was still ringing the alarm.

With every passing station the crowd of passengers thinned out. A seat freed up, but Ivan stood still, staring straight ahead, examining the mental slides, going over every step of the operation.

No, not the panic room. Something else. The armored vest? No.

The investigation? No. Even if Popov had made a call about his plumber, it would lead to a false name. And they would never find the camera in the ceiling.

Ivan dove back into his memory, but none of the images, neither from the apartment nor from the street, offered any explanation for his unease. The job ended with a clean exit, but his palms were still moist, his body reacting to a subconscious clue.

At the last station on the line, everyone spilled out of the half-empty train. A talkative woman at a small market by the exit sold him a stylish trench coat. Ivan packed his old one into a shopping bag. Without the glasses and hat, he exited the subway in full view of an overhead surveillance camera—a respectable, middle-aged businessman instead of a plumber.

From the station exit, he traversed the sidewalk of a busy street that cut between blocks of flats twenty stories tall, each block exactly the same as the other. Melting ice, yellow from fresh salt, revealed black asphalt. The sidewalk led to a standalone office building with a large antenna on its flat roof.

The industrial look produced in Ivan a comfortable feeling of familiarity and helped reenter his usual role of a legitimate businessman running a legitimate company. He breathed in the crisp air, anticipating the opportunity to relax and not worry about bodyguards returning fire.

But the moment he stepped onto the office floor covered with desks, Volodya spotted him from behind one of the computer monitors and ran up with a worried expression on his youthful face.

"Ivan Denisovich, I just got a call from our customs man at St. Petersburg terminal. He says he can't clear the last Seoul shipment."

"Why not?" The words came out rough. No refuge, even here in the office. Business trouble on top of everything else. The tension never let up.

"It's not us. It's the shipping company."

Ivan checked himself with a nod: don't snap at him. These people deserved at least impartiality, not rudeness. "Let's go to my office."

In the anteroom, Irina was smiling and waving. Such a nice girl—hard not to smile back.

Ivan pushed open the door to his office, the largest enclosed space on the floor, and waved for Volodya to follow.

The youngster couldn't wait to spill the trouble. "Zamyatin says Maersk split the containers. They're missing one and can't clear the rest without it. It's going to cost us a fortune in fees if they hold the shipment until the missing container arrives."

Ivan frowned and came around his desk. Trouble all over the place. The top desk drawer was slightly open, and he slammed it shut. "What do you think went wrong?"

"I—I'm not sure."

Ivan measured the youngster with a look. Still new. Assigned to work with customs a few months ago. Young and indecisive, standing here scratching the back of his head with a guilty smile.

"Thoughts?"

Volodya hesitated. "I've been calling customs, but Zamyatin's not taking the calls anymore. I know I messed up somewhere, but I'm not sure where."

Ivan stretched his arms out in front to release tension in his shoulders; his knuckles cracked as he flexed the interlocked fingers. Stretching was good. Helped with stress. No wonder Lena kept talking about yoga. The gym was more exciting, though. Weights. Wrestling and SAMBO—plenty of stretching in both.

The soft leather of the chair hugged his shoulders when he settled back. "You're looking at this all wrong, fixing the consequences when you should be fixing the original problem. Find out what started all of this. Understand? Go to the source of the issue."

Volodya's eyes widened. "I should be talking to Maersk. And the Koreans. They're the ones who parted the shipment."

"Exactly."

"Sorry to bother you with this, Ivan Denisovich."

"No bother." It was hard to smile, but the young man needed encouragement. "Go sort it out."

Volodya closed the door carefully behind him. The youngster had good reasons to worry: the missing container was worth more than he would make in a lifetime.

Ivan pressed a button on a desk phone. "Irina? You there?"

"I'm here. I've got some invoices for you to sign."

He held the button. Such a lovely voice. Trained singer, but art didn't pay. Pity—she had real talent. And everyone thought she got hired for the looks.

He said, "No invoices today. I'm going to take off soon. Make sure no one comes through my door until I leave."

"I'll keep them off, Ivan Denisovich. It's been quiet here anyway."

His desktop computer came alive after a single stab at the keyboard. A crime blog already posted a short report: two men shot dead in the middle of traffic, more details to follow. Ivan browsed several other pages, but nobody offered anything beyond the general description of the car with two bodies inside.

His chair creaked as he sat back and wrapped his hands around his abdomen. Heavy unease churned and stirred and threatened, despite the quiet comfort of the office.

Clean the revolvers. Clear the mind.

He got up to lock the door then returned to his desk to spread out the cleaning kit. The routine of stripping and cleaning the guns never failed to calm his nerves. He eyed with pleasure the organized arrangement of the tools lined on the table: the brushes and the oil—the repetitive steps would give a reprieve.

The gentle hum coming from behind his office door accompanied the cleaning job, three dozens of his employees selling and shipping electronics, typing and making calls.

Lucky people. They could share their worries with anyone. Unthinkable—to go fifteen years without confiding in another human being.

Ivan was running a brush though slots in the revolver drums when his cell phone played an old song about roses—a cheerful soundtrack from a Soviet era movie.

Lena. She thought using this tune as a ringer for her was romantic.

She sounded upbeat. "How is everything? Your dog has been restless all day. So I'm thinking either you have been in some kind of trouble, or he's smelling the chicken."

Ivan chuckled. "He's smelling the chicken. Are you roasting it or frying it?"

"If you wanted me to fry it, you should have called and told me so."

A reprimand. All playful pretense. Probably wanted a quick call during the day. "No, no," he said. "I like it when you roast it." He paused, remembering the last time she roasted a bird. "Don't forget to rub it with garlic. Garlic is key."

"Hmm. You sound tired. Are you tired?"

He sighed. "Today's been crazy. Maersk split the shipment and we can't clear it. Always something. Otherwise, I'd be home already."

The lie sounded indistinguishable from the truth. Always easy when it's not a lie but a half-truth. Mix the lie and the truth together, and nobody knows any better.

But she almost caught the lie by picking up on his anxiety. "You shouldn't run everything by yourself. Why not promote Alexei to Director? You always say he is your smartest man. And now the food's going to be cold by the time you get here."

"I'm about to leave." He heard Bond bark in the background.

Lena giggled. "You know, sometimes I think he understands everything we say."

"That's why I named him Bond. What good is he as a spy if he can't tell what we're talking about?"

She laughed.

After disconnecting, he hid the revolvers in a safe under a square section of the parquet. Logic demanded that his bosses would want him to lay low for a good couple of months.

With a grunt, he pushed the safe back into place. Hard to believe the logic with your gut churning like this.

Downstairs in the parking lot, Ivan climbed into his car and took a deep breath. A familiar feeling, this one. Makes the hair on the back of your neck stand up. The same feeling like in Afghanistan. Just before the explosion. Just before the thunder and the blast wave. Before flying face forward into the dirt.

On the way home, he slid his favorite CD into the player. The voice of the opera singer, Bocelli, pulsed through the car. At an intersection, people hurried across the street, caught in the beams of his headlights, their outlines stark against the early winter darkness.

He punched the button to turn off the music. Bocelli. Favorite voice for so many years, now irritating.

He drove the rest of the way in silence, hoping that his instincts were wrong.

2

Matehuala, Mexico

Half the buildings on the narrow street looked like they were still under construction, some with rebar sticking up from the unfinished walls. But this one, painted ochre, stood out with its clean adobe style.

Go or no go? In a reflex action, Agent Robles put his hand on the back of his waistband. Of course, there was no pistol. Unarmed. Who the fuck goes to Mexico unarmed? Idiots, that's who.

For the second time, he read a sign painted in white above the entrance:

BAR MI LUGAR

Fucking cute. A bar name that rhymed. He mumbled, "Go time." But the words failed to encourage or excite.

Agent Garcia, tugging at the rusted bicycle chain as if to adjust it, said, "I got you covered."

"Uh-huh." Covered. Covered with what? Bicycle chain? One had to wonder if the narcos bought off the entire Mexican parliament wholesale. So convenient—just outlaw foreign agents carrying firearms and then pick them off at your leisure.

Robles clenched the straps of his backpack. A simple decision of going through a door was no longer simple, now that getting shot in the face on the other side was a real possibility.

He looked at Garcia sitting on the sidewalk, took a deep breath, and pushed through swinging doors.

Inside, the darkness struck him blind. If someone were to put a gun to his head right now and take the money, he wouldn't be able to give a description of the attacker during debrief.

Robles blinked a few times. Relax, he told himself, you're overreacting. Nothing but a simple pay-to-play operation. What had the Chief called it? Routine.

His eyes adjusted, and he scanned blue plastic chairs and tables in front of him in search of a man with a full beard—this would be an unusual sight in Mexico, an identifying feature in a country of smooth chins.

But the bar was empty. The barkeeper was in the back—moving boxes, by the sound of it.

Robles slid his sweaty hand into his trouser pocket and pulled out a cell phone to check the time: they were on schedule, half past one, sharp.

He took his backpack off and shoved it under the table furthest from the door. Here in the corner, he kept the backpack between his feet as he sat down. The man had said he'd come in through the back door behind the string curtain. La Barba. Funny name for an informant. But not so funny in an empty bar without even a pistol to cover your ass. A couple of trucks from the federal police to provide cover—that would be nice. 50 cal guns. Post one on every corner. But no. Chief Peterson had said, "Involving our Mexican partners would defeat the clandestine nature of the routine operation." Key word— clandestine. Safer to go in unarmed than let the Mexicans know what's up.

Robles wiped the sweat off his forehead. The oppressive heat wrapped him like a blanket soaked in perspiration and fear. Fuck their law. Should have brought pistols. Feds did it all the time. At least something.

The sharp smell of stale beer and urine hung thick in the balmy air. The bartender, a frail, old man with a dark face, came out from the back, wiping his hands on a soiled apron.

"Señor, que quieres?"

Shit. Drinking was against protocol. But it would look weird not to buy one.

Robles cleared his throat and pointed at a poster on the wall. "Pacífico."

Protocol my ass, he thought. In a bar, a man must have a drink.

He took a sip. Nice and cold. Condensation rolled off the bottle and formed a ring on the table as the minutes ticked by. The swinging doors at the front and the string curtain at the back didn't move.

Outside heat flowed into the dark space in waves, spread around by the blades of a ceiling fan black from grime. A fly buzzed through the silence and landed on the rim of Robles' bottle. Fieldwork, so exciting in theory, was a lot less fun in practice.

The bartender came by to collect empties. "Una mas?"

Sure.

Robles almost jumped at the sound of the string curtain rustling.

The man wore short sleeves with dress pants, glasses, and a hat—dark skin. Totally local except for the red beard. And quick, not wasting any time, sliding into a seat across the table. "Thank you for coming." Odd accent. Guttural. "We better make it quick. I have reason to believe they are watching me."

Reason to believe? Great English, for a foreigner.

Robles pushed his backpack under the table with his foot until it hit the man's shins. "We appreciate what you're doing for us."

"I am going to pull something from behind."

Better not be a gun. No, not a gun. Small book. Leather bound. How fucking old fashioned.

"Remember," the man said, head bowed as he looked over the rims of his sunglasses, "You cannot pursue this now. I will not work with you again if you do."

Robles nodded. "If your information is good, we don't need to hurry."

Half the man's mouth twisted up in a creepy smile. "Ah. It is good."

A ring from an old phone on the wall behind the bar upped the tension, La Barba pushing back and standing up, not even checking the money. Leaving without any goodbyes. Fast, through the curtains.

Robles pushed the notebook under his belt and almost took it out again. Back soaked with sweat. Better not ruin the contents after months of grooming this guy. Every gun buyer on the Gulf side. Every seller.

From outside came the roar of a revved engine and a squeal of tires.

The bartender hung up the phone without saying anything into it.

Garcia—was he still there? Robles glanced at the swinging doors. There would be noise if something happened. Without music, the bar had been dead quiet.

The old bartender limped from behind the bar, another bottle in his hand.

Robles stood up. His chair fell backward, and he failed to catch it, his fingers missing the plastic edge and clasping empty space. Fuck it. Never mind. "No, no. Gracias."

He threw a few bills on the table. Go, go, go.

Garcia was leaning with his back against the outside wall, his sombrero askew and something in his hand.

Robles squinted at his partner in the bright light: Garcia was watching the perimeter real well—the goddamn fool was texting.

"We're done. Let's go."

Garcia shoved his phone into his jeans. "What, already?"

"You're supposed to watch the fucking street and alley exit. C'mon." They hurried down the street, past cinder-block walls and gated entrances. "Whatever happened to covering my ass? This isn't fucking Cabo. You're not on a cruise."

"I look natural if I'm on the phone." Garcia's tone shifted to curiosity. "Are we all set? Did he give you the list?"

"Yeah, yeah. Hurry."

"What's the rush?"

"Something's off."

"Like what?" Mister fifty questions.

"Like—do you want to get shot? Feel free to stick around if you want to get shot."

They hurried down the street toward an intersection, and the whole time Robles looked for an SUV to jump at them, tires screeching, gunfire ripping through the mundane noise of the town.

Why did the barkeep get that call?

They crossed the street by diving into stopped traffic. Robles looked ahead, past a sign for a local bank—one more block, and they would reach their truck. The sooty exhaust from cars made his throat itch. He coughed up a slime ball and spat it out.

Garcia fell behind a step.

"Keep up. We're exposed here." The whole time, Robles fought the urge to break into a run—but that would draw attention. And so far, the drivers and a few pedestrians they passed didn't give them more than a look.

Their truck sat where they'd left it, in a parking lot behind the bank. Robles sucked in a long breath at the sight of it and said, " We made it." Here by the truck, with the two bank guards on the other side of the lot holding shotguns, everyone was more or less safe.

Robles opened the driver-side door and hopped in, digging his cell phone out of his pocket and tossing it on the dash.

The whole op looked so stupid now. No guns, no backup—it made sense in Dallas, not asking the Mexicans for help. Clandestine. The word just meant you ended up scared out of your fucking mind.

The truck engine rumbled to life, and Robles cranked the air conditioner. The book bit into his skin, pressed against the seat like this. Future Special Agent in Charge of the Division, getting soaked in butt sweat.

He stomped the pedal, and their truck shot out of the lot. Oncoming cars had to break hard, drivers laying into their horns.

Garcia pointed at the cell phone sliding across the dashboard and said, "We should call it in."

"Let's get out of this fucking town first. You don't know who's listening."

Silence hung around them. Narrow streets on the north side of town gave way to a wide expanse of desert, and Robles kicked the accelerator. The Suburban growled and sped up.

"Something freaked you out," Garcia said. "I can tell."

"The bartender got the phone call and my guy just fucking ran out."

"He has a reason to be nervous."

"So do we."

The monotone landscape of the desert around the highway was soothing to the eye. Home base, almost there. But a white sedan in front of them was slowing down. Robles caught up with it and swung left to see a long line of cars ahead.

"What is it now?" Garcia asked.

"Looks like the same federales roadblock we saw on the way in."

Robles swung the truck back into his lane. "They weren't stopping anyone on the way in."

The cars crawled toward two police trucks parked perpendicular to the highway. Cops in black armored vests were waving everyone through, looking into vehicles as they crept by.

A broad-shouldered cop wearing aviator glasses stood a car's length before the block, holding an "ALTO" sign.

Robles craned his neck to look over the sedan ahead of them, at the cars speeding off once they passed the blockade. One of them mobile blocks. Maybe something happened since they passed the same spot on the way into town—back then the highway was empty. Maybe that's what spooked La Barba. That phone call.

The cop stuck the sign out in front of their Suburban. Ignore him? What were they gonna do, shoot at a car with diplomatic plates? No way.

"They have a .50 cal on the turret," Garcia said.

"I'm not blind." Robles hit the brakes. A misunderstanding could be costly.

The cop, the one with the sign, pointed at the shoulder, at a spot in the dirt in front of a Nissan pickup.

"I don't like this," Garcia said, twisting in his seat to take a look at the cop. "We should call it in."

"That might provoke them." Robles pulled onto the shoulder. "They're probably curious. I mean, normally we'd give them the heads-up."

Robles turned off the engine, waiting for the cop to come over. But the cop seemed to lose all interest in the Suburban. He returned to the two police trucks, their hoods pointed at the highway; he waddled under the weight of his vest and a rifle slung across his chest.

Robles mumbled, "God, he must be hot under that vest."

The cop also wore a balaclava, under a helmet, in the boiling heat.

Robles fished a bottle of water from the back and drank greedily. He passed the bottle to Garcia. "Fucking dry out here."

Garcia leaned on the dashboard. "What are they doing?"

The cop had thrown the ALTO sign into the bed of the pickup and was now waving the other cars through; his taller partner was doing the same from the other side of the road. In a minute, only the two police trucks and the Suburban remained.

A gust of hot wind pushed a tumbleweed across the hardtop; it bounced off one of the police trucks. Annoying. The Suburban had diplomatic plates, for god's sake. The cop needed to ask his questions and get the fuck out of the way.

With astonishment, Robles watched both cops climb into the truck bed on the other side of the highway from the Suburban instead of walking up to him to check the papers.

"Where the fuck are they going?" Garcia said. "They stopped a diplomatic car for nothing?"

"First they flag us down and make us wait, and now they're leaving?"

"They're fucking with us 'cause we come from the other side of the border is what it is."

But the federales weren't leaving—their truck pulled alongside the Suburban on the left, dust flying from under its wheels as it came to a halt.

Garcia peered around Robles to get a better look. "Why are they—"

"Fuck!" Robles kicked the gas pedal, his eyes on the masked men in the truck bed, men in balaclavas lifting their rifles and taking aim. "Jesus! Move! Move!"

Fear galvanized his body. He slammed his foot repeatedly into the accelerator—but nothing happened.

Fucking amateur—turned the engine off after pulling over. The keys. Here. Start. Go. Go!

The engine groaned. The driver-side window exploded into his face. Shards of glass bit into his cheek and neck. With glass flying all around him, Robles snapped into gear.

Instead of reversing away from the truck blocking their way, the Suburban lunged forward—wrong gear, asshole!—and smashed into the side of the Nissan.

The airbags went off with a bang and burned his face. They deflated instantly. Glass or bullets or god-knows-what-else flew everywhere.

A woman was screaming "No! No! No!" in a piercing, staccato cry somewhere to his right. Robles flicked the car into reverse and realized the voice belonged to Garcia, who was screaming his lungs out, cowering in the front seat.

Glass shredded Robles from the left. He leaned away, looking to crawl over his incoherent partner. His seatbelt held him—he searched for the button. A tremendous punch, like a sledgehammer, hit him in his chest and threw him back, knocking out his breath.

He'd stopped thinking a while ago—he acted on reflex. He turned to look where the punch came from and another blow slammed into the side of his jaw.

Everything around him started to swim, and the noises grew distant, muffled as if someone had put headphones over his ears. He felt for his chin with his right hand, and his fingers grasped something warm and mushy that made him think of boiled spaghetti.

The screaming cut off, but Robles didn't care to check why—he was having too much trouble breathing. His lungs rattled as he tried to suck in air.

He was gasping when the driver-side door opened and a gun barrel popped in, followed by the gloved hand that yanked him out of the car. He fell sideways onto warm dirt.

There was ringing in his ears. He lay on his side and watched pairs of black boots stomp around and climb in and out of the Suburban . . . looking for something? They stepped over him as if he were a fallen tree.

Another truck pulled up, its wheels shiny with chrome. The whirring sound of the window rolling down attracted the black boots; they stepped closer to the shiny wheels.

The boots man said in Spanish, "Miguel, there's nothing in the car. No laptops, no papers. No money. Nothing. Did we make a mistake?"

From inside the truck came a thoughtful answer: "Check his body."

The boots came back and around Robles, and something tugged at his back. They were taking the list.

A moment later, this Miguel said from his car, "So, it's true. He sold them all of the buyers." He sounded mellow and a little surprised.

Robles coughed, his mind filled with alarm. Compromised. This whole operation was compromised.

The boots said, "He knows we'll look for him. He came here from Russia, didn't he? We don't know anyone in Russia."

Miguel kept silent for a moment in his truck, like he was considering the suggestion. "My man says he never goes there anymore."

Robles wondered why his throat was making this weird wheezing sound.

The black boots stood still. "Takes balls to sell us out. Why do you think he did it?"

"Can't be the money," Miguel said. "Gringos never pay well. Maybe he's buying his way into a better customer. Someone who wants Americans to go after us."

"Coño, that's clever. He'll be hiding."

"Of course he'll be hiding. He knows what I do to people who play games with me."

"He must hide well." The black boots turned. Robles looked up; a gloved hand waved at the shredded truck. "When gringos see this, they'll be looking everywhere for him, too."

For the first time, Miguel sounded irritated. "Don't be an idiot. They will be looking for us, not him. This is our territory." And after a pause: "Burn the car. Tell everyone to go to my house and stay there till I come back from the city."

The chrome wheels spun in the dirt, spraying pebbles all over agent Robles. An Escalade, Robles thought. Their fucking boss is riding in a fancy Cadillac Escalade like some gangster wannabe.

Robles was thirsty, like he could drink a swimming pool. A spasm shook his chest and belly, and he gurgled some blood. His headache disappeared.

A shadow of a bird flicked over him, but he didn't worry. He lay motionless, relaxed. He didn't care about vultures or being burned. He drew a strained breath and wondered why he couldn't smell the gasoline they were pouring two steps away.

3

Moscow, Russia

While **Lena made** breakfast, Ivan stared into the darkness outside their kitchen window while absently petting his dog. Always dark in the winter. Long months of little sunshine. Not even much of a winter: no ice on lakes and rivers. No ice and no sunshine—neither here nor there. But as much wind as you can take. February was always the worst.

Lena stood with her back to the TV where a weatherman was talking. She flipped a pancake over on the pan and echoed the weatherman's words. "The warm weather should continue. An unusual pattern."

It would be interesting to see what she'd say next. Cute—she still kept the habit of snatching random phrases from the broadcast. She always repeated it like it was a nice turn of phrase. Did all linguists do it? Something about studying languages made them like to play with words.

A commercial came on, and Lena said, "Girls kiss better than men."

Ivan chortled.

She turned from the stove in surprise—never aware of herself talking. "Why are you laughing?"

"Oh, you know, the stuff they say on TV."

She glanced at the screen and turned back to the pan, the broadcast turning to news. An overexcited correspondent announced they had a major breakthrough in the lawmaker Popov murder investigation, less than a day after the murder took place.

"Multiple witnesses," Lena muttered. "Daring crime."

Ivan stopped running his fingers through his German Shepherd's soft coat.

Bond, whose body grew stiff in response to his master's reaction, had sprung to all fours.

"Sit."

Bond sat back down under the pressure from the heavy hand.

Ivan reached for the remote, and the TV flickered off.

"Hey." Lena picked up a steel bowl and poured more pancake mix into the pan. "I'm watching that."

"Sorry." He dropped the remote to the floor and leaned forward to pick it up, moving slowly. Not slow enough for the news segment to end.

He pressed the power button, and the same correspondent filled the screen talking about Sadovoe.

"Brazen crime," Lena echoed. "In front of many."

"We have a photo," the correspondent said.

Ivan grabbed the edge of the table as if the floor gave in under his feet. At the sight of his figure, large on the screen, his insides grew cold—like drinking ice water in huge gulps.

There. That's why it all felt wrong. Major slip-up.

The nails-on-chalkboard voice of the correspondent was mind-piercing. "...looking for further evidence."

Every word from the TV ripped apart a carefully constructed life. Ivan shuddered. Say goodbye to your hopes for the future, he thought. Now Lena would know her husband was a slave. And a liar.

His heart pounded against the ribcage. No time to think of a plan, no good way to explain this. Distract her before another picture fills the screen, before another revealing close-up? And who the hell took the pictures? No dashboard cams behind Popov's car. The images had to come from somewhere else.

Ivan left his seat at the kitchen table, came up behind Lena, and wrapped his arms around her just right—his wide palms snuck under her gown and landed on top of her breasts. Warmth and love. About to be ruined.

She said with exaggerated scorn, "I can't make your pancakes when you hold me this way. If you keep this up, you'll go to work hungry."

He pressed himself into her back and kept his voice deep and low. "Maybe I'm in the mood for something other than your pancakes."

She turned her head. "Maybe you should have your breakfast first. And then we'll take care of your mood."

Drown out the news. He said into her ear, "Make sure you fry the edges crispy."

"I will if you stop fondling me."

Bond growled, and Ivan turned to look at the TV in time to see a picture of him leaning against the blue Lada, ready to shoot Mr. Popov and his bodyguard. Grainy picture. Face hidden behind the raised collar.

He closed his eyes, turned his head, and pressed his lips into her hair. Smell of home. Please, no video. Unrecognizable, in the pictures. But in the video, the body movement will give it up. The gait—she would recognize the way her boyfriend carried his large body.

Through panicked breathing, he kept his body relaxed, but his face stayed locked in a mask of rigid tension.

Relax your face, he thought. Breathe in her smell. Ignore the pictures on the screen.

The broadcast turned to the interview with a kid who'd snapped the shots from his seat on a bus. The TV shifted to a detective asking for help from the public, followed by a wide shot of the Sadovoe.

The bus—that's the mistake. Idiot. Should have waited for the bus to fall behind Popov's car.

The correspondent said, "This is the first time a witness using a cellphone managed to capture the ruthless killer in action, a political assassination."

Ivan nuzzled Lena's neck. His body responded to her sweetness, and her warm smell helped rein in the adrenaline.

There. Not so tense. Breathe.

The news anchor repeated a plea from the detective. "If you have any additional information..." The single picture from the camera phone was all they had. The voices changed to a female correspondent talking about the upcoming elections.

Ivan let go of her and went back to the kitchen table. She'd missed the broadcast, but there would be others. They'd keep a news segment like this in rotation for a while. And if she did see it—she often watched the news after he went to work—would she connect the blurry image of the suspect with her loving man?

Ivan sat and stared at the TV. Bond put his head on his lap, asking for a scratch behind the ear. Looking up with a question, the good dog. Smelling trouble.

Lena came over with a plate full of pancakes and added tea to his cup. Wisps of steam told him the tea was too hot to drink.

"What did they say about the murder?" she asked. "A politician?"

"Some guy from the Duma. They don't know the motive."

He stared into the cup between his hands. What did they have? Blurry images of a slouching large man in a workman coat, a hat, and glasses. But no video. Still a chance.

He took a cautious sip, gauging the temperature. The black tea didn't scold his lips, but its rich taste didn't satisfy. A major slip-up. Public exposure like this . . . the entire organization would watch the story. The boss himself would watch it, his trusty employee on the screen, his business a matter of public interest.

Partorg wasn't a forgiving man.

Ivan's face twitched when his cellphone buzzed on the table. Already?

Lena said, "They need you early today, huh?"

"It seems so," he said, reaching for the phone. The message read: Meet me for lunch.

So innocuous, at first glance. The owner calling his dog to heel. Everything happening too quickly. Like sailing a ship riddled with holes. Plug one, and another pops open.

"Do you have to run?" Lena came over and pushed a fresh pancake onto his plate.

He didn't answer right away, scrawling through the text messages, not really reading any. Tell her and run. If only she knew. Was it too late? Tell her to pack up a suitcase, to wait for the explanation, to trust until the dogs lost their trace. Drive to Ukraine. Everything still there. Start a new life.

He grumbled, "One of those troubles left from a previous day."

Running—stupid idea. Fedot wouldn't send the text message unless he'd seen the news. And he would run to his daddy to deliver the news the instant he saw the picture. Probably said, "See? I told you he lost it. He never had anything to teach me. Let's put down the old dog."

And what would Partorg say? He would get angry at the exposure. An ironic twist: the man owned the damn TV channel that just broadcast a report on the sloppy work of his old employee.

Ivan pushed away his phone. Hopeless. Whenever the big boss got upset, people died violent deaths. Impossible to run from him. Not with a woman in tow.

At the stove, Lena turned to the noise and studied his face. "What's wrong?"

He waved her question away. "Nothing. I might be going on another trip. I don't want to. I'd rather stay here and eat your pancakes." Good lie. But not good enough. She'd look for her man. Stubborn girl. She'd search and get in trouble.

Lena put the pan down on a trivet and stood in front of him, picking on the hem of her apron. "You're upset. I can see you don't want to go."

"I don't."

Her voice picked up some tension. "Why does it always have to be you? You own the company. Let other people do the traveling."

"No one's ready. There's too much money at stake." More lies. Disgusting.

"Money?" She shook her head. "How much money do you need to stop working yourself to death? We have more money than most. Who cares about money?"

"I don't trust anyone enough yet to send them."

"You don't trust anybody except your dog."

"I trust you."

She put her hands on her hips. "You have to learn to trust someone besides me and your dog."

This was going to be a long day. Or worse—a short day, in which case none of this mattered. He took a sip of tea, and she must have decided he was avoiding her question.

"One time your friend was too scared to help you, and you had to give up on everyone forever?"

The memory ripped open the old scars. "Too scared?" The worst morning in a long time, and now she brought up the war on top of everything else. His jaw muscles clenched so tight, he struggled to push the words through his teeth. "He wasn't too scared. He left me because I wasn't worth the risk." He dropped his cup on the table with a thud and shook his head. "I should have never told you. You don't know what you're talking about."

Her lips quivered like she was about to cry. "How can I know if you never want to talk about any of it?"

He stared at his hands. "It's better this way. If we don't talk."

Tears filled her eyes, making her blink, but she still managed to say, "Vanya, the war ended twenty years ago."

God. Talking about the war on the worst possible day to bring it up. He balled up his fists but drew a deep breath and dropped them open after meeting her gaze. "Zaichik. I promise you, I'll sell everything the first chance I get. The company, the warehouses. All of it. Just not now."

Her eyes grew wide. "You will?" She paused. "You know I'm just tired of being alone." She sounded conciliatory. "You always dream of leaving the city. We're not teenagers. It's time we start living our dreams. God knows we have enough money for that."

He sighed. If only she knew. "It's not the money. I have to finish things."

"Will we ever be able to leave?"

He nodded. "That's all I've been thinking about."

Just like that—an honest confession. Thank god she stopped crying. Clasping her hands. So hard when she cried.

He stood up and stepped closer to her, taking her hands in his. "Zaichik, believe me. From morning till night, all I think about is you and I leaving Moscow for good."

"You do?"

He wrapped his arms around her, her fists pushing against his chest. "I don't care about money. But I care about us."

He held her head gently, looked into her eyes, and pressed his lips hard to hers. Her fists unclenched, and she slid her hands up to his neck, kissing him back. Before she could protest, he scooped her up and carried her to the bedroom. Her apron and gown taken off, he laid her on the bed and kissed her and ran his tongue all over her until she pulled his body into hers.

It was like dying, like it was his last time—his last minute being alive, his last breath.

While they rested, she grew sleepy. Her smooth forehead, her half-closed eyes, her even breaths told him he'd succeeded in distracting her. And himself. At least for now.

He caressed her cheek. Her eyelids fluttered, and she opened her eyes, looked at him, and smiled. "God, you tore into me like a bear. I hope you saved some energy for tonight."

"Of course." He breathed in the smell of her hair, like on their first date when he took her to a ballet, at the Bolshoi. She had rested her head on his shoulder the way his wife used to. The scent of Lena, the gentle closeness—right there in the theatre, with the orchestra booming from the pit—that's when he felt it. A feeling of hope.

He kissed her head. "I'm sorry I snapped at you. I shouldn't have. I promise I'll watch myself."

"It's nothing." She looked up. "Aren't you late?"

She watched him dress and suggested a tie. Wearing a fresh shirt, he tied his shoelaces and straightened up only to find Lena still smiling at him, her small fist under her cheek. An impulse to climb under the covers with her made him step toward the bed.

Zaichik, he thought, you are my home.

"Go," she said. "Take the pancakes with you. The containers are in the dishwasher."

He leaned over to take her face in his hands then kissed her. The most delicious lips in the world. Before walking away, he pulled the covers up to her face to keep her warm. She giggled as she burrowed under.

In the elevator, he chambered a round into his pistol and thought: You are a delusional idiot. Creating a cover good enough to have a normal life? Trying to make money by building up a company? You would never make enough. Partorg wanted clean wet work, not a money maker.

He rolled his shoulders and cracked his neck to increase mobility. Dreams of the normal life. No chance if they'd already sent a team to put the old dog to sleep.

The floor numbers blinked on and off like years of life. Blinking too fast. One blink—the airborne division of the army, the first jump. Another blink—a kid takes a picture. The last one, and an ambulance is taking a body of the successful businessman from the garage to the morgue.

And for what? No satisfaction in any of this work, not for a long time. Used to be like stomping on a filthy cockroach. Crooks, pedophiles, thieves—Russia's new rich. Stomp. Stomp. Good feeling. Justice. Pedophiles like Popov. A lot like the mullahs in Afghanistan. The mullahs—they called their wives dirty. Unworthy. But liked raping young girls all the same. Bought them as wives. Traded cows or goats for them. Got the girls pregnant before going back to screwing boys. A harem of boys to satisfy their holy urges.

Popov had a harem too, the fat pig. Favor to humanity, a bullet to his head.

The last button blinked then went dark. Ivan covered the pistol with the flap of his long coat and stepped out of the elevator. The car sat on the far side of the garage by the wall. The concrete columns made for good cover, but if they came, they'd come with rifles and armored vests.

Useless, putting up a fight in here. Would be real short.

Ivan walked into the open and let his heavy steps echo off concrete walls, betraying his exact location. He stiffened as he neared the open space of the turn. Here. They'd be waiting here, a few shooters springing from behind parked vehicles.

Fedot, you ugly bastard. Come out. I'll take you with me, he thought. It would make the dying easier.

But the garage stayed quiet, and he made it to the car. He checked the back seat then got in.

He waited, fighting the instinct to speed off. No team here. Fifteen years of impeccable work should buy some leeway. You don't fire a good worker for one mistake if you're a good manager.

He started the engine. Still no shooters. Lunch, then. Hope, maybe. A stop by the office for the DVDs from Popov's bedroom. They'd want the DVDs. Leak the filth to the media. Make the world care a lot less about Popov. Maybe once the truth about him hit the news, the world would appreciate the work of his assassin a little more.

Damage control. The Organization was great at damage control.

Out on the street, tires split slush from snow that had fallen overnight. Cars barely moved in each lane, but under the circumstances, traffic didn't matter.

He signaled and merged into a slower lane. When lunch could end with your brain splattered all over the tablecloth, you don't hurry. You go ahead and allow yourself a few small luxuries.

He exited the boulevard and parked in front of a tobacco kiosk where an old man with yellow teeth sold the packs of Stuardessa cigarettes. Blue and white pack. Golden bird on the front. Father's favorite.

Back in the car, the warmth of the first inhalation spread into his arms and legs. His fingers tingled.

Sorry, Zaichik. Forgive me for breaking my promise to quit.

He'd gotten through half a pack by the time he parked in a lot in front of the restaurant in Solnzevo, his car the last in the row of familiar Mercedes S600 sedans.

Stepping into the slush, he grimaced at the lineup. Brothers in arms. All drove a bulky bathtub with the right logo on the grille. Symbols of success for the special few.

But all of the registration plates were local—a good sign. If the big boss had gotten angry enough to off his most experienced shooter, he would have brought in an outside team from Kazan or even Dagestan.

Ivan yanked the restaurant's heavy door open. Warm air and music spilled out like steam from a sauna. A long bar led all the way to a back room separated from the rest of the restaurant by curtains made of burgundy velvet.

Behind the curtains, a table covered in meat dishes and salads dissected the space. Bottles of wine and vodka stood guard above food. On each side of the table sat large men, most of them dressed in leather jackets, most of them with golden chains on their thick necks. Cigarette smoke drifted above their heads.

Colleagues in their business suits.

None of them mattered except for the one at the head of the

table: the black–haired, skinny twerp with a thin, handsome face ruined by a scar. Ivan eyed the ugly smile with revulsion. As always, the instinctual urge to rip out the twerp's throat made it hard to stay calm.

"Oh, look, it's our TV star," Fedot shouted over the music.

Nobody laughed.

Ivan slipped a hand into his coat pocket and found the pack. Still a few cigarettes left—the highlight of the day at this point.

Fedot raised his hand and flexed his index finger in a lazy fashion to beckon the new arrival. Always acting like a royal, the twerp.

Ivan rounded the table and sidled past the backs of four other foot soldiers, each in a varying state of inebriation. The music—the prison-themed lyrics put to pop—grew so loud, he had to lean in to hear what Fedot had to say.

"Wait for me at the bar," Fedot said. "I'll talk to you when I'm done here." He picked up a shot glass and tossed its contents into his mouth. His Adam's apple bobbed up and down, inviting a couple of strong fingers to catch the lump between the thumb and a knuckle and crush it like a rotten walnut.

Ivan pushed his hands deep into his pockets and went out the way he came. Working with Fedot . . . punishment for every mistake, every transgression, every crime. A deal with his father was a deal with the devil. Should have turned the deal down and stayed in prison. Deserved the twenty anyway.

The gangly bartender offered him a laminated menu without saying a word. Ivan nodded. Not the kind of place where patrons talked much to the staff. A long list of food, but Fedot liked to make people wait, to humiliate them. May just as well eat. Breakfast wasn't much of a breakfast.

He picked pelmenys with sour cream, the restaurant's best dish. His heart tightened: Lena's pancakes tasted great with sour cream.

All the TV sets on the back wall were showing hockey, with one screen broadcasting a football match taking place in Mexico.

The bartender brought a steaming plate over and put it down. "Anything else?"

"Tea." When the bartender came back with a cup, Ivan stuck his fork at the TV screen. "What do you think the winter's like out there?"

The bartender shrugged. "Warm, by the looks of it." He pulled out his cell phone and walked off, typing.

A beer commercial came on. It looked enticing: palm tree fronds over white sand, a cold beer bottle sticking out, dew droplets rolling off. Mexico seemed like a nice country.

Fedot took his time, and when he came, he nodded at the screen. "You know, I was glad to see you on TV this morning." He straddled a bar stool, a beer glass in his hand, alcohol on his breath.

A mean type of drunk. Liked to spike his beer with vodka. No respect for the work.

Ivan shook out a cigarette from the pack and lit it.

"They were asking for witnesses to step forward and identify you," Fedot said. "And I thought maybe I should call the number they put on the screen. They offered a reward. I could get rid of you and get paid for it. Good business. What do you think?"

Ivan kept his voice steady. "I think it's not up to you."

Fedot scowled and narrowed his eyes. "You think you're the best, old man. You think you're better than any of us. Some kind of war hero. You're not a hero. You're a nobody. Remember that. Nobody. If my father tells you to suck my dick, you'll suck my dick."

Ivan nodded. "Like I said, it's not up to you."

A crooked smile drew up half of Fedot's face. "Be on TV more often, and it will be up to me."

The jagged scar on Fedot's cheek ended at the torn lip sagging over the corner of his mouth. One of those deep scars, the kind that hurt when the weather changed. The girl did a good job fighting back, cutting the twerp so close to the eye with broken glass.

Ivan picked up a napkin and dabbed his lips. The threat in Fedot's voice came mixed with smug satisfaction. The twerp would only be this smug if an unpleasant surprise awaited his former instructor. But why bother with the edifice of lunch invitation? They could have sent a team to the apartment building or picked their target off in a car along the way or in the parking lot.

Ivan checked his wristwatch and made sure to sound casual. "Why don't you tell me the reason I'm here. Otherwise, I have to go back to work."

Fedot kept scowling. "You're here because I told you to be here." But his scowl went away the moment his phone rang.

Ivan sipped his tea and waited.

"Yes, we're at the restaurant," Fedot said then listened. "We'll leave right now." He hung up and hopped off his stool. "Let's catch some fresh air. My father wants to see you."

Father. Ivan stood up to follow him. A dozen possible scenarios, but none plausible. A ruse? A distraction? Play it like an invitation then put him down in the parking lot? No, too elaborate, with the texting and lunch. And witnesses.

Outside, all the cars were empty, not a soul in sight. Ivan hesitated, tempted to put his hand on the pistol in the armpit holster. But no signs of a setup. Not yet.

Fedot plodded over to his Mercedes, lifting his feet as if glue was sticking to them. "This shit will ruin my shoes."

Ivan walked a few steps behind on the side of the road to avoid the melting snow in the middle.

Fedot got in his car, banged the door closed, started the engine, and honked the horn.

Ivan adjusted his armpit holster. First impulse: shoot the twerp and run. Would be stupid, getting into his car. This was how ordinary people got in trouble: no trust in instincts. Everyone followed social norms instead of running when they must. But Partorg never granted audiences to condemned men, not unless he wanted something from them.

This was too elaborate for execution. A chance?

He pulled the door open and got into the back seat.

"Did you forget how to open car doors?" Fedot asked. As soon as they drove into the street, the twerp turned up the volume of the car radio—on purpose, of course. Kitschy pop music blared from the speakers.

Ivan winced at the noise and thought: This is what happens when you tell your trainee you grew up in a rural village and liked old-school folk music and opera. Later, he hates your guts and annoys you with pop. Building trust with this guy—may just as well build trust with a rabid dog.

Outside the window, gray apartment blocks matched in color the dirty snow on the sidewalks. Ivan let the bleak scenery become a blur. Another meeting with the big boss. Would this be the last? One mistake shouldn't lead to dismissal. Fifteen years of doing the man's bidding. A decade and a half of executions. Should be some trust there. Called to order the last one himself—not trusting his son with instructions. Men like Partorg, former Communist Party officials—they did everything on trust.

Fedot drove them over a bridge, past a circular freeway surrounding the city, and out of Moscow. Ivan watched the congregation of satellite towns whisk by: Podmoskovie. Under Moscow. Strange term. Not near, but under. Like with the boss. Never near, but always under.

Urban scenery changed to stretches of open fields interspersed with villages and an occasional hill, the wooded areas becoming thicker, the air cleaner, the snow whiter. Not a lot of snow—like they said on TV, winter had been unusually warm.

The traffic disappeared. Fedot exited the highway at an unmarked spot, nothing but trees and open fields around them, but the road they now took into the woods was swept clean of snow and better paved than any city street.

Ivan put the pistol on his lap and took off the safety as the woods grew denser. Gray light sifted through snow on tree branches that closed in on the road.

Whatever happened, the twerp would go first.

Out of the woods, a manned gate appeared, and a guard armed with an AKSM rifle recognized Fedot and waved him through. The guard had a dog on-leash, a Doberman. Not the best dog if the weather turned cold, with a short coat like that.

They drove around a bend and came on a high fence with surveillance cameras and high-tensile electric wires on top. Two guards stood next to a booth by a steel gate, their dogs on leashes, everyone watching the car drive up.

Fedot stopped the car but kept the engine running. "Get out. The guards will take you to him."

Ivan held his door open. "You're not coming in?"

Fedot looked away. "He doesn't want me there right now."

Something in the twerp's voice . . . a lie? Do him now or go in. Both guards had their index fingers just above the trigger wells of their rifles.

Ivan patted Fedot on the shoulder and said, "Look at you. My personal chauffeur for the day," and watched the twerp's face carefully.

Fedot gave him a smirk. "See how funny you are after you talk to him. He watches the news, you know."

Ivan slipped the pistol into his armpit holster and climbed out. One of the guards held open a narrow door welded into the much larger gate.

Two more guards covered the other side of the gate, a young one with a German Shepherd on a leash. The older one stepped out of the booth dressed in police uniform.

"Weapons?"

"A pistol."

"Give it to me."

Ivan put his hand on the pistol, the fit of the custom grip reassuring. Not a good idea, letting go of the pistol. Always the best way to take somebody's weapon: tell them they must give it up to see someone important. Then shoot them on the way in.

He handed the pistol over.

"Don't forget to pick it up on the way back." The older guard carried the pistol into the booth and came back with the metal detector.

Ivan put his hands up. The guard ran the paddle all over, and finished the search with a pat-down. Experienced. Not his first time.

The German Shepherd started with sniffing Ivan's shoes. Young, just a pup. Tempting, to pet him. But a trained dog wouldn't like it. And here was a pleasant thought—they never bothered with so many procedures when they took someone out. This wasn't an execution.

From the gate, the older guard drove them in a golf cart, a pleasant two-minute ride through a coppice of pine trees, the plot large enough to belong to the president.

The guard stopped the cart in front of a gabled entrance to the sprawling log house and nodded at the door. "Go inside. His maid will take you to him."

Ivan sized up the place. Would be a problem, doing a job in a structure of this size: it would take a backup team and a good couple of hours to clear all the rooms on two floors.

A series of short steps led to a massive, double-paneled door made of solid oak, and one panel swung open before Ivan put his hand on its brass handle. On the other side stood a plump woman wearing a laced apron. With a sweet smile, she said, "Oh, you must be Vanya. Come in."

"Only my mother called me Vanya." He stepped inside. "No, I'm sorry—my girlfriend calls me Vanya sometimes."

She chuckled. "I bet your mother called you Ivan when you misbehaved. All kids get called an adult name when they're being bad."

She turned to walk away, waving for him to follow. They walked across a thick rug, a vaulted living room the size of the basketball court, and a glass door leading to the yard.

The maid pushed and held a French door open. "He's by the pond, in the gazebo."

A staircase led down to a path made of marble flagstones, each stone dry and clean, and—judging from the melted snow on each side—heated from underneath.

Ivan breathed in the pine scent. A different setting compared to the first meeting twenty years ago. No pine scent in Kabul, just the choking stench of burnt airplane fuel. Partorg—no big change for him over time. From Communist Party boss to the boss of a crime syndicate. Still the boss. Still giving orders to other men who pull the triggers for him.

The relationship hadn't changed at all.

4

Port of Acajutla, El Salvador

"**Miguel, wake up**. They're taking off."

Miguel stirred, and his sun glasses fell on his chest. Sitting up in his chair, he blinked against bright light, sunbeams reflecting off a dark blue ocean below. He put the glasses back on. "I'm awake. Same driver, then?"

Seso nodded. "Yes. He's out at the gate. Showing paperwork."

"Give me the binoculars." The afternoon heat pressed down with invisible weight, humid air coating his skin with a film of sweat. Hard to break out of sleep in this shit.

From his chair on the balcony, the registration plates on a tractor trailer at the gates were easy to read. The driver was handing over the papers to the customs officer in a blue uniform.

Miguel fished a piece of paper out of his pocket and checked a set of numbers stenciled on the side of the trailer. Everything around the tractor trailer looked quiet. No other cars. No activity.

"Is ours the last one?"

Seso didn't hesitate. "They trucked out all the others already."

The driver picked up some paperwork and climbed back into the tractor's raised-roof cab as a black cloud of diesel exhaust shot up from its pipes.

The Freightliner rumbled off the pier, past the oil storage, on its way out of the port. Now that the wait was over, mild excitement rose up in Miguel's body. Nice feeling, this coming alive at the start of the hunt. This rush, coupled with anticipation, made for the best drug.

He put down the binoculars. "Let's see if Juan was worth the money."

Seso stuck his hand into a cooler they'd set within reach, pulled out a handful of ice, and pressed it against the top of his head. "He never failed us before."

"He's been reliable, for a Colombian. He got drunk with me in Medellin."

"He did?"

"On tequila. Kept asking me why I still do it, after all the years and the money. I told him the war was my coca."

Seso's tone was neutral, as usual. "We are good at it."

"We are."

Truth, but not all of it. 'Good' wasn't the main reason. 'Good' wasn't enough. You don't run a military style campaign day after fucking day, you don't sleep with a rifle next to you, just to be the best enforcer, the famous Zeta they make songs about or to add numbers to your bank account. You do it to feel alive. To be in control.

Miguel stood, careful not to straighten his lower back too fast. The stiff muscles throbbed with dull pain. He tightened his back brace and turned toward the door to the living room.

"Let's get moving."

Inside, Cho lounged on a sofa, his laptop making funny sounds. Miguel headed past him toward the kitchen, saying over his shoulder, "I want everyone in a car."

When he came down to the garage, wiping the water off his lips, they were in their seats, rifles at their feet. Cho was stuffing candy into his mouth, washing it down with soda. Still a kid but learning fast.

Miguel got behind the wheel and shoved a water bottle into the cup holder. But he didn't start the Escalade, instead picking up a Motorola HT off his belt. "Dado, you there?"

The radio crackled, and a deep voice came back. "I'm here."

"The container just left the port. Same truck. Same driver. He should be passing you soon. We'll see if he goes up twelve to San Julian or not. If he does, we'll know he's ours."

"My money says it's our container even if he doesn't."

Son of a bitch. Always cocksure of his bets, even the ones he ended up losing.

"It's going to cost you if it's not," Miguel said.

"I'm not gonna lose this bet," Dado said. "Out."

Cho said, "Dado still thinks he'll win."

Seso, in the passenger's seat, turned around. "My brother always thinks he'll win."

Miguel clipped the radio back to his belt and started the engine. "He's too confident."

"Maybe it's a sniper thing," Seso said.

"Maybe." Miguel checked his reflection in the mirror and ran his fingers through his hair to make the unruly black curls look neater. The noon heat made his hair glisten with sweat. "What I don't understand is why he wants my Escalade. Like he can't buy the same damn thing for himself. Did he ever tell you why?"

Seso shrugged. "He says yours has armor plates in every panel and the back door."

Miguel maneuvered through the front gate and into a narrow street lined with stone walls. The gate behind them closed after one click from a transponder. "If he plans to rob a bank, he better tell me about it."

Seso shook his head. "He said he wants to test it or something."

The few other cars on the road moved at a lazy pace, as if slowed by the tropical heat. The truck carrying the container came into view before they reached a fork in the road. Miguel dropped behind, checking the highway for other cars staying close.

"They don't even bother escorting this one. Puta madre. What the fuck do I need to do to earn some respect with these Sinaloa assholes?"

Seso said, "We take enough of what they own, and they'll respect us sooner or later."

The truck in front of them turned on its blinkers, signaling a left turn.

"He's turning north," Cho said in surprise. "He's not going back up the mountains. Does that mean it's not our truck?"

"Shit. I think my brother lost the bet," Seso said.

Traffic was busy both ways, and the truck driver waited several minutes to make the turn. Miguel stayed close. Rust showed where gray paint had peeled off the trailer.

He picked up the radio. "Dado, do you see we're turning toward the border?"

Dado's voice crackled through. "I see you. I'm pulling out. I'll let Carlos know we're taking the border route."

From the intersection, Miguel spotted Dado in his beat-up pickup shooting ahead of the container truck, gaining some distance along Highway 2, a red dirt bike lying flat in the bed. At this speed, Dado would reach his hide site with lots of time to set up for the shot.

The truck lumbered through the turn. Miguel stayed back, out of the driver's side mirrors. Not that it would be unusual for everyone to travel in the same direction here—with the Guatemala border and the port so close, the driver shouldn't worry about a vehicle keeping back while everyone else sped by.

After a few miles, the trees and thick bushes covered in creeping vines on both sides of the highway fell off, and a farm field opened: a good, long stretch of it with a hillock at the end overlooking the highway.

Miguel stared at the hillock. Dado—hidden in the green hillside, among the coffee trees, with his cheek pressed against the pad of his favorite Finnish Sako rifle, the driver of the truck in the reticle of a telescopic sight, a .338 round in the chamber.

Two tires on the right side of the container truck exploded outward with chunks of rubber.

Cho said, "I swear I heard the shots."

"Impossible," Seso said. "He's using the suppressor. It's because when you expect it, you think you can hear it."

The container truck swerved and pulled over. Miguel accelerated to pass, and the truck fell back in the rearview, the driver maybe cursing his luck, maybe thinking he drove over a piece of razor wire from a nearby fence, the barbs sharp enough to punch through worn rubber.

Miguel dropped speed and checked the rearview mirror. Another truck, hauling the same-size container, joined the first one. It stopped short of the damaged one, like a fellow trucker eager to help.

Cho craned his neck to watch the trailers line up. "Good timing from Carlos."

Miguel checked for other vehicles. "He knows what happens if he's late."

An old sedan flew by, the driver minding his own business. Miguel stopped, shifted into reverse, and sped back toward the truck's cab.

Cho and Seso were out of the Escalade before it stopped, running with their rifles pointed at the swarthy driver and his young partner who'd climbed out and stood staring at the blown tires.

Cho shouted at the men to get down.

The driver dropped right away, but his partner lingered, gawking at the assailants in shock. Miguel got out of the car and walked toward them with a roll of duct tape in his hand while Cho slammed the butt stock of his AK into the man's mouth. The young man's head jerked back, and Seso kicked his feet from under him.

Miguel tossed Seso the roll of tape. He and Cho taped the men at their ankles and hands. Cho made them step into a pair of burlap sacks they'd pulled out of the Escalade's trunk.

Miguel chuckled—sacks for beans, now sacks for beaners.

Cho ordered the men to bend forward and pulled the sacks over them.

The sun already low, Miguel checked his watch. In the dark, Dado would be less effective providing cover. They needed to hurry. Turning toward the front of the container truck, he waved at the sacks. "Put them in the Escalade."

He climbed into the cab, leaving the door open; the air inside smelled of stale sweat and fried food. The cargo manifest sat in the glove box, right next to a cell phone connected to a charger. Miguel flipped through the pages, some of them greased with thumbprints.

Rotocleaners. Brushmachines. Coffee plant equipment. As usual, the Colombian sold good information. Accurate so far.

From outside came the hiss of air-brakes, and he checked the mirrors; Carlos had already turned his truck around and was backing it up to bring the doors of the containers close together.

Miguel hopped out of the cab and walked back, the road shoulder strewn with crushed plastic bottles and pieces of blown tires. The men Carlos brought climbed out, one of them carrying a bolt cutter. They all wore long-sleeve shirts and dark pants. Two of the men were black, all of them looking like local farm workers hired for an odd job of reloading cargo from one truck to another to keep it moving.

Miguel stepped into the gap between containers to watch them snap the lock off and pull the doors open. He climbed in and pulled out a flashlight, which he flicked on and ran over a series of wooden crates. The top crate barely budged when he leaned into it.

If Juan was worth the money, and the manifest was fake, this was no coffee plant equipment. Which meant Dado would win the bet. And they would have a big problem to deal with.

Miguel wheeled and stepped toward the container entrance, where the man who'd opened it stood holding the bolt cutters. "You, give it to me." Back inside, Miguel tore the cover off a wooden crate and shone the light on the familiar plastic, on white letters printed over a box.

SAAB BOFORS DYNAMICS SWEDEN

"Puta madre."

Seso climbed in. "Everything good?" he asked, coming to stand beside Miguel.

Solid metal clasps snapped off with ease. Miguel slapped the case with disgust. "Son of a bitch—it's true. Look at this. He's selling his guns to Sinaloa now."

"He's not afraid of us. He thinks they'll protect him."

Miguel rubbed his forearm. The old pain took the sight of the guns as a cue and bit into his nerve endings.

He stood still, staring at the crates, grinding his teeth. A container full of recoilless, portable grenade launchers. Each compact enough to fit in a backpack. Highly effective against men in armored vehicles at all kinds of ranges. All going to Sinaloa.

Seso stepped away from the crate. "So now we know. El Checheño is back to selling."

Miguel stared at the smooth, green metal of the weapon for a moment then slammed the crate cover shut. "I'm going to find him and cut his legs off. Then I'll feed them to the dogs with him watching."

Seso ran the beam of his flashlight over the pile of crates. "It's a lot of firepower. He must be making good money with Sinaloa. Do you think that's why he fucked us over in Matehuala?"

"It doesn't matter why. We can't let him do this. First he hangs the Americans on us, and now he's back selling to our enemies like nothing happened. It's bad enough he's giving them the advantage in the field. He's shitting on our reputation now."

The muscles in his forearm throbbed with pain, and as if on cue, a headache joined in. He pulled a pill bottle out of his pocket and popped off its cap. In the dark, it was hard to see how many pills rolled out. He allowed himself two and swallowed them dry, turning to the exit. "I want to talk to the driver."

The pills would take a while to kick in. Mierda. This was adding to the aggravation.

He shoved the pill bottle into his pocket and unclipped his radio. "Dado, watch for army vehicles and police. Shoot the engines if they show up. I don't care what you do—keep them away. We have a container full of Carlitos here. They'll take a while to unload."

"So I won."

"I'm not giving you my Escalade until you tell me what you want it for." He put the radio back on his belt. Serious guns. Serious problem.

Carlos, leaning against the container with his hands in his jeans pockets, asked cautiously, "Miguel, what's Carlito? Something to do with me?"

Miguel waved distractedly at the container. "Nothing to do with you. These are grenade launchers. Americans call them Charlies because 'Carl Gustav' is the actual name of the gun. Dado and I call them Carlitos. Warn your men the boxes are heavy. Now hurry up and load them."

Carlos rushed to his men, shouting orders. With a wide sheet of steel, they bridged the space between containers and started moving crates. Miguel walked back to the Escalade, gesturing at Seso and Cho to get in. He spoke into the radio. "Dado, you see the small bridge where the highway cuts into the open field? I remember passing one."

Dado took a couple of seconds to respond. "I see it. What about it?"

"Anyone around there? Locals?"

"All clear across the field. Wait. There is a farm, but that's at least eight hundred meters."

"Let me know if anyone comes over while I'm there."

He took the Escalade to a beam bridge that spanned a creek and parked it in a narrow pullout next to a steep slope. A trail went down, through the bush, to water hidden in the greenery.

"Get them out," Miguel said.

Cho dragged the burlap sacks behind him. "What do you want to do with them?"

"Step aside." Miguel kicked the sacks down the slope. They crashed through branches and brush and landed somewhere on a narrow gravel bar below. Miguel climbed down, holding his back. Halfway, he turned to look up at Cho and Seso. "Tie a towing cable to the back and throw me the free end."

Cho raised his eyebrows. He looked like a child whose parent took away his favorite toy. "Aren't we going to make them fight each other?"

"I don't have time for games. Just the towing cable this time."

The air felt much cooler down by the water. On the gravel, his prisoners wiggled in their sacks.

Pungent pink flowers hung low. Flies buzzed in thick air, getting into his eyes. Waving them off, Miguel pulled out a pocket knife and knelt to cut the men out of the burlap sacks.

The pills had kicked in, and he didn't feel pain as he dragged the driver—a small, swarthy man whose moustache stuck out between layers of duct tape—to the bridge abutment and leaned him against the concrete.

No need to explain anything or ask important questions. Not yet. Important questions always worked better when the man with the information was ready to answer them.

Cho's voice sounded from above: "Jefe! Aqui esta!"

The kid tossed the towing cable down, and Miguel pulled it and tied it to the thin youth's leg, the driver's partner. He cuffed the youth's wrists to the trunk of a nearby tree no wider than the youth's shin.

Miguel returned to the driver and crouched in front of him. Fear kept the man's eyes wide, beads of sweat on his forehead.

Miguel put his hand on the man's shoulder and stared into panicky eyes. "Your name's Diego, yes?"

The man nodded.

"Good. I have a question for you, Diego. What do you think: hands, leg, or tree?"

The driver stared back with eyes full of incomprehension.

Miguel rose. "I think wrists. The tree roots run deep, and the leg has stronger tendons. Plus, the handcuffs are sharp around the edges, no? I bet his wrist will go first." He looked up toward the car and shouted, "Cho! Vamonos!"

The Escalade began to pull, and the cable snapped tight, lifting the youth off the ground. His leg, attached to the cable, pointed at the bridge, his head toward the tree.

The strung body rotated around the axis of tension in a weird pirouette, the youth's free leg twitching and groans coming louder through the tape—louder than the murmur of the water splashing over rocks.

His groans turned to muffled scream that escalated to an unbearable pitch as the cuffs cut into the wrists. With a watery popping sound, his forearms separated from his hands.

The youth fell on the sand, writhing in agony, blood squirting from the bluish stump of his wrist with each heartbeat.

Miguel returned to Diego and ripped the tape from the mouth. The driver's face was trembling, tears streaming down his cheeks. Miguel grabbed and squeezed the man's puffy face between his fingers.

"I want you to tell me everything you know about the men who own the container. Their names. The address. Everything. Start talking." He let go.

Diego was shivering. "Si, Señor. I'll talk. I'll talk." And he did, a barrage of words spilling out of him.

Miguel patted him on the shoulder. "Slow down. I don't need you to talk fast. Just tell me the truth."

Talking calmed the man. His answers became more coherent. A couple of things didn't seem right, but at least the container's destination became clear.

In the driver's phone, Miguel found a number and shoved the phone at the man. "Go ahead. Explain to them why you're late. And you know what happens if you mention anything to them but the tire."

The driver took a minute to compose himself, but he did well. He sounded tired on the phone, not scared. The conversation done, Miguel took the phone and snapped the clamshell shut.

"You never have any escort?"

The man stared. "Escort?"

"Protection? Where are your guns? I searched the cab and didn't find anything."

The driver shook his head, like the questions didn't make sense. "This is El Chapo's truck. Nobody would dare take El Chapo's truck."

Fucking farmer. Miguel squinted at the idiot. The heat, and this stupid driver, and the Gustav guns—it had been one giant insult. These men—never even entered their primitive minds that El Chapo's was just one family. That there were other families out there with reputations to maintain.

In one angry motion, Miguel stuck his hand into the wide pocket of his pants and yanked out a pistol. He aimed at the annoying face and pulled the trigger.

The bullet punched a hole between the man's eyebrows, and he slumped back. Miguel kept shooting—went through the entire magazine, shooting at both captives, his aggravation lessened by each shot.

Refreshing. Always refreshing, pumping lead into morons.

But the climb back up the slope took the feeling away. Up on the highway, they'd already packed the towing cable.

Seso said, "Carlos reported they were almost done."

Miguel wiped sweat off his face with the flap of his shirt. "He better be. Take the wheel. We're going north. We have more work to do."

"We're not escorting the guns?"

"I don't care about the guns. I only care about the asshole who sold them."

5

Podmoskovie, Russia

Ivan found the boss reclined in a chair, watching the pond from inside a white gazebo. Partorg looked relaxed in his dress shirt and belted slacks, a pair of slippers on his feet.

The past two years had left their mark: the boss had lost what little hair he used to have, and the wrinkles on his tall forehead had grown deep. The bulge around the waist developed into a respectable potbelly, but Partorg's steely blue eyes remained cold and their stare cutting.

Ivan stood near the entrance. A formal greeting would be best. "Dobry den, Victor Vasilievich." First and middle name. Respectful. Good way to keep the boss happy.

Partorg nodded at a chair to his left. "Come, sit down." His gaze went back to the wide expanse of the pond where a swan was making rounds close to the shore.

Ivan carefully lowered himself onto the comfortable pillows of the wicker chair positioned just so that both men could watch the water. Gas heaters above their heads kept the air warm. On a glass table between them sat a pack of cigarettes, a golden lighter, and an ashtray.

Partorg stayed silent for a long minute, until he shifted his bulk and said, "I'm trying to remember what I told you in Butyrka when I hired you. Do you remember it?"

Ivan hesitated. "I think you said you saw my picture in the paper and read the article. You said you understood why I did it."

"That's it." Partorg nodded. "I saw your picture. And the article reminded me how you handled the airport situation in Jalalabad. What year was it?"

"Jalalabad or the prison?"

"Jalalabad."

"Eighty eight."

Partorg grunted. "Time flies. I was against going into that airport,

43

believe it or not. But Gorbachev wanted me there talking to the Afghanis. Like it made any difference. We were getting the hell out anyway." He stared at Ivan. "I remember the way you shot that peasant who was going to blow us up. I never got to ask you how you knew he had the vest on him."

"I didn't. He looked wrong. And we could always pay off the tribe if it were a mistake."

Partorg turned back to the pond. "It was a good shot, for how far he was. We wouldn't be here if you didn't put him down. That's why I remembered you when I saw that newspaper article. You used to be very good."

A moment of silence stretched for at least a minute. From the corner of his eye, Ivan, unsure what to make of the silence, observed his boss lost in a memory. Why talk about the past? On the positive side, the boss didn't seem too upset.

Partorg picked up the pack of cigarettes from the table next to him, shook out a single one, and lit it with the lighter. "See, this is why I like veterans. You guys have the right instincts. I was hoping you'd help my son develop some of those instincts."

So this was about Fedot? "Victor Vasilievich, he didn't want my instincts. I taught him what I knew, and he still did things his way. And the way he did it, it really complicated the Litvinov case."

Partorg wrinkled his nose. "I always struggle with him. He does as I say but thinks too highly of himself. Gets too excited. I don't know what his problem is with women, but he gets all crazy with them. I lost all hope of getting him married." Partorg took a puff and blew out a jet of smoke. "I know you two don't get along. But it didn't matter to me, because you always did quality work." Partorg turned his head, his steely eyes burrowing into Ivan's. "Until yesterday."

Ivan sat still. It was like the heating lamps disappeared and the air froze, the chill gripping his bones. Goddamn kids and their cellphone cameras. "Victor Vasilievich, I'm unrecognizable in that picture. And the picture is all they'll have. And even if anyone saw something, they'll keep quiet."

Partorg frowned. "I don't care about the picture. But you know how much I dislike having my business show up on TV or in the newspapers."

"There was a time limit. I didn't want to let Popov get—"

Partorg raised his hand, his gray eyes dark with anger. "I don't need your explanations. You know your work cannot be connected to me. And you let it be connected."

Ivan felt the question bubble up into his throat: so why am I still alive? He swallowed it and nodded. "My fault, Victor Vasilievich. Nothing else I can say."

"Exactly." Partorg gently knocked the tip of his cigarette against the edge of the ashtray.

It was a relief not to look the man in the eye.

Partorg looked up. "You know better than anyone what happens to people who make me upset. But you're not like the others—you have done exactly as I asked for years. So I'm going to give you a chance to redeem yourself." The boss's attention returned to the pond.

Ivan let his hands slide to the seat; he'd been holding them across his abdomen, knuckles aching from tension.

The pond surface was black glass, the swan sliding on top, shaking its wings.

Partorg watched the bird. "Since your face is all over the TV, you should get out of the country for a while. But you don't deserve a vacation. So I'm giving you another job. And I'm not going to let you work this one alone. You'll have a partner."

A partner? Ivan tensed up in the seat. This meant working with Fedot, probably. A disaster.

Partorg drew on his cigarette and exhaled. "His record is as good as yours, as far as I know. Or better, given your recent mistake. Supposed to be a very talented man."

Ivan sunk into the chair. No one—not even his father—would call Fedot 'a very talented man', which meant Partorg was talking about someone else. Krivonosov? Sheyanov? They were good, but neither of them fit Partorg's description of 'talented'.

"Sheyanov would make a good partner," Ivan said cautiously.

"This man's supposed to be much better than Sheyanov. He's an American. So your English will be useful. And you'll need a lot more than your English, by the way. You're going after a real artist." Partorg winced as if from a toothache. "Kazbek's not like Popov or even Litvinov. You'll need help."

"Kazbek?"

"Your new target. He's Chechen."

Ivan nodded. A real artist. Interesting. The boss was showing some trust here. A target that was different from the likes of Popov and Litvinov, one a fat pedophile full of himself, another a crook dumb enough to take a taxi to Sheremetyevo airport hoping to blend in with the passengers in the waiting area.

Partorg crossed his legs, and his foot twitched. "The man you're after crossed me back when Yeltsin was still president. It's been years." He frowned. "I bet he thinks I forgot about him." Partorg shoved his cigarette into the ashtray, grinding it into the glass. "How he betrayed me isn't important. Here's what you need to know: he's an arms trader, sold Izevsk and Saab guns in Central and South America. Unfortunately, I couldn't trace him from the manufacturer's side. So I bought a couple of banks in the Caymans I heard laundered drug money."

"He works with the Mexicans?"

"He does. The banks were a good idea, but it took a long time until my investment paid off. He must have grown comfortable. He wouldn't have dared to show his face otherwise."

"He's still in Mexico?"

"He's on the run. He should be in Los Angeles, if my bank's correct."

"We don't know for certain?"

"He pulled some kind of con in Mexico, and a couple of government people died. The blame fell on the Mexicans—this is typical Chechen trickery." Partorg chuckled and shook his head. "And he went ahead and bought himself a luxury car. He always had a weakness for fast cons and fast cars."

"He races them?"

"He likes to own them. And this one's his favorite. He used to own one here in Moscow." Partorg picked up his pack and shook out a fresh cigarette. "I bought it for him once, believe it or not."

"Should be simple, then. I find the car—I find him. Is it up to me how I take him out?"

"You're not taking him out."

"No?" Ivan couldn't help but stare at the boss.

"You will bring him to me."

"Extraction? I ship him? Put him in a crate and ship him?"

"When you have him, I will fly to the States myself. I'll let you know where to bring him. Las Vegas, probably. I have some business there." Partorg's voice carried no emotion, but his eyes were full of threat. "I want him alive, you understand? You can hurt him, but he must be conscious when you deliver him to me. I want him to be able to talk."

The white swan glided slowly from some reeds toward a patch of lilies in front of the gazebo, the movement of the graceful bird corrugating the water surface. Partorg, using his free hand, reached into his pant pocket for a piece of dried bread and tossed it to the bird.

The bird's movement seemed to calm the boss. He sounded business-like when he spoke again. "Keep in mind—I waited a long time to find him. Pick him up and bring him to me. No mistakes. And the Mexicans are looking for him too, so there's competition. You'll have to move quickly."

"I understand."

"Good. Ah. I should mention something else." Partorg put his cigarette on the ashtray and shook the crumbs off his palms. "The contractor I'm giving you is an unusual man. But Fedot tells me he's done great work for us, so you'll have to disregard his eccentricities."

So, this guy was Fedot's connection. Nothing good would come of that. Eccentricities? A drinker, perhaps? Or a gambler? The most important assignment in years, and it was someone without discipline.

Partorg sat back, watching a wisp of smoke coil in the air above the cigarette. When he looked up, he said, "Listen. You and I are not young. We've made our mistakes. But I believe in second chances. You've always done good work for me—since Jalalabad. So from my point of view, I should let you make amends."

Ivan nodded politely. Make amends. Lena's face, her nose red from tears. They had a chance, after all. Good choice—not to run. "How do I know I have the right man? Do we have a picture?"

"It's good you reminded me. I'm getting old." Partorg brushed ash off the front of his shirt and stuck his fingers into his chest pocket. "He'll have a tattoo."

"He sat out time in prison?"

"Many years ago. Back then they used sewing needles to make tattoos. But you'd be surprised at the quality."

Partorg pulled out a photograph and tossed it on the glass table.

Ivan picked it up and stared at the black-and-white image of a bare-chested man on the beach, yellow splotches betraying the picture's age. Large tattoo, belly to shoulders, on the man's chest: a tiger coming through the reeds.

Ivan hid the picture in the inside pocket of his coat. "When do I leave?"

"Now," Partorg said, watching the swan swim in circles around where the bread had landed. "You're leaving now."

Ivan stood up. The picnic was over, a vote of confidence for a long-time employee. Now it was time for the employee to prove he was worth the gesture. Or invest into a plot at the local cemetery.

6

Outskirts of San Francisco Menéndez, El Salvador

In the still, moist air of the container, Miguel studied his men's dark faces. A good crew, and it should be big enough to deal with El Chapo's cousin. Their faces were black with paint, the whites of their eyes stark in the dim light cast by a portable lantern taped to the ceiling. They sat on empty crates and eyeballed him, bulky in their vests, their rifles checked, fresh sweat on their greasy skin.

He swept them with his gaze. "One more time—this is not what you are used to. But I warn you, I want everyone you find inside those cabins alive, you understand? I want my information, and one of those maricónes has it. So make sure nobody dies until I say they die. Claro?"

They echoed, "Claro," and a few of them nodded.

He climbed out of the container, and helped one of the men pull the door closed from the inside.

Cho, with the most resemblance to the original driver of the Freightliner, sat at the wheel wearing a dirty shirt he found in the sleeper.

Miguel climbed in and shut the door. "Go slow. I don't want you to jackknife this thing."

The engine shook the cab, the brakes disengaged, and the truck pulled off paved highway and onto a dirt road snaking through thick brush, canyon walls high on both sides. Insects danced in the beams of the headlights.

Miguel rolled the passenger-side window down. The sour odor of fermented coffee fruit grew stronger the further down the road they went. Dado, who'd gone up the ridge early to survey the coffee plantation from above, had reported they should see the single smokestack long before they reached the gate.

"There it is." Miguel leaned toward the windshield. In the early-morning light the stack and the silos looked out of place, odd footprints of industry in a lush forest.

The truck lumbered past boulders in the first gear.

Cho said, "Assholes built the plant but forgot about the road."

"They didn't forget. This plant isn't here for coffee."

Miguel stared at the steel gate straight ahead, yellow-gray in the headlights. The dead trucker had made the call about his blown tires, which would explain the delay; it was possible the guard might open the gate at the sound of the approaching truck.

He sat back and clicked the button on his radio. "Dado, what's the guard doing?"

Dado sounded amused. "He was asleep, but he heard you. He's got an AK on his back, hanging from a sling."

Miguel felt a familiar buzz of excitement in his chest. This was the ideal scenario—the guard swings the doors open for the truck to go right through. The trucker said he'd only been to the plant once and hardly talked to anyone.

Dark enough outside for Cho to pass as a driver. They'd roll in without raising an alarm, wrap everything up in under an hour, and get out before anyone else got involved.

The gate, painted light blue, showed a growing crack in the middle. These people—downright stupid.

Miguel smiled and said, "This is working so well, it's making me horny." He check-twisted his gun's suppressor, racked the pistol, and leaned sideways on the seat to hide from view as Cho guided the tractor through the gate.

"It's funny," Cho said. "They only have one guard."

"Don't look at him. Watch him from the corner of your eye." The sky looked milky with the muted morning sunlight.

"He's by the gate, on my side of the container."

"Keep going to the parking lot. I'll take care of him."

Miguel pushed his door open and slipped out of the cabin with the truck still on the move. No chance the guard was anyone important, so killing him didn't matter. The important people would be asleep in their cabins.

He walked back, as the container rolled by, and shot the guard in the temple as the man pushed the gate closed behind the trailer, oblivious.

Miguel put the radio to his lips. "Seso. Venga."

The truck rolled forward while the assault team spilled from the back, fanning out toward the cabins and storage sheds, sweeping their sectors. Once Cho killed the engine, an orchestra of cicadas and frogs took over making noise.

They took a few minutes to clear the grounds, Dado's description so accurate they found the cabins and rounded up the inhabitants with minimum fuss.

Some of the captives, groggy and disheveled, walked, directed by gun barrels. Others had to be dragged by their shirts or hair. Seso lined up the disoriented, frightened men by ordering them to kneel in the dirt of a large parking lot, in front of the truck.

Miguel walked the line, shining his flashlight into their faces, and at the last man spat on the ground.

"Puta madre—this is going to be difficult."

All of the captives, most middle-aged and of wiry build, looked much like any other farmer or plant worker. Some were going bald. All were dark, most of them in underwear, two in crumpled pants and shirts they hadn't bothered to take off before going to sleep. None looked anywhere near important enough to be El Chapo's cousin.

Miguel stepped toward the fattest of the captives and kicked him in the belly, the tip of the boot smashing deep into the soft triangle of his solar plexus. The man let out a gasp and collapsed, curled up like a millipede. His hair felt soft when Miguel wrapped it around his fingers and yanked the man upright.

"That's to wake you up. You own this place?"

The man tried to get the words out between gasps. "No—I—run—the machines."

"I see." Miguel let go of the man's hair and wiped his hand on his trouser. He eyed the line of prisoners in dim light on their knees, their hands zip-tied, and raised his voice. "Which one of you assholes is waiting for the container full of guns?"

Nobody spoke. Miguel pulled out the phone he'd taken from the dead trucker and dialed. With no wind and everyone silent, all could hear the ringer coming from the gate, from the dead guard.

Shit. The doorman could have been useful, after all.

Miguel shoved his phone back into the front pocket on his flack vest and spoke loud enough for everyone to hear. "I'm Miguel Alvarado. I bet you all know who I am."

At the sound of his name, he could hear hope draining from their lungs, the gasps. It was satisfying to watch them react like that to a name. Took a lot of dead bodies to build a reputation like that.

He watched the captured men carefully, sweeping them with the flashlight. Their heads hung low while all of them gazed at the dirt. But one of them, a bare-chested youth with short black hair, the one of two wearing pants, was now showing a growing dark spot around his

50

groin.

Miguel stepped closer to him. "I want to talk to El Chapo's cousin. Point him out, and I will let you join one of my sicarios. I give you my word. My driver used to be like you—young and scared. Now he is brave, and I treat him like my son. Tell me what I want to know, and I'll make a real man out of you."

The bare-chested youth never dared raise his eyes as he blurted out, "He is not here. He is not—"

An older man to his right burst into a rapid speech, a warning to keep silent. The youngster faltered.

Annoying. Miguel raised his pistol. A single shot into the talkative man's grizzled head split his skull in half.

The youngster stared in shock at the collapsing body, at the wet gap in the man's head, at the flap of skin dripping with bloody goo. In shock. Useless.

Miguel put the flashlight under his arm and found his radio. "Dado, did you see anyone running?"

"I would have seen them climb the fence. No one exited the perimeter."

Miguel gestured at Seso. "Give me your canteen." Holding the youth by his neck, he forced the canteen into his mouth and made him take a few gulps. Drinking took care of the shock. Miguel held him by the chin. "What do you mean 'he is not here'?"

Shivering lips and tears promised little by the way of information, but the youth surprised Miguel with a complete sentence. "Señor Ruiz stays in his cabin because he likes to smoke by the pool."

"The pool?"

Miguel turned to Seso who had his helmet off, smoking. Seso shrugged. "Cho is still there. It was his sector."

"What's he doing?"

"I have no idea."

Miguel nodded at the captives. "Talk to them. See if they open up."

He took a path of compacted dirt—lined with strings like it was about to be paved—to the only cabin with a pool. On a porch, an ashtray held an extinguished cigar. The house smelled of fresh paint and plaster, the bathroom still without tile or light fixtures, the sink without a tap.

In a bedroom, near a window facing the pool, Cho was sifting through plastic packages spread all over a huge bed under a fancy chandelier. The kid showed promise. But still very little discipline.

51

"Puta, you're supposed to clear your sector and report. What's all this?"

Cho's submachine gun dangled from his neck as he turned. "Jefe, I'm trying to find the right size."

"Of what?"

The kid was beaming with excitement. "The panties. I found a whole drawer of them. I'm going to pick some up for the girls."

Miguel rolled his eyes. "Cabron, we're still looking for El Chapo's cousin. Stop thinking about sex. One of the farmers says our man should be here, in this cabin."

"Jefe, he was here. Look." Cho stepped over to a chest of drawers and pulled off the top a long tape of condoms, one package torn open. He held up the tape, pointed at the torn one, and giggled. "He's been fucking. But I think he left with the girl."

"Idiot, he's not going to leave with the truck coming. Not because of some whore." A shirt hung from the back of a chair in the room. Miguel stuck his gun at it. "Look at his shirt." He kicked the chair over. A pair of shoes with socks stuck inside stood askew. "See?"

Cho had his kid face on, his startled look—his mouth and cheek like someone squished them and they never straightened out. "Emil and I checked everywhere. Even the outhouse."

"Any fresh food in the kitchen?"

Cho scratched his head, quiet. Always quiet when he was guilty. Killed like an adult, but still thought like a kid.

Miguel wheeled and stepped out into the hallway. "You're supposed to look everywhere, no? How many times do I have to tell you?"

The fridge was full of meats and fresh vegetables, bottles of white wine lining the door. On the table stood a glass of water, half full, a torn packet of medicine next to it.

Miguel read the label and tossed it on the table with disgust. "Puta, he's right here!" He moved to the doorway and waved at Cho, who still looked clueless. "Show me the outhouse. I bet you a million he's still in the hole."

The outhouse was a simple pit toilet built with wooden boards, a temporary solution while the cabin's more civilized bathroom was being built. The door stood open, fresh cigarette butts on the ground in front.

Miguel turned to Cho. "You took a shit, didn't you? You are the only asshole I know who likes to shit with the door open."

The sun was already up but not over the ridge yet, not giving enough light to see anything inside the hole. Miguel ignored the stench and knelt in front of the hole with his flashlight.

In the yellow ring of light, black, curly hair smeared with shit stood out amidst brown sludge. The man was in the shit up to his neck, in the corner of the square dugout, holding on to a log that formed part of the foundation.

Miguel kept his tone friendly. "Buenos dias, Señor. It's a pleasure to meet you. I'm in charge of the men who scared you down the drain."

Cho giggled from behind. The man, squinting into the light, said nothing.

To take a break from the stench, Miguel stood up and turned away from the hole, covering his nose with his forearm. "I don't want to drag him out. He's covered in shit up to his ears. I need him to talk, though." He spat. "The fucking stink is killing me."

"Jefe, we can shoot a flare in there. The flare smoke is better, no?"

"It will be shit-smoke, stupid." He thought of it for a second. They had to deal with the smell. "Go get his cigars from the cabin."

It took five lit cigars spread around the hole to make the stench bearable. Miguel squatted by the opening and waved a lit cigar at the man inside. "You tell me your name, and I give you a smoke. I bet you want one."

"Ramon." First thing out of the man's mouth, in a tired voice.

"Good. Ramon. Now catch." Miguel threw the cigar, aiming at his head, but Ramon didn't move for it. His hands stayed on the log. The cigar bounced off his black curls and fizzed out in the shit.

Miguel nodded. "You're tired. I understand. A long night of diarrhea. Then we come along and it becomes a very long night. Look, I know who you are—an important man. So I'm not going to kill you if you tell me where I can find the asshole who sold you the guns. That's all I want. You tell me about him, and I'm going to trade you back to your cousin."

Ramon sounded hoarse. "And who are you?"

"Does it matter?"

"I'm not saying anything until I know."

"Fine." Miguel sighed. "I'm Miguel. Miguel Alvarado."

"Dios mio . . ." The man seemed to sink deeper. "You kill me no matter what I say."

Miguel kept his tone pleasant. "I'm not so bad. You shouldn't believe the rumors. I don't need to kill you. I'd rather tell your cousin you lost his guns and went swimming in the shit to save yourself. This way, I will humiliate him and make him pay me good money when I trade you. See? It's a good deal for me. Better than just killing you. So tell me about the man who sells you the guns, and I'll have you out of the shit in seconds."

Ramon mumbled something without looking up. Hard to hear him like that—Miguel overcame his disgust and annoyance and leaned into the stench, holding his back. "What? Say it again."

The whites of Ramon's eyes showed. "You're lying. You don't trade. I know all about you. If I tell you what you want, you'll kill me."

"I see." Miguel stood up and turned to Cho. "I saw some barrels by the plant, next to the weird looking machine with a number on it. It's diesel fuel. Go get it. And don't forget the gasoline from the generator."

"I know, I know," Cho said, nodding and walking away. "I just forgot to mix it the last time."

"Yes you did."

"He still talked though, even if he didn't burn in the barrel."

"Yes, yes. Get going. And bring your flare gun."

Miguel stomped on the cigars around the hole to put them out and pissed on them for good measure.

Cho brought a drum of diesel in a golf cart. They dumped it into the hole, which didn't help with the stench. The added gasoline formed a layer on top. The gasoline was more volatile and, mixing in with shit fumes, smelled so foul that Miguel had to talk through his sleeve when he leaned into the hole.

"Ramon. Last chance. Tell me about El Checheño, or I'll burn you alive in this shit. You know I'm not joking."

Ramon's face was black from dried feces and fuel when he looked up, his eyes two white spots. "I saw him once. Only El Chapo met him. I understand he doesn't like to show his face too much."

It was hard not to gag. Miguel stepped out to take a breath.

Cho stood there, waiting with the flare gun. "Is he talking?"

"Not sure it's worth the stink." He motioned for Cho to hand over the gun. "I'll be smelling like shit after this for a long time." He returned to the hole, gagging. "Ramon. I'm back. Go on. What else do you know?"

"He came to us. We didn't know him before, just heard of him. He flew in from Los Angeles and told us how he had you kill two Americans after he took their money. He said the Americans will always be looking for you because of that. El Chapo liked that. He thought it was funny."

El Chapo, laughing.

Miguel slid a flare into the gun and flicked the barrel up to arm it, the temptation to fire a shot into the hole damn near irresistible. The injury to reputation was maddening—El Chapo and his men, laughing and making jokes.

Nobody afraid of Miguel Alvarado anymore. Miguel was weak. He was nothing to worry about. Anyone could fool him.

Miguel clenched his teeth as hard as his jaw muscles would let him. Anger, welling up and mixing with revulsion, sent him into the bush, retching, spitting saliva and chunks of half-digested bread.

This El Checheño problem. Had to put an end to it, and soon. In this business, the day you look weak was the day you died.

"Here you go, boss." Cho was standing behind, holding a cigar and a lighter, flicking the flint wheel. "You need a smoke."

Miguel thrust his hand at him—he wanted to say "STOP" but had to first spit out the mix of saliva and vomit. That cost him a second. And a second was all it took.

Cho flicked the wheel. The spark lit the lighter. The lighter lit Cho's hand and sleeve soaked with fuel.

The kid screamed and jerked his burning hand upward. The cigar flew in a wide arc and fell on the steps in front of the outhouse. Orange-blue flame ran inside.

Miguel tackled the idiot in one lunge, and as they fell, the saturated air inside the shithole exploded, a volcano of flame shooting into the sky, its vile heat slapping and scorching them.

He rolled away from the giant torch, from black smoke billowing into the brightening sky.

Cho, screaming, got up and ran toward the half-full barrel of diesel fuel and stuck his whole upper body inside, coming up drenched and smoking but no longer burning.

"Idiota!" Miguel, blinking in rage, raised his pistol at the pathetic figure. He shook his head and put the pistol away.

Dumb kid. Not worth the bullet. Standing there, pathetic, with diesel dripping from his nose and hands.

He rose from the dirt and walked down the path, answering questions from everyone on the radio.

By the lineup of captives, Seso stared like he saw something new. "Shit, Jefe, your eyebrows are gone."

"I'm lucky I still have a face. The fucking kid is going to kill me someday." The sickening stench reached into Miguel's throat, all the way to the stomach. He folded forward, coughing and spitting in an effort to eject the filth. He straightened up with a grimace. "Anyone say anything?"

"No"

"Give me your rifle."

Seso unclipped the gun from his sling and handed it over.

Miguel flipped the safety and strafed the captives, ignoring the recoil that went from shoulder to spine and pinched his lower back. A few bodies slumped face forward into the dirt; the kid who'd pissed his pants tilted and fell backward, knees up in convulsions.

Miguel ejected and tossed aside an empty magazine then took a new one Seso held out without a prompt. After a few short bursts into each body, he handed the rifle back to Seso, who asked, "Are we leaving?"

"After I find a working shower. It's a miracle we got anything useful out of this shit."

"Do we know how to get to the Chechen? The cousin talked?"

"The asshole is in Los Angeles. I guess you can say we almost know." Miguel looked down at his vest, grimacing in disgust at the specs of feces and vomit. "I swear, the kid's like a monkey sometimes. Just grabs things without thinking."

Seso chuckled. "You're the one who adopted him. He's crazy. Which is why you like him."

"You all like him because he's crazy. I like him because he's fearless. Anyway. We need to put the word out to everyone we know on the Pacific side. Tell them who we're looking for."

"I can put a contract out to the maras. Say, half a million, American. That's big money to them."

"Make it a million. Whatever it fucking takes. I lost my eyebrows, and I'm covered in shit. And all I have is the name of the city."

"My mother used to say 'thick layer of shit makes for good vegetables'."

"Is this what we're doing, spreading shit to grow vegetables? Your wisdoms are making it worse, Seso."

"I'm just trying to make it smell a little better for you, boss."

"You know what'll make it smell better? A shower." Miguel said into the radio. "Dado, give me ten minutes and get off the perch. We're done here."

"That was a pretty explosion. Went straight up, like a rocket."

"Yes. Make sure to thank the little idiot for the shit volcano. Out."

"You know, I always wanted to visit the states," Seso said wistfully.

"So you will." Miguel handed him the radio. "You're in charge while I wash up." He walked to a cabin in the trees to his right, one that looked finished with fresh paint. On the way, he unclipped his gear.

A favorite harness, ruined with a deluge of shit. Stupid kid. Fearless, though. Stupid, but fearless. But maybe he'd grow up and learn someday.

The shower was an immediate improvement. Miguel stood under cold water, letting the chill calm his mind.

The city name should be enough of a clue to get to the Chechen asshole. Make him pay, make a video out of it as a warning to everyone. A good video, something creative, not just some stupid beheading. Everybody was already used to those.

7

Los Angeles, California

Ivan fidgeted in his airliner seat. They were showing a movie in which some idiot ran back and forth through Vietcong-infested jungle with an enemy bullet lodged in his ass, like it was a minor wound.

An explosion flashed on the screen, and Ivan grimaced in disgust. The intrepid hero was now running another lap through thick vegetation, on his shoulder a fellow soldier. Pure nonsense.

He looked away from the screen to the window, to the silver sky streaked with white wisps. Nobody could run with a gunshot wound like that, let alone carry anyone. Once a bullet from the Kalash hits you in the butt, all running becomes impossible. Even the silly pancake commercial was better than this.

He shifted his weight. The film had brought into focus an old wound already aching from sitting for twelve hours. He slid his hand under his rump and squeezed the large muscle, which responded with a stab of pain—a reminder of the 7.62 mm bullet fired by an Afghani, the real bullet that tore out a good chunk of muscle. It hurt whenever the weather changed or from too much sitting.

Ivan turned off the screen. Life was nothing like the movies. When a mojahed shoots you in the ass, you don't save anyone or run anywhere. You writhe in the dirt like a bloodied worm. Best you can do is crawl away from the burning personnel carrier and beg for your buddy not to leave you behind.

A chime sounded and a flight attendant announced their approach to Los Angeles International and mentioned something about the weather being dry. Her American accent left the broadcast unclear.

He closed his eyes to process the words. The standard British accent Lena used when she taught English was so much easier to understand.

Lena. She really helped with learning English for the Malta job.

58

Shouldn't have flirted with her. Was supposed to be a few lessons.

His chest felt warm from thinking of her. She'd given so much more than English.

Outside the window, the brown wall of mountains split the carpet of cities. The plane banked. A few skyscrapers stood in a tight crowd near a stadium. Southward, the city stretched into the horizon, smaller towns blended together into a giant human hive.

Ivan followed the lines of the freeways with his gaze. Good-sized city. The bigger the crowd, the safer you were when the shooting started. Though San Francisco or San Diego would have made a safer landing point. It wasn't good for the boss to be in a rush: when the usual rules didn't apply, the risk went up exponentially.

He eyed a cup on his neighbor's tray, the leftovers of red wine. Here's to hoping nobody would care about a wealthy businessman with a clean record.

Off the plane, on the concourse, immigration police dogs sniffed every disembarking passenger, one of the dogs a German Shepherd. A good sign—a dog like Bond lined up for greeting in Los Angeles. Ivan paused for a second and let the animal nuzzle his coat.

Further into the building, curious looks from several attractive women confirmed the success of the presentable look he'd put together: the four thousand dollar Armani business suit, a cashmere coat thrown casually over his arm, a silk scarf, and a felt hat to complete the wardrobe.

He didn't rush toward the checkpoint. Old, cracked linoleum reflected bleak fluorescent light from ceiling lamps and stuck to his shoes. This place was no better than Sheremetyevo. Shabby.

An immigration official with a sad moustache waved for the next passenger, and Ivan stepped up to the counter. The man leafed through Ivan's passport until his visa came up.

"Purpose of your visit, Mister . . . Klimov?"

"Business, all business." Ivan added obligingly, "Acquisition. We bought a company here. I am taking over. I have some brochures if you want."

He jiggled the long handle of his suitcase, for the official's benefit. Go ahead, ask for it. A folder full of technical drawings of the actual drill. Partorg owned a lot of them. An extensive business background, right here. Layers deep. Lestniza. Peel one layer to find another.

The man worked his keyboard. "What kind of business did you say it was?"

"Oil. Crude."

"Oil?" He stopped typing and stared with eyes full of cold interest. "In Los Angeles?"

Ivan chuckled and screwed his lips into a smile. "I know. You say 'Los Angeles' and everybody thinks about Hollywood. But there is oil here, under the city. You can hit gold even if you are not a movie star."

The official nodded, looking down at the paperwork, his hands busy under the counter. A heavy thud of the stamp came. He looked up and pushed the passport across the counter.

"Strike gold, Mr. Klimov. That's the expression. Not 'hit gold' but 'strike gold'. Welcome to Los Angeles."

"Thank you, officer."

The man responded with a smile.

Interesting. Ivan grabbed the passport and walked off. So, it was true. Just like the research said: they all liked to be called 'officer'. At home, calling a customs official 'officer' would produce at best a look of surprise. At worst, he'd look for a reason to make your life difficult.

The arrivals lobby gave Ivan a pause. Fat people. A lot of them. Real fat. A lady in a shirt big enough for two women of regular size. Riding a special cart of some sort. So fat she can't walk? You don't see this in Sheremetyevo.

Ivan strolled forward until another odd sight slowed his step: a smartly dressed young man from the same flight—who'd spent nine hours looking at Forex currency charts on his laptop—was locked in a passionate kiss with a man in tight shorts.

Brezhnev. The General Secretary of the Communist Party. He used to kiss visiting officials this way, slobbering over them in his senile affection. But this wasn't senile. Passionate. Back in Moscow, a kiss like this would get you beaten bloody.

Stepping past sliding gates, Ivan breathed in a lungful of dry air tinged with exhaust fumes from the endless caravan of buses and cars. Still fresher than the recycled waste inside the plane.

The bus to the rental agency had carpeted seats. He rolled out of the rental lot in the most expensive sedan available, the navigation system guiding him downtown. Rays of mid-afternoon sun reflected off windshields with surprising intensity. Sunglasses helped, the custom lenses thick enough to withstand impact from a spent casing ejected from the chamber.

California—closer to the equator. The sun brighter. The glare more painful. Not so bad with glasses. Cheerful. Better than gloomy February back home. Unless you were aiming into the sunlight.

The GPS's female voice suggested to go north first and then east.

An endless stream of cars on the freeway supported the claim from the local newspaper he read on the plane that called Los Angeles 'the gridlocked city where traffic stymied everyone's lives'.

Ivan chuckled at cars drifting by and thought: These people don't know traffic. They should try driving through Moscow in the middle of a workday afternoon. It would be a relief to get shot.

He parked in a lot next to an office building downtown, the wall of glass going up so high his neck cracked trying to see the top. Using a cell phone tied to a clean company, he made a call to his office back home. The message on the answering machine would say the executive arrived safely and found the office in good standing.

With duct tape from a small roll, he attached the cell phone behind the bumper of a stranger's car parked in the same row as his. If FSB, Interpol, or any other agency were to look into the whereabouts of Mister Klimov through this phone, they would get the impression he'd been making a regular commute to and from work.

On the twelfth floor of the office building, one of the doors bore the name Sovoil, a Russian American joint venture. A female secretary bloomed with exaggerated enthusiasm as soon as he stepped through into the office's glass doors, a practiced smile pulling her cheeks way up.

"Can I help you?" The badge on her suit read: Stephanie Wong. Except she didn't look anything like a Stephanie. Kioko, maybe. Or Zheng. But certainly not Stephanie.

"My name is Klimov. I am here to see Ruslan."

"Oh, of course."

She scampered from behind her desk and led the way to an office hidden behind an ordinary door with an extraordinary ability to shut off all sound. The small man inside sprung to his feet from behind a desk, thanked her, and made sure the door closed when she left.

He switched to Russian.

"I'm Ruslan. They call me Ruski over here, which is kind of funny." He looked at Ivan inquisitively, as if to check if 'funny' was something the new arrival would approve. Ruslan's eyes were eager, his arms pressed to the sides of his body, his nervous fingers flexing.

Ivan studied the man for a second. Short. Intimidated—a common reaction. Play him friendly. "Russki? Yes, it sure is funny. I think Americans would simply call me Ivan. It's hard to make a nickname for Ivan."

"They think it's the most popular name in Russia. Like John."

"Then nobody here will believe me if I tell them the most popular name in Russia is Alexander, not Ivan." He pulled up a chair and sat down. With his hands on his knees, he leaned forward to stretch his back still stiff from the flight.

Ruslan was nodding. "It's that Rocky movie. Rocky was fighting that huge blond guy. That movie made Ivan a synonym for Russian." He waved at the window. "So, what do you think of Los Angeles so far?"

Ivan shrugged. "I haven't seen enough yet. But I've been here for an hour, and I already noticed that everybody smiles all the time." Ivan nodded at the door. "Like your secretary. Nice smile, but her eyes tell me she doesn't care."

Ruslan cackled. "Welcome to America. They all smile at you like you are their best friend. It means nothing. My landlord smiled the whole time he was telling me I couldn't have a dog in my apartment."

Ivan shook his head. "I can't live without my dog. What breed is yours?"

"A Jack Russell."

Ivan whistled. "I feel bad for your carpet."

"I know. I had to find a place with hardwood floors." Ruslan sighed and stared outside his window. After a distracted pause, he caught himself and perked up. "I have your equipment ready. And your car."

Ivan stood. "I'll take it."

Ruslan pulled open one of the drawers of his modern desk and produced a set of keys and several credit cards, each from a different company. "My instructions are to finance whatever you do. For your expenses, these cards have a limit that would be hard to reach." He handed Ivan the car key. "Lincoln Town Car. It's big enough, like you asked. It's in guest parking in the lot outside."

Two cell phones wrapped in cables attached to chargers came out of the same drawer. Ruslan pushed them across the desk. "These are brand-new, prepaid. Let me know when you need more of them." He rose to his feet in one quick, nervous motion and walked to the corner of the room where a black gear case stood with its cover shut, a tripod sitting on top.

"This all came for you a couple of days ago."

"Did you get the toy car as I asked?"

"It's in there. Do you need help with anything else?"

"No," Ivan said and went to the case, put the phones inside, and shut the cover. The crate's wheels rolled silently along the carpet, the handle nice and solid. "I will stay in touch."

"I can get whatever you need," Ruslan said. "I understand you are in a rush and there is competition." He yanked the door open for him. "Anything you need. Things are easy to get in this country."

The meeting had taken less than two minutes. On the way out, the receptionist beamed with another dazzling smile, and Ivan did his best to smile back. When in America, do as Americans do. But the strain of faking a grin felt weird. Like an actor in a TV commercial for pancakes, the one from the plane. "I'm gonna go try them now!" the actor says, grinning like an idiot.

Ivan frowned as he stood in the elevator. The frown helped with feeling normal again.

8

Puerto Vallarta, Mexico

Antonio let the wicker chair swallow his small frame. From the balcony of the hotel's dining room, sailboats looked like white napkins folded in half, tucked into the deep pocket of the ocean cove.

He shook his head—Jorge's hotel was a marvel. With a view like this, no wonder the tourists poured in even during off-season.

A pang of envy made his cheeks feel hot. It was shameful, to feel bitter about life on the other side of the border. A good life. But it was all silly, to sit in front of a TV in East Los Angeles and shake your head at the news from Mexico. Plain silly. Look at this paradise—how could anyone in their right mind trade this for LA? Marisol used to say the family was better off in LA. Now she wasn't sure herself, having a great time here with her sister.

Antonio looked to where ocean met sky. Was LA ever home? The landscaping business took off, yes, after years of back-breaking work. New life in United States. An American dream. Looked like a big lie from this balcony. A slogan to make you feel better about being an immigrant. And meanwhile, here in Mexico, so much change everywhere. Everyone with a business now.

Antonio fingered the silverware on the table in front of him. Jorge—he did so well with his hotels. Landscaping was pitiful business by comparison. It's impossible wealth, a hotel this size. And Jorge as the owner—nobody would believe it twenty years ago when Jorge borrowed his bicycle to get to the market.

Antonio picked up a pastry off a plate and bit off a piece, careful not to spill the topping crumbs on his best dress shirt. Pan dulce, the taste of childhood from Mexico—the real home where people treated you with respect. In the states, they always reminded you of your origins, especially the blacks. They liked to hint at where you came from. Nobody did that here in Puerto Vallarta. None of that nonsense. And every priest here delivered sermons in Spanish, the language of home.

Antonio reached for his coffee cup, and his fingers almost slipped off the ceramic. Shaking like an old man—no, not that old. Decades of trimming hedges and repotting plants gave strength, not weakness. Nervous about this second cousin of Jorge. Miguel? Manuel? Jorge called him what? Un hombre de honor. A decorated veteran with a talent for real estate business, someone who could make Antonio's retirement happen with a snap of his fingers—today, if he wanted. Today. A rare chance.

Miguel—the name did sound familiar. He must have been from Carmelita's side of the family. It was true; they were all military and police.

A seagull alighted on the balcony railing, its cold eyes on the pastry. Antonio waved a napkin at it, and the bird took off. A hungry beast. Everyone wanted something. But this business meeting—who had business meetings with relatives? Jorge called it a rare business opportunity. Important enough to send the women off to shop and put on the dress shirt and pants.

Over to the right, a waiter had rushed to a table and babbled excuses in broken English to an American couple enjoying the view. The waiter, mixing Spanish and English, bowed to a heavyset wife and her husband who wore a preposterous Hawaiian shirt emblazoned with bright orange pattern of palm trees. Like other gringos here, the man's skin looked pink with sunburn.

"Why is he asking us to leave," the woman said. "We are staying at this hotel. He cannot do that."

The waiter was a fountain of words, of apologies, and as he spoke he looked further into the room. Antonio followed his line of sight into the dim interior where a swarthy man was talking to a manager.

"Let's just go," the husband said, taking a napkin from his lap and throwing it on the table. "He's not going to leave us alone."

The waiter picked up the whole table and carried it off the balcony the moment they left their chairs.

Time to leave as well? Antonio began to rise, but the waiter, a chair in each hand, said, "Oh, no, no, please, stay. Please." And he ran off.

A voice came from behind Antonio. "Señor Vargas? Miguel Alvarado."

Antonio turned to the voice, the man from the back of the room here now, by the table. And good looking, with trimmed moustache and a full head of neatly cut curls. Too bad pockmarks ruined his handsome face.

Miguel offered his hand. "Great pleasure in knowing you, Señor."

An old fashioned greeting, polite. They shook hands. Miguel looked back into the room as if expecting something, and sure enough, the doors swung wide and two waiters brought in a large armchair, the men almost at a run. They put it down by their table, and Miguel carefully lowered himself into it—odd for such a young man—and crossed his legs. "Jorge tells me you both were born here, no?" He waved at the view. "He says he wants you back home."

Nice smile, this Miguel. Should be easy to remember a man with such a nice smile. Antonio sighed and adjusted the collar of his shirt. "My wife wants us here. She wants to be with her brother and sisters."

"Of course." The smile slipped off Miguel's gaunt face. "Family is everything. For me, it's great luck Jorge and you are so close." The look of understanding in his black eyes.

Antonio wiped his fingers with a napkin. "I'm not sure how I can be of help. I'm not even sure it's the same person."

Miguel grinned and waved off the concern as he leaned back. "Oh, I'm sure it is. When Jorge told me you work for the man with the tiger tattoo, I couldn't believe my luck. I've been going around telling everyone—the man is a thief. Do not do business with him. He will take your money and run. But nobody knows him. Just you. I can't tell you—I'm so excited."

Antonio shifted uneasily in his chair. This Miguel, so polite. Wore his suit with a casual elegance of the real estate tycoon. But what kind of tycoon went around offering reward for men with tattoos?

"Why not let the authorities deal with him?" Antonio asked.

Miguel chuckled, a smile pulling at the corner of his mouth. "When was the last time the government did anything for anyone who lost money to a crook? And we are talking about the United States, on top of everything. The day they help a Mexican—" he said, nodding toward the ocean, "—that water will turn into wine."

So true. 'Spic' was the word the cops in LA used for Latinos. Sounded like 'spit'.

Antonio picked up a fresh napkin and wiped his neck. "I don't know how I can help. I can tell you where he lives—you wouldn't owe me anything for that. He lives in huge house. Always security around, all these big black men."

Miguel scowled. "He stole enough to afford them." He leaned forward. "Señor Vargas, this is why I'm here asking for your help." He held his palms together as if in prayer. "If you help me meet him so I can reason with him, I will be forever in your debt." His black eyes had a strong, earnest look in them.

Antonio shook his head. "He has all these men guarding him and his wife. I can't bring you to his house—"

Miguel put his palms up. "No, no, Señor. I wouldn't want you to do that. I'll try to meet him at the restaurant or at the store where there are people and police around. Perhaps, you tell me when he goes out, and I meet him and tell him face-to-face: no more running."

Antonio sighed. "If I do this, I may just as well close my business." He felt pressure in his chest—too much, this. Too much. Cowardly, but it was wise to probe, to ask. "This man, he dared to take other people's money. Could it be more prudent to pay the police to handle this matter? Thieves can be dangerous."

Miguel frowned and sat back, his gaze going to the ocean. "He's no more dangerous than a snake—that's why he's hiding." He shrugged, and his gaze returned with a smile. "But when he finds that we know his address, where is he going to go? Easier to give the money back."

Antonio nodded—made sense when he put it like that. The man from the villa, he owned things, antique cars. With all this, easier to pay than run. But what about other considerations, the unpleasant ones? "Señor, I know I'm repeating myself. But if you ever talk to him, my business will die. No one is going to hire my men if people find out I spy on them when I cut their grass."

Miguel adjusted his cufflinks and looked up with focus. "I would be happy to buy your business and your house. Carmelita wants property in Los Angeles for her niece. Why not your house?"

Antonio looked down at his hands. Mind buzzing with thoughts—everything happening so quickly. Sell everything? The house and the business? For how much?

Words came from afar. "Jorge tells me your wife loves the house where you're staying. I can have my attorney get the paperwork ready by end of the week. The house will be yours. Plus whatever you say I'll owe you for ruining your business. A great deal, no?"

Antonio's face turned hot despite the cool breeze from the ocean. He reached for his cup, but it was empty.

"More coffee?" Miguel asked.

"No, water, please."

Miguel turned toward the room and snapped his fingers. The manager—not the waiter—stepped closer. He'd been standing nearby the whole time.

"Bring a jug of water and a beer for me," Miguel said.

When the drinks arrived, Miguel sent the manager away and poured the water from the jug into Antonio's glass. The water, with lemon and ice in it, was refreshing.

Miguel's face split into a white grin. He leaned forward to give Antonio a pat on the shoulder. "It's a little too much, I know. But Jorge is right. This could be your lucky day." He sat back, his grin wider. "It's like your patron saint is looking out for you."

Antonio put down the cup and looked down at the callouses on his hands. Anyone deserved to retire after this much work. A lifetime of being virtuous. Paying everyone a decent wage, even if they didn't have the papers.

In the distance, a church bell tolled for noon. He looked up. Maybe God himself had finally noticed this humble servant's sacrifices. No. It was sacrilege to think such thoughts.

"Señor Vargas, look around you." Miguel swept the room with his arm. "Jorge and I have partners in our hotel business, and look how well he's done. I told him I would like to have you keep the hotel cars you and Marisol are driving. As a gift from me. Regardless of what you decide. We're all one family. It would be a pleasure to have you and your wife come back to Puerto Vallarta."

So, that was why the cars were new. That was why Marisol giggled with excitement when Jorge gave her the keys and whispered something to her. Jorge had been up to his old tricks.

Antonio heaved a sigh. "Bueno. I help."

Miguel looked toward the room, and the manager was at once by their side, leaning in as if to hear better. "Bring Partida Elegante, the whole bottle. We're celebrating."

The manager departed quicker than Antonio could muster the strength to say, "I would like something to eat."

Miguel frowned. "Oh, I have been rude. I should have asked."

"It's not a—"

Snapping his fingers again, at someone behind them. "You know, Jorge tells me he has a new chef, from Oaxaca. Let's see what he's got for lunch. If we're lucky, he's as good as the man who runs my restaurant there."

The manager returned and described the dishes in excited tones, until Miguel cut him off.

"Señor Vargas, would you like to try any of that?"

Try what? Didn't matter. Jorge had been right. An honorable man. "I'd like some fish. Fish would be nice."

"Bueno," the manager said and then left them.

Soon the square bottle arrived. Sunlight turned the tequila the color of gold.

Antonio savored the first sip, its pleasant warmth pushing away all worries. Truly, a lucky day. Finally. A lucky day for an old man who earned it.

9

Los Angeles, California

Ivan wiped the sweat off his face with a towel. The best weapon against the jet lag? A punishing workout followed by a thick steak, cooked medium rare, with broccoli or something else green on the side. And you've got to earn your meal.

He dropped into a push-up position. Stolnik was such a good workout routine. Perfect for a hotel room. A hundred of everything: a hundred pushups, a hundred sit-ups, and a hundred squats with suitcases as weights.

With the air conditioning turned off, sunlight heated the room enough to keep his muscles loose. He worked through the count, stopping only to towel off. The time difference increased the difficulty by taking some strength out of his muscles, and they screamed for rest, but he kept the number of repetitions to a perfect hundred. Either do it right, or not at all.

Sweat bit into his eyes by the time he'd completed the squats. One last thing: the pendulum. Hopping side to side, he oscillated his upper body, the muscles along his torso contracting in quick succession, shoulders swinging.

He finished the last oscillation and fingered the scar on the outside of his ribcage. A real life-saver, this technique. They probably didn't teach this anymore in counter-intelligence courses since it's such a hard trick, doing the pendulum on the run while maintaining a good aim.

He didn't doubt the movement's effectiveness. The scar was a grazing wound that could have been a penetrating one instead. The old man was right—it's no easy task to aim at an advancing shooter who moves this way.

In the shower, the water wasn't cold enough to resemble a winter swim. The guidebook mentioned snow and lakes up the mountains, but those were over two hours away. Ivan struggled to ignore the unsettling warmth of the water and its smell of chemicals. Out of habit, he counted to a hundred before turning off the tap.

Hopefully, this job wouldn't take too long. Find the Chechen, pick him up, and go back to the winter routines.

The steak at the hotel restaurant tasted fresher, juicier, and the waiters were more pleasant. But their friendliness did little to alleviate a major concern: this partnering with the contractor. Partorg had twice described him as eccentric, and that could mean a lot of things. The last partnering with Fedot could fit under the term—the twerp took way too much pleasure in hurting the woman instead of letting her leave.

Back in his room, Ivan turned on his laptop and found the right classified ad.

"Super tall gorgeous girl wants to meet a friendly guy with a sexy Eastern European accent. Must love dancing. Must be athletic. Must be rich and drive a fast car. Lame losers need not reply."

He typed up the message from memory.

"I'm free tonight, Friday. I have a Russian accent. Let's have a date."

Instructions came back in under a minute.

"Meet me at Trunks at nine pm. It's on Santa Monica boulevard. Grab a seat at the bar. Look Russian, and I'll find you."

Ivan studied the words. To anyone coming across the message, the exchange would look innocent: two people flirting before a playful blind date. But how would one recognize a Russian? Look Russian. What kind of look was that?

He Googled 'Russian look'. Girls in provocative poses and men with missing teeth came up. Partorg had said the local pro was good, which could mean the man paid attention to every detail and made sure everything was in the right place. Or it could mean the man had no fear and did every job with his nose full of coke. With a contractor, you never know what you're going to get.

The gear in the box Ruslan had provided needed rearranging. Every requested item sat in a foam cutout, but some of the tools were still in plastic. Sorting it out could wait. The contractor's suggestion to look Russian required a couple of stops, so it made sense to leave early.

The GPS unit suggested taking a freeway, but Ivan chose a street route instead. He took in the view as he drove in his Lincoln: straight streets crowded with cars and billboards, some palm trees, and occasionally a view of distant mountains; the mountains would make for easy navigation without the GPS.

On Santa Monica boulevard, shortly after La Brea, shop signs changed from English to Russian. West Hollywood wasn't exactly Little Russia, but it didn't have to be, as long as it sold the right clothes.

Ivan parked on a street crowded with small businesses, one of them a travel agency, another a grocery store advertising caviar. A shopkeeper in a knitted vest and wearing a star of David on his neck spoke Russian with an Odessa accent and tried to strike up a conversation but gave up after his questions went unanswered; he took no offense and sold a black leather jacket at a good price.

Ivan walked out wearing it over a black t-shirt, his new black slacks and pointy shoes making the ridiculous mobster impression complete. A quick stop at a jewelry store, and now from his neck gleamed a fake golden chain. Combined with thick shoulders, this was as close as it was going to get to the Eastern European look.

He grimaced at his reflection in a shop window. Back in Russia, only small-time thugs dressed this way.

He circled the block around the club. No bouncers, no lines of revelers working their way toward the door of the brick building. Parking signs were hard to interpret; none of them made much sense, but they all said 'tow away' at the top. In Moscow, on a street like this, parking would be free.

A commercial parking lot would have to do—one without gates so it'd be easy to leave in a hurry.

From the lot, Ivan walked two blocks to the club and stood on the other side of the street. A few men, young and old, sauntered in and out without hindrance. He crossed over and stepped through the door.

Inside, a few brass lamps shone muted light onto several pool tables, two of the tables surrounded by a group of men in dress shirts and tailored trousers, some of them wearing stylish glasses, all of them boasting neat haircuts.

Ivan took a deep breath that confirmed his surprising observation: nobody was smoking. Unbelievable. Any Russian club would be blue with smoke.

On his way to the bar, several of the men gave him a curious look. A skinny guy in a fedora raised his eyebrows as if surprised by the new arrival's appearance.

Ivan counted steps as he walked. Eighteen from the main door to the first barstool. Four and a half seconds if running. Two exits. Enough people here to start a stampede should things go wrong.

Two women sat on a leather sofa that stretched along the wall opposite the bar, both sipping on cocktails. One, brunette, was shorter, with hair down to her shoulders. The other one looked dark and lanky, with thick eye lashes.

Ivan picked a spot near the bar that let him keep the women behind him. Women—always a safer choice in confined space where you had to turn your back on somebody.

He used a brass footrest to give himself a lift to a cushy barstool. The barkeeper, a fit young man dressed in a black t-shirt that hugged his biceps, took the order and brought a bottle of Heineken.

"First time here?"

Ivan nodded. That should have sent the barkeeper on his way; but for some reason he lingered, a friendly, interested smile on his face.

Ivan studied the brunette's reflection in a mirror set behind the bar's plentiful array of alcohol bottles. Brown hair, shoulder length. Could be Lena, out for a drink. Holding her wine glass the same way, the bottom flat on her palm.

He caught himself staring, and jerked his head away to check the room. No professional should ever allocate this much attention to a woman—the least capable person here. Don't lose focus. Unacceptable, on such unfamiliar ground.

The bartender, on his way to mix a drink for another customer, offered another dazzling smile. "One more Heineken?"

Ivan stared at him with incomprehension then lowered his eyes to the bottle in front of him. Only a sip left. Had gulped down the contents, unaware. Head in the wrong place.

He shook his head, and the barkeeper left. Two new arrivals entered the club, one too skinny, another too old for wet work. Ivan continued to scan the room with sideways glances, finding no signs of the local pro. He pulled out his cell phone. They were well past the rendezvous time.

The skinny new arrival in old-fashioned glasses and a corduroy jacket came over, climbed onto an adjacent barstool, and ordered a cocktail. He brushed a long strand of hair out of his effeminate face and stared at Ivan.

"Like your macho look. A little retro, but you're working it. Fierce."

The realization hit like a whip—it was a fucking gay bar. Ivan smarted from the self-accusation: you would have figured it out earlier if you weren't so busy thinking about your girlfriend.

The thought of being negligent stung, and the oily scent of the cologne wafting off the homosexual was nauseating.

Ivan looked straight ahead and let his discipline kick in. A deep breath relaxed his tightened jaw. Half-closed eyes and a yawn helped with looking peaceful. Bored. Bored people never attracted any attention.

He looked past the youngster and swept the room with a lazy glance, a picture of boredom on the outside, growing resentment on the inside. Two male patrons in the back were laughing, holding hands. No doubt about it—the local pro had scheduled a meet in a club full of homosexuals.

Ivan glanced to his left, at the bartender who beamed with good cheer, showing a row of brilliant white teeth. Too friendly. Definitely a homo.

Anger pushed blood into Ivan's face. The late appointment now felt like a taunt. Other men cast curious glances at him and some smiled invitingly. One laughed and shouted something with a whiny twang.

Everyone flirting. This contractor—he would have to explain his choice of location. And his running late. And how that fit into being a professional.

"Long day at work?" The perfumed youngster on the stool to the right waited for his answer while sucking on his brilliant green drink through a straw. He kept his drink's tiny umbrella away from his face by pushing it aside with his pinkie.

Ivan looked at the youngster's painted nails and took another deep, slow breath then gave the question a short nod of confirmation.

"I figured," the youngster said. "You look tense. Your shoulders are way tight." He waved his tall glass. "You should try my cocktail. It always makes me feel better after a long day." He put it down and pushed it along the bar, rainbow umbrella and all. "Try it."

Ivan stopped the advance of the umbrella drink with a raised palm. "Thank you. I am fine."

The youngster shrugged. "Suit yourself. You're missing out."

Another quick glance at the clock confirmed the local specialist was now insultingly late. Unless he'd run into some trouble. In this line of work, trouble was never too far behind, chasing everyone. Smart men stayed ahead of the chasing party. Stupid ones died.

Ivan shifted his weight on the barstool by pushing his right foot into the floor to take the pressure off his old wound.

His neighbor noticed the movement. "Definitely tense. You need a massage. You want a massage?"

Ivan trained his eyes on the drinks lining the bar's shelf, like he was lost in thought. "No, I don't need a massage."

The mirror wall behind the bottles showed movement at the table occupied by the brunette and the blonde. The brunette had stood up and was walking away while her exotic friend headed for the bar.

A delicate, orchid-like scent of perfume reached Ivan's nostrils first. And then the woman's voice arrived, as pleasant and velvety as her fragrance.

"This seat isn't taken, is it?" She stood to his left and a bit behind, leaning forward to put her delicate hand on the bar.

He hesitated. Under ordinary circumstances, it would be best to keep the seat free by saying something like, "I am waiting for somebody." But in this club now filled with flirting, gallivanting homos, the sudden arrival of a female specimen had offered great relief.

"No, it is not taken. My friend is late." This could be misunderstood. "He is just a friend. We work together. He said this was a nice place."

The woman flashed him an understanding smile, her bright red lips parting to show perfect teeth. A strand of her long hair brushed against his arm as she sat down. She ordered a martini, studying him with unrestrained curiosity from under long eyelashes.

"Your friend never told you this was very much a gay club, did he?"

"No." Voice betraying some of his frustration. Control it.

She played with a lock of her hair. "But this is a nice place. I come here with my girlfriend because the drinks are good and the guys are gorgeous."

The barkeeper brought her martini. She took a sip, her long nails matching the color of her lips. She put her hand on his shoulder and—as if to confess a secret—leaned in. "This is a tough place for both of us, you know."

"It is?" From the corner of his eye, he saw her smiling mischievously as she withdrew. "How so?"

"Well, yes." She swirled her martini by moving the olive around with a toothpick. "For a girl, it's hard to look at all these gorgeous guys and find every one of them not interested." She sighed. "So gay, and so unavailable."

"So why come here?"

She shrugged. "This is kind of like window shopping. The guys don't bother me while I check them out."

"Look but not touch."

"Exactly." She took another sip of her martini and wrinkled her nose the way girls do when they taste something bitter.

"Why you drink martini if you don't like it?"

"This way I take small sips and never get drunk."

"What is wrong with drunk?"

"Nothing," she said. "But I prefer to stay sober when I'm working."

"Working?"

This didn't make sense. Ivan stared at the girl's thin face, her jawline rounding nicely at her small chin.

"Ivan, don't be silly," she said, her head tilted. "Of course I'm working. You're here because I told you to come here. I'm supposed to be helping you and all that." Her stare, now sharp, contrasted with a coy smile playing on her lips.

A brief moment of confusion. A barrage of questions. Hard to form a cohesive protest in a foreign language. "This is wrong. You were supposed to be a he."

"And you're supposed to be a professional and not give a shit," she countered without raising her voice. She took another sip from her martini. "Yes, I'm in drag. So what. You should consider yourself lucky—you get to work with someone who can walk on both sides of the aisle."

They sat in silence, side-by-side, an odd couple. She, a tall, elegant woman with the outline of muscle development on her long arms—he, an angry man with tense shoulders and fists clenched. Her dress, burgundy, widened at the shoulders to form frills that hid possibly thicker muscles. The dress went down almost to her ankles and draped around long thighs.

"So you are one of them . . . homos," Ivan spat out in disgust. He nodded at the room filled with well-dressed men.

Her voice turned cold. "Easy there, big guy. You're playing in my sandbox, so try not to shit in it. Use the 'h' word again, and I'll disappear your sweet ass faster than you can say 'motherfucking Russia'."

Ivan's neck grew rigid as he leaned forward. His elbows rested on the steel plate of the bar, his fists tight, his body charged with anger.

Wrong, all wrong. The wrong partner. Must have been Fedot's plan all along—partnership with a homosexual. Everything wrong. The place wrong. The contractor's outfit. The people. Everything.

The young man on the right mumbled something and pulled

money out of his wallet, his fingers peeling off bills in haste. He left without finishing food he'd ordered. The barkeeper stayed away, too. Meanwhile, the man-woman casually swirled her drink, her fingers wrapped around the stem of her martini glass, the olive on a toothpick in her other hand.

She took a sip and put the glass down. "Control yourself. We've got work to do. Not gonna do well if you play angry."

"I'm not angry."

"Then relax and stop scaring people. You look like you're about to murder somebody."

Ivan put aside his beer bottle. No need to squeeze it so hard. "This is interesting." A disco tune thumping through the club drowned the words.

She leaned forward. "What did you say? I can't hear you."

"This is interesting!"

"What is?"

"Why he chose you for this job."

"You mean your boss? How about because I'm good at it?" Her voice low, no longer sounding like a woman's.

Ivan looked at the array of bottles behind the bar again to get a reprieve; the discrepancy between her female looks and male voice was unsettling.

"Your Party man liked my record," she said. "You wanna hire someone you can trust."

"My Party Man?"

"Your boss. I can't spell his name right. Par-Tor? Party Man sounds better, wouldn't you say?"

Ivan shook his head. Was it worth the trouble, telling this—man? woman?—to stop being disrespectful? His anger had dissipated, and it was easy to think in clear, precise thoughts.

He even chuckled, albeit internally, at the name: The Party Man. Funny, and also appropriate. Partorg certainly had the Communist Party background.

Ivan rolled his shoulders to loosen up. "What am I supposed to call you?"

"You call me Foxy."

"Foxy," he echoed, as if testing with his tongue an unfamiliar concept. "So you have perfect record. And so we are to work together."

"Better believe it." She signaled for another martini. "Let's talk about you."

Ivan shrugged. "What about me?"

"The Party Man told me you like revenge kills. Correct?"

"So?"

"Explain it to me."

In all this weirdness, getting to know each other. "I like justice. That is how I started."

Foxy nodded and ran her index finger around the martini glass to collect some salt before licking it slowly. "He said before you snuff them out, you like to remind them what a little shit they've been."

"Sure. I like it. Without justice it's all just . . ." Ivan paused to look for the right word. "Butchering. I'm not a butcher."

Foxy's lips curved in a thin smile. "Is that what you tell yourself so you can sleep well at night?"

"I don't have to tell myself nothing. It's true."

"Right." She bit the olive off the toothpick and said, while chewing, "I guess this is why he did it."

"Did what?"

"Sent you here. This is a revenge hit, the kind you like. I bet he's got someone else to do the work you wouldn't be good for. Real dirty work that would make you feel guilty."

Ivan nodded. "His son, who recommended you." His words came out steeped in sarcasm.

"Oh, yeah. Fedya."

"Fedot is what we call him. He likes to make a mess. He has a thing for women. Wives, girlfriends. He thinks it's a good way to create distractions for detectives who blame the boyfriend or a husband. But that's only his excuse."

"That's why Party Man's the boss," she said. "He knows how to pick the right Bob for the right job. He wouldn't send his son here— he sent you."

Full of opinions. "You think you're the right man. A man who looks like a woman." Ivan waved his hand at her dress. "Are you going to be wearing this always?"

She picked off the last olive, chewed it slowly while staring, and swallowed. "I'm gay, not stupid. I'm a woman when I need to be."

Ivan shook his head. "This is weird shit."

She waved the toothpick at him. "Yeah, keep shaking your head. You wouldn't know what weird means. Your Party Man warned me about you. He told me you're so buttoned-down you should be teaching girls at a catholic school."

"I am not buttoned."

"Yes you are! Look at you. All angry because you have to sit next to—"

"A homo."

"There you go. Your new favorite word. Your English's getting better by the minute, huh?" She tossed her hair back and raised her chin. "Now look at yourself—all red in the face 'cause you have to sit next to a gay man in drag. Talk about pencil-straight."

"Better straight than homo." Too tired of this shit to hold back.

She leaned forward and said in a perfectly cold, male voice, "Listen up, Boy Scout. You will not call me homo. Ever. The correct term is gay. I'm putting up with your fat bigot crap because your boss is paying me enough to cover it. But I won't let you disrespect me. So either you get up and walk away, right now, and fly back to your Mother Russia, or you get over yourself and get to work." She leaned back and picked up her martini glass. "Your choice. You have until I finish my drink."

"I'm not fat," Ivan said. "I have thick muscles. You are a man wearing a dress, like a crazy."

"You just jealous," Foxy said and pushed her hair over her ear in a perfect feminine gesture. "You know I'm better than you. You've spent all this time talking to me without having a clue. I could have walked you out to my car and cut you down before you could figure what's what."

Ivan rolled his beer bottle back and forth between his palms. The sensation was relaxing. No point arguing with this 'Foxy'. A homosexual, calling himself a pro. Absurd. Everyone knew homos were half-men, neither here nor there. Weaklings. This was all Fedot's doing, no doubt. The twerp, setting his former instructor up for a failure.

The weirdness of the situation in itself didn't constitute the problem. But this weirdness could affect the quality of their work. With all the discomfort and oddness, the job would suffer as a result.

Ivan stood up. "I need to think about this."

Foxy raised her thin eyebrow. "Don't forget, we're on a schedule here, big guy. We've got competition. A lot of work ahead of us."

A cluster of men was on the floor, dancing to ABBA. Ivan pushed through, holding his breath to avoid breathing in their cologne. Good song, but these men ruined it with their gyrations. Like the one in a hat with a disco ball attached, the light arrays bouncing off his head. Clowns.

He kicked the door open. The whole thing was a joke, and there was nothing funny about it.

10

Matamoros, Mexico

The armored truck didn't stop but merely slowed down as its heavy door swung open. Miguel caught the inside handle and let the truck pull him forward. The momentum lifted him for an easy step, and he dove into the truck's interior, twisted his body into the seat, and yanked the door closed.

The door shut off the blaring of the car horns, the baby's cry from the house facing the street, the piercing crow of the rooster.

The silence inside the vehicle was absolute, save for the engine's growl. Like climbing into a tank and closing the hatch. Miguel flexed his fingers, his forearm aching from the pull.

Air conditioning vents spouted frigid air that dried fresh sweat on his black police uniform. He shivered and snapped the vents shut.

The driver, in a helmet with goggles over a black mask, drove without speaking. It wasn't his place to speak. The men in the back were silent as well as the truck heaved and swayed over speed bumps.

Guards at the federal building recognized the vehicle and sprung into motion, pulling hard on gate handles, a line of razor wire at the top broken apart. The truck lurched into the parking lot.

To avoid the strain on his lower back, Miguel clicked the door lock before the truck stopped and let inertia swing the door open. Old pain taught you all kinds of little tricks.

As he walked through busy corridors inside, men and women in uniform saluted him all the way to the quietest, biggest office in the building, the only office with a single desk. Fernando, with bleary eyes, stared from behind it, a stack of papers in his hands. The stack thudded against his desk.

"Are you sure you want to risk it?" He asked, straightening the pile of papers. "A lot of risk for such a small thing."

Miguel pulled off his helmet and mask for a brief reprieve from the stifling disguise. "I am here, am I not?"

The stack went on top of another one, the desk like a model of a city block, piles for buildings. Running federal police involved a lot of paperwork. "Then I suppose I should call them," Fernando said and picked up the receiver of an office phone, its cord twisted and tangled. "The gringos always get upset when they have to wait."

"Gringos are always upset. That's why they buy all the drugs. To calm themselves."

Fernando chuckled as he pressed a button, and the dial tone came through the speaker. It rang once, then the gruff voice of a Texan said, "Yes?"

"Mister Peterson, my man is ready if you're ready."

"Was there a problem? You're an hour late. We were about to get upset over here."

"No problem. But we must be safe. There were men at the bridge we didn't want. I had to send the car to make them leave."

"We saw that."

"My man is taking a big risk, no?"

"We understand. We're taking every precaution on our side as well, Sir."

"Yes. So. He's here with me. Should I send him over?"

"How long is he going to take?"

"He will be on the bridge in five minutes."

"Roger that. Five minutes."

Miguel put the helmet back on and pulled the mask over his nose. The Texan's accent was hard to reproduce, but it was fun to try. "Roger that. Roger that." He chortled on the way to the door. "Gringo likes to play war."

The same armored vehicle took him down a narrow street and out to the bridge. Two pickup trucks with mounted machine guns provided an escort, and civilian sedans scampered left and right like frightened street dogs.

Two black SUVs pulled onto the bridge from the American side as soon as the armored vehicle rolled on. They had their back seat door open for him. Miguel came out of one door and straight into the other, the gringo shaking his hand in the back seat, a tall old man with a hanging mustache.

"Mister Orosco, I'm Chief Peterson and this is agent Estevez, FBI." The black suit in the front seat half-turned his head, hanging onto the handle above his seat. The SUV was already in a U-turn. "Agent Estevez is here because of his experience with protecting our informants. Mister Orosco—what I'm trying to say is we take your safety very seriously."

The turnstiles of the border crossing swung by. Miguel pulled the mask down and took off the helmet. "I have half-hour. Not more."

"Then we better get to work."

The FBI man handed over a brown envelope from the front seat without turning his head. Peterson didn't move for it. Miguel took the envelope and pushed it inside his armored vest without checking its contents. No need. Set the right tune for them, and they'd always dance.

Peterson said, "Should you decide to pursue US Citizenship, we'd be able to fast-track your application."

Miguel nodded. "Thank you." The SUV slowed down just enough for them not to get too far from the border. Miguel stared out the window at the vast, shorn farm fields. He let the expectant silence stretch like the land outside. So satisfying, making them wait. A deep sigh would give them the impression of the final commitment. Show some fear? What did people do when they were nervous? They fidgeted and squirmed. But the gringos would assume their informant was a brave man.

He rubbed his gloved hands on his thighs. "You cannot record this, yes? I do not want accident, like they recognize my voice."

Peterson was quick. "Nobody's recording nothing in here, Mister Orozco. Nobody can make any calls from inside this vehicle."

"Good. So I tell you what I know."

"Please. We're all ears."

Miguel cleared his throat. "Your two men died because you have cut off El Chapo's weapon buys. Guns he bring through the border."

The gringo sounded incredulous. "Are you telling us this was a revenge hit?"

"You do not understand because it is difficult. El Chapo is not fighting the military. He is the friend of El Presidente. Not like the Chacalosos from Juarez or Tamaulipas. But he is fighting everyone else. He is fighting other families. So he wants best weapons."

"What does it have to do with my men?"

"I was going to say—" Miduel paused. So much pleasure to see the gringo shut up and wait eagerly for every word. "I was going to say it was about the weapons. There was a man who sells guns. He is not Mexican, as far as we know. He is from Europe. He used to sell his guns to a man who works out of Veracruz, to—how you say— operative de Golfo. But then El Chapo needed weapons because of your operation, and the European changed sides."

"And my agents got caught in the middle." Peterson clenched his hand into a fist.

"The European used your agents to earn El Chapo's trust. He set up your agents to humiliate the local bosses. You know how it is— reputation is everything. If you have reputation, you control the plazas, the business, everything. The European humiliated the bosses from Tamaulipas and Veracruz. They lost reputation. We hear El Chapo liked this very much. So now they make big business. The European sells him his guns."

"Do you have a picture of this gun seller for me?"

"No." The disappointment from the gringos was almost palpable. So satisfying. "But I have something else."

This Peterson, he didn't seem too excited with the crumpled sheet of paper Miguel pulled out of his vest. "What is this? It's dirty." The Texan grimaced and checked his fingers as he unfolded the sheet then studied it. "What am I looking at? Wait. Are these container numbers?"

"Si. Yes. You follow these containers. They take you to El Chapo's men. You wanted to know about your men, and you wanted the guns. I give you both. And the European who ships them. You have the computers, everything. You can reach everything this way, no?"

"Can you work with us on this from your side?"

"If I start following these containers, my family and I will go into what you call unmarked grave. Sinaloa men are everywhere. Someone will talk, and El Chapo's men will come after me."

"I see." Peterson passed the sheet to the FBI man in front then crossed his legs with his long fingers around his knee. His lips tightened, like he was to deliver an unpleasant truth. Even his whiskers drooped. "You must understand—I have to ask, of course. How did you come into possession of this information?"

Nice act. No threat in his voice, and so casual. "I investigated for you."

"You investigated?" His bushy eyebrows came up and formed a tent.

Miguel nodded grimly and leaned toward the driver and the FBI man, reaching with his arm between the front seats. "Señor, el papel, por favor. Un momentito."

The FBI man gave up the sheet. Miguel unfolded it carefully. The best moment of this circus. He took his time, scratching dark dust off a spot on the side of the sheet with his nail.

He held the sheet up to Peterson, close to the window. In the

84

white glare of Texan sun, the brown spot took on a lighter shade. "After you request help with my boss, I sent a man I trust to Matehuala. This is your agent's blood."

Peterson took the sheet like it was the holy shroud of Christ himself. He held it in his fingers, staring at the splotches, his mouth slightly open.

The driver, unaware of the dramatic moment in the back, banked the SUV as he made a U-turn to return to the border.

Peterson lost the sheet, his fingers snapping in the air. He caught it by the edge. "Jesus fucking Christ. Mike, slow the fuck down!"

It was hard not to laugh. Miguel turned to the monotonous scenery outside. Thank God for this boring view. This comedy with the Americans, it was more fun than any party, any good gunfight. Well worth the risk.

The dull fields helped him maintain a grim expression, but he had to wait for his lips to relax. Just in case, he pulled his balaclava over his nose.

"Mister Orozco," Peterson said, a business card in his fingers. "I can't stress enough how valuable this information is to us. If you ever need any kind of help, you call my number. Any day. Any time."

Miguel took the card, put it into the front pocket of his vest, and then said softly, "Thank you. We fight on the same side, no? I do this for mi familia. And yours. For their future."

He patted his chest, the envelope thick with the green card and his new American driver's license. Easy to buy these things. But this way, it was so much more enjoyable.

"For your family future," Miguel said. "For our children."

He leaned forward and sideways to glance ahead. The gray border installations with antennas and turnstiles rose from the horizon. The spectacle was over. He put on the helmet and busied himself with its chinstrap, a smile under his mask.

After he stepped out of the SUV onto the bridge's cracked asphalt, he straightened his back out of habit of expecting pain. But the nerve endings tickled and his muscles flexed instead of cramping up.

The satisfaction of making fools out of the gringos had trickled into his body, and what a pleasant rush. The feeling would last, no doubt. And grow, once the gringos started picking up El Chapo's guns. The fat fuck would wonder: how come the Chechen's guns never get to my men? Maybe my new Chechen friend is not a friend at all.

Miguel climbed into the armored truck, which sat waiting on the bridge, and pulled hard on the door. He smiled under the balaclava as they drove. The fun had been worth the risk of meeting the gringos on their territory. They'd keep El Chapo busy now and make him suspicious of his new gun-selling partner. And the Chechen? With El Chapo upset, he'd stay at his home in Los Angeles, thinking he was safe.

Miguel scowled. Safe. The asshole didn't even know his gardener wasn't his anymore. A big party to take place in Los Angeles. It would be a long time before the Chechen or El Chapo would share a laugh again. A long time.

11

Los Angeles, California

Ivan strained his muscles against paralysis, anxious to fight off a
faceless man in a skirt. The man didn't care, pushing a drill into
Ivan's temple, its bit grinding into his skull with a piercing buzz.
The moment the paralysis fell off, and Ivan threw himself at the man,
punching and smashing.

He woke to the buzz from the alarm clock on his bedside table.
Red numbers blinked until he slapped the button.

Time difference—it threw off his internal clock. Wouldn't need
the alarm to wake up otherwise.

A workout, a shower, and a pile of fried eggs with bacon helped
shake off the nightmare. After breakfast, Ivan dragged his gearbox out
of the wardrobe and laid out his equipment on the bed, assembling
miniature camcorders and inserting fresh batteries.

Each microphone and camera fit inside plastic molds made to
look indistinguishable from rocks and tree branches. His laptop picked
up audio and video from each piece.

Repetitive work offered mental space to examine the delicate
situation of his partnership with the man-woman. Partorg said Foxy
would provide operational support. But this Foxy appeared more
interested in wearing costumes and playing games than planning an
extraction. Meanwhile, nobody even had Kazbek's address.

Images flicked on and off in small windows on the laptop screen,
the feed from each camera coming in clean. Could this Foxy even
help? Or would he help things go wrong? In the army, everyone made
jokes about homos and their girly ways. But Partorg's orders were to
team up. The last guy who disobeyed The Party Man ended up in a
meat grinder at the local processing plant; a lot of Muscovites could
claim they'd eaten human flesh.

Possible to start without the homo, though. Gather some
intelligence and scope the terrain. A routine first-step with no need for
outside help.

Ivan checked his email for any encrypted messages. There were none. No questions about the first meeting with the local, no admonishments.

He pulled Kazbek's picture from his shirt pocket and studied the tattoo. The Chechen was smiling, his eyes shrewd, wily. Had to be wily to stay on the run for so long.

Ivan put the picture back into his pocket. The hardest assignment in years with a weakling for a partner. All Fedot's doing, no doubt. He saw a chance and went for it, the twerp. Never cared about any objectives other than his own.

This was going to be difficult.

Ivan closed his email and opened the browser to study a local map, looking for the car dealership Partorg had dug up through his bank. If Kazbek had indeed bought his Ferrari there, then they should have his address on file. Would be a logical place to start. The problem of the man-woman could wait.

The three-piece Armani suit restricted Ivan's movement. But who would go around buying Ferraris in jeans and a hoody? He slipped the toy car Ruslan had ordered from a catalogue into a jacket pocket and walked out of the room, pulling the gear case behind.

From the hotel, he drove west with the windows rolled down, the gear in the trunk. The bright, warm day didn't match the month on the calendar, the air fresh without being chilly, sun still caressing his skin. Nothing like February in Moscow. More like early September, when leaves turned yellow and red.

Traffic on Wilshire Boulevard was as bad as traffic on Tverskoy, the potholes worse. The gray box of the Ferrari dealership building stood jammed between a bank and a high-end restaurant.

Withdraw your money, buy a car, and celebrate the purchase over dinner. But first—buy the car.

Ivan parked and headed for the showroom. The moment he stepped into the spacious interior, a tall, busty blonde in a tailored jacket and short skirt launched her athletic figure from behind a desk in the corner of the showroom and headed his way, her radiant smile fit for the cover of a fashion magazine.

He didn't smile back. Ignoring her, he scanned the room in search of male salespeople: a Chechen would never enter into a business agreement with a woman given a male alternative, and there were plenty of alternatives around.

He took a step toward a desk adjacent to the front windows with a plump man behind it engaged in a phone call, but the blonde intercepted him.

"Hi there," she said, smile never leaving her lips. "You look like a Ferrari man. Are you a Ferrari man?"

"Sure. But I want a car that's not here."

Her smile sagged. A tinge of uncertainty diluted her otherwise perfect cheer. Still, she thrust her hand forward for a shake. "Brigitte. I'm pretty sure if someone else bought the car you wanted, we can order another one for you. Our delivery period is less than two weeks."

He fashioned a smile of his own. This American thing with the smiles, it took energy. "I'm looking for the car they don't build anymore. I know you sold such car. A 1972 Ferrari 246 GTS."

A flash of recognition brightened up her powdered face. "Oh, yes. I remember. In black. Louis sold it."

He loaded his words with heavy finality. "In that case, I must speak to Louis."

The woman hesitated and glanced to the plump man behind the corner desk. "I think he's on the phone—"

Ivan turned to walk over there. "Then I will wait for him to get off." Not to sound rude, he added over his shoulder, "Thank you for your assistance."

Louis, a heavyset man with cheeks like a chipmunk's, seemed surprised to see someone get past Brigitte to his desk. He put down the receiver. "How can I help you?"

Good. Not a smiling type. A slight accent, Central or South American. "I'm looking to buy a 246 GTS. I found your old listing on Internet. I want it."

Louis shrugged, his attention going back to his computer monitor. "Can't help you. Sold it to a guy who was super excited. I haven't seen a GTS like that in years."

"It is rare."

"Keep checking online. You might get lucky."

"Listen, Louis." Ivan pulled a chair and sat down on the other side of the desk, which earned him another surprised look. "What if you get me in touch with the buyer? I will make him a big offer. I will pay you a finder fee. I love that GTS. I really want it."

Louis sounded noncommittal, his gaze on the monitor. "Sure is a nice one."

Ivan stuck his hand into his pocket, pulled out the toy, and held it on his palm. "Look—black GTS. My father gave it to me when I was seven." He closed his palm. "Now I want the real one. I'll pay any price. Maybe you give me address, and I write a letter or call."

Louis shook his head. "We don't disclose the names of our buyers, see. Company policy."

"I understand." Ivan swept the room with a look, stopping at glass windows of offices lining one of the showroom walls. Brigitte—back at her desk, typing. Nobody watching.

He put his hand inside his chest pocket and produced an alligator skin wallet. Out came five bills, a hundred dollars each. He slid the stack of cash over the desk and stuck it under the corner of Louis's keyboard like it'd always been there. "Louis. I love this car. I don't care how much it will cost. I must have it."

"Sorry." Louis still sounded apologetic, but he was no longer shaking his head. And his gaze lingered on the cash. "It's a beautiful vehicle, but I just can't—"

Ivan dipped his fingers into the wallet. The five additional notes made the stack under the keyboard look a lot thicker.

Louis's quick eyes flitted from his monitor to Brigitte to the glass windows with his colleagues behind them. He breathed through his mouth now.

Silence lingered while Ivan's fingers went back into wallet. Five more notes tilted the keyboard sideways.

Louis rubbed his cheek. "You really want that GTS, huh." He cast another quick glance at the room and pulled his desk drawer open. With one sweep of his thick hand, he brushed the cash into the open drawer then slammed it shut. He straightened his keyboard. "You never mention my name or anything, okay?"

Ivan feigned indifference with a shrug. "I just want my ride."

Louis typed and clicked his mouse. Ivan moved the chair to the side to see the screen. Sales records. The letters too small to read.

Louis tore a piece of paper off a notepad, scribbled a few words on it, and passed it over. "Just keep me out of this, okay?"

"Of course." The piece fit neatly into his wallet. Ivan rose and headed for the door. On the way out, he caught a disinterested look from Brigitte.

Only cared about the ones coming in.

He turned his back on her—they would remember nothing but a stylish man with a weird accent who wore his hat nice and low on his forehead.

Back in his Lincoln, he typed the address into a smartphone from the gear case. Too bad Louis didn't provide a name, but the address was more important anyway. First foray into enemy territory.

Ivan drove north and east without haste, watching hills rise over a crowd of short, residential buildings. Strange. Such a busy city, but the buildings were only two or three stories.

The white letters of the Hollywood sign came into view and roused a soft chuckle out of him. Hollywood never got hit man characters right. They made killers flashy, their hits spectacular. They never showed the real work: the endless waiting, the preparation, or the failures lurking in the shadows of every assignment. They never showed the scars, the men stiff from old wounds.

Scars and tattoos. Interpol loved those; they made you identifiable. Like this Chechen's tiger. So stupid. He must have been in a prison gang with a tat like this. One of the Sinyaki, maybe? They loved their blue tats. No, not the Sinyaki. They always tattooed their fingers. But Partorg didn't mention this Kazbek having any finger tattoos.

Proximity to the target made license plates and pedestrian faces look sharper, distant sirens louder. Every turn and stop sign cut the distance to the man bold enough to betray Partorg and smart enough to get away with it for twenty years, tattoos and everything.

Ivan studied the traffic. Cars here took right turns on red. Brilliant—but could be a nasty surprise if you blew through an intersection in a hurry. Good, wide streets. Made for easy corners. Easy to drift in a turn. And parking spots under buildings everywhere, with open access. Drive in right off the street—nice hideout, if you needed one. The map said 'West Hollywood'. Who knew they had more than one Hollywood out here?

A few blocks closer to the hills, noisy streets gave way to quiet residential drives lined by trees and cast iron lamp posts. Shop fronts became tall hedges and neatly trimmed lawns.

He parked several blocks away from the address then changed into a track suit and running shoes.

An easy jog took him the rest of the way, to a tall stone fence, impenetrable, covered in thorny vines. A thorn drew blood from his finger with one touch. Any intruder would be shredded long before he reached the top, where other surprises would finish him off.

Ivan stole a casual glance into the grounds as he trotted by a wrought iron gate separating the street from the winding main drive. There was a guard post occupied by a young man apparently more interested in an old TV set than in a passing jogger. Here, Iven paused to place a couple of surveillance pieces for a better look at the gate and the house further in—all under the guise of tying his shoes; he took

91

off as soon as a young guard in the booth turned his head.

The presence of a guard didn't mean the job would be harder than any other. But things like tall fences and guards spoke of a certain mindset, which might translate into an expensive security setup.

Ivan jogged along the fence and around the block, checking parked cars for signs of the Mexican competition.

The cars lacked drivers. So far so good, as they said in English. An opportunity to take a better look at the grounds. And the trash. Always clues in the trash.

The topographical map on his smartphone suggested a few vantage points further uphill. He returned to the Lincoln and drove deeper into the neighborhood of towering fences and super-sized gates, the streets becoming narrow and steep. A winding drive dropped him off at the top of the ridge, and he parked in a narrow pullout.

A couple of cars zoomed by, and, once the road turned empty, he slipped into the bushes with a tripod in his hand and a camera around his neck with lenses so large he could pass for a sports photographer. Thorny branches scratched at his jacket like the hands of Afghan kids pulling on a soldier's clothes, demanding candy.

At the top, he looked down at the slopes and squares of sprawling mansions surrounded by palm trees. Palm trees—the guide said the tall ones were not native to California.

Air tickled his nostrils with the spicy smell of plants and warm dust. A boulder still hot from the day's sunlight provided a decent seat in front of the tripod.

More like a paparazzo here, not a sports photographer. Some of these private properties should belong to movie stars.

Looking through the camera, he found the driveway: flowers, booth with the guard, an old tree giving shade to an enormous swimming pool. The sun was to the right and behind, about to drop into the ocean. Perfect lighting for a rifle shot. Minimal bullet drop. No wind. Too bad it was an extraction instead of a straight hit.

He zoomed in on two large men who came from behind the house. One of them was walking a Doberman on-leash, a casual walk around the perimeter. The other split off and went toward the pool, a stocky black man in a stylish jacket over a t-shirt. The jacket flapped opened as he walked, revealing a harness with a holster.

Ivan grunted with satisfaction. Vot I priehali. First break on the case. Guards with guns. Thanks, Louis. Now he'd see who the guards worked to protect.

12

Los Angeles, California

Antonio lowered a picture frame into a cardboard box. He felt proud of himself, looking at his old wedding photo, his wife so radiant in her long dress. Marisol, mi amor. In her new house in Puerto Vallarta now, fussing over her new furniture, deciding where to put the plants.

He smiled at the memory of his wife letting out cries of joy after the lawyer picked up the signed papers, shook their hands, and wished them a happy retirement in their new home.

Everything happened so quickly. First the meeting with Miguel, then lawyers, then endless shopping. A trip to the old church was a relief, an escape. Such a nice Sunday Mass. Enchanting. Pleasant. Front row with wife and daughter, next to powerful friends. People whispering respectful things from behind.

Antonio padded the picture with bubble wrap and taped the box shut. He'd already boxed most of their personal stuff, a few pictures and clothes, her favorite brushes. Odd, the way Miguel insisted everything should be left unchanged, boxes unshipped, the landscaping business running as usual. But Miguel didn't say anything about moving in. And why would he? A man that rich would stay at the nice hotel.

Antonio's clam-shell phone vibrated and played a tune. He answered, glad not to miss the call. Could be Lucia, asking about her skirts.

An unfamiliar voice said, "Hola, Antonio? My name is Roberto Correon. I work for your cousin. Listen—are you at home right now?"

"Oh, you must be the real estate appraiser. But—"

"I'd like to stop by and take a look at things. I'm five minutes away, so why don't you wait for me, yes? Please."

Antonio sat in a kitchen chair, happy to still have the old furniture. "Do you need the address? Do you want me to wait for you by the gate?"

"No, I'll knock."

The man hung up without saying goodbye. The doorbell rang in minutes, and in came a middle-aged, chubby man in cowboy boots and hat, dark and sweaty. He insisted they close the gate behind them.

"I parked on the street," he said. His quick eyes took in the driveway and the garage. "Anyone else here?"

So confusing. "No, but why—why don't you park your car here?"

"I'm going to leave soon." He stared past Antonio. "So, this is the house?" But his gaze went to the walls surrounding the property. He pushed his hat back and walked in quick steps to the garage to lean around it and glance at the gap between the wall and fence. From there, he hopped past the plants to the other side of the house. Only then did he return to the front door, opened it, and entered without an invitation.

It was the strangest appraisal Antonio had ever seen. He walked in after the man. "Are you here to do the inspection? It's an old house—"

"Oh, there is no need. It's a family affair. We all trust each other." The man leaned forward, his hands on the kitchen table. "To Miguel, what he is paying you is nothing. He is a very important man. Very important." He noticed the box. "What's this?"

"I'm taking the pictures off the walls. Miguel said—"

But the man had already gone to the staircase, his boots banging on wood as he went up. "Yes, everything stays. No moving anything out."

Antonio followed him up the stairs, but at the top they bumped into each other, the man already heading down.

"Excellent. Everything is perfect. Are there more rooms to see?"

"Downstairs, but—"

"Vamos, vamos, let's go see."

They were back by the gate in five minutes, the man pushing buttons on his phone, putting it to his ear. Antonio stood and waited. As soon as the man hung up, Antonio said, "Are you leaving? Aren't you going to—"

"It's perfect. Just open the gate and wait."

Antonio rubbed his chin. "Wait for what?"

"For him to drive in."

The man walked onto the street and out of view. Open the gate? Was he coming back? Who was going to drive in?

Antonio pushed both sides of the gate open and was about to prop it with a brick, but an old Toyota was already turning toward him and into the driveway. It stopped in front of the garage. Miguel climbed out, stretching.

"How's it going, Tio? You can close the gate. Let me see the house you sold me."

Saying 'uncle' like a loving nephew. But he wasn't—at best a distant cousin on Carmelita's side of the family.

It was hard not to stare; only Miguel's neat haircut remained of the wealthy real estate developer from Mexico. Gone was the expensive suit and tie, the watch and the polished shoes, replaced by a plaid shirt and old jeans with a pair of dirty Nike sneakers on his feet.

Miguel turned toward the house.

Antonio pointed at the street. "But what about the real estate appra—"

"He's not coming in. Vamos. Close the gate and let's see if there are enough beds in the house."

Antonio pulled the gates closed, feeling weak from confusion. Enough beds? Was the rest of Carmelita's family coming over?

He shuffled his feet, still in slippers, back to the front door. "I had no idea you were arriving today."

Miguel wrapped his arm around him. "It's better this way, Tio. Let's go inside."

For the second time, Antonio returned to his kitchen. He'd never considered the possibility that Miguel would actually move in himself. And along with other men, like they were immigrants crowding each other in a flophouse?

"I only have two beds here. You may have to buy extra," Antonio said. "When are they coming? And when should I leave?"

"Don't worry, Tio. We don't need much. And I'll send you back as soon as we're done. Right now I need you here." Miguel was already in the bedroom, his voice echoing from further inside the house. "This is good. There's enough space here."

"But how many men?"

Miguel stepped into the living room from the bedroom. "Four of us. And you." He stuck his hand into his pocket and pulled out a wad of cash. "A mattress is what, about five hundred?" He counted off the notes and handed them over. "Did you keep the truck like I asked?"

"Yes, you said you wanted—"

"Excellent. Go get two nice mattresses right now while I settle in. I don't want my men to sleep on the floor."

Antonio took the money and stared at the bills. Everything was spinning, like he was on a merry-go-around. From the kitchen came the sound of water pouring from the tap. Miguel was splashing his face when Antonio shuffled in.

Later, when Antonio came back from the store, the other three men were already at the house. He didn't know what to think. Nobody cared to introduce themselves. They sent him out again, to bring Chinese food, ignoring his talk of the good restaurant just around the corner.

He returned with a cardboard box full of food containers and put it down on the kitchen table, the men in a circle on their chairs with beers. Their energy upset Antonio. They sat like compressed springs waiting to uncoil.

The youngest was just a kid and ate with his hands, ignoring forks and napkins. "Are we going there tonight?" he asked. "I bet El Checheño is going to be surprised."

Miguel chuckled. "I want to take a look around first, before we meet our old friend."

Antonio stood still, a stack of his wife's favorite coasters in-hand. "El Checheño? Who's that?"

Miguel finished drinking his beer and licked his lips. "Tio, that's the man you work for. The thief who took my money."

"Mister Dominguez?"

Miguel smiled in a way that made Antonio uncomfortable, a scowl more than a smile. "Dominguez? Is that what he calls himself? That's funny. Very funny."

Antonio didn't see why Dominguez was a funny name. He thought El Checheño was a funny name. Strange, even. Everything was strange with Miguel's men suddenly here, playing cards, smoking, and drinking beers with the general air of people who were waiting for some big event to take place.

He went to pack the knick-knacks from upstairs—pictures and old albums stuffed into the last box. The men were loud in the kitchen. Stress shortened Antonio's breath and made him sweat. Late at night, he often had pain in his chest. But it wasn't late yet.

He carried the cardboard box to the garage. His truck was out, and the garage door stood cracked open, the light turned on inside. He pushed the door wider with the box and stepped in.

One of Miguel's men, the one they called Dado, sat on a crate, loading shells from a box into a long, black shotgun.

Antonio's knees buckled at the sight, and weakness shot into his chest and throat. The box slipped from his hands and thumped onto the floor, its cardboard edge splitting open.

Dado looked up and said, "Hola, Tio."

Out of breath, Antonio patted his pant pockets in panic. His fingers trembled as he pulled out a bottle of pills. He gripped the bottle so hard that it jumped from his fingers and fell, rattling as it rolled away.

Dado stopped the bottle with his foot and picked it up, the shotgun in his other hand.

Antonio would have gone down on the floor of his own garage, right where he dropped the pills, if Dado hadn't put the gun aside and come over to prop him and guide him to the crate.

Easing Antonio onto the improvised seat, Dado said, "Here, here, Tio. Rest a little."

The crate. That's all Antonio could think about: he was sitting on a crate full of guns. Santa María . . . All of these men. Soldiers. No wonder they did whatever Miguel told them to do, like dogs with their master.

Antonio rubbed the left side of his chest, his breath short. Tears made everything vague. No, not so lucky after all, certainly not in the way Miguel described it back in Puerto Vallarta. An old fool who fell into someone else's war.

Dado disappeared and in a minute Miguel came in and put his hand on Antonio's shoulder.

"Tio, you have nothing to worry about. My men need the guns to protect me. Every important man must have guards."

"I'm just an old gardener," Antonio said, wiping sweat from his face and neck with a kerchief.

Miguel pressed down, his grip firm and steady. "Tio, you shouldn't worry so much. Your job is to help me get into that thief's house. After that, I'll put you on a plane back to Mexico. And I'll make sure you never have to worry about money again."

Antonio nodded and rose slowly. "I should lie down. I don't feel well."

Miguel handed him a bottle of water and guided him out of the garage. Antonio smarted from the tight grip on his arm.

Old fool. Should have listened to what your heart told you in Puerto Vallarta—this great luck was too good to be true.

By the time they made it to the kitchen, Antonio wasn't sure he'd be able to mount the steps to his bedroom—great weakness had spread through his body, neck to toes: he'd fallen into the vile trap of temptation his faith had warned him all his life to avoid.

Miguel's men sat at the table where Antonio's family used to share meals, the table Antonio had built with his own hands. He stared at their tattooed arms and listened to their foul jokes. The harsh reality of his mistake squeezed his heart with iron fingers.

He gripped the wooden handrail and willed himself up the staircase to his room, his feet so heavy he could barely lift them from one step to another. His body sagged and resisted, his breath uneven, his eyes watery.

As he sat on his bed with eyes closed, he saw himself shaking Miguel's hand back at Jorge's hotel in Vallarta, Miguel's hand hard, like he was a construction worker, but with fewer calluses. A hard hand and dark eyes without any feeling in them.

Antonio washed the pills down with leftover water from the bottle and waited for them to settle in his stomach. Too early in the day to be in bed. Needing rest like an old, sick man.

He lay on the comforter, sure he wouldn't be able to sleep.

Questions banged about his head: What to do? Which way to run? What would happen? But the pills worked their magic and granted merciful oblivion, brought him to a thoughtless place away from fear and guilt.

He passed out without any answers.

13

Los Angeles Westside, California

Looking down at the villa, Ivan counted surveillance cameras protruding from the roof corners and adjacent garage. All this security would make the job of sneaking in undetected difficult or even impossible. Not one of those quick grab-and-run jobs.

He shifted his view to the yellow walls of a service building in the compound: two more modern surveillance cameras drilled into shingles, one on the front and one on the side. Clearly, the owner maintained a discipline that discouraged close contact, the kind that involved an examination of an old tattoo on a hairy chest.

Hard to blame the man for being cautious. Anyone who took the risk of crossing Partorg would be wise to hire an army.

Ivan left the camera trained on the villa and waited. The guards came in and out a few times. A small truck rolled up the drive, grapes and apples painted on the side of its refrigerated trailer. A uniformed driver unloaded a few tables and boxes with the help of the guards.

Ivan snapped a picture of the company name: BESTSIDE CATERING. Setting up for a party?

The truck left.

The sun rolled down, its rays fanning out from behind the hills, and the moment the last of them faded, the lights inside the compound came on and flooded the property. It glowed like a football stadium during a night game.

Ivan put a cap on the camera and was about to take it off the tripod. Nothing else to see here. Can't do this alone even in theory, not without disobeying Partorg's instructions and taking the risk of spooking the target. Which meant the local genius in a skirt had to get involved.

Blyad. Ivan got off the boulder, ready to leave. One last glance at the villa without help from the camera. He froze. The grounds, bathed in light, showed signs of commotion.

With one quick movement, Ivan yanked the cap off his camera

and zoomed in. A black Ferrari rolled out of the garage and stopped in front of the main entrance. A lithe, dark man stepped out and entered the villa with the authority of someone who lived in it. He wore a yellow tracksuit: three stripes on the pants, three stripes on the jacket.

Adidas, the favorite uniform of every gangster in mid-nineties Soviet Russia. Kazbek, in all his glory.

A flood of adrenaline quickened Ivan's heartbeat. A chance to get home to Lena.

He tore through the brush like a scared bear. Dry twigs and stones crunched under his feet as he ran uphill to his car, in his hand the camera still attached to its tripod.

He threw the gear into the back seat and drove off with his tires screeching. Through every turn, the heavy sedan rocked side-to-side like a boat on choppy water. He made it to the parking spot a few meters down from main entrance with the gate still closed.

Dusk made the glow of the TV screen in the guard booth visible, the guard's face highlighted by flickering light. The guard sat slumped over his desk, his hand under his cheek.

Ivan stepped out to access the gear in the trunk—a jet injector. Back in the driver's seat, he attached a gas cylinder to the bottom of the device, the cylinder itself becoming a handle. He tested the instrument on a leather pillow of the car seat and put it into his pocket.

Kazbek took a while to come out. When the Ferrari's sleek profile finally slipped through the gate, Ivan waited for it to pass and reach the end of the street. And as the Ferrari rumbled by, he spotted the same three Adidas stripes on the driver's shoulder: Kazbek, out in the open. Alone. Without any protection detail.

Ivan waited for the sports car to make it past a stop sign and took off after it. Behind him, the street stayed quiet and empty. He felt focused, sharp. A unique opportunity, and with the right gear at hand. A solid chance to deliver the goods well ahead of Partorg's expectations. And no need for men in dresses.

On the boulevard, traffic was thick, making it easy to stay close to the Ferrari without being obvious. A fast car like that, in the hands of a skilled driver, could take off and disappear in a flash.

But it never did. Kazbek drove as if his car was made of glass: he used turn signals to change lanes. He obeyed the speed limit. He made no sudden lane changes. Twice, the Chechen could have crossed the intersection on yellow with time to spare, but he'd stopped well in advance each time.

The Ferrari's sleek silhouette stood out among bulky sedans, easy to spot. Ivan dropped back. The grid of Los Angeles streets allowed for easy tailing. These young countries—square blocks and straight lines everywhere. Even when the Ferrari made a right turn at the red light and slipped out of sight, Ivan caught up with it using a side alley without speeding and becoming visible.

No longer worried about the chase, Ivan noted the turn-offs to quiet alleys they passed. At this hour, it was fair to assume Kazbek would have a single appointment. The Chechen hadn't brought any bodyguards, which meant he was going to a secure location. This would leave an in-route intercept as the only option.

Ivan scanned both sides of the street for quiet sections with few cars and few streetlights—most people took the same route on their way back as on their way there, a minor deviation notwithstanding. One quiet spot would be enough, on a street with businesses closed for the day.

Different here in West Hollywood, with so few pedestrians around. In Russia, in a residential neighborhood like this, there'd be people walking everywhere.

He drove through the familiar area, past stores with Russian names, Foxy's favorite club only a short ride away. If things went well, the skirt nonsense would be unnecessary.

Encouraged, Ivan cut his distance to the Ferrari to one block.

Kazbek pulled into a corner parking lot in front of a single-story building divided into sections, each one a small restaurant. 'Dinner with associates' hypothesis now looked more likely.

The Chechen got out and walked to a door at the end of the building where a group of men stood talking.

Ivan turned into a side street and drove by, his passenger window open. Kazbek and the men greeted each other with open arms, speaking in excited tones in a language that sounded Chechen. None of them seemed to pay any attention to the black Lincoln Town Car that slid past the parking lot.

The chain on Kazbek's neck gave off a yellow glint as he hugged a corpulent man in a business suit. The man said "Kazbek" out loud, nice and sharp, the same way Partorg did in Moscow.

A name like this. You just can't miss it.

Ivan straightened in the driver's seat and drove on to find a gap between parked cars, under a tree. The air smelled of dry leaves as he stepped out, chilly now that the sun had set. But nice weather for the middle of January. Almost too warm for wearing the track suit.

He walked toward the lights of the restaurant, his muscles limber with adrenaline.

The Ferrari sat in the spot between the curb and a Mercedes 600, the same car Fedot drove in Russia. Ivan clicked his tongue: different gang, same lack of imagination.

The darkness worked to his advantage. He could see the men inside, seated in chairs around a brightly-lit table, but they wouldn't see him. The setup only took a couple of seconds anyway—after a young couple stepped into a Thai restaurant that shared the parking lot, he slipped between the cars and kneeled next to the Ferrari's rear tire at the same time a local bus rolled by, its engine roar providing cover.

Ivan took the stem cap off and pressed the valve to let all the air out. The bus only moved a block, but the tire was already flat.

Kazbek didn't come out until well past nine, unsteady on his legs. In the dark, he climbed into his car without noticing the flat. In fact, he didn't notice it for a good while, long enough for Ivan to start worrying if the Chechen was going to notice at all. But after hitting a hard bump, the Ferrari pulled over into a residential street alongside an empty sidewalk, single-story houses behind green hedges on both sides.

Kazbek crawled out of the car's low seat, his hands clawing at the door. From down the street, with headlights on, Ivan watched the Chechen stare dumbly at the tire. Hard to believe this kind of luck. The mark all alone, with plenty of alcohol in him, and hardly any light here at all—the nearest streetlight was in the trees several blocks away.

Years in America had made the Chechen careless. First the Mexicans, then the car, and now this.

Alcohol interfered with Kazbek's reaction time as well; when Ivan pulled behind to blind the Chechen and to shield him from view of approaching cars, Kazbek squinted into the headlights with a puzzled expression.

"Flat tire?" Ivan said as he climbed out. The way he rolled his 'r', it almost sounded American. Not that it mattered. He didn't give Kazbek time to answer. A quick step to within striking distance, and he pressed the business end of the jet injector against Kazbek's neck and pulled the trigger.

The tranquilizer went in with a whisper. Kazbek said, "Hmmm—" and grabbed the top edge of the car door, unsteady like a clothing store dummy kicked out of balance. Ivan caught him and held him under the armpits. He looked up and down the street, peering into the dark. Not a soul around. The neighborhood had settled in for the night.

For a skinny man, Kazbek felt heavy. Ivan lowered him into the passenger seat of the Ferrari, the Chechen now looking drowsy, his breath slow and relaxed, his mouth slightly open. In an unlikely case of a patrol car taking interest—and in America, police cars seemed much harder to come by than patrols in Russia—the police would find a drunken man in a passenger seat, unable to speak. Kazbek's breath, full of beer, would help explain a confused look in his eyes. And who didn't look confused when they were drunk?

Ivan closed the door and went to park his Lincoln further up the street. He returned to the Ferrari with an electric tire pump in-hand. As he walked, he dialed Ruslan. The man answered with a Russian-sounding "Allo?"

"Do you have the storage space?"

"Already?"

"Do you have it or not?"

"I have it."

"Don't go anywhere and wait for my call."

Ivan hung up and squatted in front of the deflated wheel. The buzz from the pump competed with the cicadas.

He opened the driver side door. The Chechen was drooling onto his Adidas suit in the passenger seat, his head against the window.

Ivan scraped the top of his head and grunted as he climbed in. Tiny car, and the driver's seat didn't go back far enough to fit comfortably into the cramped space. The damn roadster was too small.

While the pump buzzed outside, he lowered the back rest, settling in and letting his mind flash images onto the invisible screen now darkened by the night. From the dealership to the villa, from the villa to the restaurant, from the restaurant to the dark street. All clean.

No. Not clean. Not clean at all.

His body twitched in the seat, stricken by a simple image: a guard walking his Doberman through the grounds, the villa flooded with light, all of it under the watchful eyes of the surveillance cameras.

All wrong.

With all that money and effort invested in protection, why did Kazbek have none in transit or at the arrival point? If America softened him that much, why have guards at the villa?

Ivan swung in his seat and unzipped Kazbek's track suit and lifted the shirt.

No tattoos.

A clammy chill spread through Ivan's body, making his mouth dry. He pulled out a pocket flashlight and looked again. No tiger on the chest—this would explain the lack of security in transit. Must be someone from the clan, a relative or an associate, someone close enough to Kazbek to have the privilege of driving the boss's car. Someone who looked enough like Kazbek and was stupid enough to be used as a decoy.

He patted the guy's pockets and found his wallet. A New York driver's license sat between two credit cards.

Brooklyn address. Amir Nogaev, 32, 5'6", brown eyes.

Under the flashlight, the man's chest showed no scarring from removed tattoos. Definitely not Kazbek. Ivan pushed the body aside, and the Chechen's head—was this guy even Chechen?—thunked against the window.

Ivan groaned as he leaned back. Too keen to act. Faulty assumption. Amateur stuff. Unforgivable. At best, this Amir was a relative. At worst, he was now a triggered decoy, a signal flare fired off as a warning to Kazbek, a warning that would send him running.

Ivan pinched his face, his thumb and index finger digging into his cheeks to unclench his teeth, muscles hurting from tension. This desire to wrap things up and go back to Lena—coupled with distaste for the homosexual—had colored every important judgment.

Partorg's best worker had become an opportunist.

Ivan dismissed the reprimand with a grunt. A terrible start to an operation, but only a start. This Dominguez was most likely the mark.

Clean up and regroup.

He reached to open the glove compartment. Inside were papers, a pack of cigarettes, and chewing gum. Bills and a car registration for a man named Dominguez. The real owner of the GTS, most likely.

He stepped out of the car and pulled Nogaev back into the driver's seat. The drug had taken full effect, and the man's head flopped around his neck like a ball on a rope. But with Amir's arms draped over the wheel, he would stay slumped forward as if he were asleep.

Two more injections just above his hairline guaranteed Amir Nogaev would have a terrible hangover in a few hours and wouldn't remember a thing. He wouldn't care about a small scratch on the back of his neck, hidden in his hair.

Ivan went back to the Lincoln and took off his gloves. Amir had gone drinking, which provided a perfect cover. But what if he hadn't drunk enough? Kazbek would grow suspicious, and Partorg would lose his chance at revenge.

Ivan felt his abdominal muscles spasm at the thought of what

Partorg would do if that were to happen.

He drove off, the Ferrari blending into a dark street behind, a reminder of the foolish blunder.

Idiot. Such a careless move. Luck should have no place in this work. The worst time to gamble with spontaneous approaches.

Back at the hotel, he fired off a quick email: "Hey, I found a place for us to go dancing."

He didn't hesitate before hitting send.

Foxy's reply came in a few seconds later: "Glad u still want 2 go. Trust me, you'll like my moves."

Ivan stared at the letters. God only knew if this partnership could get anything done, with one of the partners wearing dresses and such. But at this point, the normal one of the two didn't deserve the privilege of doing anything alone.

14

East Los Angeles, California

Miguel came down the stairs while his men were playing cards at the table under a hanging light. Seso looked up with a question in his eyes when Miguel entered the room.

Miguel pointed over his shoulder. "He's asleep. Old man takes strong medicine." But this didn't seem to satisfy the quiet man.

"Do we still need him? We know the address."

Miguel felt the pang of irritation. Seso, always looking into everything. "He's seen the Chechen asshole, and he's been to his house."

Seso scratched his chin. "He looked sick."

"He's old. You look bad when you're old. You take naps."

A wine bottle stood in the middle of the table, cork half-way in. Miguel picked up a glass and the bottle. Seso could be annoying with his doubts. At least the man's tone was always right. Whatever he said never undermined authority.

The wine sent mild warmth from his stomach up to his head. Miguel sat down and sloshed the wine around the glass. "We should bring a case of this back with us. I swear, this stuff from the north tastes better than anything we get back home."

"It's the fog where they grow it," Seso said. "Gives special flavor to the grape. We don't get this kind of ocean fog back home. Maybe in Baja, but that's it."

Miguel poured more wine into his glass. "The only thing they know how to do in Baja is fish and drink beer."

Cho, restless in his chair, sniffled and wiped his nose with a sleeve.

Miguel fixed him with a stare. The kid had no patience. "Relax. Dado knows how to pick the best girls. You'll get your whore."

Cho nodded eagerly. "He said an hour. I can wait an hour."

"Can you? Your cards are showing."

Cho stared at his hand. A jack of spades was facing out. He

flipped it around and said, "I just want to see if it's true."

"What's true?"

"He thinks local whores know special tricks," Seso said.

Miguel held his glass up to the light to see its deep red. "The drink is different place to place. Whores are the same everywhere."

Cho said, "But they make all the movies here, Jefe. They must have the whores from the movies."

Seso chuckled. "He told Dado to get the movie stars."

Miguel put the glass down. "He'll get what he'll get. Since when do you care—"

The radio on the table crackled, and Dado's voice came in. "I'm here. Open the gate."

Cho took off as soon as he got the nod.

"I must be old," Seso said. "I don't remember ever being so excited about girls."

"It's because you never were. Did you get the lookouts posted?"

Seso nodded at the radio. "They'll call in anything odd. It's good in this place. Especially at night. Quiet."

"I told you the old man was a godsend. We're good here for at least a few days."

Miguel added another splash to his glass. Everyone could drink as much as they wanted tonight. First day in a new place always the safest—should anyone be following, federales or sicarios from Sinaloa, they wouldn't have had time to catch up yet. And the men could use a little fun after such a long trip. Even the best crew, loyal and patient as they were, needed a distraction to keep them eager and satisfied. They would be more relaxed when the time came to do work.

The thought of work sparked excitement in him that pushed back the haze from wine. The next few days would be fun.

From the outside came the low rumble of Dado's voice, followed by peals of laughter and giggling from the girls. The first one stumbled on the doorsill and nearly fell into the kitchen, like she was already drunk.

Dado picked her up from behind. "Chica, if you want to lie down, lie down in my bed."

"I'm always falling in these heels." She sprung back to her feet, too agile to be drunk. Her black stilettos clicked on the floorboards as she turned to the table, black dress tight over her body. She threw back her hair and took in the kitchen with a confident look. Her lips, red with lipstick, folded into a coquettish smile.

She said, "Hola!"

Another girl stepped through, tall and much older than the others. A woman, really. Not a girl. Much thicker makeup, but it didn't hide the lines on her forehead. Cho had his hands on her waist, guiding her to the table.

Dado held the door open and waved at someone else outside. "Come, come." Two more girls came in, both short and a little thick.

They crowded the kitchen with the clicks of their heels and a sweet mix of perfumes thick enough to overpower the cigarette smoke.

Miguel glanced over the lineup from the other side of the table and frowned at the tall one in the middle, at Cho's hands on her waist.

Dado said, "Slow down, kid."

Cho took his hands off the woman, a guilty look on his puffy face. He hid his hands behind his back and scurried to the table to pull out the chairs.

Miguel looked from one girl to another.

The small one who stumbled met his gaze and said, "What, just wine and beer?"

She surprised him when she grabbed the bottle and his glass without invitation and poured one for herself. She took a huge draft, her eyes never leaving his face.

The glass was barely off her lips when she said, "Muchachos, what's happening? No music?" Her chocolate eyes carried no judgment.

Miguel smiled at her lack of reaction to his pockmarked face.

Her gaze left him, her black eyebrows raised, a cute crease between them.

Sassy.

Normally, he'd go for the tall one, but this morena had a quick way about her, a spark. Her eyes flashed when she glanced at him again, the glass back to her lips.

He patted his thigh. "Come, sit."

She plopped into his lap without hesitation. He put his palm on her waist, a perfect fit against the firm inward bend.

"Is that it?" she asked, looking at the table. "No perico to powder our little noses?"

He chuckled. "That's it. We are like Americans now—we eat and drink healthy. No drugs. Now, where is your accent from?"

"I don't have an accent. You have an accent."

Her insolence was amusing. He raised his eyebrow at her. "I do?"

"Of course." She nodded and screwed her small butt tighter into his lap. "You're not from Spain. But I am. She nodded at the rest of the girls. "We all are." She was sitting across his thighs, dangling her legs like her feet were in a creek.

"Come here, Española." He leaned to her neck and breathed her in. "I like your smell. What is it?"

She wiggled her shoulders. "You're tickling me. It's a lemon blossom."

"Bueno, lemon blossom. Come show me what you look like under the dress."

Cho's portable stereo played a quick salsa beat, and the current of music surged through the girl and launched her off his lap. "I love this song!" She quick-stepped, wine sloshing in her glass as she held it up while her hips swung and her hair flew.

She grabbed his hand, dancing close to him, the warmth of her body against his for a second, pulling him off the chair.

"Dance with me!"

He stared, amused. All a game to her, but without pretense. She was having fun. He shook her hand off and walked over to the bedroom door and pushed it open. But this puta was something special—she danced all the way to the door, but instead of coming through, she grabbed his arm and pulled, saying, "Baila, baila, chico!" Not giving up on the dancing idea.

"Puta, vamos!" He caught her by the wrist and yanked her into the room. Her wine spilled, and she stumbled forward. But catlike, she spun and landed with her back on the bed, laughing.

He frowned, her disobedience now irritating—a clear challenge. Time to tell her to remember her place. He stepped forward and pointed his finger at her face. "Puta, don't play games with me."

She met his gaze, giggled, and pulled the bottom of her dress down, like she was some school-girl, ashamed of herself. Next, she grabbed his finger, rubbing it. Her allure, with its hot magnetism, disarmed his anger. And her small hands went to his belt, quick to unbuckle it.

She left him with his pants falling off. Childlike, the way her attention dashed from his belt to kicking off her stilettos, to her wine glass. A smile kept her face lively as she sprung to her feet.

"Here," she said, putting her glass on the bed stand. She took his hands and pulled him toward her, guiding his hands to her hips.

Playing games, this whore. Usually, they waited to hear what the client wanted, but not this one. Cheeky. Arousing and annoying at the same time.

He let her pick up his hand and guide his fingers up to her face, their tips caressing her lips then sliding to her soft, warm neck.

He didn't like her being in control, but the impulse to yank his hand out of hers and slap her dissolved at the beckoning in her chocolate eyes, her mouth open now with a soft gasp as his hand landed on her firm breast.

He pushed her, and she fell back on the covers. "You are a whore. Stop acting as if you like it and take the dress off." Was it the wine? He didn't sound convincing to himself.

She never broke off her stare, even as she fell with her arms splayed and her hair fanning out.

The unsettled feeling went away as she pulled her dress up until the arch of her panties showed. She went slow, teasing him. Her palms stopped on the hipbones. She stared, her mouth open a little, an invitation in her eyes.

She was leading him on, the damn whore.

He got on the bed and stuck his hands under her dress, pushing it up. Her velvety, dark skin was dry and hot. Her dress slid up and caught under her arms.

She giggled. He climbed over her and ripped the dress up in one angry pull. But she wasn't pliant, like the others; she wasn't waiting for him to do with her as he pleased. As soon as he tossed her dress to the side, she sat up under him, her slender body taut with effort, and ripped his shirt open.

"Puta madre!"

He slapped her this time. She fell back on the bed, gasping. But her gaze never wavered, burning with intensity. One of his buttons fell on her chest.

He tossed his shirt off. "You want to play, you little whore?"

She wore no bra. Her breasts filled his hands with satisfying warmth as he grabbed her and squeezed hard. She moaned. But her hands were on top of his, joining in the effort, her eyes meeting his with electrifying ferocity.

He ripped her stockings off, and then her panties. Her small body flowed in smooth curves. She flexed her toes, and the muscles in her legs gave definition to her thighs. She looked at the ceiling, arms above her head. She stretched like she was ready for bed!

Her small breasts enticed his hands to return.

The pull of her—was it the smell? This morena pulled him without moving, without looking.

He took his pants off like when he was a boy of fourteen,

yearning and clueless with his first girl. When he dove into her, into a blur of delicious skin and lips, she met him with her open mouth. Her tongue flicked out and went under his lip, a teasing slide along his teeth.

An intrusion.

He grunted and pushed her face into the bed with his palm. Back to his senses, he got off of her, picked up his pants and pulled out a condom. She was as eager as he was—unbelievable, this whore. She snatched the condom out of his fingers and ripped the plastic open.

He almost slapped her again when she pulled her arm away after he reached for it, the condom in her fingers.

But her other hand was stroking him now, fingers kneading and rising up. Then her mouth joined them, and he forgot about her challenge to his dominance.

The way she worked him, the pressure between his legs demanded an immediate release. He groaned, and her lips left him. But her fingers came back, quick to unroll the cool rubber. She fell back on the bed in front of him, her arms outstretched, her eyes closed.

Finally, she was giving herself to him.

He fell on her, hungry for the heat of her body. His favorite feeling—so much hotter on the inside.

He groaned with satisfaction as he entered her, his hands grasping at her neck. Now in a frenzy, they convulsed together, his breath mixing with hers, his thoughts murky and his mind lost in the pleasure of gasping and molding her supple form under him.

Until she giggled into his ear.

She was laughing at him!

A swell of anger brought him up. He said through his teeth, "Puta, you're not going to laugh at me," and curled his fingers around her throat and kept thrusting, choking the laughter out of her, his domination now absolute as she floundered under him and the pressure spilled out of him and into her.

He fell alongside her, breathing heavily, listening to her gasps. He yanked the condom off and tossed it. "Don't you ever laugh at me."

Her breath evened out, but she didn't try to leave or even get up.

He couldn't believe it when he felt it—her hand was back between his legs, stroking and caressing.

She kept caressing him even as she pulled the duvet over them both, the room chilly with night air. He was aroused and drowsy at the same time.

A crazy thought went through his head: this was his house, and he

111

was with his woman, the two of them alone. And maybe he should ask her to make him something to eat.

15

Downtown Los Angeles, California

Ivan forked a piece of fried egg, dunked it into a smear of ketchup, and ate it with a bite of rye toast. The prospect of working with the homosexual seemed less depressing now than last night—mornings always took some weight off the problems of the previous day.

A few hotel guests shuttled to and from the hotel's breakfast buffet, most of them drinking coffee and orange juice. Americans really liked their heartburn.

He swirled a teabag in his cup, hoping for a stronger brew. Not even a few days on the road, and the thought of home already pulled at his heart. The way Lena blew on her tea to cool it, the way she pursed her lips out of fear of burning them, her eyes half-closed in childlike hesitation—impossible not to miss her.

Morning in Los Angeles, evening in Moscow. Was she watching the evening news? Repeating the words?

Two business types walked in and caught his attention: suits and ties, confident, their jackets unbuttoned. A lady in thick makeup followed, blue sweater, black skirt and stockings. None of them young enough or tall enough to be Foxy—although without heels Foxy wore at the Trunks, he wouldn't be so tall either.

The door swung open again, and a young woman in a tailored suit walked through. She was fit, tall enough, and her trousers could easily hide the thicker muscles on her legs. Foxy'd have strong legs.

The woman strutted to the salad bar. Ivan eyed the back of her suit with suspicion the whole time she moved along the buffet line. He waited for her to finish loading her tray and turn around—now that she was closer, a bigger Adam's apple should be a giveaway, no matter the disguise.

But hers was small, and her face looked much wider than Foxy's. Thicker lips.

Another young woman, dressed in a blue stewardess' outfit,

tightened her mouth when he stared at her hips longer than he should have. She had Foxy's slender arms, but her wispy hair was too thin.

Ivan's corner table gave views of the entire room, from the entrance to the food stations and windows, but none of the guests looked familiar. Without the music or dimmed lights of the dance club, Foxy wasn't going to pull the same stunt. Not here. What was the English saying? Fool me once, shame on you. Fool me twice, and I'm the village idiot.

Ivan checked another woman entering the room—too plump to be Foxy.

A business executive in a striped suit left the food station carrying a tray with a crowded plate of fried eggs and fruit, steam rising from a cup of coffee. He approached Ivan's table in confident strides.

"Mind if I land over here?" he asked, his voice deep, almost a baritone.

Most of the other tables were taken. The request made sense, the room getting busier by the minute. Ivan looked back at the executive, the man tall and lanky, golden tie, expensive watch, designer glasses. Shaved head. At least in his forties, his suit bulky.

Ivan shrugged, closed his laptop, and said, "If you want."

The man put down his tray then took off his jacket and hung it on the back of the chair before sitting down. The musky smell of his cologne wafted across the table.

A hostess came by to offer him coffee.

"No, thank you." The man kept his bespectacled eyes on his food, sharp elbows sticking out as he chewed his way through the eggs.

Ivan sipped his tea and watched the room. From the corner of his eye, he saw the man wipe his thin lips with a napkin, take off his glasses, and pick up his coffee cup.

"You really underestimate me, you know. That's the second time I snuck up on you."

Ivan stared at the man's eyes, a familiar glint in them—the damn joker with the same trick. Same bony face but wider somehow with a mustache, and his voice much huskier. The width of the shoulders also different, but that could be the suit. Glasses and no wig. That did it.

Ivan shook his head. "You with tricks again. What is next, you wear a clown suit?"

Foxy chuckled. "Just helping you lose the attitude. No need to get sore."

"I am not sore. But your dress tricks are not helping anything. We

114

need to talk business."

Foxy's mustache curled up. "I can talk business in my birthday suit, Drago." He adjusted his tie. "That's part of being a professional."

Ivan grunted. "Last time you wore dress like some call girl."

Foxy crossed his arms and leaned back. "I can be a call girl if I have to. Question is, can you?"

They were wasting time. "We work different. I don't wear dress. But the boss says you do good work. If you want to wear a dress, wear a dress."

A thin smile animated Foxy's face. "Nice of you to give me permission."

Ivan raised his palms. "I didn't mean it like that. I can say sorry. We all have our problems, yes? I'm not used to men in dresses, and you don't like Russians like me. You call me names. But we have work to do, as you said. The boss wants this done. So I can say sorry, and we can work."

Foxy grinned, his eyes shiny. "Ha. Big Russian apologizing." He sat back and crossed his legs. "I guess that counts for something." He paused. "I can be reasonable. Let's talk about our man." Foxy rubbed his cheek. "He bought the car, right?"

Ivan exhaled. Finally, talking business. "I already traced the car. I found his house." He pulled his laptop closer and flipped it open. Its screen lit up, an array of images from his surveillance taking the entire span. He turned the screen toward Foxy, who clicked on each picture to expand it.

"Where is this?" Foxy asked.

"Close to Beverly Hills. I know his name now. It's a Spanish name. Dominguez."

"Mexican." Foxy nodded, his eyes bright with screen reflection. "Are you sure it's him?"

"I followed one of his men from villa to restaurant. I heard him talking Chechen. And I went through the house trash this morning. People do that here, too. Collect bottles."

Foxy raised his eyebrows. "They didn't see you?"

"They have a guard, but he does not look."

"So our man owns a villa in a posh neighborhood, huh?"

"Yes. But also I have bad news."

"Bad news?"

"I think you call this a mansion in English, but it is like a compound." Ivan pulled the chair closer and opened a few close-up images on the screen. "Here, the guards and dogs. And a permanent guard at the gate." He scrolled to another image. "Video cameras. Last generation, cooled thermographics. Expensive. And this is his car driving in at night. I put my cameras there. Small. They look like stones. So we can download video."

Foxy narrowed his eyes at the images. "This just might be our man." He stuck his finger at the screen. "Wait. What's this?"

"From yesterday evening. This truck drove in, and they unloaded chairs from it. And tables." Ivan pointed at the laptop. "I took many pictures, but no Kazbek. He could be hiding. It was not him in the Ferrari. I checked."

"You checked?"

Ivan kept his face relaxed. "I watched him, close but safe."

Foxy kept scrolling through the pictures. "This ain't half-bad." His tone different now, without sarcasm.

"My gear is near the gates, and I can download it from the car. But I doubt we can confirm the tattoo without getting past the gates." He pulled the old photograph from his pocket and handed it to Foxy, who studied then gave it back.

"He may have removed it. I would."

"It is large. There will be scars."

Foxy didn't confirm, his finger swiping across the laptop's touchpad. "Did you get a picture of the woman in there?"

Ivan leaned back, picked up a cup, and took a sip. "You think there is a woman?"

Foxy shrugged. "Of course. There are towels on two chairs by the pool."

"I thought the same. But I was not sure."

Foxy smiled and leaned back to stretch, his arms above his hand. "Our man Kaz lives in a mansion, owns a Ferrari, and you think there isn't a woman?" He leaned forward in one quick motion, his hand back on the track pad. "I guarantee you, there's going to be a woman." His smile grew wider. "Or a man." He clicked and scrolled to an image with the catering truck, and his smile faded. "They have a party going on." He pulled out his cell phone and typed a message, checking with the image. "I have a hookup with a few catering companies. If the crowd's a decent size, they'll have a guest list. I might be able to get us invited."

Ivan sipped his tea while his new partner worked the phone, a focused expression on the gaunt face.

Foxy tossed the phone back on the table, a fresh glint in his eyes, the smile back on his thin lips. "If it turns out we can get in, we'd have to do something about your look."

"What's wrong with my look?"

Foxy rolled his eyes. "What do you think you look like?"

Ivan shrugged. "A man?"

Foxy shook his head. "Wrong. You look like a Russian mobster. If there were children here, you'd make them cry. Our man Kaz will see you coming a mile away."

Ivan thought back to his first impression of Amir in the Adidas suit. True. Russians could find Russians in any crowd. "I don't have to go in with you. I can work from the outside."

"What if he's open? Do I call your number and see if you can come in for pickup? No, if we can get in, we should both get in."

"I can't wear a dress."

"No shit. That's like putting a skirt on an elephant." Foxy's phone vibrated. He picked it up to look at the message. "It is a party." He looked up with a new expression. Uncertainty?

"What?"

"It's a special kind of party."

"Special?"

"That's what my guy is saying." Foxy scratched his cheek. "We'll figure it out. I've got to go. I'm gonna make some arrangements." He dipped his hand into his coat pocket and pulled out another cell phone. "Take this. I'll call you on it when I know what's what." He stood but didn't leave. Pensive, he stared down then motioned with his hands. "Can you stand up for a sec?"

Ivan grunted but rose to his feet. "What are you doing?"

"What are you . . . about two hundred and forty pounds? Six feet? Stretch your arms out."

"I wear extra-large," Ivan said. "That is what they call it here."

"Yeah," Foxy said, his eyes taking their own measurement. He nodded to his own conclusions and picked up his jacket and swung it around to put it on. He centered the knot of his tie. "Good talk. Tell the Party Man we're back on track."

"I don't talk to him until the job is done."

"No? His son told me he would be talking to you."

"You talked to Fedot?" Every word full of threat, but no helping it now.

Foxy stopped, looking surprised. "He's the one who got back to me, yeah. I asked for instructions, in case you wouldn't want to work with me on this thing. He said you'd come around. He was right, I guess."

Hot blood rushed up Ivan's neck "Never talk to Fedot. He will make everything worse."

"I'm sure everyone will be happy once we wrap this up." Foxy already had his car keys in his hand as he turned away. "I should be calling you tonight some time, okay? Stay put."

Ivan watched him leave before sitting down again and staring at his tea, his thoughts darker than the brew. Walking away from Foxy at the bar had been another mistake. Too emotional. And hard to blame the homosexual for getting in touch with Moscow—the man needed his instructions. And Fedot . . . without doubt, the bastard was the one driving this operation.

Ivan rolled his shoulders, anger and anxiety pushing sweat into his armpits, the collar of his shirt too tight. No one else to blame but himself. And what did Foxy say about Fedot? Something about coming around?

A chill, like a zap of cold electricity, ran down Ivan's spine. He sprang to his feet, grabbed the laptop, and took off. Back in his room, it took all but a minute to set up an encrypted call while using a headset—much better sound quality than any cell phone. And harder to trace.

Lena picked up after a couple of rings. "Hello?"

He kept his voice tired, like after a long day. "Zaichik, I forgot to ask you something."

"Oh, so good you called." She sounded relieved. "Dima says it's a temporary problem, but I don't believe him."

"Dima?"

"Yes, he said you will take care of it in no time, but he's a bad liar. Plus, he doesn't look like a bodyguard. I mean, he drives a Mercedes. Vanya, what's going on? Why do I need a bodyguard?"

"Zaichik, it's a small thing. Is he—" Ivan cleared his throat tight with emotion "—is he there? Can I talk to him for a second?"

"He's drinking that Polish vodka you brought the last time. He has policemen protecting me, but they stay in a car outside. Are you going to tell me what's going on?"

"Let me talk to him first. Everything's all right. He doesn't need to be there anymore."

"Thank god. Hang on."

Fedot came through so pleasant, like a good old friend. "Ivan, we were just talking about you. Lena says you don't drink anything strong after dinner. What's that about?"

Ivan kept his voice neutral. "I know what you are doing. I know

Foxy talked to you. He just told me so. Tell your father we found his man, and we'll be meeting him soon. So get out of my house. Now."

"Ah-huh. Glad to hear everything's settled." Fedot's tone didn't change one bit, still old friends talking to each other. "You finish the negotiations, and I'll keep an eye on Lena here so you don't have to worry. Oh, and it's getting colder. I walk your dog so Lena doesn't have to go outside. Bond and I are friends now. So you owe me one." The twerp chuckled, pleased with himself.

Ivan clenched and unclenched his fists when Lena came back on. "Dima is funny. He's trying to get Bond to shake hands, although I told him Bond doesn't play with other people, just tolerates them. So are you going to tell me what's going on?"

Ivan took in a lungful of air and let it out in one long, tired sigh. "I'm negotiating something here. I think we have a competitor, and I hear they don't play by the rules. I thought it would be best if someone kept an eye on you."

"Go ahead and agree with them on something." She paused, and a touch of sadness rang in her voice. "I miss you. I want you to be my bodyguard, not Dima."

"I'm working hard, Zaichik. It's a big contract. I get this one done, and remember how we talked? I'll let Agutin take over, so I don't have to travel so much."

"Well, hurry. Bond and I are nervous when you are not around. He's been growling at Dima the whole time."

Ivan disconnected and closed the program, his hands shaking.

Get in the car, go straight to Kazbek's villa, and walk in. Grab the Chechen and drive him straight to the desert, bodyguards or not. Screw their cameras and their guns. Enough gear to plow through the walls.

Ivan slapped his laptop shut and stood. His hip caught the table; a lamp jumped and fell sideways, but he caught it and carefully put it back, sliding the base into a round spot clear of dust.

He stood still, arrested by his recognition of the pattern of reacting instead of acting. Going in without preparation? Done enough of that already. And now Fedot was getting ideas in Moscow as a result. Still, the twerp couldn't do a thing as long as the job got done. Partorg's word was like God's word. Nobody crossed the man, not even his son. The important thing was to deliver the Chechen.

Ivan dropped into a pushup position. His knuckles dug into the carpet; he pushed his torso off then dropped back down. Patience. Planning. Patience. Planning.

The adrenaline rush gave way to muscle pain and labored breath. He kept going until his arms shook and wobbled and his abs burned.

An unfamiliar ringtone pierced the silence of the room. He collapsed onto the carpet and rolled over. There—Foxy's burner phone. Patience was already paying off.

16

East Los Angeles, California

Antonio opened his eyes. The pills had left him drowsy and disoriented. He rubbed his face. The smell of food added to his confusion, inviting the image of his wife.

Was Marisol cooking breakfast? But she hardly ever made eggs in the morning—was it morning?

Unable to tell the time, he felt for his phone on the bed stand, the fog of medicine pressing down on his forehead. Was it a full night of sleep? The drugs were strong enough to knock out a horse. But what about the memory of waking up at least twice in the night to the sound of animals howling?

His phone was out of reach, and he squinted at the gap between the curtains, at specs of dust swirling in daylight. What a strange dream—the howling couldn't have come from animals. Not in this part of town. Up in the hills, they had coyotes, sure. But not here.

And the smell of food? He sat up. Marisol was in Puerto Vallarta. Someone else was cooking.

Dios Mio. Miguel and his men.

Antonio pulled his work boots from under the bed, his heart thumping in his ears as he bent forward. He shoved his swollen feet into each boot, taking the time to lace them. A good excuse would do it. A good reason. Something convincing enough for Miguel.

He used the bedpost to stand up. The door to the bedroom across the hallway was closed. Work. Go to work. That was what the devil asked for—to keep everything the same, to keep the business running. That should be enough of an excuse to get out of the house.

Antonio listened for noises, but the house was quiet. They must have cooked the food some time ago. A droplet of hope fell on his heart—maybe they took mercy on the old, sick man and left without him.

He picked up his hat on and walked out of the room to the stairs. The second step creaked, and he froze, feeling foolish. Like a child out to steal a cookie. He tiptoed down.

In the living room, empty glasses and cups, some painted red with dried wine, littered the coffee table, cigarette butts sitting like chopped worms in a saucer they'd used for an ashtray. Plates with dried chicken bones. Beer bottles. The heavy smell of perfume and sweat.

An odd sound drew his attention, and he went rigid in shock. Past the doorway into the kitchen, his daughter stood naked facing the stove, a plate in her hand. Lost in thought, she picked at food with her fork.

His head swam at the sight. Lucia? Here? Naked?

He could see the triangle of her breast from where he stood. She was shamelessly exposed, her buttocks facing the open space of the kitchen. For a few seconds, Antonio stared at her in confusion. He hadn't seen his daughter naked since she was a little girl.

He croaked, "Lucia?"

She nearly dropped the plate at the sound of his voice but caught it. When she faced him, he blushed at her exposed breasts and the thin line of her pubic hair.

"You scared me," she said, food in her mouth slurring the words. "Who are you?"

Not Lucia, thank God. An angular face, a sharp nose, and small, curious eyes instead of Lucia's soft features.

With effort, he looked away from her breasts. A naked woman, so close. Dios mio, what would Marisol say? Hot with shame, he took off his hat, which helped avert his eyes from the girl's breasts, her nipples like two berries.

He found his voice. "I am—I live here." Now that he wasn't looking at her, it was easier to speak. "Señorita, this is my house."

"Oh. You must be his father." None of it bothered her, the way she spoke, simply curious. She must have noticed his discomfort. "Excuse me, let me put something on."

Fresh shame burned his cheeks and neck when he caught himself staring at her small buttocks as she walked into the bedroom closest to the garage door. But shame quickly gave way to fear. Miguel—was he in there?

Antonio listened to murmuring behind the closed door. Quiet otherwise. Enough time to get to the truck and leave.

He moved toward the garage but turned at the sound of a door opening behind him. The shock wasn't as bad the second time. This one was a tall blonde, her body like a cello with tiny breasts.

When their eyes met, she said, "Perdon" in a small voice.

A male voice behind her said, "Where are you going?" and she closed the door.

Antonio cringed at the voice. Still here, Miguel's men, rousing from their sleep, calling to their women.

The garage door was only steps away. His hand was on the doorknob when he heard another door open behind him. He glanced over his shoulder and regretted the impulse.

This time the girl was wearing a shirt but nothing else. She smiled and waved, and he lunged into the garage like the hounds of hell were snapping at his back.

Instead of familiar darkness, the garage was illuminated by bright light. His truck—windows rolled down, tool boxes open. A man's head popped over the tool box cover.

"Tio? Como le va?"

Antonio's heart jumped at the surprise. The quiet one, the one with the shotguns.

The man said, "Are you feeling any better?"

Antonio took his hat off and put it back on. "My heart isn't so good."

"We were worried. Is your medicine helping any?" Pretending to care, but his eyes cold, studying.

"I'm going for some air. I think I need some air." Antonio felt the man's eyes on his back as he pushed the door open and stepped into the driveway.

Sunlight and warmth on his back brought some order to his thoughts. Must have slept a long time, the sun so intense already. They took the truck, but it was only a few blocks from here to the bus stop.

A few steps brought him to the gate. Take the bus downtown. Make a connection there to another bus and keep going. But where, and then what? Still groggy, he couldn't think of a good answer. But the urge to get away drove him forward, his hand strong on the gate latch. He caught a glimpse of the quiet one watching him from the garage, wiping his hands. It was a relief to close the gate behind him.

But even past the gate, he couldn't be alone.

Just outside, in a chair with a newspaper open in his hands, sat the real estate appraiser, or whoever he was. Wearing same wide-brim hat, the man looked up in surprise as he uncrossed his legs to stand up.

"Antonio? Do you need a ride?" He reached to his belt for a radio.

Antonio waved. "No, no. I didn't feel well, so I thought I'd walk.

Clear my head."

"Walk?" The concept seemed alien to the man, his bushy eyebrows raised so high they disappeared under his cowboy hat. But his hand left the radio on his belt, and Antonio took a slow breath.

Smiling awkwardly, Antonio took a few tentative steps away from the man. The street looked all wrong: a line of red cones on each side and warning signs—Do Not Park. Street repair? Strange for it to be on both sides.

A brown sedan sat on the corner, ignoring the warnings. As Antonio walked by, the driver looked up from some gadget, his young face familiar, nodding. A radio sat on his dashboard, the same black Motorola the appraiser—what was his name?—carried on his belt.

Despite the sun, Antonio felt cold on the inside. All of them Miguel's people. All of them. Watching. Guarding. An army.

Police. It was best to call the police. At the wild thought, he quickened his step as his fingers found and tightly clenched his old phone in his jeans' pocket.

He checked the impulse to call right away. No, not here, where they watched. Some place quiet, away from the house. The corner store. Call from there.

He hurried past the block to a bodega where the grocer always sold Marisol the best poblano peppers. A truck was parked near the entrance. A man stared at Antonio through the windshield and raised a radio to his mouth.

Marisol. Antonio stopped and looked at his feet, deflated, his fingers off the cell phone, his hand falling out of his pocket. The brisk walk had cleared his head.

Marisol and Lucia. Think of the girls. What would happen to the girls?

He turned around and dragged his feet down the sidewalk. Every step, past the red cones and back to the gate, filled him with despair at the prospect of spending time with Miguel and his army. But what was the alternative? Couldn't ask for help from anywhere now, after taking their money. Plunged into a war between strangers. Trying to make Marisol happy, old fool.

Shouldn't have listened to—

Jorge. It all started with Jorge.

Antonio yanked his cell phone out and punched in Jorge's number, his finger shaking from indignation.

Jorge answered with good cheer in his voice, the scoundrel still pretending all this was luck. "Primo, how's everything with you? Are you on your way back yet?"

Santa María. Hard to believe the man's pretense. Antonio let accusation slip into his words: "Jorge, they have guns. You talked me into dealing with men who kill people!"

"Who?" A fake note now, the first one.

"Why didn't you tell me? You know how much I hate violence. They brought guns. What am I to do? They—"

Jorge's voice changed, all warmth gone. "No, no, no. Primo, you don't talk about any of that on the phone. We can talk about this when you come back."

"But how can I come back? How can you say such thing when they are all here, and I'm supposed to take them to the house?"

"So take them there." So calm, like they were talking about trimming hedges. "Take them to the thief, and you'll be back here to help your girls with the furniture. I was just with them at the store." He chuckled. "Your wife is as picky as she's ever been. Anyway. My suggestion is you do as he asks. Show him the house he wants to see."

"I don't feel well."

Jorge's voice took on metallic notes. "Primo, get it over with and you'll feel better."

"But I don't—"

Loud voices and laughter broke out, and Jorge said, "Primo, I must go now. Help him like he helped you, and we all will have a good laugh about it when you come back here."

The phone beeped as the call broke off. Antonio looked at the black plastic wet with his sweat.

He walked back to the gate in a daze. The appraiser didn't care to look up from his paper—a small measure of relief.

Antonio put his hand on the edge of the gate and pulled, murmuring the prayer: Santa María, help all who call on You in their necessities. Give me strength to get through this.

In the yard, the garage door stood open, but nobody was watching him from the inside.

Go along with what they want. Show them the house. Simple.

He looked from his truck to the front door and took a few steps. Simple, but not so simple. What would Miguel and his men do to the people in that huge house in the hills? Before the meeting in Puerto Vallarta, before this nightmare, it'd been so easy to ignore the news, la violencia. Easy to ignore stories about unmarked graves, people buried in stacks, their hands and faces missing. The stories always seemed so far-fetched.

Until now.

He reached for the handle on front door. When it opened into his face, he staggered back and almost fell.

Miguel stepped out in jeans but bare-chested, a phone in his hand. He shook his head, his gaze fiery under a frown. "Tio. What are you doing? If you need to talk to someone, you talk to me. We don't want to disappoint your wife and daughter, do we? We want to give them good news, yes?" He held the door with his left arm outstretched, waving in with the right. "Come. It's no good for you, standing in the sun."

17

Downtown Los Angeles, California

Ivan opened the door and returned to his spot in front of the TV. Foxy held a garment bag over his shoulder as he walked in. He surveyed the hotel room, from the gear box on the bed to the laptop on the desk to the closed curtains.

"Keeping it private, are we?" Foxy spread the garment bag on the bed and stared at the TV where a cocker spaniel was running in a figure eight pattern around the legs of a plump lady. "You into old ladies?"

Ivan glanced at the TV screen. "I like dogs. It is called 'obedience competition'."

"You been watching dogs the whole day? And you call me weird!"

"Not whole day. I watched local news for my English. To practice." The garment bag, the length of a man, looked stuffed with clothes. "Show me what you brought."

"No dresses, like you said." Foxy ran the zipper open and pulled out an outrageous yellow suit.

"I wear that?"

"It's either this or a dress."

"No dresses."

"Okay, then. The zoot suit's for you, the leather's for me." Foxy pulled the jacket off its hanger. "I gotcha some long-legged pants. Hope they're long enough." Clipped to the lapel hung a wide-brim fedora hat.

Ivan took the clothes into the bathroom and changed. The baggy pants and wide, padded shoulders made for a cartoonish look, but Foxy had judged his partner's size just right, down to inseam and waist.

Ivan returned to the room in time to see Foxy half-naked, in nothing but a flared leather skirt, more leather in his hands.

Foxy raised his eyebrows and nodded. "Looking good, Cholo. Now, you gonna have to help me out with this." He unfolded the leather and stuck his arms through cutouts then turned around to show his bare back.

"What do I do?"

"Jesus, you never seen a corset before? Lace it. Use the straps."

Leather gloves and tall, laced boots with stiletto heels were arranged on the bed. Ivan tied the top knot and stepped back. "These are weird outfits."

"You like the word 'weird', eh?"

"I can say 'strange'."

Foxy stuck something into the corset cups where breasts were supposed to be, and the cups filled out. He propped and mushed them. "Just don't call anyone weird when we get there. They'll be dressed up like you ain't seen before."

Ivan took off the yellow jacket and tossed it on the bed. Wasting time, talking about the wrong subject. "Clothes are not important. We need strategy for how we take Kazbek."

"We need to find him first. It ain't gonna be easy in that crowd."

Ivan nodded at the laptop. "Yes, but I want us to look at photos. The house is large, and we don't know inside, but we can study outside. Have ideas."

Foxy smoothed out the corset leather on his sides and wiggled his shoulders. "I like me a man with ideas."

But all of their ideas led to the inside of the villa and stopped there. A lot of it hinged on finding and isolating the Chechen at the party—provided he was in the building to begin with.

All they had were a few drawings on the computer screen. Foxy liked the software, but the plan was as vague as when they started. They still had to find their man. They prepared a few extraction strategies, but that was it.

Ivan felt restless when they walked out of the room, dressed in their clownish clothes. Dangerous game, this. Walking out of the hotel and straight into an improvisation.

As they walked past the reception desk, they caught a lot of stares from the guests. Ivan lowered his hat to keep the desk clerk from recognizing him, but Foxy didn't seem to care; in pink stockings and smoky eye shadow, he walked with his chin up, every step sure, hips swinging.

Ruslan, in a suit and tie, drove them to the villa in Ivan's Town Car, the traffic thick, the cars jostling for spots up the lane.

Off the freeway, Ivan rolled down his window and took in the cool air in long inhalations, watching store names in neon float by.

Private security at the party, which meant they'd search or send everyone through a metal detector. No guns. Will have to take them from the guards.

The thought of going into the Chechen's house without any weapons tightened the muscles around his gut. Another layer of risk. Vicious men, Chechens. Always messy and sadistic with their torture, always using their Wahhabi Islam to put everyone who wasn't Wahhabi on the level of dogs and pigs.

Ivan turned away from the window. "In English, you would say 'we are going in naked,' yes?"

Foxy kept adjusting his outfit, pulling on the leather around his chest. "If anything, I feel overdressed. This corset's so tight my lungs are hanging out."

Foxy, always turning everything into a joke. "You laugh. I did a job with Chechen three years ago. I was to pay ransom to him. He and his brother tied a man from Moscow to the wooden poles by the feet. When I got there, they cut him with chainsaw. They hung him upside down to keep blood in his brain while they cut him between legs. They let their dogs eat him."

Foxy's shook his head. "Not gonna happen. This is a social thing. Family fun for the regulars. We're in LA, not in Craplakistan."

"It doesn't matter where. If his men know us, we kill all but him."

Foxy narrowed his eyes. "Don't worry about me, Drago. You want me to kill'em, I kill'em."

The guard at the gate shone a flashlight at his list, checking the names off in a hurry, a line of arriving cars stretching far into the street.

"Ah, yes. Mr. Swensson, plus one." The blue beam of his flashlight shone into the car and paused at Foxy's skirt, high above the knees. "Please, drive up to the main entrance. They will show you in."

Ruslan pulled forward, gravel crunching under the tires.

Ivan nodded at a security camera over the gate. "In Russia, I sell electronics. You can say, I always worked in film."

Foxy chuckled. "I always worked around it."

Looking past Ruslan's shoulder, Ivan surveyed the limos lined up near the entrance lit with crisscrossing searchlights. The guests couldn't all be Chechens. And with so many people—a chance to blend in.

His concern receded further when they stepped out of the car in front of a stairway leading to the villa's entrance—the place looked more like a perverse masquerade ball in Venice than a Muslim fundamentalists' hangout. The way the greeters looked in their gas masks and rubber suits—they lent credence to Foxy's words from back at the hotel. They would be the most normal-looking couple here.

Greeters stood on each side of the short staircase leading to the main entrance, all of them women—that much was clear. Their large breasts protruded through cutouts in their black-rubber outfits. Metal clamps, big enough to come from some machinist workshop, were attached to their nipples.

"Stop staring," Foxy whispered in his ear. "We're supposed to be regulars at this type of thing, remember?"

"You did not say about women in gas masks and rubber suits," Ivan said quietly as they walked through the arch of the main entrance. "They wear the tools. Pliers hanging from their tits."

Foxy chortled. "Those are latex suits, man. And I warned you about this party. Get ready. You gonna see plenty more tools tonight." Foxy spoke in his woman's voice, in-tune with his outfit.

More tools. A giant panda walked by, holding hands with a zebra. The whole scene was so surreal, Foxy's high-pitched voice no longer seemed strange or bothersome.

Two security men rang them with metal detector pads on the way in, after cross-checking their names on a handheld. The men wore high-waisted black trousers and leather boots, like Nazi officers from a wartime movie. Except they were shirtless, their faces hidden behind full-head leather masks with cutouts for eyes and mouths.

Blood-colored lamps cast a red glow onto the lobby. Probably the only normal person in the entire building. Everyone here in a mask or a helmet—like that one over there, in a horse mask to go with the harness and metal bit stuck in the mouth. Freaks.

Music boomed from huge speakers over their heads.

Ivan pulled Foxy by the elbow to the bar and leaned close to his ear. "We have a problem. Masks."

"I noticed," Foxy said. He sounded amused. "We should have worn masks ourselves."

"Yes. Not enough preparation." Ivan swallowed his displeasure. "But if we can't find him, then we can study layout."

Everyone around them held glasses in their hands, so they got drinks, too. It was hard to ignore the ball gag in the bartender's mouth. Ivan gulped down a shot.

Foxy held a tall glass, something with mint leaves inside. He pulled closer. "A little early for vodka. Might slow you down."

"It does nothing. I have big body." Ivan pushed his empty glass across the bar and spoke into Foxy's ear. "You should talk to these people. We walk and you talk."

A screen on the wall behind the bar showed a muscular blonde in nothing but tall boots whipping a tied up man.

Foxy put his glass down. "Yeah. Let's study the layout and chit-chat." He pointed at the hallway entrance crowned by a sign that read:

HEAVEN IS BORING

WELCOME TO HELL

"You wanna see what's over there?" Foxy asked.

They walked through the hallway, lit by sunken ceiling lights, and turned right. Guided by the thumping sounds of club music coming from below, they found a staircase leading to a dim cellar.

"Would you look at that!" Foxy said, leaning closer. "A real dungeon."

A row of tables covered in drinks and food split the room in half. Guests, in different states of undress and wearing leather where they weren't showing skin, pecked at their plates.

Lights in the floor aligned to guide visitors into rooms to the left and right of the food isle. Ivan stopped. The music wasn't as loud down here.

Foxy turned toward the first room on their left. "I'm starting to like this place."

A giant mouth served as an entrance, pointed teeth painted to look like they were dripping with fresh blood. The instant they strolled in, past the giant teeth, Ivan forgot he wasn't supposed to speak Russian.

"Vo blyat dayut!"

Above the platform, suspended from the ceiling by a thick, black rope, hung a naked woman, hogtied. Her private parts stared at anyone walking in, strings tight on the flesh of her limbs, under the harsh glare of a yellow spotlight.

Music drowned Ivan's words, and he regained his composure by looking away from the platform, as if to admire the surroundings. But the platform was hard to ignore, lit by the only lights in the room, the periphery hidden in darkness.

Padded benches along walls resolved themselves, and he took a seat. Foxy landed alongside and tilted his head as if to better see the weights attached to the woman's nipples, pulling them hard toward the floor.

"Told ya. More tools."

In morbid fascination, Ivan watched a guy in leather chaps step onto the platform.

Foxy said, "Good Lord. He's hung like a moose."

The moose-man, fully erect, stood in front of the woman, his pelvis thrust forward. It was hard to believe, but she was licking him. He grabbed his cock and slapped the woman's face. With a handful of her hair in his hand, he then pulled her closer and shoved himself into her mouth like he was trying to knock her teeth out. From the side, Ivan could see her cheek extending out as he rammed himself in, over and over.

Ivan held on to the bench like he was trying to break it. He wanted to walk up to the guy and smash a knuckle into his temple—lay him flat, nice and quick. Then untie the girl.

But he sat still. One of two women in the corner dressed in skin-tight plastic clapped her hands and shouted "C'mon" and "Oh, yeah," and a couple on the other side, of indeterminate gender, had each other's hands between their legs.

Foxy leaned closer. "I'm learning something new today."

Ivan took a deep breath. "Yes. Same." The woman above the platform gagged, and a drip of her saliva stretched to the floor. Ivan moved to stand up. "This is wrong."

Foxy yanked his arm down. "Chill. You don't get it—she's enjoying it."

The suggestion seemed preposterous, the black rope biting into her white skin, her wrists and ankles swollen from coils of rope, a man's cock slamming into her face.

Ivan shook his head. "This is fucking wrong."

Foxy leaned so close that Ivan could feel the warmth of his breath. "Make sure you look like you are having fun, okay?"

The man in the leather chaps was doing overtime, having difficulty climaxing, beads of sweat glistening on his chest. The woman in plastic left her seat, walked up to the platform, and started fingering his balls. Other partiers wandered in and out of the room like patrons at an art gallery. A few didn't wear masks.

Ivan leaned over. "We go to other rooms. Maybe better light there to see faces."

They came out to the row of tables. A group of young men and women stood giggling near a box as big as a wardrobe by the wall on the other side of the food trays. The box had holes rimmed with white paint at varying places. All the men were too young to be Kazbek.

One of the girls, egged on by her companions, opened the door to the box and slipped inside. Ivan expected her friends to join her, but none did. Instead, the door opened a crack, and the girl's hand extended outside with a velvet cape she'd been wearing. Her hand slipped back inside before the door closed again.

What was she doing, naked and alone, locked inside the box?

Foxy tugged at his sleeve. "Hey, something's up in the middle room." Muffled shouts supported his claim.

"Wait. I want to understand." Ivan watched a potbellied man, naked except for the angel wings strapped to his saggy flesh, approach the giggling group. After a short exchange, the man stuck his hand into the box through one of the white circles. A young man from the group stuck his hand in from a different direction. Based on the way the men moved their arms, they were squeezing, reaching for the naked woman inside.

Ivan nodded at them. "They play game, I think."

Foxy followed his gaze. "Oh yeah. It's a grope box." He tugged at Ivan's arm. "Let's go check out the noise."

They stepped into a square room draped in black and stopped just past the entrance, glued to the spot. Ivan rubbed his face to hide his surprise. Impossible to fake excitement here. In the middle of the room, a tall blonde—naked except for lace-up red boots, boxer gloves, and a police cap—was weaving, ducking, and throwing punches. Fighting a man's scrotum. Jabbing. Chopping at the sack.

"What is this fucking place?" Ivan said, addressing no one in particular.

Every punch the woman threw resonated below Ivan's midsection.

Her victim, a man strapped with belts to a metal contraption, hung with his feet toward her. The contraption kept him leaning forward, spread-eagled under lights at the center of a boxing ring, the rest of the room filled with cheering spectators.

Ivan faked a cough to hide his revulsion. Hard blows like this, the pain in the man's testicles must have been beyond comprehension.

The man in straps grunted and moaned with every blow, but he never asked for the torture to stop. The women surrounding the scene hollered in delight at every punch. "Stick a finger up his ass!" one of them screamed over the music.

The female boxer smiled and threw a straight punch. Tired now, her face sweaty, her other arm dangling loose.

Foxy looked like he'd swallowed a frog. "I say we keep moving." He wheeled and headed straight for the exit.

Ivan followed, hot and sweaty in his jacket. Warm air blew from the vents in the ceiling. Too warm—probably to keep the naked people comfortable.

Back at the food tables, Foxy busied himself with choosing the right cheese for his cracker. An attendant, the only person dressed in ordinary garb, walked by with an empty tray.

Ivan caught him by the arm. "A shot of vodka?" The man pointed at an end table covered in a battery of bottles and glasses. Ivan walked over, poured two shots, and downed them in quick succession.

Foxy came over, taking bites from his cracker sandwich. "You don't need a snack with that?"

"Not hungry." Ivan put down his glass and glanced at the entrances of the rooms on the other side. He motioned in the direction of the staircase they'd taken to enter the dungeon. "I go to the restroom upstairs. You search. Look at naked people, for the tattoo."

Foxy nodded. "Sure." He watched a young man in a furry loin cloth walk by. "I'm gonna talk to some folks." He looked down the hall and added with some hesitation, "There are more rooms to visit."

"Yes. Three more."

"I wonder what's in them."

More grotesqueness, no doubt. Something worse than that boxing match. Something unimaginable.

Ivan walked up the steps to the ground floor, past the bar with the screen showing the boxer woman. A fluorescent arrow sign for the restroom, taped to a wall near the bar, directed him up one level, to a door with a plaque of a peeing devil.

The door stood ajar, yellow light showing through a crack. The previous visitor must have left the door that way. Ivan pushed in and stopped dead at the sight of a large woman in black stockings and a suspender belt. She yanked on a chain leash attached to a spiked collar around a man's neck, the man on all fours, his head centimeters away from the toilet.

With every yank of the leash, folds of skin on the woman's naked torso and hefty arms jiggled. She held two more leashes in her other hand, a fluffy dog on each end.

"Mistress, I'm thirsty," the man whined, while the little dogs sat on their haunches, watching him.

His 'mistress' sounded annoyed. "What's that? You want water? Fine. Lick it then." She put her boot on the man's naked butt and gave it a shove, just enough slack in the leash for the man to slam into the porcelain face-first.

Ivan expected a cry of pain. But the man didn't complain either, much like his counterpart downstairs. Instead, he stuck his head inside the bowl and lapped at the water.

One of the dogs barked, and Ivan took a step back. Pocket dogs, these Pomeranians. But still guarding.

The woman wheeled, and her fat face cracked into a wide smile. "Oh, ha-a-ai there! How a-a-are you!" Greeting them like the secretary at Ruslan's office, all smiles and good cheer. Ignoring the slurping behind her.

Ivan managed a "Hello." The tiny dogs barked at his voice. He remembered the standard American greeting. "And how are you?"

Her smile faded. "We're great. Almost done." She yanked on the leash, forcing the man's bald head out of the bowl. "Enough! I said lick it, not drink it!" She looked up. "He's being a bad dog." Apologizing for her animal.

Her red lips parted in another smile. "How do you like the party?"

"It's—it's good."

Absurd situation. What was the appropriate way to react to a half-naked 'mistress' whose 'man-dog' was lapping water out of the toilet bowl? Acting like she was talking to her neighbor, like they were chatting to each other at the local grocery store.

He forced a smile. "I go find another toilet."

"Oh, there's no need for that. We'll be right out." She looked down at her man-dog and raised her voice. "And then I'll drag my poodle back here if he's still thirsty!"

Poodle? The Pomeranians certainly weren't poodles, not even close. But the skinny man tugging at the leash had tufts of black hair around his shoulder blades.

She gathered the leashes in one hand and thrust her palm out. "I'm Barbara. You can call me Barby."

He shook her warm, wet hand. "Lars. Swensson." The Pomeranians didn't bark this time.

"Oh, you Scandinavian? That's so cute!" She cocked her head, giving him a long look. Flirting?

Ivan nodded in the general direction of the toilet bowl. "I need to go."

"Oh, I'm sorry." She looked down at her 'poodle', her flabby face tightening. "Heel!" she snapped and gave the leash a tug. The man scampered toward her legs. "Mine's trained better than Eva's Pomeranians, that's for sure." She sounded proud.

At this point it wasn't hard to manufacture a polite smile. "I have not met Eva."

Her blue eyes widened. "You haven't? Oh, you must." She paused. "This is your first time here, isn't it?"

Ivan measured his words. "Here, yes. We were—"

"Oh, gosh." She frowned at her pet and yanked the leash. "Behave yourself." She looked up and said in excited voice, "Eva's amazing. She throws the best parties of anyone. You should totally meet her. She's downstairs. Boxing, I think." She seemed to notice his silence. "Oh, I'm so sorry. I forgot you were here on business."

She shooed the dogs out before closing the door behind her. Ivan stood in front of the toilet, in his mind the image of the man's head disappearing into the bowl. And the slurping.

Ivan used the sink to urinate.

He took time to soap and wash his hands. This Eva lady. She must have been the wife. And if she was the wife, where was her husband? Somewhere close, with all this craziness taking place.

In the corridor, all three dogs were tangled, Barbara sorting the leashes.

Ivan reached out. "Let me help you."

She gave up the Pomeranians. "God bless you. They're driving me nuts."

A loose knot on the two leather leashes was easy to undo. He handed them back. "I saw Eva but not her husband. Is he here?"

"Oh, he hardly ever shows up. I hear he's more of a visual fella. Takes a few girls with him someplace to watch everyone play. He's the one who makes the tapes."

"The tapes?"

"Gosh, you're really new. That screen there?" She nodded toward the corridor. "They record the best plays. You can get the tape if you're the one playing. I can see you and I doing the wheel." She winked. "It'd be fun, big fella like you."

Ivan shook his head. "I'm sorry. My girlfriend wants me." He offered his hand. "It was a pleasure."

She held his hand in hers and squeezed, staring into his eyes. "Find me if you get bored, sweetie."

Bored? Not in this freakish place.

Downstairs, Foxy was still nibbling at food. "Seen anything interesting?"

"Yes."

Three women laughed by the last food table, one of them with a boxing glove over her shoulder.

"You talked?" Ivan asked.

"I did. Everyone knows the husband and wife, but nobody knows where they are. Our guy's in here somewhere, having fun."

Ivan pointed at the ceiling. "You know, the bar upstairs? The TV screen?"

Foxy eyed a lithe, black man in tiny leather shorts. "What about it?"

Ivan pointed to the nearest entrance draped in streamers made to look like blood. "Cameras in rooms to make recordings."

"Oh, shit. That's real kinky. They film all the action and let you keep the tape." Foxy sounded wistful, like he wished he wasn't working.

Ivan grunted. "Yes. And the boxer is his wife. Her name is Eva. I talked to woman who walks her dogs." He squinted at the dark end of the hall. Wisps of smoke hung around the three women.

Foxy gave the news a slow nod. "Our man Kaz is into some wicked shit." His left eyebrow arched up. "You don't think he's the guy she was—"

"No. I know Chechens. No. I bet my revolvers it was not him. But we take a risk." Ivan looked around. No one nearby. He made sure to look in the opposite direction from the boxer. "Three women at the last table. One with gloves. She's Eva."

Foxy held the glass to his lips and turned around casually to take a look.

Ivan leaned close to Foxy's ear, close enough to smell his perfume. "I think you should talk to her. Ask her what she knows."

Foxy wrinkled his nose. "And she'll lead me by the hand to her beloved husband so we can bag him. Other ideas?"

No other ideas. And the woman—right here. "You said we are in film. Talk to her. You talk a lot. Make nice. She will say something useful. We can't find her husband here without her."

Foxy didn't change his posture. He took a slow sip from his glass. "It's kinda risky."

"She has two dogs. Dogs are good topic. Or film. They film this."

Foxy put the glass down. "Gonna have to improvise this shit."

Ivan felt the tension lurch up from his abdomen into his throat. The previous improvisation didn't go so well. But no choice. Not with Fedot so close to Lena.

He stuck his hand into his pocket and pulled out a diamond stud. When he reached for the top of Foxy's corset, the man shied away. "Whoa, whatcha grabbin' my tits for?"

"Microphone." The explanation kept Foxy still. The stud clipped neatly through her leather corset. "Now I can listen."

Foxy pulled up the corset and wiggled his thighs, staring at the stud. "Kinda small for a mic. You sure you gonna hear me?"

Ivan flipped over his wristwatch, detached an earpiece, and put it in, pretending he was scratching his ear. Software muted the music, and the voices came through clear enough. "Everything. It is very good."

Foxy glanced over his shoulder. "Okay, then. I guess I better do some talkin'." He ran his hands down his skirt as if to smooth the tight leather and looked up. "Wish me luck." Without waiting, he turned and walked along the line of tables toward the women.

Ivan pushed the speaker deeper into his ear to hear Foxy sing softly:

"Lights. Camera. Action. Lights. Camera—" Foxy's voiced hitched as he reached the women. He sounded like he was one of them. "Oh, hi!"

"Hi yourself," a female voice said.

Ivan glanced down the hall. The boxer woman, Eva. Facing him. This 'Hi yourself'—strange greeting. Not a good opening line.

Do it, funny man. Do it. Improvise. We need a good start.

18

East Los Angeles, California

Seso came into the house through the door leading to a garage, and Miguel turned to look at him from the kitchen table where he was playing cards with Cho and Dado. It'd gotten dark out. Seso and the old man had been working in the garage since noon.

The big thinker wiped his hands with a cloth. "We're almost done."

"Both the frame and the engine bay?" Miguel asked. "It's a beat-up truck."

"Tio helped. Steel plates should hold even if we drive it through a wall."

Good effort, this, but wasn't the old man sick? Miguel looked past Seso, at the door. "And Tio? Did he complain?"

Seso shrugged on his way to the sink to wash his hands. "He's scared. But now he thinks he's safe working with me on the truck, so he pushes hard."

"Make sure he doesn't strain too much. I told you I need him."

"I don't let him lift anything. He's more scared than sick."

"Keep him calm. Tell him I won't take him with us tonight."

"Sure." Seso wiped his hands on a towel, leaning his back against the counter. "But what about tomorrow?"

"He doesn't need to worry about tomorrow." Miguel reached for the beer he'd been drinking but put it down. The bottle was warm. "Keep him busy."

Miguel checked his watch then pushed his chair back and waved at the kid and Dado, who were studying their cards without much interest. "Bueno. Enough doing nothing. Let's go see where the asshole lives."

They tossed their cards and sprung to their feet, impatient, Dado stretching and saying, "I hate waiting. It's boring, without the girls."

Miguel got in the front, the kid next to him in the passenger seat, and Dado climbed in the back. Seso opened the gate for them.

Miguel reached to open the glove box. Someone had mentioned Americans always kept their papers in there. In this Toyota, the glove box was small. But what could you expect from a shitty car? He tossed in the registration slip and slapped the lid shut. Truly Mr. Orozco now, a fresh immigrant to California. Cheap cars only.

The air conditioner wheezed musty air, so he rolled down the windows.

Dado said from the back, "I like the truck better."

"Say something I don't know," Miguel said.

The navigation system told them to turn right. He gave the lookout by the gate a nod before driving off.

"Why don't we get a truck," Dado said. "Americans like their trucks. We won't stand out."

Miguel adjusted the rearview mirror to see Dado's face. "Let's talk about trucks. What is it with you and my Escalade?"

Cho giggled and said, "I know why he wanted your truck, Jefe."

Dado kicked the kid's seat so hard, the kid's head jerked forward. "Shut up. I brought you your Hollywood whore, so you owe me."

Miguel found it hard not to smile, everyone still in high spirits after last night's fun. War and sex weren't so different if you heard men talking after a shootout and a wild night with girls. Everyone giddy from the promise of action. It was a good idea to let them have a party. And what a surprise—the whore had been so much fun. Even better in the morning. Didn't want to leave.

At the light, he looked in the mirror. "Dado. You know he'll tell me sooner or later what you did with my Escalade. He's like the whore you got him—can't keep his mouth shut."

Dado had his hand on the kid's shoulder. "You say anything, and I'm not getting you any girls anymore."

At the freeway entrance, a crooked sign showed a human figure with a red belt across its chest. Miguel grunted, rolled the windows up, and put on his seatbelt: Not like Mexico—police here cared about that sort of thing. And nobody wanted a conversation with police right now.

"Dado," he said, "the kind of girl you got him, he can get himself. She was old enough to be his mother."

A fruity smell filled the air. The kid was unwrapping a stick of chewing gum.

They took an onramp and merged into a busy lane. Miguel smiled at a sudden realization—fun to say the English words:

"Cho, you are a 'mother fucker'."

From the corner of his eye, he saw the kid stare at him.

"What?" The kid had his mouth open, not chewing.

"That's what they call people like you in America," Dado said. "You fucked a mother. Now you are called 'mother fucker'. They say it all the time in your movies, don't they?"

Cho said, "I thought it means 'asshole'." For a moment, the kid seemed lost in thought. "What's wrong with fucking mothers? I liked her. She was really good with her tongue."

Miguel chuckled. "Nothing wrong with that."

He turned the radio on and let music play at high volume until the navigation system said they were near their exit. But he raised the volume again when the fast voice on the radio started talking about the weather, something about possible rain.

He rolled the window down and smelled the air. Hot and dry. Rain would be good. People closed windows and doors in the rain, which kept them from hearing noise they weren't supposed to hear.

Off the freeway, the streets were bright with lights from small shops and gas stations. Miguel glanced at the pumps as he drove by. No attendants here. Unlike in Mexico, people here pumped their own gas.

The shops disappeared when the navigation brought them up a quiet street, opulent houses towering over expansive lawns. Some didn't have gates or fences. The residents didn't seem worried about kidnappings.

"They don't do security like back home," Dado said.

"Maybe here they are small fish, and so they don't worry," Miguel said. "There is more money here. Clean money. But I bet our European friend is worried."

Dado leaned over the center console to stare ahead. "You know, Jefe, that's a lot of cars."

A narrow street led them uphill—no more traffic lights, just houses and gardens and signs for playing children—but in front of them stretched a long line of red brake lights.

Cho pointed at a stretched car taking a slow turn. "Jefe, look. It's a limousine."

"I think we are all going to the same place," Dado said.

And they were. The navigation told them to take the same turn.

Miguel checked their location on his phone. "I don't like it. We stick out." He broke off to the left and drove up a few blocks, away from the procession of limousines. Parking was easy. Probably because the signs asked for some kind of permit.

He shut off the engine. "We're four blocks south. Go. I'll tell our man we're here."

They got out and split in different directions. Dado's smartphone cast blue light on his face as he checked the map at the corner.

Miguel stepped out. Too quiet here. Not a good place to walk. Too noticeable without any other pedestrians. But with all those limousines around, the cheap Toyota would also draw too much attention near the Chechen's house.

He waited and smoked a cigarette.

Dado reported in first. "Jefe, it's clean here. But the house has something going on—that's where all the cars are going. Come take a look. But there are cameras on the walls."

"Any lookouts?"

"Not that I can see."

Street lamps cast yellow light on wide sidewalks. A bucket truck with a City of Los Angeles insignia on its doors stood next to a pole with a transformer at the top, orange cones behind it to warn drivers.

Miguel went to the truck and yanked the passenger door open. The man inside, listening to music, merely turned off the radio.

"You are Jose?" Miguel asked.

A nod.

"Do you have the work order for this place as I asked?"

Another nod. "It's on the record."

Miguel climbed in. "Take me as close as you can." They drove past a few houses and a long fence. The truck swayed from side to side, and the gear in the back banged as they turned a corner and stopped.

"Clothes?"

Jose reached behind him and offered a yellow vest and hard hat. The hat smelled of sweat. Miguel grimaced and put it on.

"Put me up, as high as you can."

"Anything higher than the transformer isn't good."

"That's fine."

"Be careful not to touch the wires."

Jose took a few seconds to maneuver the bucket on the crane once they climbed inside, and the damn thing swung and shook like it was broken. Miguel held on to the railing as the engine struggled, its noise loud over the street.

"We are a little heavy for the crane," Jose called out.

As the machine lifted them to the electric wires, close to the transformer, Miguel spotted cameras mounted on top of the villa's fence. Unnerving. But in the dark, at this distance, the cameras wouldn't pick up any detailed features. And in any case, the feed would show city electricians in yellow vests and hard hats, up a pole to fix a transformer.

The bucket stopped and shook like it was about to fall off.

"Coño!" Miguel held on, unsteady on his feet. Back home, the municipal police would do the legwork. Should have sent Dado up in this thing. But then, what better way to see where the rat went to hide?

"Is this good?"

Miguel looked over the fence, at the bright lights inside the property. "Yes. This will work."

Inside the villa grounds, cars crawled up the driveway toward greeters who met new arrivals by the entrance. Miguel clenched the bucket railing. The Chechen asshole threw parties here like any regular person. Like he wasn't a thief, spending money he didn't earn.

But the cameras—Miguel reached into the tool compartment for a flashlight and a screwdriver, to wave them around. An electrician.

He exchanged the screwdriver for a monocular and shone the light at the cameras to blind them, using the blinding effect to steal a better look at the house through the optics. He mumbled, "What is that?"

The greeters by the entrance looked strange, wearing gas masks for some reason. But the guests were also dressed in odd clothes. Ah, yes. A dress party. Like one of those carnivals in Brazil. Yes—a huge guy in a screaming yellow suit and hat going into the house, a skinny bitch in tight leathers hanging on his arm.

Miguel looked for signs of security: only the greeters and a guard booth by the gate. Tio said he'd only seen the asshole once in three weeks. The lack of guards could mean the Chechen wasn't even home. And what an insult—the bastard didn't seem to worry too much about trouble, letting all these strangers walk into his home.

Miguel looked at the front gate. Not too strong—nothing that a reinforced truck couldn't handle. And as for the house, the front door was wood. Shoot it off the hinges with a shotgun and go in.

He put away the flashlight and scope. The frontal assault should be easy. A bit of noise wouldn't matter much with the property so large and covered by the tall fence and bushes. Maybe post a construction truck outside to explain the noise to the neighbors. That should do it. The hard part was finding out whether the bastard was home.

"Take me down."

After all the shaking, it was nice to step onto solid ground again.

Jose finished with the levers and said, "Do you need me to stay here?"

"No. I've seen enough. You can leave."

The man got back into the cab without asking any more questions. Seso's people here were good.

Back in the Toyota, Cho was the first to return.

Miguel turned on the interior lights and handed the kid paper and a pen. "You ready to give me your report?"

The kid nodded and drew a roundabout and a few square boxes. "This is the street that goes down to the main street. If he travels by car, we post three cars. Here and here, and here. Block him here, if he drives a single car."

"And if not?"

"Then we don't use cars."

"You're learning." Miguel turned the light off as he saw Dado walking up.

Dado got in and said, "You want me to drive?"

"No. You always drive it like it's a race. I hate it how you throw the car around."

They stayed quiet, until he glanced at Dado as they returned to the busy street. "What do you think?"

"I'd have to be much higher in the hills to be useful with my rifle," Dado said. "I can scout it up there, but from the angles, I should be down here with you, going in."

Miguel nodded. "We stick together."

"Anything interesting from up close?" Dado asked.

"The main gate is a joke. After that, a driveway to a wooden door. No bollards, nothing. He doesn't even have lookouts posted outside his property."

"He's not afraid here."

"Asshole throws parties. I can't believe it. I'll show him a party."

"Don't we want to know if he's inside?" Cho said cautiously.

"How much do you want to bet he's there?" Dado said.

"I'll bet whatever you bet."

"You don't have any money left after you paid your whore."

Bickering like children. "Shut up. Nobody is betting anything." Miguel caught Dado's eyes in the mirror. "Not until you tell me why you wanted my truck."

Dado kept quiet.

Miguel looked at him in the mirror again. "So?"

"You're not going to like it, Jefe."

"You won it on a bet. Of course I don't like it. But I haven't seen you drive it. Where is it?" He waited. "Say it, god damn it. Or I'll have the kid tell me."

"I shot it up."

"What?"

"I'm testing new rounds on it. New loads on my .308. I wanted to use it against armor and your—"

"Cabron, you took my truck, and you're using it for target practice?" They fell silent, the way they always did when he was angry.

Miguel turned the radio on. Dado—he didn't deserve the anger. Good shooter, always fooling around with his ammo. Then why the anger? The answer came up as a scene with the party goers pouring into the Chechen's cozy home.

Back on the freeway, all of the lanes were packed with evening traffic. The stop-and-go movement frayed Miguel's nerves—should have let Dado drive. How did people here handle this every day without shooting at each other? The crawling pace was maddening.

Miguel skipped from one radio station to another, but the music brought little relief.

He swung right—the right lane moved faster for some reason.

"Jefe, should we get the guns and come back to the house?" Cho asked. "He must be there with all those important people coming in."

"No, it's too loud. You must remember: just because your organization is strong, it doesn't mean you show everyone how strong it is. You make noise only if it serves a purpose. Here, it would serve no purpose."

"But aren't we going to make an example of him?"

"That's for the people back home. We have a camera for that."

"And what if he tries to leave?"

Miguel sighed with irritation: the kid was full of questions. "That's what we have our lookouts for, no?"

"So—we wait?"

"Until we're done with reconnaissance. Tio has his regular appointment to cut grass. Tomorrow, or the day after, I think. I'm going with him to take a look."

Miguel drummed his fingers on the wheel. Teaching the kid patience but feeling just as eager. Always a lot more exciting, to go in without any preparation.

He said, "All we have to do is make sure he's there."

The kid grinned. "Then we have a real party."

"Yes. The real one. The kind everyone will remember."

19

San Fernando Valley, Los Angeles, California

The San Fernando Valley was even warmer than West Hollywood, the mountains blocking the cool ocean air from coming in. Thankfully, the bungalow Foxy had found for them to set up as the filming location had a functioning air conditioning unit. Ivan checked the thermostat and looked around the living room, at tripods, trolleys, and the crown jewel—a compact digital camera favored by local filmmakers, from the famous Red company. A fake shoot, looking real. A day and a half after the deal struck at the party certainly wasn't enough time to set up a foolproof operation. Easy to miss something important. That said, Foxy certainly earned his pay by finding the place on such a short notice.

Ivan played the recording from the party again.

Eva's voice sounded crisp over ambient noise. "Let's say I talk my husband into it. You said script. What kind of script?"

Foxy came on much louder than Eva. "Anything from ancient Greece to Tarzan to science fiction. You get to be actors in your own film. Dialogue and everything."

That's where Foxy hooked her—Eva's voice changed to sincere excitement. "God, I love historical stuff. I always wanted to play that French woman—what's her name?"

"Jeanna D'Arc."

"That's her. I always wanted to play her. Like, the way they strung her up on the cross and everything, all those men ripping her clothes off. They wanted to fuck her. But they burnt her instead because she wouldn't let them fuck her. Because she didn't want to be their little whore."

Foxy didn't sound affected by the crazy speech. Speaking matter-of-factly, he said, "I can have the costumes and everything."

"My husband would love to be the dom in that scene. Can you do a script for that?"

"It's funny you say that," Foxy said, his voice smooth. "We just built a set just like that indoors, but the clients went with an outdoors scene instead. We haven't broken down anything yet. I'll only charge you half our usual fee if we film you on the same set."

Ivan fast-forwarded through the recording. Foxy had played the game just right, and she was coming over, so their banter didn't matter. Only her expectations mattered.

Ivan pressed the play button.

"I would want it like they did it in the movie," Eva said, "with the podium and the cross or whatever, and she's on the wooden beam. And my husband can be the priest."

Ivan stopped the recording. That was it: the podium and the cross. And the costumes.

He went to the wooden frame and ran his hand over the beams. It took an hour to sand them to make sure she wouldn't get any splinters. Enjoyable work, carpentry. But all of this construction, thirty hours or so of running around gathering gear and putting the set together in this bungalow—it could've been for nothing. The only guarantee of Eva's coming over was her excitement about the film. Would she bring the Chechen to an unfamiliar house? Even if she did, he could be the wrong one.

Foxy walked in the front door, pulling a suitcase behind him, a cup of coffee in his other hand. He eyed the set. "Looks good. You got the camera working?"

"Yes. Did you hear anything?"

"Not since yesterday. We're assuming she'll come. But she's rich, and rich people don't have a problem with fucking people over, so who knows."

"We get ready and see."

"And speaking of . . ." Foxy propped his suitcase up and jiggled the handle. "I brought my makeup kit. We still have to make you look less Russian."

Another worrisome part. If the wife did bring Kazbek, they couldn't afford even the slightest chance of Kazbek thinking a Russian was involved in making the film.

Foxy smiled and said, "A lot of you guys look this way. Must be something in the water back in Mother Russia."

"There is nothing in the water in Russia. Moscow has good water. Here, tap water smells like it's from swimming pool." Ivan nodded at the suitcase. "You think your paint is enough? I cannot become smaller."

"Nobody's afraid of old people. Old and frail should do it. Old and wrinkled, and fat. A new you. And you can stoop, like an old person."

"Stoop?"

"Bend forward. Should be convincing enough with the makeup."

Makeup. A disturbing thought. Lena would have had a good laugh. Big change from a fake mustache or wig for disguise. Eye shadow? Rouge? Definitely something from Foxy's repertoire, another trick from the homosexual.

Ivan visualized Eva, Kazbek, and their guards walking around, watching everything. No helping it—to be here, inside the bungalow with Eva and everyone else in such close quarters, everything must look right to avoid suspicion. Foxy's makeup was the obvious solution.

"All right," he said. "As you say in English—may as well try it. But do it quick."

"That's the spirit."

Foxy's suitcase was actually two cases stacked on top of each other and attached to the same frame. Foxy unfastened the belts connecting the cases and popped each one open. They expanded from inside out, sub-shelves opening like books.

Ivan thought of his gear case. Not much difference. But instead of microphones and miniature cameras, Foxy had brushes, bottles with liquids of different color, powders, and scissors, along with a beard trimmer.

One of the bigger bottles had a LATEX label. Foxy directed light from a stage lamp at an empty chair. "Take a seat. I'm going to show you the magic. Something tells me this is a new thing for you."

"You're wrong." Ivan took his seat and squinted at the bright stage light Foxy had pointed at his face. "I wore a fake beard and glasses many times. I know disguise."

"With all due respect, you don't know shit," Foxy said and rolled a tray with a mirror on it close to Ivan. "A fake beard is child's play."

Foxy left and brought an office chair from an adjacent room and sat directly opposite Ivan, the makeup case by his side. The way he studied Ivan's face—he looked like a cosmetic surgeon, that calculating look of a man about to rearrange some things.

"I'll describe every step to you," Foxy said. "You can watch my brushwork in the mirror. Who knows how many times we'll be filming before our man Kaz shows up. You might have to do this by yourself. Also, makeup on this scale will require touch-ups."

Ivan grunted at the thought of having to endure this on multiple occasions.

"We have to change your body outline, too, in case you get tired and straighten up." Foxy let out a chuckle. "I can kinda see it. A Russki bear, rearing up on his hind legs, all the guards shooting at you, like it's some western."

"I cannot shrink."

"True, but I've got something that'll dial down the fear factor."

Foxy's mischievous wink promised something highly unpleasant. The promise came true when the trickster scooped a small amount of milk-and-coffee colored goop out of a round jar with a tip of his finger and began to smear it on Ivan's face.

Ivan wrinkled his nose in revulsion—the sensation of Foxy's fingers stroking his nose and cheeks made the situation nearly unbearable.

"Keep your face still," Foxy said. "Put on your Russian face, but without the frown."

What was a Russian face? Something like Partorg's face probably—rigid, even the eyes unsmiling.

"That's more like it," Foxy said, spreading goop with wide strokes. "Keep it up."

Ivan resigned himself to the torture, but his unease soon began to dissipate; with deft touches of his angled brushes, Foxy had accentuated the flab in the jowls and deepened every wrinkle. A barely noticeable application of latex fluid made Ivan's cheeks look saggy, the bags under his eyes puffy with age and ill health.

After applying the latex, Foxy stepped back, stared at his creation, and said, "Behold. I aged your ass twenty years in under twenty minutes."

Ivan stared at his reflection, admiring the skilled work. "This is impressive." The familiar face—gone, replaced by a face from the past. The resemblance was uncanny. Suspicion churned in his belly.

"Did Partorg give you a file on me?"

Foxy, about to continue, paused with the brush. "No. Why?"

"I look like my father."

"That's expected. I didn't fuck with your bone structure." Foxy stuck his hand into the bottom drawer of his kit and pulled out a skin-colored sack filled with misshapen pieces of plastic. "Try this on. Should be your size."

Ivan got off his chair, grabbed the stretchy sack, and spread it out. Now it looked more like a matronly bathing suit.

"What's this?"

Foxy shook his head. "You do high profile work, correct? You use disguises?"

"I don't wear bathing suits." Ivan held up the misshapen garment, and it sagged and stretched under its weight.

Foxy rolled his eyes. "Yeah, yeah. It's a fat suit, not a bathing suit. This thing is full of foam. Go ahead. Put it on. Let's see if it needs more padding. It should give you a nice pot belly."

Ivan retreated to an empty bedroom, undressed, and pulled the suit tight over his skin. Like wearing a winter coat, if you put a long-sleeve shirt and jeans on top of it. Hot and uncomfortable.

But back in the living room, he admired the remarkable transformation reflected in the mirror. Between the makeup and the suit, he looked ages older, almost feeble when he hunched his shoulders enough. Definitely not threatening.

"You do good work for this, for disguise. I have to give you credit."

One of Foxy's thin eyebrows went up, like he questioned the compliment, deciding, perhaps, if it had been genuine. Then the corners of his mouth turned up. "As they say, let's not suck each other's dicks just yet."

"Here you go with the homo stuff." Ivan patted his new potbelly. "But I don't care." He checked himself in the mirror one more time, enjoying the illusion. "All I care is you did good work."

"I'd rather you don't use the 'h' word," Foxy said, rolling the case back to the wall.

"Sorry."

"You don't sound sorry." Foxy closed the drawers of his makeup kit, tightened the buckles, and straightened up. "Just remember not to touch your face. It takes time to get used to wearing makeup."

Ivan was already counting steps from the door to the chair by the wall and from his post at the camera to the hallway. "I got it. I want to discuss strategy."

Foxy reached for a barstool and sat down. "I'll take care of Eva and keep the conversation running with her and Kazbek."

"And I will stay quiet. A quiet cameraman is normal."

"But you might have to say a word or two."

"I can stutter. Stutter will hide accent."

Foxy nodded. "That'll work."

"We must decide weapons. If she comes alone and brings bodyguards, it is one thing. But if Kazbek comes, too, they will search us and this house."

Ivan walked over to the thermostat and reset the temperature until the fan kicked in. Sixty degrees should be cool enough in this fat-suit thing. "We need zones of control. When I work with others, I always choose zones, and then I know weapon access."

Foxy shrugged. "We can do that, sure."

"We start with bedrooms." Ivan checked the watch. This part of the work always settled his nerves if there was any uncertainty. And in this job, uncertainty was everywhere. Who would come? How well-armed? Where would they stand?

They split the house into two zones each of them could cover in a gunfight without crossing over. As they talked about movement, Ivan caught himself enjoying the discussion. He'd worked alone for so long, he had forgotten about the advantage of extra manpower.

"You sound like you trained in kill houses before," Foxy said after they examined the layout of each room together, judging movement and attack angles. "You all up on the lingo."

"Afghanistan. And Speznaz drills. They were good. Last year, we had an SAS man come to Moscow to work with us. His technique was different. We trained with him the whole month in abandoned village. He talked about Seal Team training a lot. Kill houses and everything. He had worked with them in Iraq."

"A two-timer?"

"Retired. Needed money." Ivan shrugged. "Partorg paid him enough."

"The brotherhood shit doesn't matter to people these days. Money does." Foxy picked up a flat plastic crate off the floor and put it flat on the barstool. "Here's what I've got for weapons. Make your choice." The latches clicked under his thumbs, and he flipped the cover.

Ivan looked in and frowned. Several Glocks and M&P9 Shield pistols. "I don't like these."

"Why not?"

"I prefer revolvers."

"Wheel guns? Really? What's next—you gonna use a musket? Or one of them flintlock pistols?"

Ivan palmed one of the Glocks and wrapped his fingers around its grip. "This is too small for my hand. And these do not work well with suppressors."

"Jesus, man, we can't use suppressors here. We need small guns so we can hide them. And didn't you soundproof the doors and windows? It's fucking noisy outside, too."

Ivan nodded. "Yes. The freeway."

"And the airport. You asked for a house with noise, and I gave you noise. We have enough noise outside to drown out large calibers, never mind the Glocks. I've put a clip through each. They're ready."

Ivan popped the slide open and checked the chamber. "They are over-oiled," he said with disdain. "They'll jam."

"You can strip and clean them if you want. Nobody stopping ya."

The reset on the Glock felt tactile, solid. Ivan dry fired it several times and checked the ammo Foxy had brought—Federal. Better than most Russian brands. There was no reason to act picky.

He put the ammo down. "All right. It's not good to argue now. I can do it with small pistols."

Discussing communication took time. But they had to—in case they had to go room to room in the fight with the guards. Deciding on gun placement took another half-hour. After that, they ran more drills and practiced clearing the rooms until Foxy said he was hungry and went to get food.

They ate next to the set. "I like to have soup for lunch," Ivan said, hesitating over the burger. "Borsh with a slice of rye bread."

"You Russians are weird." Foxy picked a fry and popped it into his mouth. "I bet for dinner you pluck a chicken and roast it on a spit back home."

"I used to. When I lived on a farm."

"'Cept we ain't got time for no chicken."

Ivan unwrapped a burger, took a bite, and stared at the mess of wilted lettuce and ground beef sticking out. "Soup is better," he said with his mouth full. He swallowed what felt like a wad of paper. "This tastes dry."

Foxy picked up a cup off the floor and handed it over. "That's what the Coke's for."

The sugary drink coated Ivan's mouth like bad cough medicine but helped him swallow the rest of the burger. Ivan waved at the hall to the left of them. "Let's do one more run."

Foxy sucked on a straw and stared. "We've drilled a thousand times. You worried I won't back you up or something?"

"I'm always worried. That is why I am still alive. I like things the right way or not at all."

"Fine. You be the boss."

Ivan stood and took a long draught of his soda, emptying the cup. More caffeine for quicker reflexes. The possible raise in his body temperature, adding heat to the already sweat-inducing fat suit, seemed well worth it.

They cleared the house all over again, this time with lights off and rolls of cloth Foxy called 'do-rags' tied over their eyes. They moved from one room to another, bumping into doorways with their elbows and sometimes heads, the goal of the drill to etch the house's entire layout into their memories.

He had Foxy take point, due to Foxy's narrow frame, but he kept his free hand on Foxy's shoulder to track Foxy's position and the direction in which he pointed his weapon.

They were coming into the kitchen, blind, when Foxy ran face-first into the fridge.

"Fuck it," Foxy said grimly. "I'm done with this. We're just hurting the appliances at this point."

They took off their blindfolds. Ivan pointed at the hallway behind them. "We must do the exits. We must do it right to be ready, in case—"

"In case what, they poke our eyes out with dildos? Jesus, man, how much prep do you wanna do?"

"Till perfect. I cannot afford a mistake."

"Nothing's ever perfect. But feel free to roam around." Foxy headed to the living room. "We got the drill down. We're all set. I'm gonna finish my fries."

Ivan opened and closed his mouth. Criticism would inject discord into an already difficult situation. Best let the man be and check everything else—put more tape over black paper on the windows.

He was playing with the foot switch he'd wired to control the stage lights and the ceiling lamp when Foxy's cell phone buzzed on the kitchen counter.

"Did you move my phone?" Foxy asked, going into the kitchen to pick it up.

"Because you left it in the bedroom."

Foxy returned to the living room. "Eva says she's leaving soon. We've got her, at least." He picked up his drink off the chair.

"No husband?"

"She didn't say." Foxy looked around. "Fuck. I sure hope it's our man, after all the prep we've done."

Ivan eyed the buckets with props. They'd planned well. Their setup inspired confidence with its taped windows and professional film gear. Also, by suggesting creative gun placement, Foxy had redeemed himself for quitting the drill—the man was flamboyant, but his eccentric thinking produced an ingenious solution.

Gambling was a fool's favorite pastime. But it was a good bet that the guards, if they were to search the place, would never find the guns.

Ivan said, "It's a good trap. And we rehearsed."

Foxy slurped the last of his drink and said, "Yap. Looks like we're done with rehearsals, Russki Bear. Time to play out the script."

"How long before she comes?"

"The traffic wasn't bad. Should be about forty minutes."

Ivan picked up his French fries, took a seat in the chair near the camera, and opened his laptop. The miniature surveillance videos from the villa's gate came out nice and crisp. He fast forwarded through a few until a maintenance truck caught his eye; he slowed the footage to real time.

He clenched his teeth and sucked in a deep breath.

"Foxy. Come here."

"What?"

"We have complication."

Foxy's eyebrow came up. "What kind of complication?"

"The kind that travels from Mexico."

20

Los Angeles, California

Did **Miguel hide** those shotguns in the back?
Antonio drove his maintenance truck past the corner store, past one of Miguel's men sitting in a car on the corner.

"Tio," Miguel said from the passanger seat, "your truck can go faster than this."

Already impatient, probably from waiting an extra day. But it was his idea to go to the villa on a scheduled appointment, as if they were the usual maintenance crew.

They stopped at a light before the on-ramp, and Antonio looked at the cars on his left. Jump out and run. Hide behind other cars all the way to the bus stop. Miguel wouldn't care to give chase. And his men—where were they?

In the side-view mirror, two of the cars looked familiar. The light changed, and Antonio drove on.

The freeway was packed with morning commuters. Antonio stayed quiet, lost in worry, while Miguel seemed focused on downtown skyscrapers floating by.

Antonio rubbed his chest. The traffic was pure torture, the way it stretched his anxiety over each mile from home to the hills.

"Tio, you are sweating too much. Are you sick? Take your pill. You look blue. Like a dead chicken."

"I'm not sick, no."

Lie to him. But lying's a sin—enough sin here already without lying, God knows. Antonio hesitated then said in a weak voice, "I'm afraid."

"Afraid of what?"

"I'm afraid you'll shoot a person. I saw the way you talk to your men. And the guns you brought."

Skyscraper windows blinked in the morning sun. Miguel slid on a pair of sunglasses. "I'm still a soldier, Tio. I'm supposed to shoot my enemies. I've been shot twice myself." He slapped his abdomen.

156

"Once in the belly, with a pistol, the bullet all the way to my back. And once in my forearm, when I was a kid."

Antonio sighed and wiped his sweaty hand on his old jeans. "This is terrible. All the violence."

Miguel shrugged. "Violence keeps things in check." He pointed behind them with his thumb. "In Mexico, we need violence. El Checheño killed two Americans in Matehuala. Two good men, dead in the desert. And now he's selling his guns everywhere again, like nothing happened. He's throwing fancy parties for all those rich people—I saw them arrive in their limousines. Someone has to stop him, no? Someone has to give him justice."

Miguel sounded like the priest from the church, the conviction in his tone more upsetting than the thought of the guns.

Antonio glanced sideways in apprehension and found himself reflected in Miguel's dark glasses. "You're so calm. Aren't you afraid of God's punishment? Killing is a sin, no matter why you do it."

"Everything is God's work, Tio. Everything. My first time killing somebody—I didn't even know what I was doing. I was seven."

"Dios Mio," Antonio mumbled. "Just a child."

"Sure. One of seven." Miguel paused and smiled. "I remember it well. I was digging through trash at the scrapyard in Juarez for stuff to sell when they started shooting on the street. Two cars, blocked and shot at from all sides. We ran there when we heard the shots. Bom! Bom! Bom! My friends and I, we raced each other to where it happened."

"Why would you go there?"

"Because it's exciting, Tio! First time I saw a man bleeding like that—blood dripping out of the car into the dirt. Thick liquid, smelly, you know, like when you slaughter a pig. And my friend Alberto said, 'Look, he is still holding his rifle.' And I knew the police wouldn't come soon, so I came closer, and I see his rifle, and I want it."

Antonio stared straight ahead. The excitement in Miguel's voice promised a terrifying punch line, something full of ugliness and sin.

"I was never scared, even back then. But I was stupid." Miguel chuckled. "So I was about to grab the rifle, but this older kid shoved me aside, and I shoved him back, you know? We both reached for it at the same time. He got the rifle by the belt. Guess what I got?"

"I don't know," Antonio mumbled, afraid of what he would hear next. Miguel's story made him queasy, the way Miguel spoke about it like he was describing a child's first trip to the ice-cream parlor, excited by the memory.

"I got my hands around the grip. The safety must have been off because as soon as I tightened my fingers around the rifle, it went off—BOOM!—like thunder. That older kid, his chest just exploded. And his eyes turned huge, like black buttons. I didn't mean to kill him, Tio. But it was all God's work. When God says you die, you die."

Antonio glanced in the side-view mirror, at the reflection of the truck's tool boxes. Guns brought nothing but death. Perhaps Miguel would be watering the plants around the villa. Or cutting the grass. And Mr. Dominguez—or whatever that man's real name was—would walk out the same way he did sometimes, in his bathrobe. And Miguel would pull out that shotgun and shoot him in the chest.

Antonio's armpits and neck grew clammy at the thought: If anyone died at the villa today, it would be my fault. My sin.

He looked at the statue of the Virgin of Guadalupe glued to the dashboard, hoping for advice, for clarity. Refuse to help Miguel? But what would happen to Marisol?

As they drove through the villa's neighborhood, Antonio prayed for the guards not to let them inside. The young guard in the booth, Danny. Would he recognize the truck? Would he open the gate the same way he always did? It was against reason to hope for the gate to stay closed.

They pulled around a corner and in front of the villa. Danny came out from the guard booth, a radio in his hand. He locked eyes with Antonio, and Antonio whispered before he could catch himself, "Please, don't open it."

"What?" Miguel asked.

"Nothing, I . . . nothing."

Antonio pushed his door open and climbed out. As usual, Danny tried out his heavily-accented Spanish.

"Antonio, como estas? Are you here to clean up?"

Antonio felt Miguel's eyes on his back. "It's the third week. Just the lawn and the hedges."

Danny shook his head. "No can do."

Antonio couldn't believe the miracle. For the first time in his long life, he was encouraged by rejection. "No?"

"Let me check. We had a huge party a couple of days ago. They wanted some quiet." He leaned into the booth and picked up his Motorola. "Jordan, you there?"

A voice rattled through the radio. "What's up?"

"The gardener is here to cut grass and such. Should I let him in?"

Antonio rubbed the palms of his hands against his jeans and

looked past the electric wires, into the endless blue sky. Please, no. Please.

The voice from the radio, distorted by interference, said, "Yeah, sure. We'll be leaving soon."

Danny said, "Cool," and went back into his booth, and the gate swung open.

Deflated, Antonio got back into the truck and drove toward two guards sitting in front of the main entrance in a pair of chairs.

Antonio stared at them through the windshield.

Leave. Leave now.

Miguel took his glasses off. "Tio, would the owners come out into the yard this early?"

"I don't see Señor Dominguez outside much." Antonio sensed the guard's eyes on their truck as they passed.

"How come?"

"He stays in his half of the house, in the south wing. He doesn't swim in the pool. But his wife is often around—she likes to play with her dogs out on the lawn."

"She goes to the pool?" Miguel said, nodding at the turquoise water ahead. "To sunbathe?"

"Sometimes even when my men and I are working. They tell me she likes it when they look. I tell them not to, but she's a beautiful woman. They can't help it."

Antonio parked the truck and swung his door open, ready to step out. But Miguel grabbed his arm.

"Tio." He was looking at the main building, at the side door. "I need to know if he's here." He narrowed his eyes. "It's like we talked about: your job is to get inside the house and find out."

Antonio shivered under Miguel's stare. "But it will be strange if I go inside and work the courtyard before we cut the grass. I never do that."

"We cut the grass, then." Miguel let go, turned to the door, and pushed it open.

They opened the tailgate together, Miguel climbing in first to pull the mower closer to the gate.

Once they unloaded the machine, Miguel grabbed its handle. "I'll do it. You find out if our thief is here." He looked over the grounds, as if deciding where to go with the mower.

Antonio waved at the row of plants by the outer wall of the house. "I'll trim the hedges first. Water the roses."

Miguel stared at the villa's arched windows. "Make sure you talk to the woman if you see her."

From where they'd parked, Antonio could see a white sofa inside the living room. "And you?" he asked, hoping his voice didn't show his fear.

"I will cut the grass and look around."

Antonio climbed into the truck bed to get the trimmers and a rake, the guards still watching them. He grabbed his favorite pair of hedge shears, and when he climbed out, Miguel was fiddling with the mower like he didn't know what to do with it.

Antonio put the shears down and helped Miguel prime the pump. Nothing unusual about any of it, but Miguel being useless must have attracted the guards' attention—every time Antonio looked up, the men were looking at them.

"When was the last time you cut grass?" Antonio asked in a low voice.

Miguel had unscrewed the gas tank and was now peeking in. "How hard can it be? You just push it all over the lawn."

"No, you don't understand." Antonio heard the rasping worry in his own voice. He coughed to clear his throat. "No gardener just pushes his mower all over. You have to cut header strips around walkways and flowerbeds. Then you cut back and forth between header strips. And you overlap the strips. You cut to keep the grass from bending." As he spoke, he pointed at flagstones and flowerbeds.

"Tio, stop pointing," Miguel said coldly. "You're drawing too much attention. And I don't care about your strips. I'll just cut the damn grass. And your job is to find out if my man is here. So go find out."

Miguel bent toward the mower, probably looking for the start button. His shirt hiked up and exposed the small of his back, revealing a black pistol tucked into his belt.

Antonio squatted next to him and pointed out the starter with his shaking index finger. "You have to pull this."

The sight of the pistol had heightened his anxiety; the guards would notice how awkward Miguel was with his equipment. And what would Miguel do if they confronted him?

Miguel yanked the starter so hard the mower's motor sprung to life with a high-pitch buzz.

Antonio felt old as he shuffled toward the hedge surrounding the house. The shears were heavier than normal, his every step laborious. He prayed for Miguel to be thorough in mowing the lawn. The guards weren't stupid. They would know.

And they did.

One of the men leaped from his chair and strode toward Miguel, who, oblivious to the guard's approach, pushed the mower in a somewhat-straight line.

The gun or the mowing—it didn't matter now what attracted the guard; with sickness rising up his throat, Antonio watched as Miguel noticed the guard's approach and straightened up.

The mower buzzed at Miguel's feet, but he didn't seem to care to shut it down.

Antonio rubbed his chest and shifted his weight from one foot to the other, fighting the weakness in his knees. He wanted to look away but couldn't. The guard yelled something over the noise, right into Miguel's face.

Miguel's hand went to the back of his shirt, and Antonio heard the shears clank as they fell from his shaking hands.

"Santa María," he mumbled, "defend us from all dangers."

But his words lacked the usual conviction. The prayer wouldn't help; it was certainly too late now to pray for mercy. A moment of greed in Puerto Vallarta had created a bond to all this evil. He who offended against one commandment, offended against them all.

The guard's shouting continued, but instead of pulling out his gun, Miguel pulled down the back of his shirt.

The guard pointed at the ground. Miguel turned off the mower, and Antonio caught the guard's words:

"—fucking pipes!"

The sprinklers. Miguel must have chopped off the sprinklers. Antonio started walking over as quickly as he could manage. From a few steps away, he said, "I'm sorry, Sir. My man's new. I just hired him. I promise you, we'll replace every sprinkler head he broke."

The guard turned to face him. "Is he stupid? I don't cut lawn, and even I can see them."

Antonio waved his shaking hand at the jagged pieces of plastic on the grass. "I'm sorry. I've replaced these before. The soil's a little soggy in spots, so the blades cut low. I should have warned him."

From his spot in the middle of the pitch, Antonio saw the other guard rise up from his chair, curious. Did Miguel do this on purpose to create a scene and draw the owner out of the house? Antonio's heart jumped to his throat. He looked at the guard and quickly said, "We'll go pick up the new heads from the store. I'll put them in myself." He looked at Miguel, but Miguel was staring toward the villa.

Antonio followed his line of sight all the way to the main

entrance, and his heart fell. Another guard had come through the door, his hair in cornrows, and a striking blonde followed him with two dogs on leashes.

Antonio whispered, "Señora Dominguez. No."

"Fix the fucking sprinklers, man," the guard snapped, turning around to leave.

Miguel rubbed his chin. "She is the wife, isn't she?"

Antonio felt the blood drain from his face and neck, his hands like ice. Señora had been nice, always respectful, always asking about the kids.

"Tio, let's go. We are leaving." Miguel grabbed the mower's handle and dragged it toward the pickup with such force, Antonio had a hard time keeping up.

In the cab, Miguel stared at the side-view mirror. Antonio checked his side—the lady and one of her bodyguards were fussing to get the dogs into a white Mercedes.

"Tio. Here is what you do: where she goes, you follow."

"But the sprinklers—"

"Tio, when I say follow her, you follow her."

The Mercedes was already backing out of the garage. Antonio hoped for somebody to join Señora Dominguez, to protect her. It was a relief to see the guards get into a black SUV parked next to her.

Antonio exited through the gate and caught up with the SUV at the light, two other cars between them. "They know my truck," he said meekly.

Miguel, busy dialing a number on his phone, looked up. "Relax. Just stay behind them. They are private security taking a rich lady on a shopping trip or to a restaurant. They won't care about you. Not in this traffic." Miguel spoke into his phone. "Dado, stay back. We are going to pick up his wife. She's in the Mercedes coupe. But let's see where she's going first."

A kidnapping! Antonio's breath hitched. His hands sweated so much his fingers slipped off the steering wheel during a sharp turn.

He glanced at the man to his right: Miguel seemed darker, like a tornado of evil pulling in everything and everyone.

Run! Run away! But how? And where? Miguel's men could find anyone, anywhere. It would take a miracle to escape.

With his sleeve, Antonio wiped the sweat off his brow. His gaze went to the statuette mounted on the dashboard, his Virgin of Guadalupe, watching him from under a rosary hanging from the mirror.

162

The Virgin would know a pious man who deserved a divine rescue, a good Christian who hadn't missed a Sunday mass in years, always honest in his confessions.

They were back on the freeway now, speeding northward, the gear rumbling in the back with every bump. Antonio silently begged the Virgin to give him strength. The statuette shook forward and back, nodding.

21

San Fernando Valley, Los Angeles, California

Ivan listened to himself repeating the name, "Lars, Lars, Lars," until it felt right on his tongue. Lars Swensson. Camera man.

He stood in the doorway and watched Foxy greet the new arrivals out in the front yard. Eva's car pulled straight into the empty driveway, the second car close behind and Foxy guiding them, waving his arms excitedly like a good host.

Two cars. Easy to box them in if necessary. Ivan looked past the curb, past a single tree on the neighbor's lawn, toward the first intersection. Nobody following. No sign of the Mexicans. At least not yet. The Mexicans would know how to box people in, too. An attack here in the front yard would be a disaster, with all the weapons back at the house.

Through the windshield, Eva was visible in the passenger seat, rummaging through her purse. Her driver climbed out first—a well-built black man with a diamond earring and his hair in cornrows.

The SUV behind him disgorged a pair of tall guys in black suits worn over black t-shirts. They closed around Eva when she climbed out, and they all walked toward the house as a tight group, the three men towering over their client whose two fluffy dogs strained their pink leashes.

The dogs looked ridiculous, with pink bows tied into their manes.

Ivan cringed at the memory of the collared man lapping water from a toilet bowl next to the Pomeranians. No human pets here, thank god. But no Kazbek either.

"Hello, hello!" Foxy opened his arms and dashed past the guards toward Eva. A quick hug, and they did this weird thing—going cheek to cheek, lips pursed as if about to kiss but never kissing.

Foxy, a jaunty cap on top of his head, motioned toward the house. "This is it, darling. This is where the magic happens!"

"It's cute! Is the set inside?"

"Sure is!" Foxy sounded every bit like a flamboyant film producer.

Ivan stretched his lips—smiling time. Though nothing here to smile about, with Kazbek not showing up. Did he sense trouble? A lot of the Chechens had the right instincts, those who lived to their forties and fifties. Those who didn't died young.

Foxy bent down and pet the dogs at his feet. He spoke in a thin, feminine voice. "Oh, you brought your babies! They're so cute! Are they Pomeranians? I bet they are! Do they have names?"

"The smaller one is Boo-Boo," Eva said. "And the big one is Honey."

Her bodyguards stood around them like they didn't know what to do. Which was the first bit of good news. Ivan adjusted a digital light meter and a camera hanging from his neck, the belts cutting into his skin.

He sized up the bodyguards through his thick-rimmed glasses: Tall, heavy-set men, looking more like former heavy weight boxers than experienced soldiers. Perfect targets if the situation turned hot in any of the rooms inside the house. Head shots would be near impossible in the dark interior, which meant shooting center mass.

The guard with cornrows glanced at him then looked away. Reassured by the slouching and makeup?

"Mike," the guard said. "The house, man. Go."

His colleague, who was scanning the porch and the yard with an impassive look, nodded and headed for the front door.

"Sweetie, just don't touch the filming equipment," Foxy called after Mike, who was already mounting the steps. "You break it, your paycheck won't be enough to cover it."

Ivan pushed the door open and stepped aside. The stocky guard stomped by, giving off a sour smell of sweat; he stopped in front of the living room, gaping at the wooden rack in the middle of the set. Mike certainly seemed to lack the wits needed to find the hidden guns.

Eva—whose silky blond ponytail swung over a blue cardigan—looked a lot more feminine without boxing gloves. A matching skirt hugged her nicely rounded hips, and she wore high heels well; she walked alongside Foxy with steady steps, her hips sumptuously moving side-to-side, tight fabric of the mid-thigh skirt accentuating the outline of her thighs.

At the bottom of the stairs, she handed the leashes over to the guard with the earring and looked at Foxy. "Patrick, you'll have to excuse my security guys." A tired smile appeared on her face. "My husband's a very important man."

"Darling, that's okay," Foxy said. "That makes you a very

important woman."

"Maybe we should credit me this way in the film."

Foxy beamed at her. "I'd be delighted. Your husband didn't make it here today?"

Eva rolled her eyes skyward. "He's always busy with something or other."

Foxy moved right past the bad news. "Oh, I shouldn't forget." He pointed up at the doorway. "Eva, this is Lars, my videographer and sound specialist extraordinaire."

Ivan walked down the steps and offered her his hand. Her handshake was firm, her silvery blue eyes without shyness or reservation. No surprise, the kind of parties she threw.

"It's a pleasure," she said, her smile genuine, the corners of her eyes joining in.

From the sidelines, Foxy gave a slight nod of expectation—a reminder. Yes. Stuttering.

"It's a—it's a—all mine."

Eva's eyes grew thoughtful. "Oh, I knew a girl in high school who stuttered. Poor thing." Her slight accent—she wasn't Russian but not a 'home-grown American' either.

"Lars doesn't speak much, but he's great with the camera. He makes everyone in his shots look their best." Foxy glanced at the doorway then back at Eva. "Should we all go inside and take a look at the set?"

"Hang on." The cornrows man beckoned with his fingers the second of the two large bodyguards, who was poking the ground with his foot, to come closer. "Sam. Sam!" His eyes shifted person to person. "We have to ring you for weapons, guys. Let me know if you have anything metal on you. Sorry about that."

The apology sounded more like a perfunctory statement polished by thousands of repetitions.

"Jordan, is that really necessary?" Annoyance crept into Eva's voice, her head tilted slightly to her shoulder. "You're embarrassing me."

"Oh, that's fine," Foxy chimed in, and gave the man a dazzling smile. "You can ring me up all you want."

Ivan shrugged with feigned indifference in support of Foxy's statement, but he felt tense. This Sam, would he limit his search to ringing them with the paddle of the metal detector? Or would he frisk everyone as well? If anything buzzed, Sam might decide to do a pat down; he might pinch or feel for anything that bulged out. The foam inside the fat suit might pique his curiosity.

Ivan brushed his belly with his hand. The bulges of the suit felt different from skin. They didn't welcome prying hands.

He glanced from Sam to Jordan. Their jackets looked thicker on the left, around their left armpits. Holsters there. If a fight were to break out in the yard, the bodyguards would have a significant advantage.

Sam stepped up and raised the paddle.

Time to distract the man. When the tip of the paddle touched his ribcage for the first time, Ivan stuttered, "You t-t-t-tickling m-m-e." The stutter flowed naturally, bringing up memories.

"My bad," Sam said indifferently. The paddle didn't stop moving. In a couple of spots, Sam patted Ivan but never squeezed. The pat-down was over in a minute.

With Foxy, who struck a glamorous pose to help the guard run the paddle, Sam hardly cared to do a thorough job—no touching, no standing close.

"All clear, boss."

Jordan turned and walked toward the doorway. His quick movements betrayed regular exercise, but he didn't seem bothered by turning his back on the filmmakers. His colleague, Sam, looking to get rid of the metal detector, went to the car and left Eva alone.

Ivan exchanged another look with Foxy. Stupid of the guards to leave Eva unprotected like this. Definitely no government experience. Amateurs, all three of them.

"I suppose we can all go in now," Foxy said. With his arm wrapped around Eva's, he escorted her up the stairs and into the living room.

Ivan paused in the doorway. All good, so far. Everyone inside the house, in a controlled setting, away from the competition. He glanced over his shoulder at the street before closing the door. No new cars, so no Mexicans. Yet.

On the set, lights flooded the improvised stage with intense, yellow light. Foxy was already waving script pages at Eva; her dogs sniffed the tripods, wrapping the leashes around Foxy's feet. Nothing suspicious anywhere. Like Foxy said earlier, just another porn shoot in the valley.

Ivan walked up to the camera and turned it on. Filming explained everything, all the insulation on the windows and doors, all the soundproofing. Foxy's improvisation was working out well, with the important exception of Kazbek not showing up.

Nice trap, but no mouse.

Ivan took the gear off his neck, put headphones on, and swung the camera on its pivot back and forth, like a camera man in a documentary he'd watched in preparation.

The slow guard, Mike emerged from the hall. "The rooms are empty, boss. Just chairs and clothing here." Mike spoke in a deep baritone, clearly hot in his jacket, sweat on his forehead. He flicked his thumb at the backyard door. "Nothin' outside. Just the pool."

Jordan's eyes darted between plastic tubs filled with cuffs and whips and vibrators, and the impressive wooden frame in the middle of the filming area—the torture rack, in upright position. "Did you check the toys?" His eyes drifted over the bucket filled with dildos of every imaginable size. The biggest one in the middle glistened with lube.

"Ah—sure, boss," Mike said and his wide face wrinkled in revulsion. "Them plastic dicks in there and shit. Fake pussies, too."

"Okay," Jordan said, his attention returning to the rack. "We cool then."

Ivan relaxed his grip. Another score for the local team. He trained the camera on chains hanging from the crossbar of the torture rack, the padded cuffs hinting at the nature of the scene to be filmed. A dramatically oversized winch linked to the chains stuck out from the side of the frame. It was impossible to look at the winch and not imagine a body being hoisted up and up, away from the floor.

With Eva's dogs tied to a chair in the corner, Foxy got her looking at the script; they flipped through the pages and giggled. In the end, Foxy waved the script in the air like a flag and raised his voice. "Lars. We gonna do a few close-ups."

Ivan gave it a thumbs-up. The rigmarole of making a private film could still rope Kazbek in through his wife, as long as the Mexicans stayed out of the way and Foxy played the game right.

"Darling," Foxy said to Eva, "let's see how you look in digital." He waved at the guards. "Out, boys. Out. Everybody out. Go watch the TV."

Jordan opened his mouth, but Eva said, "It's okay. He's going to put make up all over me."

She was naked before Foxy reopened his makeup case. Foxy told her jokes as he worked and dazzled her with his skill of concealing her skin's every blemish. Eva didn't have a lot to conceal: it was a pleasure to photograph her naked body, bathed in bright light.

Ivan showed them the pictures on a large monitor. Foxy smacked his lips with appreciation and said, "You look fabulous, darling."

"Oh, you are such a flatterer," Eva said. But she looked pleased, smiling.

Foxy handed her a robe then picked up the script from a tray and leafed through a few pages. "Aha! This is where your husband winches you up." And after flipping through another page: "This is where we film your husband whipping you—you'd have to cry out in a sexy voice, but with good amount of pain."

Eva pointed at the torture rack and said playfully, "I bet you and Lars have already tried those cuffs."

Foxy waved the suggestion off. "Oh no, I look dreadful on film. I don't have your smooth skin or wonderful hair." He sighed. "I'm so sorry your husband couldn't come. We could've filmed a short scene. We have everything set up." He sighed again with added drama. "Without your husband, all we can do is b-roll." The corners of his mouth drooped as he tossed the script back on the tray. "I guess we can't film a discipline play without a good-looking dom."

Eva tightened her lips. "And if I get you one? Can we shoot at least one scene if I get you one right now?"

Foxy's eyes flashed at Ivan; they might still get Kazbek to come over. Eva was watching him, too.

"I-I-I-I'm g-g-good to go," Ivan stuttered.

Foxy turned back to her. "You think he'll drive over? The traffic shouldn't—"

Eva shook her head. "No, not my husband."

"No? Who do you have in mind?"

Ivan took a step away from the lamp, the heat cooking the side of his face. Really. Who was she talking about?

"Jordan will do it," she said. "We have a short scene with the mask. He can do that one." She was already walking off, through the doorway and into the hall, toward the bedroom where the bodyguards were watching TV, her stilettos clicking on the wooden floor.

With Eva out of the room, Foxy said quietly, "And there I was, selling her on a family film."

"Maybe we get the husband jealous. It may work."

Eva returned with Jordan in tow. He was mid-speech as they entered the room:

"...you know I'm down, but this shit's on tape. I don't know if—"

Eva waved at Foxy and said, "Patrick, could you show him the mask? The one you made for the couple who cancelled."

"Sure." Foxy went to the small chest in the corner and pulled out a prop that must have come from the set of *The Man in The Iron Mask*. The shiny thing was lined on the inside with soft velvet.

"Put it on," Eva demanded as she handed the mask to Jordan. "Put it on and take a look at yourself in the mirror. You'll see it covers your whole head. Even if we use the footage, nobody will recognize you."

Jordan looked at Foxy in a plea for support, but Foxy shrugged as if to say, "She's your boss. I guess you have to do what she says."

"Damn," Jordan said. "I wore a mask for Halloween, but this is way different." He put the mask to his face, and Eva helped him close it around his head and lock it. Jordan's voice came out of the mask's mouth as if he were speaking through a tube. "This thing is pretty soft, huh."

Behind the camera, Ivan met Eva's stare. "How's that?" she asked. "Does it look good?"

He nodded. "G-g-good."

"But darling," Foxy said. "Your gladiator here hasn't even read the script."

Eva's chin went up. "We'll shoot the part where he ties me up. If the footage comes out perfect, I'll show my husband. Then he'll see what he's missing."

Foxy, his arms crossed over his chest, studied Jordan for a moment. The man looked strangely menacing in his black suit and a shiny metal mask wrapped around his head.

"Okay, dear," Foxy said, smiling at Eva. "Let's get you up on the rack. We'll shoot you au naturel first, and then if the footage looks good, we'll have your man read the script and rehearse it."

A simple scene, less than two minutes long, but it took time to set up properly. Ivan took some shots with his camera first. Then they had Jordan change into a medieval executioner outfit that went along with the mask: studded leather belts crisscrossing his chest, hooded robe, and leather gloves with flared cuffs. Eva took off her gown and put on a vest with cutouts for her breasts, a steel gag in her mouth.

They finished by filming Jordan fitting Eva into the rack and winching her up.

The lights made everyone hot and sweaty, but Eva, who must have been the most uncomfortable of them all, didn't issue a single complaint despite her painful position on the rack, her wrists in shackles, her legs spread out by two ropes pulling on her ankles. Where her smooth skin wasn't covered by leather, it was moist from sweat.

Jordan had winched her twice from the floor up, and for each take she made soft moans of pain, just as the script demanded. She looked good in leather, her large breasts crowned with nipples of dark chocolate.

Ivan wiped the sweat off his forehead. A beautiful woman looking her most tempting in digital. But with these stage lights heating up the air, it was impossible to appreciate her attractive qualities.

He checked the time stamp on the monitor. Time for Foxy to finish things. The husband was the one who should be in the spotlight, not the guard. He caught Foxy's attention by raising his hand.

"Okay, cut," Foxy said. "Guys, help me lower her."

They lowered Eva—gagged—to the floor together, Jordan on the winch, Eva's wrists still shackled while Foxy fussed around her feet, saying he'd unscrew the shackles in a second but they should put some oil on her wrists.

Ivan reached for the bottle of water on the tray. The stage lights were impossibly hot when you were so close to them.

"Hey, man, what's wrong with your face?" Jordan asked, staring through his mask.

"Nothing is wrong," Ivan said. "I am just hot."

The words rolled off his tongue, his mind already processing the mistake. Two mistakes, actually. The makeup—he'd wiped it along with the sweat—and the stutter. The damn lights—hotter than the sun in Afghanistan, or Spain, or Niger.

And now everything was ruined because of them and the damn fat suit.

Ivan wiped the sweat out of his eyes and glanced at his sleeve, gray smears of makeup all over it. He took a slow breath—all this work, for nothing. At least this was the right position to start things off.

He rolled his shoulders to loosen the muscles in his back, Jordan staring through his mask from his spot near the winch, surprised the camera man was no longer stooping.

"Motherfucker," Jordan said, "you're not really old, are you? And you don't fucking stutter."

"I used to stutter in school." Ivan took a step toward the bucket with the props. Foxy was on the move as well, leaving Eva hanging.

Eva moaned, but no one paid her any attention. Patrick and Lars, the aspiring filmmakers, were gone. It was going to be Foxy and Ivan from now on.

As if on cue, the Pomeranians broke out barking.

22

San Fernando Valley, Los Angeles, California

"That's her car," Miguel said, "right there. Órale, you almost lost her. Take the next turn and park so I can see the building."

Antonio brought the truck around. The single-story houses on both sides of the street reflected the modest income of their inhabitants, nothing like the opulence of El Checheño's villa.

Miguel eyed splotchy paint peeling off an attached garage. The street didn't have the right look for El Checheño's wife. Her white Mercedes, parked in a bungalow's driveway, seemed out of place. The bungalow itself had a grass lawn in front but only a tiny patch of it, pockmarked with brown spots. What was the wife doing here?

He turned to the old man. "Tio, what do you know about this place?"

The old man looked down at his hands, fearful, as usual. "I'm just a gardener. I know nothing of her business. I only spoke to her—" He flinched when a car passed by. "I only spoke to her a couple of times. She was always nice."

"What did you talk about?"

Tio raised his watery eyes, blinking. "She asked about my family—what part of Mexico I was from. She was nice to me. Very smart. She knew Puerto Vallarta was in Jalisco. She told me she'd been to Bahia many times on vacation. She stayed at local resorts."

"They vacation in Bahia?" Anger rose in Miguel's chest. "Her husband has some balls. He takes my money, makes me look like a joke, and then sends his wife to tan her ass on our sand like nothing happened."

The old man shrunk into his seat, his hands clasped, and Miguel reminded himself to keep his anger in check. The man was just like the rest of his farmer types: timid, hobbled by his stupid religion. Keeping figurines of Christian saints everywhere. Like any of those plastic dolls were going to help him.

173

Miguel patted him on the back. "I'm not angry at you, Tio. I'm angry at them—" He nodded at the bungalow. "—for making a fool out of my family. They betrayed me, you know. You like to talk about sin. That's what I consider the biggest sin of all. Betrayal. I'm going to punish them for betrayal."

The old man cleared his throat. "I swear, I don't know anything of what they do. I've never even spoken to her husband—his manager handles all the housekeeping. He drives her husband's car sometimes."

A manager taking care of El Checheño's business?

"What does this manager look like?" Miguel asked.

"Like . . . like Señor Dominguez himself."

Miguel nodded. Another Chechen, maybe. Someone to do the books, to run the errands. The wife should know all about it.

Miguel pointed at the bungalow. "Do you think the manager is in there with her?"

"I don't know. He was not at the villa."

"Doesn't matter." Miguel waved at the house. "His wife will tell us everything."

An old Toyota turned onto the street, Dado at the wheel. Miguel pulled a radio from the glove box. "Dado, she's in the blue house. Three more men with her, all black, private security. Small arms. I'm not sure who else is in the house."

"Are we covering this exit or others, too?" Dado asked through the radio.

"Just this one. The white coupe is hers, so I bet she'll be coming out of the front door. Park and set up to take down the men when they all come out. Tell Cho and Seso to pick her up after you put down her guards then grab her quickly. I don't want her screaming all over the place. They should move in on her the same time you put down the guards."

Miguel tossed the radio on the dashboard and glanced at Antonio. The old man was crying, wiping away tears with the heel of his palm.

Miguel clenched his teeth. Farmers. Weak and pathetic. And this one was old, too. But useful, so far. And he might be useful again.

He put his arm around the old fool. "Tio, I'm not going to hurt the woman, I promise you. I know you like her. I'll let her go as soon as her thief of a husband pays for his sins."

The old man nodded and pulled a kerchief from his pocket and blew his nose into it.

Miguel turned the truck's radio on and tuned into a local Spanish station, the DJ sounding much like the ones back in Mexico. The

174

music here almost the same, too. Only the commercials were different, advertising products he'd never heard of. He let a few songs play then changed the station. He was on the fourth one when a street vendor went by, pushing his fruit cart, a man as old and as wrinkled as Antonio.

Miguel watched his slow progress down the street. "I swear to god, it's like I'm back in Matamoros." He pointed at the vendor. "Even his cart is the same wooden piece of shit. You know, Tio, I think California will be Mexico again someday." He leaned back, his arms folded behind his head, his eyes half-closed. "Thank god for music, Tio. Whatever El Checheño's woman is doing in that house, she is taking her time."

Half an hour passed, and Dado's voice rattled from the radio. "Jefe, do you want us to go in?" Itching to do some shooting.

"I said wait for her to come out. And tell the kid he needs to learn patience."

His monocular was still in the glove box. Miguel got it out and used it to zoom in on the windows. Black curtains were drawn in each one. Was she fucking the guards there? He chuckled at the thought. That would be something, if they stormed the house and found the blonde on a bed, fucked by three black men. Like one of those videos on Cho's computer.

Down the street, the fruit vendor reached Dado's car and approached, exchanging words with Cho, who had taken the driver's seat after Dado moved back to set up with the rifle.

"Hijo de puta, he wants to eat fruit now?" Miguel frowned when the vendor uncovered the fruit box. The damn kid was buying strawberries; the vendor pulled out a basket and leaned toward the car's window, eager to spare Cho the effort of reaching out.

What if the woman came out right this moment? The kid never thought of details like that, even after all the training.

But he was fast, the little devil. Stupid, but fast. When the vendor saw what he shouldn't have and staggered backward, Cho was already out of his car, whipping his compact body around the open door.

23

San Fernando Valley, Los Angeles, California

The guard, Jordan, went for his gun. He made a quick move to the chair where he had hung his holster and harness after they told him to get undressed for the part.

Quick, but not quick enough to beat hours of preparation and planning.

Ivan stomped on a button near his camera tripod. At once, all the lights in the house went out, including the TV in the bedroom. Ivan dropped to one knee. Safer, in case Eva's men got any random shots off.

The dogs went berserk when Jordan yelled, "Mike, get over here! It's a fucking setup!"

The darkness was absolute.

From his position near the camera, just behind the microphone crane, Ivan stuck his hand over the tub with props and caught a big dildo sticking from the middle. The disgusting thing, lubed at the top to deter the bodyguards from ever checking the contents of the bucket, guided his hand straight to the pistol at the bottom.

Foxy, the weird partner. But also creative.

"Mike, get moving!" Jordan bellowed.

Jordan's panicked cry made things easier. Foxy must have thought the same—he left Jordan alone, and it didn't take long for Sam and Mike—the other two giants—to stomp out of the bedroom and into the hall. They were heading for the living room, the amateurs, making a lot of noise, their heavy feet banging on the hardwood; they used their cell phones as ineffective flashlights.

The hall funneled them straight toward the choke point.

Ivan saw the hall entrance in his mind's eye and raised the pistol. When the dancing cell phone lights and the banging of the guards' feet reached the doorway, he fired. Muzzle flashes revealed the startled outlines of the guards' bodies.

Mike, upfront, caught two shots to the chest and slumped,

bleeding out.

From the side, Foxy fired an ambitious shot, its accuracy improved by muzzle flashes and weak light from the phone in Sam's hand: the bullet ripped out Mike's throat.

Ivan, shooting, checked on Jordan, who was now hugging the floor, far enough from the chair that had the holster hanging from it.

The second guard, Sam, further in the hall, backpedaled as the bullets tore through his jacket and shirt and crumpled backward.

With the last muzzle flash, Ivan took note of Jordan's position again. What? Moving away from his gun? Ivan kicked the light switch, and the lights made him squint just as Jordan bounded off the floor, crashing clear through a door and into the backyard.

Foxy held one hand over his ear—smart of him to protect his hearing like this—and shouted, "All yours!" The grimace on his face was easy to read: Your mistake. You fix it.

Ivan sprinted after Jordan. The fat suit restrained his movement, its fabric fighting the stretch in his groin. Once outside, he reflexively aimed at a crouched figure on the tiles near a reclined lounge chair—easier to shoot the target than to run him down. But here the gunfire would boom over the neighborhood.

"Stop! Stay!" Ivan shouted, not sure what else to say in English.

Jordan scrambled to his feet on the tiled path, lunged forward, stumbled, and fell straight into the blue square of the pool.

Ivan walked alongside the pool and watched Jordan slice his way through the short span of water, unhindered by his boots and the mask he still wore. Jordan's arms came up and down in a windmill motion, his head low in the water. The man swam like he was in the Olympics.

Jordan popped out of the pool at the end, saw his pursuer, and turned to swim in the opposite direction.

Shock-induced lunacy? Ivan walked back toward the house, alongside the pool. Easy target, this guy. One problem, though—the lack of suppressor on the Glock. The Stechkin revolvers, they'd be perfect here. The damn Glock would be too loud. A neighbor might hear the shot and dial the cops. Everything bad enough already.

But this Jordan, still in the pool and intent on swimming away from trouble instead of running away, had to be dealt with.

Knife him? No, he might scream. Drown him?

Foxy stepped through the broken door and took in the situation, shaking his head at Jordan turning around for another lap. "Would ya' look at that—a brother trying to swim away from his problems."

Ivan dove into the pool headfirst, pistol in-hand. He resurfaced right next to the bodyguard and grabbed the oblivious swimmer by the clothes. No use trying to drown the good athlete; before Jordan could realize what was happening, Ivan wrapped his left arm around the guard's torso, brought the barrel end close to his body, and fired four quick shots underwater into the guard's chest, careful not to push back the slide by contact.

The pool had turned red by the time he climbed out.

"Real nifty," Foxy grumbled. "Now we have a bloody fish tank with dead fish." He turned around and went back into the house.

Ivan followed, stepping around growing pools of blood spilling into the living room from the two bodies in the hall. Foxy checked their pulses.

The house smelled of feces now, and of urine, and of burnt gunpowder. A smell of violent death.

Ivan glanced at Eva, who was still cuffed to the rack, her eyes huge and darting from her barking dogs to the pistol in his hand.

Foxy stood up, pulled out his phone, and dialed. He spoke loudly over the noise. "Hey, it's me. Listen, I need you to keep an eye on the dispatch log. I want to know if anyone calls in the noise. We've been a little loud here. Let me know if the local precinct gets wind of it. They tend to be quick."

He hung up and stared at the pool of water forming around Ivan's feet. "You're drippin' all over the floor."

Ivan nodded. They were no longer shouting, the ringing in their ears subsiding by the second. He glanced at the casings on the floor— enough shots to go deaf. "You have someone listening to the police?"

"What? Yeah. We'll have the heads-up. But we have a bigger problem, don't we?" Foxy nodded at Eva.

Ivan kept his breathing even. "I need to think. I will change into dry clothes." Big mess. Would need a big solution. He turned to leave the room.

"Yeah, you think about it," Foxy said gloomily to his back. "You think real good."

"I will."

Ivan went into the bedroom where he'd left the clothes he wore before changing into the fat suit. The problem with partnerships—they often soured when work went wrong. Who would take the blame? Clear answer in this case. No need for a reminder.

Ivan ripped his wet shirt open, not bothering with the buttons. The loss of concentration was inexcusable. Such a foolish mistake, wiping off the makeup. What now? The original plan, gone. The perfect setup? Ruined. Forget the setup—three dead bodies in the house, and Eva a witness. If Kazbek ever got the wind of this, he'd disappear forever. And with Kazbek gone, there would be more bodies going into the ground, in Los Angeles and in Moscow.

His clothes sat in a pile on the floor, which he kicked and sent thumping into the wall. Unforgivable. A total failure with something so simple as stutter and cosmetics. And now the operation was delayed indefinitely.

His abdomen had contracted into a tight knot. Stuck here now, with this 'partner'.

He bent forward, like a runner out of breath—hands over knees—and closed his eyes. Blame—it wouldn't do. Think.

Inhale. Exhale. Attentive breaths.

He shut off the judging voice.

Inhale. Exhale. Into the emptiness came a solution, a vague idea at first. But as he opened his eyes and started to dress, a new chain of events formed in his mind, one possible action leading to another.

First—explain the disappearance of Kazbek's wife and her bodyguards. Eva, a witness still alive, should be an advantage, not a disadvantage. Jordan—a security guy who would know Kazbek's protocol—had gone swimming. That left Eva. She knew just as much or more about her husband's routines.

How do you interrogate a sadist?

He took time, tying his sneakers. This would be tricky, with all the pretense. But it was the only path available.

He returned to the living room. The Pomeranians, freaked out by the shooting but unable to flee due to being tied, cowered in the corner. Foxy, on a foldable chair, was feeding them treats. Eva, the metal gag in her mouth, was still stuck on the rack.

She made a gurgling noise at the sight of him.

Ivan walked over and stood in front of her, turning the pistol over so she could see it clearly. "I will let you talk. But if you scream, I will shoot you." He waved the pistol at the bodies. "Like them. Understand?"

She nodded.

Foxy stepped up beside him, standing with his arms crossed. "I assume you know what you're doing?"

"Yes. No more movies. We do everything real now." Voice gruff, with Eva listening. He unclasped the buckle that held the gag in place and pulled it gently out of her mouth.

Eva licked her dry lips then said, "I'll do whatever you want. Please, don't shoot me."

"Stay quiet until we tell you to talk," Ivan said.

"I'm sorry, darling," Foxy said. "It looks like our production turned into a snuff film thanks to Mr. Self-Confident here."

Eva just stared.

Foxy sighed and cast a cold look at Ivan. "You plan on telling me what it is you have in mind?"

Ivan gestured at the broken door, and they walked into the backyard. The guard's body was at the bottom of the lit pool, his golden mask glinting through the reddish murk.

"I'm all ears," Foxy said.

This was the delicate part. "For the front assault on his villa—do you have a team?"

Foxy rolled his eyes skyward. "Pfft. Hell no. I contract people. That's why I'm not on anybody's radar."

"Then we use the wife. We put pressure on her." Ivan nodded at the house. "She is wife to the man we want, and we have her. She'll know where he goes, what he does."

"So?"

"We let her go. We tell her to watch him and tell us when he leaves the villa."

"Right. And how do you suggest we keep her honest?"

"We threaten her. She saw what we can do."

"Threaten her with what, exactly? She kicks men in the nuts for a hobby."

"We take her dogs."

Foxy narrowed his eyes. "I doubt that's enough."

"I saw how she watched you when you fed them. She watched them during film. And now, she never looks at dead guards. Just her dogs. They are her children."

Foxy pointed at the house. "And the bodies? I mean, how do you suggest we explain three men leaking fluids all over this place?"

"We put them on the Mexican from the surveillance."

"We don't know who he is. He could be a random."

"He carries himself like a soldier. But it's not important—we just need description and story. Kazbek knows Mexicans want him. He will believe they killed his men. Eva just needs escape, like she hid then ran."

Foxy's gaze grew distant. "A failed kidnapping, huh? Mexicans have quite the reputation for it."

"Exactly." Ivan nodded. "We make everything look like it was them."

Foxy scratched his chin. "We have a lot of filming gear here. How would you explain that?"

"I have solution for this. But we must scare her first. Have her cooperate."

Foxy stared with a searching look. "You prepared to bet your life on how much she loves her dogs?"

Ivan returned the stare. "I have a dog. His name is Bond. Like James Bond. And if you put a gun to my head and give me a chance to save him, I will take my chance."

A thin smile appeared on Foxy's face. "A dog person, eh? What do ya know, the tough Russki has a soft spot for pooches." He propped his chin with his hand, fingers hugging his cheek like he had a toothache. He dropped the hand. "Okay. Say I like your plan. Who's going to play the bad cop and lay down the law for her? You or me? We'll have to be convincing."

"I will scare her," Ivan said.

Foxy tilted his head, his gaze judging. "You're no Mister Rogers, but—"

"Who is Rogers?"

Foxy shook his head. "Never mind. What I mean is—"

"I can scare her. I can play bad cop. Trust me."

"I did." Foxy's eyes flashed. "Until you fucked this up."

There, the partnership problem. Ivan put his hand up. "I understand. I say, you check when I tell her what she must do. And your English is better, and she liked you. So you act good cop when I scare her."

A corner of Foxy's mouth curved up. "Look who's improvising now." He looked away, his gaze going across the back yard, over the crimson pool, to the broken door. "A kidnapping, huh." He stood still for a moment. "Okay, fine. Let's see what she says."

There were only a few details that needed further discussion.

Back in the living room, Foxy picked up a bottle of water and held it to Eva's lips. She drank in quick, greedy gulps.

"Darling," Foxy said, his voice heavy with friendliness, "it looks like we have a predicament on our hands." He put the bottle down and nodded at the bodies. "Are you wondering why you're still alive?"

"I can't feel my arms," Eva said.

"I'm sorry." Foxy reached for the screws on the shackles. "I never got to these with all the fuss."

Eva, with her arms free, slid into a crouch, arms folded on her knees, hands limp.

"The truth is," Foxy said, "we're here because of your husband. Too bad he didn't show up. You see—he owes our employer a lot of money." He waved his hand at the bodies. "Nobody would have died if he came over. We'd simply make him pay us back then leave."

"If you are after my husband, I can tell you everything you want to know," Eva said firmly.

Ivan studied her face. Sounded like she'd regained some strength, bolstered by new hope. Everything depended on her now. She had to stay coherent. It helped the plan that she wasn't hysterical.

"Tell us why he didn't come," Foxy said. "After our little talk at the party, you had me believe he'd be interested in doing the private film."

"I lied." She coughed, and Foxy gave her more water. She was looking up at him when she said in a weak voice, "I don't know if anyone told you this, but my husband and I live very different lives. I was the one interested. He'd never show his face on the film." She coughed and wiped her mouth against her forearm. "All he ever cares about is his work. He acts like I don't exist."

Eva looked at her dogs, like she wanted to approach them but didn't dare. Ivan walked over to the Pomeranians and stood next to them, the Glock still in his hand. Eva watched him without blinking.

"Eva, why don't you get dressed?" Foxy said. "Would you like to check on your babies? You can do that. We don't mind."

Eva stood slowly, her wrists bearing ugly red marks from where they'd been squeezed by the cuffs. She ignored her clothes piled on a chair and headed straight for her dogs. They whimpered as she kneeled to hug and kiss them.

Ivan looked at Foxy, who raised his eyebrow. Your turn, bad cop.

Careful to avoid a pool of blood spreading from one of the dead bodyguards, Eva walked barefoot back to the chairs and pulled on her skirt and blouse. She sat down to put her shoes on, her hands slow, eyes staying on the Pomeranians.

Ivan put the gun away and untied their leashes. The bad cop. Time to scare Eva into compliance or lose the mission.

Foxy stepped around Eva's chair and put his hands on her shoulders. "Now, darling. Lars is going to do an illustration for you."

Ivan sunk his fingers into the dogs' fur, gathered folds of skin, and picked them by the scruffs of their necks. They squirmed and snarled as he held them up for Eva to see. She twitched up in her

182

chair, but Foxy pressed down and held her in place.

Ivan opened his arms like he was about to smash the dogs together right in front of her face.

"Don't hold them like that!" Eva shrieked.

Foxy leaned to her ear. "Eva. Listen to me." She was trying to stand up, and he leaned into her. "I said listen to me!"

"Let them go!"

Ivan put the dogs down. She was scared enough. He gathered both leashes in his hand. The way she reacted, she'd be receptive to anything. Totally attached to her dogs.

"We need you to understand something," Foxy said, raising his voice. "Eva! My big friend here—" He extended his index fingers towards Ivan "—owns a butcher shop. They sell a lot of ground beef in his shop. He is a butcher. Do you understand?"

She nodded, breathing hard, eyes on the dogs.

"Okay. Now. He has a machine in his shop that can grind a cow, hooves, and bone—everything—into pulp in under a minute. And if you don't do exactly as we say, he'll put your dogs through that machine."

Ivan pulled the dogs closer, picked them up again, and raised and lowered the poor creatures like he was dropping them into the imaginary grinder. He kept his 'Russian face' on the whole time.

She cried out, "Oh my god, let them go already!"

Ivan lifted them even higher, Foxy saying into her ear, "Are you going to work with us or no?"

Eva nodded, tears leaving streaks on her cheeks. "I will, I will, just let them go!"

Foxy let go of her shoulders. "Okay, then."

Ivan put the dogs down gently and let them scamper to their owner. The smaller one jumped into Eva's lap. Her tears matted its fur as she hugged and kissed it. Real suffering. Proof of new loyalty.

Ivan held the leashes as he stared down at her. "How did you meet your husband?"

"My god, what do you care?" She glared up at him. Ivan returned the look, which cowed her. "We met at a party. He sent me flowers. Roses. A huge bouquet. We went on dates. He said he wanted to marry me. He said he was so wealthy, I would never have to worry about money."

"I see," Ivan said. "An arrangement."

"So?" she said, truculent. "I married an asshole for his money, and now we fight all the time. He hits me, and I hit back."

Ivan grunted. "My boss wants his money. I will take your dogs. If you want your dogs back, you must help us arrange a meeting."

"I'll do whatever you want," she said flatly, clutching the small dog. "I don't know what my husband does, but I know it's illegal. This is all his fault. He can go to hell for all I care." She pressed the squirming Pomeranian against her chest and buried her face in its red fur.

Ivan exchanged a quick nod with Foxy. Not bad.

"Will your husband come if you call him and tell him to come over?" Foxy said.

She shook her head. "He stopped leaving the house after his last trip to Mexico. He's afraid of someone from over there." She looked up. "Are you the people he's afraid of?"

"No," Foxy said. "But if your husband never leaves the house, then you'll have to help us find a way to meet him."

"Now, we will let you go," Ivan said.

Eva looked up in surprise, eyes showing a lack of belief but with new hope. "You will?"

"Yes. But I keep your dogs."

"You will keep my dogs," Eva echoed in an incredulous tone.

Foxy added, "And we'll be keeping a close eye on you."

Ivan pulled on the leashes. Eva stared as if he were a monster about to rip her dogs to pieces. Meanwhile, she was the one choking the smaller of the two fluff balls.

He put together the scariest thing he could say and gave Foxy a nod.

Foxy put his hands back on Eva's shoulders.

Nasty, but no other choice. Ivan snatched the dogs out of her lap. He pressed his gaze into hers and loaded his words with threat. "Now listen. You make mistake or trouble, and I grind your dogs into burgers and make you eat them."

Not Hollywood grade, but convincing enough—Eva went white. Diminished, she curled up in her chair, arms at her chest. "I'll do it," she said weakly. "I'll do whatever you want."

"We start now," Ivan said. "A thing you must do is make a story."

She nodded, fresh tears in her eyes. "What is it? What story?"

He loosened the leashes to let the dogs reach her feet where she could pet them. "I will explain. It is only a little hard. But now you know—it's important you don't make mistakes."

184

24

San Fernando Valley, Los Angeles, California

Miguel shook his head. "The damn kid has no control. If he doesn't handle this before she comes out—"

Cho acted as if he heard the words. He stepped toward the vendor, who was adjusting his hat and backpedaling, his lips moving.

Watching the scene from the cab of the truck, Miguel felt his annoyance mix with curiosity—another problem the kid had brought on himself. What would he do to solve it?.

Cho gave the vendor a hug with one hand while his other stayed hidden from view. Judging by the way the old vendor shuddered and sagged, Cho had used a knife.

Miguel frowned. "Now what? He's got a body in the middle of the street."

Locked in tight embrace with Cho's chin on the vendor's shoulder, the two men moved as one when Cho stepped back, taking the vendor with him, swinging the limp body around the car door. They were like two dancers, one supporting the other.

Cho was small in stature but had plenty of strength to lower the vendor into the front seat of the Toyota, lifting the man's feet off the ground and tucking them into the foot well. The vendor's hat had slipped off, but Cho picked it up and looked up and down the street to check for any onlookers.

"What is he doing with the hat?" Miguel muttered, amused. He got his answer when Cho made it look like the old man was at the wheel of the Toyota, sleeping, holding the hat to his chest.

Miguel chuckled at the sight: the hat was hanging from the knife's handle, the blade still inside him to keep the blood from dripping all over.

Miguel picked up the radio. "Dado, how's the moron going to drive you with the body in the front seat?"

"He said he is going to move it," Dado said. "I told him not to buy the fucking strawberries. I think the fruit man shit his pants when he saw my rifle. It stinks in here."

"Move the body where? Hijo de puta, what is he doing with the cart?"

The kid was pulling the fruit cart closer to the Toyota. He dug inside and pulled out a stack of strawberry cartons. Miguel held the radio close to his lips. "Dado. Tell him if we miss the wife, I will make him eat the cardboard."

Cho had his arms in the cart up to his shoulders. He kept unloading strawberries into the back seat.

Miguel slowly shook his head. Fucking fruit fly. Not even watching the street.

But Cho straightened and looked around. Satisfied, he dove into the Toyota and lifted the old man from the seat.

Miguel leaned closer to the windshield. "Where is he taking him?"

Cho answered the question by folding the vendor in half and pushing him straight down into the cart with impressive strength. The vendor's arms and legs stuck out, but Cho shoved them inside, pushing hands and feet in with the lid.

"Diantre!" Dado said on the radio. "Jefe, he fit him in!"

"I know, I saw it." Miguel heard mumbling from the passenger seat and turned to see Tio shaking and crying. Worse than a child with his crying and fear. Miguel patted him on the arm. "Tio, the man killed himself. He shouldn't look into peoples' cars like that."

This didn't seem to calm the old fool. A lot of similarity here, come to think of it. Tio and the vendor—about the same age and build. Both belong in the box, really.

Miguel put his hand on the old man's shoulder. "Tio. Trust me. Nobody's going to hurt you. You are family."

Tio's reaction was odd: he stuck his hand out at the windshield. "Dios mio!"

Miguel looked where the old man pointed. Black smoke billowed out of one of the windows in the blue house.

"Caray!" He picked up the radio. "Dado, there's a fire."

"I see it. She should be coming out now."

"Get ready."

"I'm ready." Dado sounded calm. The man would be calm even if he was the one inside that fire. The kid was ready as well, for once, back at the wheel of the Toyota.

Miguel expected the bungalow's front door to swing open. A minute passed. Even the old man stopped shivering, watching the house in astonishment. A window exploded, and black smoke poured into the late-noon sky, orange flames lapping at the shingles.

He picked up the radio. "Seso, did you see anyone from your side go by?"

"One car. Asian man in a Honda."

"When?"

"Eight minutes."

Miguel stared at the front door of the bungalow. The woman and her bodyguards should have already run out. So where were they? Smoke from the window grew into a thick column, black mixing with orange from the flame.

"Everyone," Miguel said into the radio, "stay in position and keep watch. I'm going around the block."

But in the back, nobody was climbing over the tall fence, the street as quiet as when he drove through the first time, except for thickening smoke now coming from inside the property, the crackle of fire growing louder.

From the passenger seat, Tio said, "We should call nine-one-one."

"Somebody already did." The sound of sirens was clear in the distance. Miguel said into the radio, "Dado, get out of there. The firemen are coming. Meet me back at the house."

They were rounding the corner when the radio crackled and Dado spat out, "Jefe, she's climbing out of the garage window."

Miguel stomped the brake pedal and swung to the curb. "Is she alone? Tell Cho to take her and cover him."

Dado sounded amused. "I think she's stuck! Her legs and her ass are hanging outside, but she can't pull her shoulders through."

"Stop talking and tell the kid to fucking get her."

The sirens were getting louder.

Miguel squeezed the radio. "What are you doing?" No answer. He swung out and drove around the corner and back to the front of the burning house.

Rounding the second corner, he saw Cho by the garage, pulling on a nice pair of white and bare legs, no skirt or pants, just black underwear. Cho propped the woman by the ankles, holding them above his head, staring into her crotch.

"I'm going to kill him this time," Miguel mumbled. "I swear."

But Cho was struggling, not playing. The woman had wiggled her butt out and most of her waist, but the widow clenched her around the armpits, the weight of her legs pulling her down and jamming the shoulders against the top sill.

The kid pushed her up to keep her level and help her work the rest of her body out. Miguel looked from the end of the street and back to Cho pulling and pushing.

Seso came on the radio. "I have fire trucks."

Miguel slapped the wheel. "Just pull the bitch out already!" He was about to tell Seso to help when the first fire truck rolled in, sirens blaring and lights flashing.

Firemen rushed out in their yellow jackets and pants, two of them in a sprint toward Cho. They shooed him away from her legs—he walked away quickly to the Toyota.

Miguel clicked on his radio. "Everyone, go home."

"They will take her to the hospital," Dado's crackling voice came back. "Should we follow?"

"They will notice the fucking fruit cart. We'll stay out of it for now."

He drove off, fuming, but the situation was too strange to stay angry for long. All these questions: Why was the bungalow on fire? Why was El Checheño's wife climbing ass-first out of the garage window? Where were her bodyguards?

Back in traffic on the freeway, Miguel tried making sense of what he'd seen, but nothing worked. He turned the music on.

The woman didn't matter. What mattered was getting into her villa.

He glanced at the old man. "Tio, we are going back to the villa tomorrow. We were supposed to fix that sprinkler, no?"

The old man stayed silent, and Miguel nodded to confirm his own decision: Go to the villa tomorrow when the wife is back home and find out what's going on. Get the layout of the building then suit up, go in, and kill her husband regardless of who climbed out of what window.

People did stupid things all the time. One could go crazy trying to figure out why.

25

South Los Angeles, California

The safe house smelled of rotting wood. On a cot in the musty living room, Ivan turned over and stared at the ceiling. He'd had little sleep, awake for the most part with the Pomeranians roaming the empty rooms, their nails loud on the old wood floors. And it wasn't just the dogs that kept him awake. Questions jolted and prodded and pushed away his drowsiness: Did Eva make it out of the fire? Would the cops believe her? And a real big one: would Kazbek take off, spooked by the kidnapping attempt on his wife?

Foxy said Kazbek wouldn't go anywhere, not with the LAPD Robbery Homicide investigating the bodies at the bungalow. But still. If Kazbek took off, that would be the end of it.

Ivan gave up on sleep and rolled off his cot. It was an impossible wait, with so much at stake and nothing to do about it. An empty house, Eva's dogs, and the silence.

The bigger of the two Pomeranians, Honey, came over, and Ivan ran his hand through its fur. The dogs had gotten used to him after he groomed them and played with them last night. After some practice, they responded well to simple commands.

The dog's pretty coat and warmth offered some comfort for his mind. Honey was definitely the friendlier of the two.

He went to the kitchen, the dogs following him, happy to eat steak he'd bought them yesterday—raw meat was always a better option than commercial dog food. Too much filler in manufactured stuff. Bad for their stomachs.

Ivan ate the same steak, fried, off a paper plate, using a cardboard box as a kitchen table.

He glanced at the wall from time to time as he ate, at the fat suit hanging from a nail—a silent reprimand, a humiliating reminder of a simple task bungled.

Disguise. Telling Foxy, "Yes, I know disguise." And then, like an amateur, rubbing the make-up off with sweat. Pathetic.

189

He walked over to the wall, took off his pants and shirt, and put the suit on, covering it with clothes. Using the laptop camera, he filmed himself walking across the room, back and forth. He slouched and waddled until his fake belly appeared so heavy, it affected his movement.

He checked the footage and nodded at himself. Wear the damn thing from now on, until the end of this job. Punishment for losing focus.

He walked the dogs on the quiet, bleak street. The dilapidated safe house Foxy had provided stood next to similar wrecks, their windows boarded with plywood or secured with steel bars. An old Pontiac red with rust sat on deflated tires by the curb. The Pomeranians peed on the back wheel.

The walk brought some clarity—no point sitting in the empty house, waiting for the phone to ring, when the cameras had fresh surveillance footage. The Mexicans might show up again. And it wouldn't hurt to check on Eva coming and going.

The drive to the hills took a while. Foxy's safe house was east and south of downtown, along the major commuter route. Despite the early hour, the freeway was already filled with cars, their drivers looking glum.

Miserable morning for everyone.

In Kazbek's neighborhood, the sidewalks were wet from sprinkler spray. At the villa, one thing was different—a police cruiser sat near the gate. A sign of encouragement, perhaps. Eva's story about the Mexican kidnappers would keep police close. But the truth would keep them even closer.

Ivan drove past the cruiser and parked a good distance down the road, behind another sedan, and sat watching the gate and a cop in the cruiser through glasses with lens and video magnifier built in. He was barely within range for his surveillance cameras to dump footage on his laptop.

Being so close to Kazbek helped dispel some uncertainty. The cops wouldn't be here if the residents were gone. Ivan glanced at the empty cup in the cup holder—should have stopped and bought coffee. From this far, the download would take a while.

The smell of fried bacon from down the street wafted into his nostrils. Could be Kazbek's bacon. Unlikely, though. Muslims wouldn't eat pork. But they wouldn't host torture sex parties either, so different rules here.

The prospect of running into the Mexican from the earlier video worked as a substitute for coffee, pushing away the drowsiness. The man was no electrician—no tool belt, and so awkward in the lift cage, like it was his first time.

Ivan's phone buzzed and jingled. He fished it out of his pocket and answered.

"I've got some news from Eva," Foxy said, skipping a greeting. "She gave cops the description of the Mexican from your surveillance tape, like I told her, and she says they bought it because it's so detailed. She says they posted a cruiser outside her house."

"I see it right now."

"You feelin' nervous?" Foxy asked.

"Kazbek takes off, we are dead. Partorg doesn't forgive."

"Let's not overdramatize the situation. We've got police watching him now. By the way—apparently Kaz recognized the Mexican Eva described to him and the cops. She says her hubby got really worried when she mentioned the pockmarks. Worried enough to bring in a bunch of his men."

"Chechens are no cowards," Ivan said heavily. "If he's worried about the Mexican, we should be worried, too."

"Jesus, man. Lighten up and give yourself some credit. You spotted the guy."

"I do not deserve credit." Ivan's fingers bit into the plastic of the steering wheel, knuckles white, nails digging in. Complications from his mistakes at the porn shoot were snowballing. "It is not good. It will be harder to reach Kazbek now."

"But you had the right idea—the Mexican makes for a good decoy. He'll take the fall for the burnt bodies in the valley, and for whatever happens next."

"Kazbek might run."

"He can't go nowhere with the cops watching, not with involvement in a triple homicide. Meanwhile, we have a mole on the inside. Eva will keep an eye on him for us even if he makes a move. It's perfect."

"Nothing perfect about it," Ivan said. "We don't know anything about this Mexican. Chechens don't scare easy. This Mexican must be working for someone heavy, with a big crew. Heavy enough to interfere with our work."

"But what's your Mexican gonna do? This isn't Tijuana. I like the way this is playing out. Everyone is thinking about the Mexican while we do our work through Eva. Funny, isn't it? I'm beginning to like this job. It's got an interesting twist."

"It is not interesting. It is difficult. Even if Kazbek comes out, the Mexican will be waiting for him, too."

"But now with all the cops snooping around, they'll have to back off. Which gives us some room. Eva says Kazbek might have some business in the city next week. Any opening she finds, she'll let us know right away."

Ivan took a deep breath. "This is a long wait." Too much vagueness and uncertainty while Lena was alone in Moscow—worse than alone, with Fedot. "Maybe we find another way."

"Maybe. But for now, Eva says you have to make sure the dogs drink lots of water and get walked three times a day. You were right—all she cares about is her dogs. Keep them happy."

"I know dogs. Dogs are not our problem. Access to Kazbek is our problem. I cannot wait forever."

"Actually, I can wait a little bit. I have some family business to take care of."

"We cannot have distractions."

"It's not a distraction. My ma has some problems with her club. I was gonna take care of it after you left, but it's gotten worse with her. And since we got nothing else to—"

There was movement at the gates. Ivan said, "Someone is here. I must go," and hung up.

An unmarked, black Crown Victoria with an antenna on the roof pulled into the property. Detectives, most likely. Foxy was right, with so many cops around, the Mexican would stay away.

A notification popped up on the laptop, the first of the files downloaded. Ivan pushed the glasses up on his forehead and opened the footage; it showed the area around the main gate. He fast-forwarded through a few cars arriving and leaving, but he had to pause the video due to more movement at the gate.

He put the glasses back on and zoomed in. A pickup truck. Magnified, the driver's skin looked dark, his face lined with deep wrinkles. Lawnmower handlebars, a ladder, and some rakes sticking over the truck bed.

The pickup looked familiar—from the earlier footage? Ivan returned to the laptop and rewound the last clip from yesterday and found the same pickup truck pulling in, same old driver.

Two days in a row? A lot of landscaping.

The new guard at the gate must have thought the same; he approached the driver's side and said something short and quick, waving impatiently at the truck.

The old driver talked to somebody in the cab. The pickup backed away from the closing gate and headed down the street, getting closer.

Ivan put on a baseball cap from the back seat and picked up an empty cup. He put the cup to his lips once the pickup got closer and took a quick glance at the man in the passenger seat.

One glance was enough.

The fake electrician from the surveillance footage.

The pickup turned the corner, and Ivan picked up his laptop. That one video—he fast-forwarded through the footage until he found Eva and her guards leaving. The pickup followed them. Maybe even to the blue bungalow.

A video search brought up a clip from a different camera for the same time period. It showed the cars entering and leaving from up close, its lens trained about window-level. For the pickup, the camera only caught the passenger's arm hanging out the window.

Ivan stopped the playback and expanded the shot screen-wide: this round scar—the burn a bullet makes when it blasts through skin.

He opened the glove compartment, pulled out a pistol, and racked it. The pistol fit snug under his fat suit. The damn thing held it tight and was thick enough to avoid printing. This self-punishment was useful in more ways than one.

Pulling out of his parking spot, he dialed Foxy, who sounded amused when he picked up.

"Did you miss me?"

"No." Ivan accelerated down the street to catch a green light, the pickup crawling through a busy intersection two lights away. "I am looking at our Mexican."

Foxy didn't sound worried. "Oh, yeah? What's he doing?"

"He drives a truck and has access to Kazbek. I mean had—I think the guard turned them away."

"What do you mean 'has access'?"

"The Mexican works with a gardener. I have video. They came in and out yesterday. Right after Eva. I am behind them right now. We should take care of them."

"Hold on—did you say the guard turned them away?"

"Yes. I think."

"Then we got nothing to worry about. They can't—"

"You wrong. If he went in, he knows layout. He was watching the place for attack. This is serious. He is no simple maintenance man. He has seen action."

"How do you figure that?"

"I saw him close. He has bullet scars on arm."

"I see. Does he know you made him?"

"No. But I am following them."

"You gonna do something?"

"Can you back me with more men?"

"I told you, I don't have a team. And I don't see why we should bother anyway. They aren't going to shoot their way in with all the cops around."

"Then I find where he hides. We can delay them. And after, we hurry with our work."

"We can't hurry. We're on Eva's schedule now."

"Yes, we can. I have ideas."

"And you gotta sit on them. I'm on my way to Pomona. I told you I got family problems."

"Is it bad?"

"She's being harassed by a couple of cops. The crooked variety."

"We solve your problems, and then return to our work. Let me help."

Foxy's voice oozed sarcasm. "You mean like you helped yesterday?"

Hard to hear. But feelings had no say in this work. And Foxy's problems could become solutions. "It's true, I was bad with disguise. But I work good with electronics and weapons."

It was a guess, but the way Foxy spoke of his family trouble—and with him lacking a team—there was a chance the man would bite.

"Electronics, huh?"

So he did bite. "I caught Mexican on my video. My electronics."

Foxy's silence was promising. "Let me think on it."

"I will call back."

"Fine."

Ivan hung up.

Between following the pickup and engaging Foxy in English, he was sweating. Exhausting, these conversations. Hard not to offend people in English. Russian, translated directly into English, sounded rude. Politeness took too much effort. And right now, everything was too busy to be polite. Only two lights left before the onramp to the freeway.

Ivan pulled behind a long row of cars waiting for the light, the pickup second car from the front. A good opportunity here.

He stepped out of the Lincoln and came around the back, diving into the trunk, sorting through his surveillance kit.

The driver behind him honked; in some ways, drivers in Los Angeles were no different from drivers in Moscow.

Ivan pulled out the tracker box, closed the trunk, got back behind the wheel, and put the box on the passenger seat. He opened it as he drove. The tracker fit neatly in his palm, like a flip-phone. He slipped its SIM card in and put the device into a magnetic case. At the next light, he pulled up behind the Mexicans, close enough to see the tools in the pickup: rakes and a leaf blower.

The leaf blower—they pushed trash and dust through streets here, dry leaves flying in every direction. What was the point? Lena would hate that, with her asthma.

Ivan checked the driver in the rear view. A woman, texting. She wouldn't care.

He got out and came around the hood of his car, bending under it like he was checking for a problem. The pickup truck took off while he still had his arm under it. But the tracker was already attached to the pickup's undercarriage.

He let the Mexicans speed ahead, out of view. Then he got back into his car and followed them onto the freeway, staying way back. A few miles later, the laptop map showed them slowing down—a residential neighborhood east of downtown.

Cracked cement on the exit ramp shook his car, the road surface corrugated like a washboard. Ivan pulled over after the first intersection, in front of a corner store, and watched the tracker dot zigzag across the map displayed on his laptop.

He typed the address of his safe house into the search window. Almost neighbors, Foxy's safehouse further south by a few miles.

The GPS dot veered off the street and stopped. The standard satellite map showed a fenced yard next to a house.

Ivan pulled away from the curb. Would their location be easy to approach?

Two blocks down the street, he rounded a corner and cruised past a row of houses hidden behind iron or chain-link fences.

From one tall porch, a few young men in basketball shirts too large for their bodies watched him attentively as he drove by. Too attentively. One even stood up to take a better look, his neck covered with tattoos.

Although the pickup was still a few blocks away, Ivan turned around at the next crossing and drove back to the freeway. The Mexicans would post a watcher on one of these corners; it was foolish—pushing closer without a good reason. Not the time to get close. Not yet.

The presence of Mexicans was highly alarming. They didn't get into the villa today, and maybe the cops and the guards would keep them away, but that would push them toward more radical solutions. Delay them? But any action would alert them and squander the advantage of surprise. Action must be tied perfectly to open the window for picking up the Chechen.

The sun was heating the car, and Ivan jabbed the air conditioner button.

On the freeway, a billboard floated by, the text in Spanish.

Ivan fingered his cell phone. Mexico was only a few hours away, with its extensive crime syndicates backed by limitless financing. Foxy was too optimistic. There wasn't time for family problems. It was time to take action or risk losing the Chechen to competition.

26

West Hollywood, Los Angeles, California

When the new guard came out of his booth behind the gate, Antonio didn't know what to think. The guard—a dark man with a bulbous nose—turned sideways to pass through the gap and approached the pickup from the driver's side, leaning close, drilling the new arrivals with his charcoal eyes.

"What do you want?"

What happened to Danny? This new gatekeeper, he was much bigger, with leather belts under his jacket—when he leaned into the window, holstered pistols nosed out from under his armpits.

Antonio pointed at the grounds beyond the gate. "Sir, we were here yesterday to cut the lawn. We brought new sprinkler heads."

The man, leaning away, flicked his wrist dismissively. "Get lost. No maintenance today. We don't let anyone in." Weird accent, too. Saying 'we' like 've'.

Miguel moved in his seat, and Antonio said hastily, "But we never fixed the sprinklers. I was supposed to come back and—"

But the guard was already walking away.

"They brought in new people, didn't they," Miguel said, staring forward and cocking his head as if to see past the wrought iron. "The police is here, and new guards. This one has a hook nose, like he is an Arab."

Antonio nodded. An image of Cho, the craziest of Miguel's men, floated into his mind: Cho lifting the dead fruit vendor, folding and pushing the body into the cart, shoving legs inside, smashing lifeless hands with the lid.

If Miguel couldn't get in as a maintenance worker, he would have no need for his 'uncle'.

Antonio drew a shallow breath, hopelessness sucking vigor out of his body. Maybe Miguel would let his 'uncle' go. What did he say? A family. But a family of monsters. Ghouls. Laughing and joking and making fun of Cho for failing to pull the wife out of the window by

197

her naked legs. None of them ever mentioned the dead man in the cart, like he didn't exist.

"Tio, get going," Miguel said. "No use sitting here."

Antonio shifted into reverse and pulled away from the gate. He drove around the block to the first light, thinking how they'd never let him see his girls again. The crazy one would cut him down and shove him into some box or a garbage bin. Marisol wouldn't even know what happened. Whatever Miguel said in the beginning about the plane to Puerto Vallarta—it was all a lie.

Miguel's words broke the reverie. "Tio, what are you waiting for? It's green. Go."

Antonio moved slowly through congested streets. Oh, how quickly sometimes did the Lord's punishment follow the sin. Days. Mere days after getting greedy at Jorge's mention of the reward, at the promise of easy retirement wrapped in a package of catching a thief.

Offend against one commandment, and offend against them all. Greed, simple greed, leading straight to Miguel and his demons. God worked in mysterious ways sometimes, but this wouldn't be one of those times. The wages of sin were death.

Antonio drove without changing lanes, without rushing through yellow lights. And Miguel—the devil didn't seem to care about their slow progress, quiet in his seat; he either looked out the window or kept adjusting the mirrors as if he was the one driving. Not a word from him the whole time.

The cars on the freeway hurried along, traffic thinning out, morning rush now over. Antonio stared ahead, numbed by questions: What would the knife feel like? How much would it hurt?

When they pulled into the driveway, Miguel let the passenger door swing itself open and hopped out. In a hurry, the devil. Unhappy. Going straight into the house without saying a word.

Antonio climbed out and went rigid with fear at the sight of Cho coming through the doorway seconds after Miguel went in.

Here it was—the old man's punishment for the deadly sin of greed. And no chance for confession—everything happening so quickly. Antonio stood motionless, his hat in hand, his legs refusing to move.

"It's you and me, Tio," Cho said and spat on the ground. He rubbed his palms, warming them for the devil's work.

Antonio gave him a beseeching look. "I would like it done quickly. If I could say a prayer first, and then you do it—that's all I ask."

"Como?" The little demon seemed puzzled, staring with his mouth open. "How long is it going to take?" His thick lips puckered in displeasure. "Jefe is not going to be happy about this. He wants it done, no delays."

"Can I at least say a prayer?" Antonio cried in desperation. "I've done everything you asked me! How evil do you have to be not to let a man say a prayer before you take his life?"

Cho waved the plea off with his hand. "Tio, stop rambling. Let's go to the garage and get to it." He was frowning, rubbing the narrow strip of hair on top of his head that always made him look like a Mayan warrior.

Antonio followed Cho across the front yard, stumbling, looking at his feet through tears. He stopped inside the garage and stared at a red pickup truck, the insignia of Los Angeles Fire Department painted on its doors.

The steel side boomed when Cho patted it. "Jefe says not thick enough. Seso and I brought more steel sheets. We need to weld them into the doors and reinforce the inside of the tool boxes. Things might get hot in that villa because the Chechen brought in new soldiers." He pushed his chest forward proudly. "I used to be a welder. My father taught me. Do we need to refill your tanks, or are they fresh?"

His words, once their meaning took root, weakened Antonio's legs, the energy from his fear dissipating. He leaned against the cool metal of the truck.

They wanted their old man alive. Welding. Helping.

Antonio wiped his eyes, ashamed of his weakness. "No, there is no need for refill. The tanks are still at least half-full."

The work helped his heart settle down, quieted the flutter. They cut steel into measured strips and were taking the paneling off the doors when Antonio's cell phone rang.

He stared at the number. Did Señor Dominguez find out? No, they wouldn't be calling their landscaper if that was the case. They would send the police. A much simpler explanation: the sprinklers, the timer at the villa had turned them on.

"Yes?"

A male voice, one he'd never heard before, said, "Are you the groundskeeper for Dominguez property?"

"Yes?"

"You need to send someone here right now. The grass is flooded." Somebody was swearing in the background in a strange language. "You must repair what your men broke."

Cho put down a screwdriver he'd been holding, trying to listen in.

"I'm in the middle of something," Antonio said. "I was at your gate in the morning. The gatekeeper didn't let us enter the grounds."

"I don't care what you're doing. It's your fault, so you have to do repairs."

Cho nodded at him, so Antonio said, "We'll come back. An hour maybe, depending on traffic."

"No 'we'. Come alone. This should be a simple repair. The guard will let you in, but nobody else. We had a security problem. Only people we know can come in." The man hung up on Antonio before he could say anything else.

In the kitchen, Miguel looked up from his cards when Antonio came in through the door to the garage. "You finished with the truck already?" He turned to a quiet one. "I told you the kid is better with the welding than you are."

Everyone at the table was smoking, the smoke so thick Antonio had to clear his throat before speaking. "We cut the steel sheets to size and took the paneling off. It's a lot of work."

"The sooner you finish, the sooner you go home to your wife, Tio."

"Miguel, it's not that. I got a call from the villa. They say the sprinklers flooded their lawn. They want me to come back."

"Good. I still want to know why that house was on fire." Miguel put down his cards and stood up. "Let's get going. Cho and Seso will finish with the truck."

In God's name, this was the time to be brave. "The man on the phone said they had a security problem, so they won't let anyone inside but me. Because they know me."

"A security problem?" Miguel narrowed his eyes, his cold gaze like a draft of winter air. Antonio held his breath until Miguel shifted his gaze away to Seso. "Did we get all the gear in yet?"

"Some of it," Seso said. "The rest should get here soon."

Miguel sat down and took up his cards. "Go fix those sprinklers, Tio. But do me a favor: Get inside the house. Talk to the wife. See if she tells you about the fire."

Antonio's heart sang with new hope. He turned to the door, new energy coursing through his body. A chance for penance, for confession—all of it still possible, God's mercy infinite to those who embraced him.

"Tio. Wait." Miguel said, his voice like a dagger in the back.

Antonio turned.

"Count how many men they have outside and inside. And pay attention to the inside of the house—I will be asking you about it."

Walking out to his old truck, Antonio hardly felt his legs. Alive. Alive! All of this was a design made by holy providence itself.

He drove out of the gate, meeting the watchman's stare straight-on.

I'm brave now, he thought. There was no fear among His flock.

The same billboards that drifted by in the morning flew by in the afternoon. And there He was, The Lord himself talking from the billboard above a tall apartment building:

I WAS A STRANGER AND YOU WELCOMED ME.

Antonio's heart trembled at the sight of the message, the Bible's language so clear—it was up to men to welcome God's commandments and deliver themselves from sin. The call from the villa was God's call to make amends.

Antonio pressed on the accelerator, intent to hurry toward redemption.

No more cowardice. No more compliance with the demons' wishes while innocents died. Time to answer His call. At the highest cost, if need be. Serve Him and no one else.

27

South Los Angeles, California

The Pomeranians barked their fluffy heads off when Ivan stepped into the house, and he waited for them to settle down. When they didn't, he closed their mouths to let them know he didn't like them making so much noise.

Honey earned a treat by staying quiet—this one deserved its name. Ivan wasn't sure what the name 'Boo-Boo' meant, but judging by the second dog's behavior, it wasn't anything good.

He checked the Mexican truck's position on the map. For now, they were right where he'd left them.

The dogs fussed around his feet. Take them out for a walk? But Boo-Boo might take it as a reward for barking. To lessen his own anxiety, Ivan considered calling Lena, but the clock said it was too late to call Moscow; she was already asleep. Time difference split them worse than the distance.

His stomach rumbled; he had gone too long without a meal. He looked at the Pomeranians, and they perked up their ears, sensing an opportunity. The dogs needed relief, and the problem of Mexicans getting close to Kazbek demanded careful consideration. Walking would be good for that.

The dogs yelped and barked as he fastened their pink leashes to their harnesses.

Outside, the Pomeranians dashed in different directions, pink bows in their manes. They resisted his pulling them toward the avenue where he'd seen a yellow sign for a fast-food restaurant, but he dragged them along, past rusty cars and razor-wire fences. The dogs watered the telephone poles; the street lacked any trees.

At the avenue, Ivan turned left and walked by a gas station where a pudgy man in a baseball hat and a woman in a long skirt were fueling their sedans. They stared at him as if he were an apparition.

He looked around: The only white man here. And traveling on foot—so un-American.

The sidewalk disappeared at times, as if the city didn't expect anyone to ever walk. The dogs peed happily on the fence of an automotive repair shop and on the corner of a square building Ivan took at first for dry-cleaners.

He looked closer at a crude sign. A church? But looking more like a prison. Nowhere in Russia would you find a church in such an ugly, utilitarian building. Americans seemed to have a rather practical approach to god.

He didn't feel bad when Boo-Boo peed on the far corner as they went by.

The walk offered little pleasure—ugliness was everywhere, from cracked concrete and peeling paint, to trash and dried grass. Hard to find an area this ugly anywhere in Moscow, even in the sleeper neighborhoods of concrete towers. Although, Moscow did get this ugly when the snow turned to brown slush in the spring. Or uglier, with all the dog shit revealed by melting snow.

He found the fast-food restaurant and walked in with his dogs in tow.

A small girl seated at a plastic table across from her mother pointed at the dogs and broke out in loud Spanish, "Mommy, mira!" Her index finger trembled with excitement. "El Gordo con perros!"

The mother shouted "No," but the girl was already off her seat and running toward the Pomeranians.

Ivan let her pet them. Last night, the dogs hated his brushing their fur—may just as well let the girl enjoy their fluffy coats.

Ivan glanced at the mother, at the dark-blue circles around her eyes, lashes thick with clumps of mascara.

Makeup was hard for men and women alike.

He turned and stepped toward the counter, the scratched, old menu above his head. The air, this close to the kitchen, stank of rancid grease and old socks.

The server, a tired kid in a shirt covered with oily spots, moved around in a daze. The food trays needed a wash, and every step Ivan took stuck a bit to the floor. A restaurant from the same chain in Russia was luxurious by comparison. Did they forget how to care around here?

At a table in the corner, Ivan unwrapped a burger and stared at the squished bun, at black rot around the lettuce. He tore off and tossed a piece of the patty to the dogs. They jostled for it, but after sniffing, let it lie on the floor.

A sip of a milkshake induced a grimace, all sugar and water. Ivan's teeth hurt.

The front door swung open, and two younger men walked in, one dressed in shorts that came down to his ankles and a hooded sweatshirt, the other in baggy pants and a blue basketball jersey. The basketball man had a bandanna tied around his shaved head. Their skin, where visible, was blue with tattoos.

The mother picked up her girl and walked out. Ivan pulled the dogs closer and quickly ate the rest of his fries. The youngsters had a nervous energy about them. Ivan kept his gaze on the tray as he ate. Wise, avoiding eye contact with young men when they're in a tight group like this.

The men argued by the counter, and Ivan glanced at their backs. The skinny one with a bandanna adjusted his pants, his right hand then quick to the back but not touching anything. A pistol inside the belt?

Bandanna said, "Smells like shit in here."

The stocky one in a sweatshirt said, "You're the one who wanted a fucking shake. So get a fucking shake."

Time to go. Ivan shooed the dogs toward the exit but slowed by the bin to deposit his trash. Their leashes slacked enough for Boo-Boo to scamper off.

He heard one of the men say, "Homes, check out the little fucker. Ten spot says I can make him bite my shoe."

Ivan turned around. The skinny lowlife hadn't waited for his buddy to take the bet: he jerked and shook his sneaker in front of Boo-Boo's nose.

The movement would excite the dog—Ivan yanked the leash, but it was too late; Boo-Boo sunk his teeth into the man's foot like it was a rat.

The man hollered, "Oh, shit! He bites strong! Get off, bitch! Off!" He shook the dog off his sneaker.

"Sorry." Ivan jerked Boo-Boo back to avoid a possible kick just as the skinny thug bent forward and reached to catch the Pomeranian.

Ivan pulled harder on the leash to keep the dog out of man's reach.

Their eyes met only for a moment, and the baldy said, "The fuck you looking at, fag?"

Ugly with cheap bravado, and a teardrop tattoo not helping the impression. The teardrop just an outline, not filled with color. The bastard hadn't killed anyone yet.

Ivan turned and was half way through the door, herding the dogs out, when the baldy shouted, "Yo, fatty! You owe me money. Your fucking dog bit my—"

The door closed and cut off the rest.

Terrible time for local disagreements. But the thugs offered an idea worth exploring.

Ivan pulled the dogs away from the restaurant, past the parked cars. The Pomeranians, oblivious to danger, spread out, Boo-Boo disappearing under a green sedan.

Ivan pulled on the leash, reeling in the silly fluff-ball. Fag? A vaguely familiar word. An insult, most certainly.

A bell over the restaurant door chimed, marking the passage of customers.

Of course. The idiots here shouldn't be any different from the ones back home. On instinct, Ivan sent his palm to the pistol on his right side, where it sat snug against the fat suit. Would be a favor to the neighborhood. But too close to the safe house. On foot, with dogs—no, out of the question.

Unless—

The skinny thug in a bandanna was already stepping closer in a rush to get his great speech out. "Yo, you don't walk when I say you owe me." His shaved head was moving side-to-side, snake-like as he spoke. He poked the air with his fingers in a weird gesture. "You coming here to my hood with your faggy dogs? Da fuck you think you are? Bulletproof?"

His buddy flared from behind his leader, a united front of morons. They didn't seem to even consider encircling their target to lock him between the two parked cars. Full of bluster. But throwing furtive glances to the street. Afraid of the police?

The stocky one, shaped like an over-pressured oil barrel, did the same weird thing with his fingers as he spoke—he had something to say as well, apparently. "I think this fat puta here is confused. The homo come to our house looking like a bitch, walking fag dogs on pink leashes."

"I'm gonna unconfuse his bitch ass right here," the one with the bandana said. He had pistol potential and deserved attention.

Ivan looked straight into the man's brown eyes and waited.

The thug glanced at the road, like he was checking for witnesses.

Without taking his eyes off the man's ugly face, Ivan looped the tied-up leashes over the side mirror of a parked car.

At last, the thug got his pistol out. A 1911 Sig Sauer, white letters over black frame. Poor choice, really, for standing so close to the target. A long take-up on the trigger, two hitches before trigger release, and a heavy trigger pull.

Eye contact was key, until Ivan broke it and looked behind the thug, to the street, and said, "Police."

Next to impossible for a man, primed for something, not to look where the eye of another points.

The thug's gaze went to his left. Ivan swung right, out of line of fire, and caught the slide with his palm. Good contact. Easy push. The slide and barrel would disengage the sear.

The lowlife jerked the trigger and learned that his gun was out-of-battery.

Nice of him to keep the finger in the trigger well; Ivan rotated the pistol and pushed it down in one swift motion until the bone snapped.

"A-a-h-g—"

Ivan ripped the pistol free and put it in his pocket, watching the stocky man for movement. No gun yet. Just passive astonishment.

Ivan took the whimpering baldy by the head and smashed his skull into the car. Once. Twice, for extra insurance. And to teach a lesson.

The stocky man took a step back.

Backing up now? Going where? Moving forward, Ivan took the trophy pistol out. "Stop." What did they say here for hands? "Hands—up!" He waved the barrel, and the man obeyed.

Ivan took a big step, opened his hips, and put all of his recent failures and all of his weight into the straight punch.

Crunch of cartilage.

The man dropped like he had no legs. The Pomeranians kept barking the entire time, two tireless noise machines.

Ivan checked his surroundings—just cars, and the restaurant's surveillance camera stayed pointed to the side. He tucked the trophy pistol on the other side of the fat suit and searched their clothes. The skinny one had two plastic bags with crystals inside. Methamphetamine, probably. It would do.

Ivan picked up the leashes. Boo-boo, always the feisty one, sniffed the prostrate body between the cars and lifted its leg to take a piss.

"Poidem." Ah. Russian wouldn't work. "Stop playing. Let's go."

But Boo-Boo resisted the leash, sniffing and licking something that fell out of the stocky man's pocket. Pills? Ivan yanked the leash.

"No. No!"

He pulled the dog closer, caught him and checked his mouth, spreading its small jaws apart. Empty. Silly dog.

The baldy said, "Kahhh." A kick to his temple ended the nascent speech. Ivan pulled the dogs away, toward the sidewalk. They had to hurry, but after a few steps, Boo-Boo slipped between the bars of a fence and into the auto repair shop's yard. Honey joined him, of course. The tiny brats had no walking discipline whatsoever.

Did Eva train them to follow the leader at all?

He pulled the dogs back gently and guided each one through the gap with his hands. The lack of pedestrians helped, but people in passing cars still stared at him and the dogs as he pulled them back onto the sidewalk and moved along quickly.

Around the corner and away from the main street, the dogs scampered ahead of him, recognizing what had become home and expecting food. Ivan listened for police sirens as he walked. Would anyone report the fight? In this type of neighborhood, people should keep to themselves and not get involved. And it would be awhile before the thugs recovered from their concussions. But with their pride injured, they would come looking for revenge at some point.

No more walks.

In the kitchen, he refilled the water bowl. Boo-Boo was by the stove, sniffing for steak, but Honey lapped the water greedily, flicking droplets onto his short snout.

Ivan checked the map on his laptop and felt a chill run up his spine.

"Suka, oni na zahvat poshli!"

At the sound of his voice, Honey stopped lapping water, and Boo-Boo barked.

Ivan, staring at the map, dialed Foxy. Too long a drive to get there in time. Call the local police? What was their response time?

"What is it?" Foxy said when he answered.

"They are at the house."

"What?"

"My tracker. Mexicans are with Kazbek. At the villa."

"Fuck. Okay. Let me call Eva. I'll call you back."

Ivan wanted to hurl the phone into the kitchen wall. Family business? Everything out of control—this was no time for family business. Told him, too. Intercept them, delay them. But no. And now the cops and Kazbek's men were the only hope of Kazbek surviving the assault.

A police scanner. If the Mexicans went in already, the cops by the gate would die first.

Ivan went to the room, to the crate with gear and picked up the

207

scanner and turned it on. But his phone rang before he could tune in.

28

Los Angeles, California

White crosses stared at Antonio from the steeples and walls of the churches as he drove back to Beverly Hills.

"Santa María," he whispered. "I've never seen so many crosses before."

Every cross reminded him of his guilt, of his sin. The old truck shook and rattled, unhappy about being pushed past its limit, but Antonio kept his foot firm on the gas.

Señora Domínguez—she didn't deserve to fall into Miguel's hands. The call from the villa, it was providence. A chance at redemption.

The tools in the back clanged on the incline when Antonio reached the villa's driveway. Coming out of his booth, the gruff gatekeeper looked as if he knew about Miguel, about the guns and the violence.

Antonio met the guard's gaze without flinching—so much easier to be here without Miguel in the passenger seat.

The guard came around for a cursory check of the gardening tools in the truck bed.

"Go," he said, waving. "Go in and talk to Amir."

From the driveway, the lawn looked darker in some areas. Water in the puddle where Miguel had cut the sprinkler shimmered with late sunlight.

Antonio parked in the same spot, to the left of the main entrance to the villa. He'd just pulled the pin out to open the tailgate when a man strolled over, dressed in a white track suit, three black stripes over the sleeves and shoulders. The same man who drove the owner's car and never responded to greetings.

Antonio stared in surprise; this one always ignored the workers, like they were trees or umbrellas around the swimming pool. And now he wanted to talk?

"You here to fix the sprinkler?"

"Yes. Are you Amir? You called me—you said the lawn was flooded." Antonio offered his hand. "I'm sorry—we've never been introduced."

The man ignored the offered hand. "Why did you take so long? Come, I show you." He waved a cigarette stuck between his fingers, ashes breaking off. "Let's go."

Antonio followed Amir across the yard, their feet sinking into soggy soil.

"Million dollar house," Amir said over his shoulder, "and no one knows how to fix sprinklers."

The short walk tired Antonio more than it should have. He looked for signs of Señora Dominguez as he walked: her car, or her dogs, or maybe a towel on a lounge chair by the pool. But there was nothing. The thought of Miguel's men grabbing her brought sticky sweat to his armpits and forehead. He wiped his face with his sleeve and glanced at the house. No. Nothing.

Amir looked toward the house, too. He shouted something in a foreign language, and another guard—another new one?—came out of the garage, a jug of motor oil in his hand.

Amir stopped short of the sprinkler and pointed at Antonio. "You. Wait." Sounding like Miguel, every word an order. "Wait for Ramzan to call the dog."

Antonio perked up with a surge of hope. The dog? Which dog? The little one? Then Señora shouldn't be far.

Amir shouted something else, the words sounding guttural and angry, and the man from the garage whistled.

From behind a tree, a few steps away from them, a heap of black and white exploded into a bear of an animal. It was covered in a thick coat from the snout to its long, fluffy tail, its ears hidden inside a huge mane.

"Dios Mio," Antonio mumbled. "What kind of animal is this?"

"It's dog. Just a big one," Amir said.

The beast sauntered toward the garage entrance. Amir nodded at it trotting away. "Was waiting for us. Likes to hunt."

"It's—it's like a bear."

Amir seemed proud, like he owned the beast. "It's Kavkazets."

Antonio shook his head. Strange word for a strange dog. The mane, like that of lion. Nothing ever normal here.

They walked past where the lawn had a natural dip in the surface. Amir pointed at it and said, "Kavkazets hides and attacks. Very dangerous."

Antonio noticed water at the bottom and bent his knee to stick his hand into the puddle. "It's clean, cold water. The flooding isn't going to hurt the grass."

"Just fix it." Amir took a drag of his cigarette, his eyes narrow from smoke. "Make it like before. Dry."

Antonio glanced at the house. Gus used to help with the shutoff valves. "Where is Gus?"

"No Gus." Amir turned and walked away, his white tracksuit making a swishing sound with each step.

Antonio glanced at the pool area, where another new guard had just sat down on a chair. All of these new men could be from the same family, the way their dark faces matched, with their bulbous noses and the black stubble on dark cheeks. Black hair, like Miguel's. Black eyes. The one at the table near the pool wore a bomber jacket.

Antonio trudged his way to the manifold to shut off the water and afterward to the truck to grab tools, encouraged by the guards ignoring him. Crossing the grounds, he gave himself time to watch for signs of Señora Dominguez showing up. At the wall, working on the manifold, he listened for her little dogs—they used to bark a lot. But everything was quiet inside.

He gathered his courage and waved at Amir, who'd joined the other guard at the pool. Come. Come over.

The man spoke with the cigarette in his mouth when he arrived, his hands in the pockets of his track suit. "What?" Again, the strange accent, 'what' sounding like 'vat'.

"Should I water the plants in the house?"

"Did I say anything about plants? You fix pipes. Nobody goes into the house."

Antonio nodded. Patience. Señora used to walk her little dogs outside all the time. She'd come out.

He climbed into the truck, opened the toolbox, and banged the tools around. This close to the windows, she might hear it and grow curious.

Antonio felt it in his back, the look. He turned in time to see a curtain fall behind an upstairs window.

Señora!

But he couldn't see her anymore, the curtain no longer moving.

He didn't know whether to run to the front door or shout, and he didn't dare shout. But at least she was inside, watching. Redemption was close, and real.

His heart protested against the exercise as he climbed out of the truck bed. He stood gathering strength, casting an occasional glance at the guards.

The only thing left to do was find a way into the house and deliver the warning.

29

South Los Angeles, California

At the safe house, Ivan, sitting on a foldable chair, held his phone in his left hand while petting Honey with the right.

At the other end of the line, Foxy sounded confident. "She says it's just one man. The old gardener."

"He works with them."

"I'm not telling her that. I told her we're watching her house. That's it."

"Why is he there?"

"Something with the pipes. He's their maintenance guy."

"The scout."

"Sure, but he ain't gonna do much. Relax. She says all the men her husband brought in have guns."

"Mexicans have guns, too. We must act. And I know how."

"Fine. Let me wrap it up here, and I'll come over."

"How long?"

"I don't know yet."

"And if I help?"

"Your electronics, huh." Foxy paused the same way as the last time they talked. "Do you have extra gear to record something in a room? Like a small piece?"

"I have everything. Small as what I gave you at Kazbek party."

"Hmm. I suppose. Wait—who's gonna look after her dogs?"

"Video to my phone. Anything happens, I come back."

"Video, huh." Another pause. "Fine. I'll text you the address. But don't even think about bringing any guns."

"It's public?"

"Yes and no. And I'm about an hour away from you. So get going." Foxy hung up.

Ivan closed his eyes. Foxy made it sound like he was just making up his mind. But that was just for pretense. The man had made up his mind long before the conversation.

He stood and went to the gear case. Preparations were quick and easy: he fed the dogs the rest of the steak, plugged in two cameras to watch them in the living room and in the kitchen, and locked the doors to other rooms. Next, he routed the camera feed to an easily accessible server.

Before leaving, Ivan petted Honey, who seemed indifferent to a belly rub and sauntered off to lap at the water bowl. Boo-Boo wasn't interested in petting at all after eating most of the steak; he lay on his side, sleeping.

The car's suspension sagged under the weight of the gear, a large case going into the trunk. Everything but the guns. Odd, Foxy's request. Because of the family?

Late afternoon sunlight flashed from windshields of oncoming cars. Ivan played music all the way to Pomona and repeated the lyrics in English where he could.

The city looked indistinguishable from the rest of the urban sprawl. In Russia, each city had an end, a freeway circle behind which lay woods or fields. Here, it was impossible to tell without the GPS where one city ended and another began.

Foxy's night club sat wedged between clothing stores, each business a sliver of the larger building that looked like a former warehouse or a factory. The area had a relaxed feel to it, the people on the street walking like they had places to be and no one to impress. Different from the men in West Hollywood who strutted their stuff like peacocks.

But the men here also looked much more likely to carry.

He parked and walked around the corner to a narrow alley separating two identical buildings. A rolling gate kept the back alley shut off from pedestrian traffic or random motorists taking a shortcut.

Good news—no lock. The gate would also give extra cover for anything taking place in the alley between the tall walls.

The gate slid aside with a rumble, and Ivan went through, looking for the right door; it had a peephole and a light over it and a sign with the club's name. He took the cover off the light and unscrewed the bulb. Next, he pulled the dumpster closer from the opposite side of the alley and looked inside. Enough space for a couple of bodies. Perfect.

He circled the building. Posters on the front door showed women in heavy makeup dancing on stage, kicking up their long legs. One looked like Foxy: the same jaw outline, the same shoulder width. Another homosexual. Some partner, Foxy. A cabaret dancer with a killing streak. And good at it, too.

Ivan reached for the handle. The door opened on a dark lobby with a box office to the left. Two steps in, he stopped to take in the surroundings: just ahead, a catwalk jutted like a breakwater into an open dance floor. The stage took most of the back wall, lights and lamps hanging over it on a trellis.

The high-ceilinged place looked asleep—too early for the patrons and staff. But the clicking of a calculator and the thin buzz of a printer confirmed someone was home.

A tired looking man in a loose shirt sat at a round table near the bar, a stack of papers by his elbow. Light from his laptop accentuated his sagging cheeks, aging the man well past half a century.

The door behind Ivan clanged closed, and the man looked up from the calculator, staring over stylish square glasses, his eyebrows raised. "Can I help you?"

"I am looking for Foxy." Ivan came closer, surveying the space along the way, looking for the back alley exit. It was nice, the way they marked exits in the United States: often a sign on the door or over the hallway, pointing at the escape route, should you need one.

In Moscow, finding a back exit was always like taking a tour of the place. And no guarantee the exit wouldn't be nailed shut or locked, the padlock rusty from a decade of neglect. In this club, the sign for the exit was easy to see, just left of the stage.

"Oh, you must be Ivan," the man said, smiling, glasses on the tip of his nose. "He mentioned you look like a bear. You're a cameraman, right?"

Ivan nodded. The man must have been an accountant, a roll of print thick on top of his calculator. "Foxy not here?"

"I sent him to the store. We're low on ice and napkins. I'm Laverne," the man said, offering a hand.

"La—" Ivan, uncertain about the name, paused mid-handshake.

The man smiled. "You say it like 'love earn'. Love-earn. Lavern. It's okay, people get it wrong all the time. Take a seat. I could use some company."

Ivan pulled a chair closer. "My name, you say it with an 'e' in the front. People here say, 'ai-vun', like an iPhone, you know. Or iPod. But it's 'e-vahn'. 'E' like in 'Email'. But nobody says it correctly."

"Foxy said your English was good. It is."

This accountant was someone close. Could be Foxy's older brother. What was the phrase? "Thank you. I appreciate the compliment." Ivan grabbed his stomach as it rumbled in the quiet of the large space.

Laverne turned toward the bar and shouted, "Terence! Terence!"

"What?" A head popped through the door on the other side of the bar. The face of a young man.

"Can you make us some wings, dear? Sauce on the side?" The head disappeared, and Laverne turned to Ivan. "You like spicy food?"

"Sure. My girlfriend grows red peppers in a pot. They are spicy." In one of the framed pictures on the wall behind Laverne, a boy in tights and a tank top was dancing. Ivan motioned at the picture with his chin. "That boy looks like Foxy."

Laverne twisted in his chair. "Oh, that's him all right. Back then, he was into ballet. I had him take classes, he liked it so much. These days, he wouldn't dance if I begged him. Kids are wonderful, don't you think?" After a sigh, he added, "Too bad they grow up. You have any kids?"

"No. I hope, in the future. So you are the father?"

"Well, they all call me mother, but for better or worse, I'm both. I'm all they've got."

Ivan looked at the pictures of kids and men, white and black, some dancing, others in university gowns. What was the set up here? Laverne—clearly a man. But calling himself a mother. Everything bizarre—Los Angeles like a strange planet full of aliens, fathers acting like mothers, men wearing collars like dogs. But no point in expecting normalcy from an abnormal place. Best ignore it and move on with the work.

Ivan nodded. "You adopt them. Orphans. I understand. Not a real mother."

"Oh, gosh, he warned me you were awfully straight. Sweetie, at your age, you should know already the only real mother is the one who raised you. Plenty of parents out there kicking their kids out on the street. Blood don't mean a thing in this world. Only love does."

"I did not mean any offense," Ivan said. "It is hard to be polite in English. I am not rude in Russian."

"Oh, I know you didn't mean it. You strike me more like Jimmy." Laverne turned and pointed at the skinny kid in the picture with Foxy, their hands on each other's shoulders. "That's him—he was my one good boy, never gave me any headaches. Foxy was the one getting him in trouble all the time." Laverne smiled. "I guess he found someone else he can get in trouble, asking you to come here to record everything."

"It is okay. I am good with cameras. I like to help." Ivan rubbed

216

his cheek. Laverne, talking about recording. Meaning the cops?

"I hate asking him for help." Laverne picked up the stack of papers and shook them into an orderly pile. "I know it would be easier to just pay them off. But the last time they came, they were so mean I decided I wouldn't pay them another dime. Still, they scare me. I've seen my share of the local blue, and these two are meaner than most."

Ivan gave it a half-shrug. "Mean is no problem. We can deal with mean."

"Oh, that's what worries me. Foxy said the same thing. But I hate trouble. God knows, I've seen enough of it."

"So we help," Ivan said, and added quickly, "with equipment."

Laverne took his glasses off and rested his eyes against his wrist. "Foxy says if we get evidence against them they will leave us alone. They threatened me in plain English. So, I guess he thought of you and your cameras. All that equipment you use in film." Laverne sighed. "Now we're making our own crime show."

The young man walked out of the door behind the bar, a bowl of chicken wings in one hand, a bottle of sauce in the other. He put the food on the table and smiled. "Here you go."

Ivan picked up a piece of chicken but dropped it back into the bowl, the food so hot that it burned his fingers.

"Give them a minute," Laverne said. "He always brings them hot."

Ivan picked up a napkin and wrapped it around the tip of the bone and picked up the drumstick that way.

Laverne laughed at the maneuver. "That's one way to do it."

Ivan bit into the meat. Weird place, America. Why eat chicken wings when there was better meat on the rest of the chicken, like the thighs, or the breast? Not some bony wings, fried to a crisp.

Some of the hot juice spilled on his chin and fingers. Crunchy skin, but soft meat on the inside. He picked up another piece.

"They're good, aren't they?"

Ivan nodded, chewing.

"Glad you like it." Laverne rubbed his eyes. "Don't tell Foxy, but I feel bad for bothering him. He's always traveling, always busy. These days we only go to him when it's serious."

Ivan put the bone down on the edge of the plate. "How bad is this?"

Laverne picked up a glass of water, took a sip, and then put it down. "The cops said they can file a report saying we deal drugs in here. If that happens, I'll lose the club. The kids will lose their home."

Ivan wiped his mouth with a napkin and looked at the photographs on the wall. "So, Foxy was orphan?"

"Worse off than most." Laverne gave a tired smile, wrinkles gathering around the eyes. "Not a lot of people out there looking to raise a gay black child." No accusation in Laverne's words and no protest. Just tiredness. "How about you? You parents still in Russia or here?"

"They died. Long ago."

Laverne's smile faded. "I'm sorry to hear that."

"It's okay. Everybody dies some time."

"That's a very Russian thing to say." Laverne was smiling again, but the look in her eyes triggered in Ivan an old memory of being small and lost, standing by the side of a coffin, unsure of what to do. He was glad to look away from Laverne when, from behind the stage, came the sound of a door banging shut.

Foxy walked in with a cardboard box in his hands and carried it behind the bar where he dropped it on the floor with a thud. He came back around and kissed Laverne on the cheek. "All set, ma."

"Ivan likes our chicken wings," Laverne said. "I was telling him about you and Jimmy—he was asking about the pictures."

Foxy picked up a wing out of the bowl. "So, you two getting along, huh?" He waved the food at the stage to their right. "C'mon, Russki Bear. Let me show you the office where you put the camera."

They came up a steel stairway to a second floor balcony wrapping around the dance floor below. Walking along, Foxy said quietly, "What's the deal with the fat suit? You like it so much you gonna wear it everywhere?"

"I don't like it. But when I make mistakes, I practice. I made mistakes at the bungalow."

"Yeah, just don't overdo it. Don't go all *Crime and Punishment* on your ass. We got other shit to worry about."

"There is no ass in that book."

Foxy opened the door to a small office. "There was in the movie. Patrick Dempsey was real hot."

The office had a window near the door and an old desk at the far end, underneath metal bookshelves. Elaborate, feathered masks and photographs of people in outrageous outfits decorated the walls.

Foxy plopped into the office chair behind the desk and bit off a piece of meat. "Well, what's the big idea?" The food garbled his words.

Ivan looked through the window at the balcony and lights and speakers hanging over the dance floor. Once the show started, the

218

noise would drown out everything that happens in this office.

Ivan grabbed a chair from a line of them at the wall and stepped to the desk to sit down. "We take the police. Take their uniforms and gear. Everything. And go inside to arrest Kazbek. The Chechens will not fight police."

Foxy rolled his eyes. "Jesus, I fucking knew it. You saw the cops at the villa and decided you can just walk in, didn't you?" Foxy shook his head, his face gathered in a grimace like he'd licked a lemon. "Listen, it's a good plan, but if I wanted to take down the assholes harassing my mother, I would have done so myself." He tossed the bones into a trash can. "This isn't Moscow. You can't just snuff out a couple of uniforms. If we gonna go into Kazbek's house as cops, we gonna have to get the gear elsewhere."

Ivan nodded—start with agreement, and people will listen. "I understand. But we can do it clean. They deserve it. They hurt your mother."

Foxy's eyes flashed. "I fucking know they hurt my mother—don't you think I know that? Which is why we can't touch them. The fuckers are tied to her now." Foxy yanked a tissue out of a box sitting on the desk and wiped his fingers. "I was thinking more like you use one of your gadgets and film them. This will give me evidence, so I can tell them to go fuck themselves."

Ivan shook his head. "Not good, just recording. My way—we can plan it right, and you will have alibi. And they will never come back. My way is guaranteed. Your way, they may still hurt him—I mean her. I like Laverne. I can help."

Foxy's eyebrows flew up. "You don't like my approach, but you like my mother? That's your argument? Do you like me, too, now?"

"You improvise well."

Foxy raised his arms palms up in a theatrical gesture. The man liked to clown around—his gaze turned to the ceiling as he cried, "Ladies and Gentleman, Captain Red October here is okay with the gay. Praise Jesus, for it is a miracle above miracles." Foxy's tone changed back to normal. "Do you have any idea what kind of heat we'll be looking at if anyone gets a whiff of you and me disappearing a couple of cops? Clearly not, because if you did, you wouldn't be sitting here telling me it's your great plan."

"I always use a good plan. Or many plans. This is good opportunity. I can set it up—"

Foxy raised his hand. "Russki. Look. You know what this really is?"

"What?"

"A good opportunity for you to practice sound recording. You're not doing anything else. Got it?"

Ivan nodded. "All right." No need to argue. Still early for that.

"Peachy." Foxy rubbed his forehead with the back of his hand, like he had a headache. "Just set it up near her desk. She says they don't hold back when they talk. And if she says they threatened her, it means they fucking really threatened her because she tends to downplay her troubles."

Foxy, the cool operative, no longer cool. Understandable—hard for him to keep his composure with Laverne in danger. But everything here smelled of an opportunity; a lot could happen in a charged situation like this. It made sense to agree with everything and stay close to the cops.

Ivan looked around the room. "Do the cops come here or another office?"

"This is the only one."

Ivan stood up. "I will go to get gear."

When he came back, Foxy was still in the office chair, checking his phone. He said, "Eva just texted me. Says she got in a fight with her husband. He says it's her fault the dogs got taken."

"Trouble in the family. We can use that." The gear case took half the table surface. Ivan clicked the latches open and pulled out the trays with cutouts, all the electronics cradled in foam. "You know, large family is nice. My grandmother was like Laverne. Always kids around her. She loved taking care of everyone."

Foxy put his phone away. "Unfortunately, I'm the only one here to take care of mom, you know what I mean?"

"The oldest son. One who takes care of the parents."

"Tell me about it."

The camera unit needed good placement. The shelves above Foxy's head? After considering the books and a set of speakers, Ivan stuck the camera into a binder sitting on top of the cabinets. Recording through a round hole in the binder's spine, the fish lens covered the entire span of the room.

He popped the unit cover open to put the battery in. "I don't mean any offense, but I want to understand. Why do you call Laverne 'she' if she is a 'he'? It is confusing."

"Because gender has nothing to do with it." Foxy looked out on the balcony. "She brought me up in the world. Taught me how to change myself." The cover snapped in with a crack, and Foxy pointed at the plastic package. "Those look like watch batteries."

"They are. But can I ask—you mean Laverne taught you disguise?"

"Jesus. It's not always about work. She taught me transformation."

Ivan picked up a binder and checked if the camera would fit. "Transformation is from electricity. I don't understand."

"That doesn't surprise me."

Ivan dug into the case, looking for glue. Sarcasm, the brother of insecurity. "I like to understand people. You and Laverne are not like—"

"The rest of you Russians?"

"Not like anyone I know."

"You should get out more."

Ivan shrugged off the joke. "She's nice. Not like you or me. She cares. Most people do not care."

Foxy stared in silence then said, "She changed me. I was a street hustler." A corner of his mouth went up. "You know what she called me?"

"'Foxy'?"

"I already had that name when she picked me up. No. She called me a 'confident human being with unlimited potential'. I didn't even know what the fuck that meant. She taught me the meaning of it, though. I'd be dead right now if she didn't."

"I will remember to say 'she'."

Foxy snickered. "I'm surprised you haven't called my mother a homo yet."

Ivan taped the camera to the inside of the binder and powered it then closed the binder and put it back on the shelf. "I'm not going to call anyone homo. I did that because of Afghans. The mullahs there used children. But you are not like the mullahs. So it is my mistake."

Foxy squinted at him. "Did you have an epiphany or something? You're all nice today."

"Russians are nice people, even if they don't smile." Ivan powered the laptop, got the application paired up with the camera, and handed the laptop over. "Go downstairs, but slowly. Tell me if the feed stops. This way we know how far the laptop can be."

"I thought your cameras download the feed?"

"At the villa, yes. Not this one."

Foxy nodded and stepped out of the office, holding the laptop flat on his palm.

Now was the time. Ivan took out a remote and played with the camera zoom. It made just enough noise to draw attention—a perfect way to upset the cops who wouldn't expect being recorded. Crooked cops belonged in the garbage container.

He shut the gear case after pulling out a cardioid microphone. Foxy wasn't thinking clearly, yet he would have no choice but to accept the outcome. Laverne would be safer this way. She deserved to be safe.

He stuck his head out of the door. "Is it good?"

From downstairs, Foxy said, "It's grainy, but it's recording."

"I will come down. We must put a microphone on your mother."

Downstairs, Laverne gently held the mic between her thumbs. "It's so tiny."

"For good sound, it should be on your clothes," Ivan said.

Laverne looked at Foxy. "I have that dress with a large flower on it. It'll fit, won't it?"

Foxy nodded. "As long as the color is right."

And it was, black and gold. Foxy left, and Ivan chatted with Laverne about Russian food while fitting the mic under fake flower petals. The more they talked, the more Ivan thought of Laverne as 'her': Laverne, even after she changed into a dress and put on makeup, didn't provoke in him the same rejection Foxy did when they first met.

When Laverne scolded Terrence for not wearing a clean shirt, Ivan recognized the feeling emanating from Laverne in every direction; she was exactly like his grandmother: she fussed and worried but never stopped giving everyone hugs.

When the club filled up with people, the DJ turned the music on. From his seat at the end of the bar, Ivan watched Foxy float through the crowd, greeting people, until everyone erupted in applause at a huge figure that emerged from behind the curtain and took the stage. A woman, or a man? Hard to say with all the makeup, Victorian dress, and the wig sparkling in a spotlight.

Foxy sauntered over and leaned closer to say over the singing, "I'm gonna go beat my face. I'm supposed to be one of the performers."

"What?"

"Makeup. We call it 'beating the face'." Foxy nodded at the stage. "I oughta look like one of the girls when the cops come."

"Then I wait upstairs in the room."

"You can't be in the same room with us."

"Why not?"

"Why do you think? 'cause you don't look the part."

"Hoody and jeans is normal, yes?"

"Look around." Foxy tilted his head toward the people in the dancehall. "The cops will expect everyone to be in drag. One look at you, and they'll tell you to fuck off. You don't belong. I'm asking Terrence to come up."

"I should be in the room. I'm better than Terrence. Terrence is a cook."

"You don't know what ya' talking about." Foxy pointed at the singer who, up close, looked like a woman from Leo Tolstoy book, a matron at the ball or something. "Look at him. Do you see yourself wearing that?"

"I can wear anything. Two cops coming, yes? You need two of us to match. And I can wear a dress for disguise. It is like fat suit. If I am in dress, the cops will think I am weak. It is good this way."

Foxy's lips curled up. "Same way you thought I was weak when we met at the Trunks, huh?"

"So I was wrong. And they will be wrong, too."

Foxy rubbed his chin, his lips in a tight line. "Fucking fine. It bugs you the way you fucked up is what it is. Okay. C'mon."

On the way to the dressing room, they passed clothes racks, all manner of clothes on the hangers. Ivan imagined himself putting them on. Who cared if it was a dress, or a fat suit, or a wig? The most important part was being in the same room with the cops after they showed up. And the dresses offered an added advantage—they would be easier to take off and put on a body. No need to bother with pants.

Foxy held the dressing room door open. "You just want to prove to yourself you can do what I do, don't you? That you can rock a dress if you have to. I know your type—you can't get over a mistake."

Ivan stepped past him into a bright lit room full of mirrors. All the shouting over the music made his throat sore. "I can get over it. And I can learn. Like you say in English: old dog can learn things."

A whiny voice said, "Hey, Foxy. I didn't know you were singing tonight." The voice came from a stocky man getting dressed at the end of the room by a clothing rack. Speaking with weird affectation.

"Hey, darling," Foxy said. "So great to see you. No, I'm not singing, just hanging out. Teaching my new friend some style."

"That's too bad—we could do duets, like the last time."

"That was great, wasn't it?" Foxy motioned to the stocky man. "Ivan, this is Marcel. Best soprano on the West Coast."

They shook hands like normal people. Wide stockings hugged

Marcel's hams, the pads visible—like those in the fat suit. They rounded his hips. Marcel sure looked like a man—potbellied, thick hair, and wide in the shoulders—but a man without a penis. Nothing but a crease there. Hard not to stare.

"Well, I better hurry," Marcel said. "Denise doesn't have a follow-up."

"Oh, no. Don't let us keep you then," Foxy said.

Marcel picked a red dress off the top of the rack.

Foxy pointed at the chair in front of a mirror. "Let's make you look like a regular."

The chair was comfortable, unlike the sensation of Foxy's fingers spreading cream over Ivan's skin, picking at his eyes with brushes, picking at his eyelids. As bad as the first time at the bungalow.

When the door closed behind Marcel, Ivan raised his hand.

Foxy pulled away. "What?"

Ivan nodded toward the door. "Him—Marcel. What happened to him? Did he cut it off?"

Foxy stepped back, a pencil in his hand. "What are you talking about? Cut what off?"

"The balls. He had no balls or dick."

Foxy rolled his eyes. "Oh, God. Here we go. He tucked them in. We are gay, not crazy. You just can't see them." He picked up a tub of powder and a brush.

"The dress, I can wear. But I'm not doing the thing with the balls."

"You should. It will look good on you."

"No."

Foxy tossed the brush into a cup, handle first, like a javelin. "You can do whatever you want. You shouldn't even be here, you know what I mean?"

"We work for the same boss. So I am here."

"Let me tell you, your boss is the only reason you are here." Foxy put his hands on his hips and stared at their reflection in the mirror. "I say, this should do it." He walked toward the clothes rack. "Now. You wanted a dress, so let's put you in a dress."

The image in the mirror was wrong. "But it's not good." This time the makeup was crude, thick, with bright paint lines for lips and eyes. And the eyelashes were huge, ludicrous, and irritating. "Not as good as at the bungalow."

"It's drag. It's not meant to be subtle. Come here. I think this one will work." Foxy held up a dress with a long skirt.

"Pink?"

"It'll suit ya."

Ivan shook his head. Fooling around, the clown. Looking for a way to take a dig, get a reaction. Rushing, too. Saying, "Let's go. The cops will be here any minute now."

Turned out the cops didn't come until an hour after the show started. So, they just stood there in their stupid dresses and makeup. Nobody as much as gave them a look, though. Laverne stopped by and said, "It's a lovely dress. But watch out with the chicken cutlets."

"What?"

"Your breasts, sweetie. They are slipping out."

Ivan looked down. The inserts that gave him huge boobs were showing. He shoved them deeper under the dress. "Thank you."

It was strange: the longer he wore his ridiculous outfit, the more it felt normal to him. He even got better at not touching his face or keeping the crumbs of his sandwich from falling into his cleavage. Like Foxy said, this was about transformation. This club, it was a world with different rules. Anyone could be anything here. Growing up in a place like this would make anyone stealthy.

Ivan stared at a man in bright yellow pants gyrating on the dance floor. If I wanted to, he thought, I could be one of these freaks, and they'd all accept me. Laverne already did, treating me like one of her children.

He sprung off his barstool when Foxy spotted the cops and gestured, and they filtered through the crowd of cheering, dancing patrons, Laverne already in her office upstairs.

They stopped by the DJ's booth to check if the laptop was recording. Foxy said, "You know what's driving me fucking crazy?"

Ivan opened a window on the screen to lower the volume for the earpiece. "What?"

"The fucking pigs made her so nervous, she asked Terrence for a scotch."

"Why is this bad?"

"She's been sober three years," Foxy said through his teeth.

Ivan held the door open as they came out of the booth. "Do not worry. We are both here. Important thing we stay close."

Pure truth. Two scenarios, and both required staying close to Laverne and the cops.

They walked along the balcony, the cops still downstairs, talking to Terrence at the bar. Ivan's sneakers felt nice and tight, the dress not long enough to constrain movement—mobility would be important for the second scenario.

In the office, Foxy said to Laverne, "They just got here."

Laverne nodded, her face reddening. She twisted the large ring on her finger back and forth.

They sat in the chairs by the wall, and not long after, the door opened as if it was kicked in from the outside. The cops strode into the room, their chins high with belligerent condescension. Ivan sized them up: one white and another Hispanic, the white one much wider, with more girth. Slow but strong. The Hispanic one had a trim figure and tight posture. Quick, athletic.

Ivan glanced at Foxy, who nodded. These were the guests they had been expecting.

The white cop took a step toward Laverne from the door and stopped, frowning at Ivan and Foxy. "And who the fuck are you?"

The Hispanic one, on the heels of his partner, looked down on Ivan, grimaced, and said, "God, you're fat. Time to cut down on your Taco Bell visits, Gordita."

Ivan looked down at his belly. What were you supposed to do as a girl if they called you ugly? Play embarrassed? He gathered loose folds of his skirt around his ankles to cover the sneakers; they didn't quite match the rest of his outfit.

Laverne cleared her throat. "They're my dancers. I want them here with me."

The white cop—the brass nameplate on his shirt reading 'Hoffman'—glanced at her but went back to them to jerk his thumb at the door. "Get the fuck out." And after they didn't move: "I said, let's go. Out. Both of ya faggies. Don't make me slap the cuffs on ya."

Foxy's face blanched. Laverne must have noticed it because she said, "Boys, why don't you just wait outside?"

Foxy rose slowly and gave Ivan a sideway glance, followed by motion of his head toward the door. "Okay. We step out. Like the man said."

"I'll be all right," Laverne said, her voice trembling.

Ivan let Foxy leave first and watched the Hispanic cop pinch Foxy's buttock. "Great ass, Mamacita." Foxy's back grew rigid.

Ivan, behind and to the left of them, stooped to grab the hem of his skirt. Sometimes you don't need a plan. Sometimes, everyone plays to your advantage. It's rare, but it happens.

He put his free hand on the loose fold of the dress on top of his belly. Let's go, he thought. Let's play it out, right here, in this room; it would all be quick and quiet, and no one would feel a thing.

30

Los Angeles Westside, California

U sing a shovel, Antonio pried up a section of soaked turf around the sprinkler. A burp bubbled up his throat. The bitterness and burning in his lower chest demanded some antacid, but he'd left the medicine at home.

The effort of digging his way to the water supply pipe kept his breath short and his arms and shoulders aching. He was almost happy to answer his cell phone when it rang, but the sound of Miguel's voice pushed the burning sensation into his throat and spread into his jaw.

"Tio, have you talked to the wife yet? What is she saying?"

"I am replacing the sprinkler," Antonio said, cupping his hand around the phone. "I haven't seen her yet—they have all these new people. I'm waiting for her to come out."

"I told you to count the men and find the wife. Hurry up."

Miguel disconnected, and Antonio felt so dizzy he sat down on the soggy grass and waited for his mind to clear.

If only there was a safe way of reaching out to the lady of the house.

He got back to working on the chopped sprinkler, watching the house in his periphery. The thing refused to come off the pipe at first, and the effort weakened him; he plopped on the grass, panting, and looked to the house, to the window where the curtains had moved earlier.

Find the wife. Sure, but only to warn her.

Antonio shuddered at the thought of disobeying the devil. What would happen to anyone who went against Miguel and his demons? The pictures in the papers would show a pile of severed heads, the bodies dangling from some bridge.

He looked into the cloudless sky. What did it say in the Bible? Whoever wishes to save his life will lose it. Whoever loses his life for my sake, he is the one saved.

With his hands weak and shaking, Antonio replaced the turf and screwed the new sprinkler head in its place. The manifold controlling the sprinkler system was across the lawn, on the side of the house; he rose to his feet and hesitated—the guard was playing catch with his beast, throwing a football, which disappeared into the dog's huge maw whenever it picked the ball up. They were playing right across the path to the manifold.

Antonio took several tentative steps toward the house and stopped, hoping for the guard to notice him and call the dog to heel. But neither man nor his beast paid any attention, so Antonio called out, "Please, sir, hold the dog?"

At the sound of his voice, the animal—on its way to pick up the ball—changed its mind and veered off-course, picking up speed in a gallop.

It was attacking!

Antonio stumbled backward, gasping and flailing his arms.

The dog accelerated, the great mass of fur bounding toward him in relentless motion. It was impossible to look away—the dog's body stretched and contracted with each leap, huge and menacing; its snout showed the ivory of bared teeth flecked with saliva.

The sprinkler Antonio had just fixed caught his shoe. Drawing a frantic, constrained breath, he fell backward into the soft grass. A loud snarl came from up close, from near his feet.

He looked up—he didn't hear the guard call the dog off, but the beast dug its massive hind legs into the grass and stopped an arm's-reach away. There it turned and trotted back to its owner, who stood bent over in laughter, gesturing at another guard and shouting words in his foreign language, pointing. The man petted his dog as it came close then sent it to get the ball still out on the grass.

Antonio scrambled to his feet. The dog had frightened all the breath out of him, and he had to bend and keep his palms on his knees until the air returned to his lungs. He wheezed, and the pain in his chest radiated through his arm. His shirt, wet around the back and elbows, stuck uncomfortably to his skin.

His cross slipped through his collar. Antonio fingered the old silver before tucking it under his shirt, and his heart settled into a calmer rhythm.

God loved his men but tested their faith. God's love was worth any pain.

He brushed the dirt off his pants and made a couple of tentative steps toward the house, watching the dog go after the ball. The guard saw him moving but this time ordered his dog to sit.

Thank you.

Encouraged, Antonio hurried, watching the dog from the corner of his eye. He was ten or so steps away from the manifold when the guard let go of the dog's collar. The animal sprung forward and accelerated with renewed vigor toward its feeble target.

Again? Will it stop this time?

Antonio managed a backward step and looked around wildly. Run? But where? No chance of escape with an animal like this.

He dropped his toolkit and closed his eyes, clutching his silver cross. If Señora Dominguez learned of Miguel in time, none of this would be in vain.

The dog's growl got closer, and then came the shout of a foreign word. The growling ceased.

Antonio opened his eyes. The dog, in its easy stride, was returning to the guard. Loud laughter and cheering came from the men at a table near the pool. The guard, once his dog had trotted back to him and sat down by his leg, fed his beast something from his palm.

Antonio's entire body shook from anger and resentment; these men used a real person as a toy for them and their dog. But the anger was empowering. Antonio covered the rest of the distance to the house on pure determination, ignoring his weak legs. His heart fluttered like a bird struggling to unfold its wings inside his ribcage, flapping its way into his throat. His toolkit felt many times heavier, pulling him down; he had to carry it the rest of the way with both hands. But he walked on.

He pushed the kit into the truck bed, and the temptation to get in and leave descended on him. An old quote sprung into his mind: God, I am so tired, strengthen me with your word.

No time for cowardice. He shivered and let go of the tailgate, not caring to close it. Leaving the truck behind, he walked to a narrow flowerbed. Wide, green leaves hid the manifold, and he kneeled next to it.

Fear weakened his knees, more now that he'd accepted the consequences of what he was about to do.

The guard kept throwing the ball in different directions, until it landed further out into the greens, close enough to a sprinkler. The dog went after it. At once, Antonio opened the valves to the fullest. The water gushed out all over the grounds, spray hitting his torturer and the dog, jets of water crisscrossing the lawn in every direction.

Now.

Too weak to run, Antonio walked as fast as he could toward the main entrance. He was wheezing by the time he wrapped his fingers around the handle and clicked the lock open.

Angry cries sounded from behind, and he turned to look—the guard was coming fast, pointing at him, no longer distracted. But the guard didn't matter—the dog did, streaking across the lawn in giant strides.

Desperate, Antonio leaned into the heavy door, squeezing his body into the widening crack. He got through and pushed the other way as hard as he could, gasping.

He came so close to engaging the lock, he imagined he heard it click closed. But in the next second, the door hit him in the face, and he fell backward, dazed. The dog snarled and pushed through the gap, nails scratching, teeth snapping at his feet.

He rolled over to crawl away, crying out in terror, "Señora! Señora!"

Sharp pain shot through his ankle, and he felt the tugging. Despair rushed out of his lungs in one high-pitched wail once the dog's teeth clamped onto his back:

"Señ-o-o-o-ra!"

More snarling, and he felt himself dragged back to the door. There wasn't pain in his back now, only in his chest, like a surge of electricity shooting into his jaw and left hand.

Antonio wanted to cry out more, but the world turned blurry and all the sounds came at him from afar, the shouting and snarling. A penetrating weakness took over and kept him motionless, his eyes closed, until cold fingers pushed his eyelids apart and a bright light shone into his left eye and then his right.

Everything was disorienting. Someone put cold plastic on his face while repetitive noise hissed into his right ear. Some kind of machine.

His eyes adjusted at the same time he was lifted—and carried?— by men. He was on a gurney. Doctors!

A metal object chilled the skin on his chest. A belt or a strap held his head in place and restrained him from looking down. A mask covered his mouth and hushed his words. And then a thrill went through his body at the sound of her voice: Señora Dominguez, shouting at someone.

His chest shuddered as he called to her, but the mask muted his words, and he raised his hand to rip it off.

"Señora!"

Voices came at him from two sides, and a hand pushed the mask back on his face. But in the next second, she leaned over him. Antonio ripped the mask off a second time, straining to breathe out the words:

"Señora. You are in danger. You need to leave. They are coming. They are monsters, they will—"

A male voice said, "Mister Vargas, please, try not to speak."

The mask returned, and this time the hand stayed on it, and someone else kept his hands away from his face.

The last thing he heard before they pushed him under the bright lights of an ambulance—strange dials and tanks everywhere—was Señora Dominguez saying, "Antonio. Don't worry. It will all be okay!"

His tears turned her beautiful face vague.

Kindness. Finally, someone with kindness.

He wanted to reach out to her, but they were doing something to his arm, and then the sounds and the light melted away.

31

Pomona, California

From the balcony outside of Laverne's office, Ivan peeked in through the window. She seemed smaller behind her desk, her cheeks flushed red, her mouth tight with nervousness. Foxy was already on his way to the DJ's booth, no doubt to watch the feed on the laptop. Ivan moved past the window to follow him.

Out of view of the cops, he pushed the earpiece in and heard the white one, Hoffman, say, "Laverne, your bitches are getting uglier and uglier. I should charge you with public nuisance."

In the DJ's booth, the laptop streamed clear video. Ivan wedged himself next to Foxy in time to watch Hoffman plop his sizable butt onto the chair facing Laverne's desk. The camera showed Hoffman in all his glory, with saggy jowls, splotchy skin, and burst blood vessels on his nose.

The second cop, Fernandez, stood behind his partner with arms crossed, his feet about shoulder-width apart—a practiced stance. Meant to intimidate. Probably learned it at the police academy.

Fernandez stood and stared, rocking on his feet, while Hoffman leaned forward and slapped the surface of the table with his palms.

"What the fuck?" Foxy mumbled.

Hoffman stared at the empty space between his hands with theatrical bewilderment and said, "I don't see nothin' here. And I know there should be somethin'."

Foxy, listening in through the headphones, grumbled, "Motherfucker fancies himself an actor."

Ivan flexed his wrists and neck to warm up the muscles. Nine steps from here to the office. Three seconds to the door, one to open it. Laverne was right to ask her son to come over.

Foxy sat with his gaze glued to the screen. "Fucker called us ugly."

"They talk too much. Call names."

"How does it make you feel?"

Ivan shrugged. "Makes me feel nothing. You should let me kill him." Not joking, but Foxy ignored it.

Laverne said to Hoffman, "I'm not paying you another dime." Her voice came through nice and clear. Fernandez stopped rocking on his feet. The camera in the binder was giving a wide shot of both cops and the back of Laverne's head. Hoffman winced and narrowed his porcine eyes. "Say that again?"

"You heard me. You take my money, eat my food, and drink my liquor. And it's never enough. I'm not gonna let you bankrupt me." Laverne's voice grew stronger as she spoke. "And if you write up my club for loitering or whatever other spurious charges you two trump up, I'll go straight to the city council." She leaned back, the camera showing the thin hair on top of her head.

The silence in the room didn't last long. Hoffman slammed his fists on the table so hard that everyone jumped. Ivan felt dizzy for a second—the bang, reproduced by the earpiece, punched his brain.

On the screen, Hoffman's eyes narrowed into slits. "Bitch, you fucking pay me when I say you pay me."

"I want you to leave," Laverne said, clear indignation in her voice. "You aren't welcome here anymore." She turned her head to her right, to Fernandez. "Both of you."

Ivan flexed his thighs a couple of times. This Hoffman, he was red in the face with anger. And Laverne was looking at Fernandez, unaware of the way Hoffman was getting worked up—which was why she missed the movement in front of her. She leaned back when she saw it, but it was too late.

The whale of a cop charged right toward the camera and grabbed Laverne's dress with one hand and her hair with the other, and then yanked her down, smashing her face into the desk.

Foxy was already out of the booth in a sprint.

Poshel, poshel. Ivan's sneakers slipped a little on the steel floor as he chased Foxy along the balcony handrail, music drowning out the banging of their feet.

Foxy crashed into the door and disappeared inside. Ivan kept his right hand under his skirt—on the injector—as he moved through the doorway, his sneakers now squeaking on linoleum.

Ivan took in the room: Fernandez was within easy reach. Foxy would take care of Hoffman—everything playing out better than expected. No need to explain anything or deal with Foxy's anger.

Laverne sat dazed in her chair, holding her face, a trickle of blood coming out of her nose, her glasses askew.

233

Foxy jumped up and sailed high with his knees together and drove them into Hoffman's upper back. The blow sent Hoffman, about to turn around, slamming into the desk.

Ivan moved left, watching Fernandez go for his pistol. The cop was clearly distracted by Foxy's high-jump in a fancy dress, palming his holster.

Too slow.

Fernandez never got his pistol out. Ivan gathered speed in two steps and drove his shoulder into the cop, pinning him to the wall.

Injector to the neck. Sedative into the muscle. Elbow to the face.

Fernandez bounced off the wall and slumped to the floor.

Ivan brushed the cop's hand away from the holster and picked up the cop's Glock. The pistol fit nicely under the fat suit.

Foxy had already flipped Hoffman to the floor and was throwing a leg over to straddle him. From his quick movements and the way Foxy sucked air through his teeth, he looked ready to punch Hoffman's brains out.

Laverne, holding a hand to her nose, shouted "Stop it!" a second after Foxy smashed his fist into the cop's head. The punch connected with the cop's temple, his head jerking sideways. Another punch like that, and they'd have a dead cop in Laverne's office. Not the worst of outcomes.

Laverne didn't think so. "Stop hurting him!"

Nice person, Foxy's mother. Seemed more upset about the cop getting hurt than her own injuries. Ivan, stepping forward, put his tranquilizer gun back under the spandex. No time for asking nicely— he grabbed Foxy from behind and threw him off the stunned cop.

Foxy roared in frustration and threw a right hook, fast and sneaky. But the attack hadn't been well planned, and Ivan leaned back to let Foxy's fist fly by.

Grab his neck. Exhale. Pull. Knee into solar plexus—easy upward swing, much easier in a skirt than pants. Good connection, all soft tissue. This would cool him off.

Foxy folded in half, and Ivan lowered him gently to the floor and turned to Hoffman, unconscious on the floor, arms rigid above his head. Two injections for this one.

Ivan walked over to a water cooler in the corner for a cup of water for Laverne. She was in tears, hands shaking so hard he had to hold the cup for her while she drank.

Foxy gasped for air, his hands on his thighs. But he recovered after a few breaths and now struggled to unfold himself. He said in a raspy voice, "Christ. You put a lot of hip in your straight knee."

"I have weight. Sorry. I had to cool you down." Ivan left Laverne and walked past Foxy to the door to check the balcony. He found it empty. Downstairs, the show was in full swing, the thundering beat of the music making him grimace. It was a pleasure to close the door.

He locked it and went to check if Hoffman's radio was on or off. Hopefully, Pomona police did things differently from their brethren in Moscow and extorted money on their private time, not during their regular shift.

Hoffman's radio was off. Same with Fernandez's. Kneeling, Ivan injected both one more time. When he straightened up, he caught Laverne on her feet, staring at him in horror.

Foxy, unsteady and still grimacing, held onto her desk. "Mother, you okay?"

Laverne turned on him with tears in her eyes. "You said he was a cameraman. What kind of cameraman kills people with a stapler?"

"Mother, he didn't kill them. He just gave them nasty dreams. Let me check your nose." Foxy took Laverne by the arm, pulling the chair closer for her to sit down. But Laverne yanked her arm out of his grasp.

"Nothing wrong with my nose. The bleeding will stop on its own." She pulled a tissue out of a box and held it to her nose. "What were you thinking?" She waved the tissue at Hoffman in the middle of the floor. You could have killed him!" She sounded congested and angry at the same time.

Anger was better than shock, and healthier. Ivan unclipped the microphone from the walkie clip on Hoffman and turned to Foxy. "Their radios are off. What is local protocol? They are in uniforms. Are they on duty? We must check if radio in their car is on."

"You bet your ass they're on duty," Foxy said. "How long did you put them out for?"

"Fifteen to twenty minutes on one injection."

"Will they remember anything?"

"Not if I give them more shots. It is like drinking vodka mixed with champagne until you lose consciousness." The word consciousness was hard to pronounce.

Foxy wrinkled his nose at Hoffman. "Fucker don't deserve something so fabulous."

"They will have bad headache. Now we should change clothes with them."

"What?"

"We change clothes. I brought drugs to put on them. We pretend they did drugs and lost their uniforms and gear. I researched on Internet what happens when cops use drugs and lose service weapons. Department will investigate. They will never come here again."

Foxy narrowed his eyes at Ivan. "You planned this shit, didn't ya'?"

Ivan returned a straight look. "I plan for contingencies. You started this." He swung his palm, flipped up like a tray, over the mess in the room.

Foxy's gaze followed the gesture. "You could have mentioned your contingency plans to me in more detail, ya' know."

"I tried." Ivan frowned for emphasis. "You don't listen."

"I was distracted."

"Yes." Ivan bent over Hoffman and slid his fingers under the cop's neck to check for a broken spine. "It's bad to be distracted. Next time, I talk and you listen."

"Bullshit! I'm not your fucking dog." Foxy glanced at the unconscious cop. "So, how is he?"

"You did not break his spine." Ivan went to the cabinet, pulled the camera out of the binder, and turned it off.

Laverne, holding a bloodied tissue to her nose, said, "I can't believe they attacked me. They're criminals. They should be prosecuted."

"Mother, I hate to say it, but his plan is better." Foxy sounded conciliatory. "It'll keep you out of this. We don't want you to be in the middle of an investigation."

"But the recording . . ." Laverne said. She stared at the blood-soaked tissue in her hand. "Oh God." She raised her eyes. "I want them to pay for this."

"They'll pay plenty. We'll keep the recording. But it's better if you stay out of it for now," Foxy said with a grimace, rubbing his solar plexus and surveying the prostrated bodies in front of him.

Fernandez moved, and Ivan came over to inject him below his hairline one more time. He checked the cop's ankles for holsters. "We must move them out so no one sees. The back alley is good—I looked. Does balcony connect to window that opens to alley?"

Foxy frowned. "You want to throw them out of the window?"

"The lights point down on the dance floor. Nobody will see us if we use the balcony. Only DJ. And trash container is full of cardboard boxes. Like pillows. Will be good for landing." He stepped over to Hoffman and started to work the pants off the man, wrinkling his nose at white undies stained with fresh urine.

"I see you did your homework." Foxy looked to Laverne. "Mother, you want anything? I can go get you a—"

"I don't want anything."

Foxy nodded. "Okay." He walked over to Fernandez and started undressing him. "Let's take the trash out. I have some ideas 'bout how that's gonna go."

Ivan took a deep breath, savoring the moment. Foxy going along with the plan was a bonus, given the man's mercurial nature. The irony of it—Foxy's temper had made everything work.

Hoffman's uniform fit tight in the belly with the fat suit on but looser in the shoulders. Ivan adjusted the belt and turned to Laverne. "I'm sorry they hurt you." He paused to construct a polite sentence in his head. "Would you like to see video? It will make good evidence if you need it. I can put it on flash drive for you to keep."

Laverne, picking up a fresh tissue, stared at him. She moved her head side-to-side in a slow, disbelieving shake.

Ivan hesitated. "Something wrong?"

"Your makeup, honey. It's like a show all on its own."

Foxy, hopping foot-to-foot as he put the cop's pants on, said, "You should see yourself. You look like The Joker, the Russian version."

Laverne pulled out a drawer of her desk and withdrew a mirror. When she held it out, his reflection showed a wig pulled askance and makeup smeared as if half his face was melting. This, on top of a perfectly clean police uniform.

Ivan looked at Foxy. "I cannot go around like this. The police doesn't look like this."

"They do in zombie movies."

"Here." Laverne, still pressing tissues against her nose with one hand, opened another drawer. She pulled out a bottle of clear liquid and a soft cloth. "Wet the cloth with this and use it to wipe it off."

The stuff smelled of lavender and mint, and its fragrance lingered after Ivan wiped off the heavy makeup. America was delivering all kinds of new experiences. Before America, a cosmetic hadn't touched his face once. In Russia, a thing like this went with being called a bitch. But not here.

Ivan looked at Foxy. "My plan—we put the cops in the trash container. I will bring my car to the back, load them, take them to quiet place, and call ambulance. Doctors will find drugs."

Foxy finished buttoning his shirt. "I have a better idea. A little more creative and with a more dramatic outcome. We'll use their cruiser."

Ivan shook his head. "No. I want the police car for—"

"We can't take this one. I need to use it here." Foxy raised his hand as if to stop the inevitable protest. "Don't worry. I can get us another one."

They half-dragged, half-carried the cops to the balcony, around the DJ's booth, and into a cramped room filled with cleaning supplies and boxes of liquor. As they dropped Hoffman through the window into the container below, right on top of Fernandez, Foxy said, "See, I want to damage their reputation. With my setup, the fuckers will avoid this place like the plague." He patted his pockets and pulled out a set of car keys. "I bet they parked in a disabled spot in front. I'm gonna bring it around."

Ivan rubbed the top of his head. It was nice, not wearing a wig. "Hurry. I will show Laverne the video. Text me when you are ready with your setup. I will bring drugs."

Foxy, walking to the door, turned to glance back, his hand on the handle. "Where did you get the drugs? I don't see you talking to a slinger."

"I took it from local youths. They kicked Boo-Boo."

Foxy stared. "No shit? Someone kicked the dog you were walking?" Shaking his head, he turned and pulled the door open, music flooding the room.

Back in Laverne's office, Ivan put the laptop in front of her and stood straight. "Do I look all right?"

Laverne looked him over. "The shirt's tight in the waist. Otherwise you look nice in blue."

Ivan leaned toward the laptop. "I know uniforms. I used to be in police, after the army. The money was not good, but we never blackmailed anyone. We did private security for extra pay." He restarted the recording, but Laverne pointed at another, smaller window at the top of the screen.

"What's that?"

"That is a Pomeranian. His name is Boo-Boo. I watch my dogs over Internet. Through camera at home."

"He's cute." Laverne waved at the video of the cops, Hoffman's face large and ugly. "Close it. I've seen enough of them." She pointed at Boo-Boo, who lay curled in a chair. "His fur is really thick."

Ivan nodded. "I brushed it."

"He let you?" Laverne looked up at Ivan in surprise. "I hear

Pomeranians have a temper."

"I train them." Ivan clicked a couple of buttons and leaned closer to the laptop. "Boo-Boo," he said in a steady voice. "Come." On the screen, the dog perked up its ears.

Laverne put her hand over the mouth. "Oh my goodness, he can hear you?"

Ivan's cell phone vibrated in his pocket. He checked the message. "I must help Foxy. Can I leave the laptop here?"

"Sure." Laverne stared at the screen. "I like him. He's cute." Boo-Boo sniffed the camera, his nose looming large.

Ivan was on his way to the door when Laverne said, "Oh my god, there is another one! They look almost the same!"

In the alley, Foxy was still busy arranging the cops—each one in a dress now—inside the cruiser. With a square bottle of Jack Daniels in one hand, Foxy opened Hoffman's mouth and poured some whiskey into it then did the same with Fernandez in the passenger seat. The whiskey spilled when Foxy tossed the bottle into the foot well next to Fernandez's feet.

Ivan tossed the plastic baggie with crystals onto Hoffman's lap. A drip of saliva in Hoffman's mouth made for a perfect 'hopped up and drunk' impression.

Foxy leaned into the car from the other side. "You know what's ironic? They told Laverne they would make arrests inside the club for possession of narcotics and take away her business license. And I would love to shoot them up with some smack right now and sprinkle the needles around, but I ain't got no access to no smack, because the goddamn club has always been clean."

"I saw. Nobody even smokes. Too clean for club."

Foxy finished positioning the cop by placing Hoffman's limp hand on the steering wheel. "Do you have a camera that can take a decent picture of these two through the windshield?"

"I have tourist camera in the case. It takes good pictures."

"Can you bring it here real quick?"

In the office, Laverne was making funny sounds at the laptop. She looked up when Ivan came in, and she said, "Boo-Boo is so curious. He keeps sniffing the camera every time I make some noise."

Ivan chuckled. "If you like them, you can take them. They give me headaches."

When he returned to the car, Foxy was staring at his cell phone, his gaunt face and the brass name tag on his shirt highlighted by light from the screen.

"I have some reading to do—Eva texted me a bunch of stuff. She says she's real upset without her dogs. Her husband's not letting her leave the house, but when he does, she wants to see them." He pushed the phone back into his pocket. "That's the problem with rich women. They complain."

"Call. Tell her she can see her dogs tomorrow morning. We must tell her what to do after we decide on plan. We can't do it over the phone. I need to see her reaction."

Foxy shrugged and pulled the phone out again. "Fine by me. We'd have to keep it tight, if we go out in the open with her." He typed a message on his phone before diving back into the police cruiser. In the dark, it was hard to tell what he was up to. From outside the car, it seemed like Foxy was making the white cop lean over the lap of the man in the driver's seat.

After a minute, Foxy straightened up and shut the car door. "All set. Would you mind taking a couple of pictures of them from the front, like you just came out and saw something funny going on in the front seat?"

Ivan walked around the hood and pointed the camera at the cruiser. The flash revealed a scene that fit into the 'homo stuff' category. He showed Foxy the pictures using the camera's small screen.

Foxy flipped through the pictures. "Mm-mm. Pomona's finest, sucking each other off." Putting the camera into his pocket, he added with satisfaction, "And who knew you can get an erection under anesthesia? I certainly didn't."

"Will they lose jobs?"

"Depends on how they behave when they wake up."

"The shot damages memory if you use a lot. I used a lot. Big dose."

"They fucking deserve it," Foxy said. "You play fucked up games, you win fucked up prizes."

The sound of the radio from inside the cruiser reverberated and bounced off the alley walls. The radio crackled and a woman came on. "One–Charlie-twelve, what's your twenty?"

Foxy looked up and down the gated alley, the nearest street lamp far, its yellow light dim. "Perfect timing. I'm thinking you go back to the dressing room and put on street clothes and head home, while I give local news a call. They need to tell the public there's quite a story happening in their backyard."

Ivan motioned at the cruiser with his chin. "You like big show.

You should be in show business."

Foxy smiled. "Why do you think I do drag?" A buzz came from his pocket. He pulled out his phone and took the call. "Mother, we are almost done. I'll—"

Foxy's face turned grim, his thin eyebrows together to form a crease. "Wait, hold on." He handed the phone to Ivan.

Laverne sounded shrill. "The little one keeps falling down. I think he's sick. It's terrible! The poor thing tries to stand up and falls back down. His little legs are shaking!"

Ivan handed the phone to Foxy, wheeled, and took off for the backdoor. Foxy asked something from behind, but there was no time for talking.

Pizdets. If Boo-Boo or Honey got sick and died, there was no telling what Eva would do.

Ivan ran up the stairs, the uniform restraining his movement. And to think that Foxy just texted Eva, telling her they should meet and talk and they'd bring the dogs over to keep her happy.

He banged his way through the door to Laverne's office the same way Foxy did when Hoffman turned nasty.

These little dogs. They always started the biggest troubles.

32

Los Angeles Westside, California

The wail of the siren sounded distant, as if it came from a different ambulance. Antonio's head felt like an empty bucket with the same thought rolling around:

Did Señora understand my warning?

When they wheeled him out, doctors were everywhere, saying words in English, but it sounded like a foreign language. Ischemia? Stenosis?

Antonio stiffened on the gurney the moment he caught sight of the old Toyota in the hospital's driveway. Miguel? Here, already? But it was a common car, millions of them everywhere.

The doors swished open, and they wheeled him through. Antonio found it odd, looking at the ceiling this way, at the lamps and tiles. Nobody ever looks at the ceiling unless they have to.

The doctors and nurses fussed over him like he was a baby—his pain didn't deserve this much attention. Incredible kindness, and perhaps it was God's way of rewarding him for trying to save an innocent woman.

After all the fuss, they moved him to a room upstairs. Before leaving, the nurse turned off the ceiling lights. "Mister Vargas. Try to rest. The doctor will be here shortly." Antonio fidgeted in his bed, and something hard wrinkled under the thin sheets.

Plastic, in case the patient wet himself. How appropriate—a visit from Miguel would make anyone wet the bed.

Miguel—the name was nauseating, like spoiled pork. It brought up vomit. What would they do after their old uncle didn't come home for the night? They might think he ran away or betrayed them. They would retaliate, the ghouls.

The thought made Antonio's heart flutter, the machine beeping faster. He searched his mind for prayer, if only to calm himself. Santa María, he prayed, I trust in you for all times. You are my only refuge.

The machine beeped and beeped, each sound like a measure of

his thoughts: Give Miguel an explanation. Make a good excuse. Call and warn Marisol.

No, it was impossible to tell her anything—the girls wouldn't have anywhere to go. Which left going back to Miguel and playing along as the only option. What did Señora say? Everything will be okay. Like she understood. Safer to go back to Miguel for now.

Unless she already did something, and Miguel found out about his uncle's betrayal.

High on the pillows, Antonio looked around the room. It would be so much nicer to stay here. Yellow light from the bedside stand made the space feel cozy and safe, if he ignored the equipment and beeping. One beep for each heartbeat. But how many left?

He shivered when the doctor came through the door. Tall lady, and so intense in her blue scrubs and cap. She came in looking at a stack of printouts in her hand and sat down on a wheeled stool by his bed.

"Mister Vargas, I'm doctor Lee. I'll be taking care of you." She rolled her chair closer to the computer near his bed and typed something. He watched, her confidence so comforting that his heart rate started to slow down.

She took her eyes off the swivel-mounted monitor and swung around on her chair. Her smooth forehead creased as she looked at him over the narrow frames of her glasses. "You must have been quite uncomfortable before passing out—why didn't you take your medication?"

He gave her a guilty smile. "I thought my lunch was no good. I thought it was coming up—you know, heartburn."

She shook her head. "You were under a lot of stress. We both know it's not your food that's hurting you. You're supposed to take your medicine and rest, not try to power through whatever's bothering you. You may not get away with it the next time."

She swung back to her computer, her fingers clicking on the keyboard.

His breath eased up with relief: she didn't mention the dog dragging him, making him go wild with fear. The dog attack would bring in the police, and then Miguel. People would die.

Without turning her head, she said, "I'll prescribe the oral spray for you. The pills may be hard to swallow—use the spray instead. You can pick up the spray from our pharmacy before you get discharged tomorrow."

The door clicked open, and a nurse popped her head in.

"Doctor—Mister Vargas has a visitor—should I bring him in?"

Doctor Lee looked up from the monitor. "Sure, I'm almost done here." The door closed. She glanced at him. "Looks like you relatives finally found you."

Antonio shrunk in his bed, cold with fear. So quickly?

The beeping from the machine picked up, and Doctor Lee's eyes went to it. "Excited your family's here, aren't you?" She went back to her keyboard but turned when the door opened.

Miguel stepped in, wearing jeans and a stylish black shirt, his long hair smooth and shiny. A successful businessman from Puerto Vallarta again, down to his black shoes with the golden crosses embossed into the leather.

Antonio pulled his blanket up, which sat heavy on his chest like the sheets of steel he used to reinforce his truck.

Miguel looked around the room, his black eyes coming back to the doctor. "Hello. I am Antonio's nephew." He held a bunch of brochures in his left hand and flowers in his right, his accent thick now that he spoke English.

Doctor Lee waved her thin hand. "Come on in." Adjusting a stethoscope on her neck, she spun on her stool to type.

Antonio leaned back into the pillow. Dios Mio—she believed him.

Miguel came over and put the flowers down on the bedside tray. With abrupt motion, Doctor Lee turned on her stool. "Your uncle gave everyone quite a scare."

"Is it bad?" Miguel asked.

She took her glasses off and stared at her patient with scorn. "It will be if he doesn't take care of himself."

"I'm sorry," Antonio said. "I—"

"He's doing very well," she said, talking over him. "He's had a minor episode of acute angina. We're going to keep him overnight for observation. Don't tire him, okay?"

"Yes." Miguel said, shaking her hand. "And thank you." His smile was disarming, showing the brilliance of his white teeth. He held up a brochure in his hand. "They gave me this about him."

"Good." She nodded. "Read it. I like it when the family members understand what's going on."

Antonio clutched the nurse-call remote like it was his only hope. The nurse had said, "Press the button, and someone will come." He kept his thumb on the call button.

Miguel was staring at the doctor like he wanted her to leave, but she wasn't leaving. She put her glasses on and resumed typing.

Miguel's hand went to the back of his black shirt, the bottom untucked.

A pistol! Antonio gasped at the thought, weakness pushing into his left arm. The numbness again—it crept into his shoulder and chest.

"Tio, how do you feel?" Miguel asked in Spanish.

Antonio licked his lips. "Tired. I feel—tired."

The devil looked so genuine, so concerned. But what about the fruit vendor, the poor man's legs sticking up from the cart? Lies, every word of it. And the doctor—she knew nothing.

Antonio threw a panicked glance at her. Warn her? The devil would shoot both of them. But it's a big hospital. He wouldn't dare shoot here, would he? Or he brought one of those quiet guns.

Dr. Lee turned on her stool and Antonio locked eyes with her, pleading with her in silence: Go. Leave.

But her attention was on the papers in her hands. "I'll check in tomorrow before they discharge you." Her eyes came up. "Don't hesitate to call the nurses, okay?" She stood up and offered her hand to Miguel. "Nice meeting you. Keep your uncle happy."

Antonio coughed, his throat and mouth dry from when the nurse announced Miguel's arrival. He reached for a cup on the mobile tray suspended over his thighs, the clamp from the machine hanging from his finger, an IV stuck in his arm.

His hand was shaking so much, the cup almost slipped out of his fingers. Thank God this sickness provided a good excuse for the shakes. The devil mustn't think his 'uncle' was guilty. Only guilty people acted nervous.

Miguel's smile vanished as soon as the doctor left. He walked around the bed and peered past the curtain separating the room into two sides. The bed on the other side was empty.

Miguel sounded pleased. "Bueno. It's good we're alone."

To kill me? Antonio took a sip of his water through a straw and cleared his throat. "I'm sorry I didn't call. Their dog bit me. And then my heart—I couldn't move. And then the ambulance took me."

Pleading, but what good was pleading with the devil? All for nothing, too; Miguel didn't seem to care—he went to the door and glanced into the corridor as if to check for someone standing outside. He looked satisfied when he returned to the bed and stood next to the IV rack, staring at the bag of fluids.

Miguel's lips moved like he was reading the English words in his mind; he flicked his nail at the plastic valve a couple of times.

Antonio pushed his back against the folded mattress to sit up higher. "It's not—it's not supposed to go fast."

Devil's eyes so thoughtful. "Does this stuff help?"

Keep talking to him. Delay. "It makes my head heavy." Antonio smiled weakly. "Like I've been drinking bad tequila. And now my thoughts go in different directions."

Miguel held the regulator for the drip between his fingers, his voice thoughtful. "Can this stuff kill you if you get too much or not enough?"

"The nurse knows." Hoarse from fear. Was this it? By drug, not a gun? Press the call button. But he'd kill the nurses. Like the fruit vendor.

Miguel's fingers slid down the IV line, and then he let go.

Aside from the monitor beeps, the room was quiet. Antonio heard the wheels of the stool squeak under Miguel's weight, the devil sitting now where Doctor Lee had been a minute ago. At least not reaching for his gun—not yet.

"Tell me what happened at the villa," Miguel said.

The interrogator. Antonio caressed the call button. "I fixed the sprinkler. But then the new guard brought this dog—big, like a bear. He kept sending it after me. Like a game."

Miguel frowned. "A game? Gringo put a dog on you for a game?"

"He played with it first. With the ball. And then he made it run after me. The others watched. They weren't gringos."

"No?"

"Morenos. Dark skin, but not black. Not like the guard you saw at the gate." Antonio took another sip from his water cup. This seemed safe, talking. Safety in words.

"How many of them did you see? I want the exact number."

"I'll try." Antonio closed his eyes—easier to remember this way. He counted the faces of the men in the yard, and when he got to the guard with the dog, the one with the mean scowl, the memory made him so uncomfortable he cringed and fidgeted in his bed. "Six or seven, I don't—"

He opened his eyes to avoid the discomfort and froze. Miguel was standing next to him, a pillow in his hands.

Kill me with it? Choke me?

Antonio's heart flew into his throat—the beeps betraying him. No, he thought. Marisol. Lucia. My girls!

The machine beeped faster. His thumb dug into a call button under the blanket. And he felt guilty.

246

Miguel bent closer. "Tio. Lean forward." He slid the pillow into the opening behind Antonio's head, propping him up. "You need to calm down. Don't think about the dog or whatever. I just want the exact number."

Antonio grabbed the cup and sucked the rest of the water out. The door swung open, and a nurse came in. Her wide, round face looked worried. What to say? He raised his cup and said in a weak voice, "I'm sorry. Can I have water?"

Miguel took the cup from his hand and passed it to the nurse. When she brought the cup back, Antonio drank greedily to show it was all true.

The door closed behind the nurse, and Miguel said with a sigh, "You are useless, Tio." His hand went under the back of his shirt and pushed the fabric aside.

Antonio closed his eyes.

"Tio, look at me."

Miguel was shaking his head, pulling his pants up with both hands. "Why do you not take your medicine like the doctor said? You are so sick, you are useless. I'm lucky I have other men to watch the house." He walked over to the window and lifted the shutters. "Take your damn pills. I have to go."

The shutters rattled when Miguel dropped them. He turned. "The doctor will let you out tomorrow, yes? There is a flight to Puerto Vallarta at ten in the morning, and another one at two. I want you to get on that plane, Tio. You understand?"

Antonio pulled in a breath, the air sweet and cool. Such an incredible idea—the devil never cared to kill anyone here. He'd come for information.

In a daze of relief, Antonio watched Miguel walk to the door and disappear through it. He didn't dare move, afraid for the dream to end. Another huge scare, like with Cho, and again nothing came of it. Just an old man's fearful imagination.

Beeps measured the time, dozens of them, hundreds. Nothing bothered Antonio, not even the weird hospital bed with a plastic wrapper under his sheets in case he pissed himself. He felt at ease, sleepy.

God's reward—a gift of safety. Tomorrow, a confession. And then the plane, the sky, and the salty breath of the ocean.

The tall hills of Puerto Vallarta.

33

Huntington Park, Los Angeles, California

Ivan woke up with a start in his waiting room chair when the veterinarian came through the door. A wall clock confirmed they had long ago crossed the midnight mark. She had a crew cut, like in the army. He searched her face for good news. Or bad. Plenty of that running around.

The vet pulled off latex gloves with a snap and tossed them into the trash bin. Her focused impression gave out nothing but tired concentration. She offered no encouragement, only a furrowed brow and tight lips.

Ivan stood up. Only one possible reason for her to look this way: Boo-Boo was done for. Time for a contingency plan. Take Honey to the meet and lie to Eva about Boo-Boo. But would she believe it? Would she do as they ask without seeing the second dog?

The vet leveled her gray eyes at him. "Mister Larssen, I cleaned Boo-Boo's stomach. Now, I'd like to ask you a question you may refuse to answer. But first let me assure you that—"

"So, he is all right?"

"He should be fine." A tired smile, but her eyes retained their weariness and alarm.

Finally, some good news. "I can take him home?"

She adjusted her necklace like it was irritating her. "Of course. But it's important we talk about what happened. When you brought him in, I assumed it was a chocolate poisoning. You told me he might have eaten kitchen food or trash from the garbage can. But I found something in Boo-Boo's stomach and urine that we must discuss."

"Discuss?" At the end of the long day, his ability to pick up subtext in English was fading. He needed to stretch his body on a bed, not solve riddles.

"Like I was saying—I want to assure you I will not be reporting anything to the police. We are under no obligation—"

Ivan frowned. "Police? Why they care about my dog?" The

microchip. Boo-Boo must have carried a chip with owner information. Stolen dog. She wasn't giving Boo-boo back.

She sighed. "They don't care. I do."

Speaking in riddles. Ivan looked her in the eye, and the vet stared back like he murdered dogs for a living. She was watching for his reaction. But a reaction to what?

Her voice was full of accusation. "I found a half-digested pill casing in his stomach. Prozac. Which is why you saw him falling on his side." She waited.

"Pills? This is wrong. I do not use pills."

She hesitated, and for the first time her cheeks showed some red. "I'm saying I don't have to report it so we can be honest with each other. I also found methamphetamine in his system. We keep a basic drug test panel here. It's not unusual for pets to ingest their owner's drugs."

He rubbed his forehead. "So Boo-Boo ate drugs." The thought zapped him. "Wait. I know where he ate it. The youths. I mean gangster—" He waved the thought away with a tired gesture. "It's a mistake. How do you say—misunderstanding."

"The gangster?"

He nodded. "Long story. I pulled him away, but too late, I think. So, what do I do? Can I take him for walks?"

She sighed. "Well, with Prozac, Boo-Boo will remain heavily sedated, so you should let him rest until the drug wears off. Make sure he has his water bowl filled—he'd be drinking a lot."

Ivan pulled out his wallet. "He needs rest. I understand. How much do I pay?"

She sent him to the front desk. After paying, he picked up the Pomeranian, the little dog limp and sluggish but licking his hand.

Exhausted, Ivan drove back to the safe house. Foxy—he'd want an update. Even this late. Or early. Didn't they call it early morning in English, even if it was dark outside?

"He ate what?" Foxy said over the phone. "Jesus, that poor thing must be tripping major balls. Prozac and meth—that's a big party for a small dog."

Ivan looked into the rearview mirror, at Boo-Boo bundled in a blanket on the back seat. "We can't take him to Eva like that. So I'll bring Honey, and we tell her I'm keeping Boo-Boo at home for insurance."

"Man, she's gonna lose her shit. She told me she wants to see the dogs before we do anything. She said it'll give her courage."

Ivan glanced back: Boo-Boo yawned then coiled into a tighter ball of fur in the blanket. "Or she will want to help us more."

"Well, we do have her babies."

"As you say—she has no room. So, we finish the job tomorrow." A billboard came into view, an advertisement for a local news station. "How is Laverne? Did your trick work?"

"Yeah, it worked all right." Foxy chuckled. "The news crew came out. I think the police is gonna stay away for a while. They got burned real good. And we got the tape, should they poke in again."

At the safe house, Ivan put Boo-Boo in a chair and fed Honey some steak. The little guy kept jumping and scratching at his leg, running around, excited to have company.

Ivan lay down on his cot. The fluff-ball climbed on and burrowed into the tight space between his arm and chest. Honey was a friendly one. Boo-Boo—that one was a drug addict.

With the light off, thoughts and images crowded his mind. Busy day. Busy night. This would be a good time to call Lena and tell her the business trip was almost done. No, too tired. Tomorrow.

His body sagged into the thin mattress, Honey warm and soft by his side, breathing quietly.

Sleep was an uninterrupted stretch of black until the alarm rang. Honey jumped off and ran to the kitchen, nails clicking on old wood. The fluff-ball came back holding his food dish between its teeth. Boo-Boo showed no interest in getting out from under his blanket, still on the chair.

Honey ate the last of the steak, ground right through it with its small jaws. Almost like a big dog. Ivan checked the time and fell forward for a few pushups. Do a full workout? No, not today. If the plan of picking up Kazbek developed complications, a fresh body would make a difference.

He frowned. Getting older—these days, the recovery time from the routine took more than a hearty meal and a short rest.

He washed himself in the backyard, using cold water from a garden hose. The fixtures in the bathroom had been ripped out and the pipes plugged, but as dilapidated as the house was, at least it had water. And electricity. And tall cinderblock walls sheltering the backyard from curious neighbors.

Foxy's text came in: "We have the cruiser. Eva leaving at 9.30."

Ivan texted back: "Switch phones." He pulled out the battery and SIM card then tossed the phone in the trash. No phone could be considered secure after a few calls.

250

Honey scurried around his legs, and he bent to rub its fluffy belly. "You ready for a walk?" The word sent the dog running and barking and twirling on the spot.

Close to Eva's neighborhood, Ivan looked for the coffee shop with free Wi-Fi and found one right next to Sunset Boulevard. With Honey tied to a tree near the car, he fired up his laptop for a video call, careful to position the laptop to show nothing but himself and the car seat.

Lena was all smiles at first, saying in mock accusation, "It's cold! You left—and it's now real winter, of course. You took the warm weather with you."

"I packed it in my luggage."

"At least it's snowing. Months late, but we got the real winter. I had to wear my fur coat to take Bond out."

"We can all go winter swimming once I get back. My Polar Bear club guys will be at the lake come Sunday, if the ice had set."

She laughed. "You can go swimming all you want. Bond and I are staying in our fur coats." Bond's snout barged into the picture, and she said, "Who's in the computer? Can you see who's in there?"

The dog sniffed the screen, ears up, alert.

Ivan switched to a more serious tone. "Zaichik, I think I'm almost done here. Everything is being sorted out. I have one more meeting today and that's it. I only have a minute to talk, but I thought I'd tell you."

"My god, you can be here—what are you saying? You can be here tomorrow?"

"Not tomorrow, but I should be able to fly out the day after. It's possible. It's just one more meeting. That's it."

Like during his previous trips, he expected her to giggle and make plans for what they would eat when he got back, to talk in excited tones. Whenever he was away, they made light of the situation by talking about what they'd do once he was back home. But this time she was quiet. She hugged Bond's neck and stared into the camera.

Tears. Tears streaked her cheeks—and she was quick to wipe them, smiling a guilty smile.

His guts churned with sudden worry. "Zaichik, what's wrong?"

She reached for something out of the camera's view. A tissue. After blowing her nose, she said, "I didn't want to worry you. I thought I could tell you when you get back." Bond licked her face, and she pushed him off. "Stop."

"Tell me what?"

She stared at the napkin she crumpled in her hand. "I'm pregnant."

A chill came over his whole body, the same sensation as diving into a frozen lake. But in the next second, his skin flushed hot. His lungs forgot how to pull in air. The street noises—car engines, a helicopter somewhere—grew muffled while his thoughts became louder. Like being choked out in a SAMBO fight at a competition—everything from far away. Only thoughts drumming in the temples.

A bus roared by, and its loud engine shook him into clarity. He swallowed and rubbed his chest and neck. "I should be—I should be home with you."

He must have been wearing the dumbest look, because when Lena raised her eyes to look into the camera, a weak smile lit her face. "I'm sorry. I wanted to wait till you were here to tell you. But you said 'I'm almost done,' and I don't know what happened—and now I'm crying like a fool."

Pregnant. They were going to have a child. "Zaichik, you are not a fool." He worked hard to keep his voice sweet while pushing words through the lump in his throat.

"I'm crying like one."

Ivan stared past the screen, through the windshield, at the people inside the coffee shop. Get out of here. Finish everything. Move.

The dryness in his mouth was the same as during his first skydive, his tongue sandpaper. He felt as weak as when he stood up from the bench to jump out of the plane. He glanced at the clock: less than an hour left to run reconnaissance for the meeting. Must be thorough now. More than ever.

"You look so stressed," Lena said. "There must be people waiting for you. Go." She wiped her tears with the tissue, waving her hand at the screen. "I'll be fine. Don't worry about me. Finish your talks and come back."

"I wish I could kiss you right now."

She smiled and looked down to her side, to where Bond's ears popped into the camera's view. "I would have to kiss Bond for now. He licks my face every time I cry."

"I will lick your face when I get back."

She looked at the camera and smiled. "Good. His breath stinks."

A child. A child! The thought pulsed in his mind as he drove uphill, to the address Foxy had texted. A child. A new life, after years of killing people.

Here it was, a dog park—looked right. Low fence. Signs.

The thought of having a child was overwhelming. He parked and gripped the wheel, squeezing it until his wrists hurt. The job. Get it done. Now. He rubbed his face until his cheeks burned. Step one: reconnaissance. No mistakes.

A short walk up the steps with Honey on a leash brought his heart rate up. The cool air and movement helped him gather thoughts. Honey jerked the leash every time another dog went by, but he kept the leash short.

It was nice how they dispensed bags for dog poop here from green boxes. Easy to pretend you were picking up after your dog.

On each corner, he left a small, fisheye camera fixed inside a plastic casing made to look like old dog poop. Don't clean up after me, he thought. At least not now.

For extra insurance, he took pictures of the cars in each street around the park; it always paid to keep an eye on the new arrivals when everyone gathered for the meeting.

The tracker dot on his laptop map showed the Mexicans as parked by the hospital. An injury? It matched Foxy's text that said there had been a mix up with Eva's gardener.

Ivan drove to the villa and waited until the gates moved and Eva's new Mercedes coupe rolled out. How she managed to ditch the bodyguards remained to be seen, but no other cars followed.

He kept his distance. An easy task, since he knew where she was going. No other cars stayed close to them for any significant period of time. It was unlikely the Mexicans were passing them one car to another, but not impossible.

Foxy called and said, "It's quiet here. What do you think?"

"You watch for new cars?"

"Yep. You tailing her?"

"Nobody followed."

"So? Yay or nay? Are we doing it?"

Eva found a spot, got out, and walked into the park through a small gate. "She is here. Go join her. I will see if anyone moves."

From the car, he watched Foxy enter the enclosure. Stylish jacket, a little large. Space for holsters.

Eva sat on a bench, her body rigid and her back straight. She stood up, but Foxy put a hand on her shoulder, and they both sat down. The feed from the cameras showed no new cars. Eva didn't get this address until late, and Foxy said he would change the location at the last minute. Even if she had alerted the cops, they would have a hard time staying invisible.

The minutes dragged on. "Spokoino," Ivan said aloud, mostly for his own benefit, but Honey let out another whimper in the back. Both of them impatient.

Foxy and Eva looked like two dog owners, chatting. Ivan stepped out and carried Honey in his hands into the dog run. If Eva set them up, the police would be moving in; he stole a glance behind him as he lowered the Pomeranian to the ground inside the fence.

The dog took off toward Eva, who picked it up and started kissing its head, hugging the squirming ball of fur against her chest.

Look casual. Ivan walked with hands in his pockets, casting glances here and there. Two other dog owners with their dogs inside the run showed little interest in Eva or Foxy. A woman in a long skirt let her Doberman off-leash and pushed a stroller toward another bench. Everyone looked local, relaxed.

Odd movement inside the stroller—instead of a baby, a small cocker spaniel. Bolnye. Who puts dogs into a stroller? Hollywood was truly a crazy place.

Ivan carried his laptop folded, screen facing out, the feed from the cameras running on the screen in several windows.

Eva sounded upset. "I did everything you wanted me to do. Why do you have to be so cruel?"

Foxy shook his head. "You've got it all wrong. We're careful. We can't just give you back both your dogs and hope for the best. And besides, if everything goes well, you'll have both pups back today. The plan is we go pick up your husband for a chat in a couple of hours."

Ivan sat down on the other side of her. Eva barely gave him a glance, petting Honey in her lap. Ivan checked the screen. Still no new cars joining them.

As soon as Foxy said 'today', Eva stopped rubbing Honey's fur. "You're insane. He brought all these new men—they're all armed! They have a huge guard dog—one of the idiots thought it would be fun to send it after the gardener."

The tracker location. This explained the hospital. Ivan said, "When was gardener at your house?"

She glanced at him, her lips shaking. "Last night. Why? You want to torture him too?"

"Hey," Foxy said. "Nobody is torturing anybody. He's just asking. He's been nice to your dogs."

She turned to Foxy. "The sprinkler flooded the lawn. Antonio came to fix it, and the dog chased him into the house."

"So, what happened?" Foxy said. "Was he hurt?"

"My god, it was terrible. I had to call the ambulance. They took him to the emergency room. He's an old man, and he looked like he was having a heart attack."

Eva lowered Honey to the ground. Ivan felt edgy. Not wise, with a few large dogs running around. Tell her? A comment like this might give her the impression he owned her dog. She seemed tense as it was.

Honey trotted off to sniff a slightly larger poodle. Eva watched the two dogs get acquainted and absently said, "I felt terrible. Antonio was scared out of his mind, mumbling on the gurney when they loaded him into the ambulance." She turned to face Foxy. "He left his truck behind."

"What happened to it?" Ivan asked.

She threw a glance at him. "The truck? I had the idiot with the dog drive it to the hospital."

An opportunity to check if she was lying. "Do you know which hospital?"

"God, why is it so important? Cedars Sinai. Happy now?"

Foxy put his hands up. "Hey, guys. Let's play nice. We don't trust your gardener is all."

"That's funny you say that." She picked at the nail polish on her thumbnail, her lips pressed together.

"How so?" Foxy sounded mildly curious.

"Antonio actually said I was in danger. He must have thought the dog was going to bite me when it broke into the house. It's one of those huge Caucasian Shepherd dogs with a great coat and cropped ears."

"Kavkazets," Ivan said.

"Never mind the dog," Foxy said, waving the topic away. "I'm happy everyone's okay, but we need to talk about your husband." Foxy put his hand on her arm. "I'll need you to put on your best performance yet. Do you think you can do that?"

"Will you give me my dogs back?"

"You'll have them back as soon as we come in and arrest your husband."

"Arrest him?" She sounded puzzled. "I don't see how you can—"

Foxy raised his palm. "Hear me out. It's a little risky, unfortunately. You'll have to get your husband real angry."

Eva clasped her hands. Her shoulders hunched, making her look smaller. "He's already angry. I wasn't supposed to leave the house."

"I know," Foxy said. "That's all part of the plan. But when you get home, you gotta get him real mad. Mad enough to slap you."

"Oh, that's easy. He likes hitting women. But why?"

"Domestic abuse. You call us, and we come in as cops to arrest him. This way, no one gets hurt, and our boss gets to have a talk with him."

"Oh my god." She took her glasses off and stared at them. "He didn't—he's not going to expect that." She looked at Foxy. "If I do it—when do I get my dogs?"

"We'll bring them with us in a different car and park it someplace close. I'll tell you where after we drive off with your husband."

A loud yelp and growling came from the opposite end of the dog run: a Doberman was harassing the poodle Honey had made an acquaintance of earlier. The poodle's owner ran along the chain-link fence in a race to save her pet—in the game of 'Doberman vs. Poodle', the Doberman was winning.

Ivan leaned backward to look at Foxy behind Eva's back. "We need to hurry. Tell her what to do."

Foxy nodded and looked back to Eva. "After we're done here, go do your hair. Take your time, make your husband real mad. Then, when you get back home, do you best and get him to hit you at least once. That's key. As soon as he does, pretend like you're really mad at him. Do that even if he doesn't hit you."

"That's easy. I've done that plenty."

"Good. Keep it natural. Walk away in a huff. If he hits you, yell about an ugly bruise he gave you."

"And then what?"

"When you're far enough to be safe, lock yourself in the bathroom or someplace he can't hear you and dial 911. When the operator picks up, tell her you have a bad headache. She'll tell you it's an emergency-only line. Ask her what the number is for non-emergency calls. Pretend you're dumb."

"I can call you instead. Why can't I call you?"

"Because if he grabs your phone at some point or looks at the log on the web, it must show a long 911 call. That's your insurance. And ours. He'll know without doubt that cops are coming in."

Eva hesitated. "I hope I can say the right thing on the phone."

"Don't worry. The 911 operators get these calls all the time. And once you've talked to them, it's better if you don't talk to your husband at all. Just tell your guards the cops are on the way and text me then delete the text, as always. We'll come right over. Do you think you can do this?"

She returned Foxy's stare. "Sure I can. I've got bruises. And he's hit me before. But if I do this for you, you have to come right away and bring my dogs."

Foxy's voice rang with sincerity. "We will. Trust me, we've got other things to do besides babysitting your Pomeranians. Now, repeat to me everything I just told you."

As Eva went through the steps, Ivan kept his eyes on Honey, listening to Eva's steady voice. She hardly missed anything, her memory and focus nearly perfect. And she asked clarifying questions. Brave, putting herself in danger like this. If Kazbek had a temper, she'd be playing with fire, calling the cops on him.

"Your husband knows cops can arrest him on domestic violence charge," Foxy said, leaning close. "He also knows he'll be out on bail in no time—so he'll tell his goons to stay back. The whole thing should go down silky smooth."

Eva nodded. "I can do it. But I want my dogs as soon as you arrest him, you understand? I want them there. I'm doing everything you asked me to do."

"Sure," Foxy said. "Don't worry about your puppies so much. Ivan's been real good to them."

"He has?" Eva turned to look.

Having a hard time believing it. Ivan nodded to confirm. Protective of her dogs, but who could blame her? Dogs made better relatives than people.

"I am good with dogs," Ivan said.

Foxy echoed, "He's very good. Show her."

"Show me what?" Eva said, looking from one man to another.

Ivan called Honey to come, and the Pomeranian trotted over without delay.

"Sit," Ivan said, and the dog obeyed. "Speak." The Pomeranian barked once. "Turn." The dog twirled on the spot and sat down again. Ivan leaned forward, and the dog tried to lick his face. "He is hungry. I give him steak."

"You trained him," Eva said, a mix of jealousy and surprise in her voice. "He wants to lick you. He's never wanted to lick anybody."

Ivan shrugged. "Dogs lick your face when they recognize your dominance. Or when they are hungry. That is all. I am not his favorite."

Eva watched Honey scamper off. "I didn't know dominance worked for them."

Foxy chuckled. "Yeah, I guess dogs and people aren't that different after all."

No time for idle talk. Ivan rose to his feet. "We have to go."

Over in the yard, the same Doberman that harassed the poodle kept eluding its owner.

Foxy said to Eva, "Just remember to stay on the line with the operator long enough. It must sound believable to him."

The owner of the Doberman looked hapless as she chased her pet, surrender written all over her flabby face. Long-haired and in her skirt and loose shirt of rainbow colors, she tried to corner her dog and grab its collar. The Doberman paid her no heed.

"I'll pick up the dog." Ivan was about to turn and call Honey to come, but Eva didn't let him.

"No. I want to walk him," she said. "You don't have to be such an asshole about taking him, okay?"

The Doberman looked wrong: it stood still, its neck rigid as it watched the Pomeranian. Ivan said, "I'm not asshole. I just want—"

He didn't get to finish his sentence. The Doberman launched toward Honey, and in a second, Honey was on the ground, yelping, wriggling its way out of snapping jaws. The Doberman worked to pin it down with a paw.

Eva screamed, "Oh my god!"

So here it was—the whole operation falling apart because of one aggressive, poorly-trained dog whose owner didn't even dare to interfere. "Mimi, stop!" the woman shouted from a safe distance. "Stop, Mimi! You're being a bad girl!"

"I don't think fucking Mimi is planning to stop," Foxy said from behind.

Ivan glanced at his partner: Foxy's hand hovering behind his waist. But too many witnesses for a shooting. Too big a mess. Just when they had everything lined up.

Eva stood with her mouth open, wringing her hands.

Ivan turned to the dogs and took off in accelerating strides. These past couple of days—first Boo-Boo and now Honey. Just impossible to get a break with them.

In seconds, he reached the snarling, yelping dogs and swung his laptop in an arc, bringing it down hard on the Doberman's head and neck. The blow wouldn't hurt the dog or stop the attack: the breed was much too strong to be stopped this way, its neck thick with muscles. But good enough to stun.

Mimi gave a confused snarl but launched a counterattack, its jaws clamping on the offered laptop.

Wind up. Downward. Knuckles to the top of its head. Parietal, closer to occipital. The dog snorted as Ivan's fist connected with its head and fell head-first to the dirt.

Ivan picked up the Pomeranian and ran his fingers over its small body, feeling bones for fractures, for broken skin and bleeding. Eva stared at him with her hands in fists over her mouth.

"He is fine," Ivan shouted. "Not hurt."

He held the dog like a baby in the crook of his arm. The fluff-ball tried to squirm out, but he didn't let it—enough adventures for everybody. He turned around and walked away, the laptop under his armpit. No telling if it'd boot up. But it wouldn't matter as long as Eva did as they asked.

From behind, the lady owner was yelping as bad as Honey had. "Mimi, Mimi, baby, what's wrong?" Ivan glanced at her while closing the gate as he left the park. She was traipsing over to the Doberman, hampered by pink plastic sandals.

The Doberman was still in a daze, shaking its head and snorting and sneezing. Would recover, their bones so thick. Ivan said, "Tupaya suka." Feeling bad for the Doberman—another great protector dog ruined by a clueless owner.

Foxy's call came in as Ivan rounded the corner in a Lincoln. "Hey, nicely done. Is the pooch okay?"

Ivan grunted. "Fine. Eva?"

"Yeah, just freaked out."

"I'm heading for the hospital."

"I thought you said we're ahead of them."

"Extra guarantee."

"If you say so. Watch the clock, though."

"I will." He stopped at a light, his adrenaline settling, his fingers vibrating on the wheel—and not from the car's engine. "I should pay more attention. That Doberman was trouble from the beginning."

"You took care of it. As my ma says, don't dwell, Terrel."

After disconnecting, Ivan rolled his windows down to let some fresh air in. The operation was picking up pace. Everything was heating up: the black interior of his car, the news from back home, the traffic on the boulevard.

His reflection in the mirror showed a permanent frown. Nothing good about any of this, all this quick improvising. Not enough alternatives, not enough backup. Gambling at the worst time, with the highest stakes.

Gambling—with a new life.

34

Los Angeles Westside, California

In the morning, Dr. Lee came into Antonio's room, and then the nurse, and then a Spanish-speaking social worker. They said things like: "Antonio, are you under a lot of stress?" and "Let's talk about your nutritional choices." They discussed his cholesterol and his medicines and sorted his prescriptions while he sat on his bed, itching to leave.

A plump nurse organizing his discharge wanted to know if he had any family picking him up, and he said no. She was about to call him a taxi from the nurse station but came back to his room, saying, "Your family brought the car over for you. It's in the visitor's parking lot." She seemed uneasy about it, her eyes avoiding him.

Antonio stared at her. "My car? This must be a mistake."

"They left the key for you." She opened her fist and handed him the keys to his truck. "I'm sorry they didn't come." A thought brightened her expression. "But I checked with your primary doctor, and she said you're okay to drive." She paused, and her smile vanished. "But you'll have to pay the parking fee."

The discharge took so long that by the time they wheeled him out of the hospital, Antonio was already late for the morning flight Miguel had mentioned. He walked slowly to the hospital's restricted parking lot, where his truck towered over nearby cars.

He checked his old cell phone: plenty of time to bring the truck back home. No, not home. Not anymore.

He climbed in and put the key in the ignition but didn't turn it. Drive the truck there and leave it for Miguel and his men? Their truck, really. Dangerous, going there now, after the warning. But the pictures—the wedding picture, Marisol would want that one. And the one with Lucia in the swimming pool. Pick up those and leave the rest.

Antonio started the engine and pulled out of the parking lot. He called Miguel from the road. "It's Antonio. I'm bringing the truck back."

Miguel sounded distracted. "Ah, bueno. I was going to send Seso to pick it up. Park it in the driveway."

So, no danger. One last visit to the house.

The trip from the hospital, with a short stop at the travel agency, tugged at Antonio's heart. Years spent here in Los Angeles—and so much work. All coming to an end.

He checked the clock: plenty of time remained before the afternoon flight. As he drove through the city, his eyes prickled with tears at the sight of the rose window on the Sacred Heart Catholic Church. Go in now and ask for forgiveness? No, much better to do it in Mexico, at the church in Puerto Vallarta. La Iglesia De Nuestra Señora de Guadalupe. What better way to start life back home than with a confession?

A 'closed' sign hung on the door of the restaurant where years ago they held his daughter's quinceañera celebration. An excited flutter rose in Antonio's chest at the thought of seeing his family soon; he rubbed and kneaded it with his fingers. Take your medicine, he thought. Watch what you eat. As the social worker had said, "Follow your doctor's advice, Mister Vargas. You do that, and you'd live long enough to enjoy the music at your granddaughter's quinceañera."

At the corner near his house, a stranger sat on a chair, playing with his phone. When the man looked up, he stared at the truck for a second and picked a radio off his belt. Another one of Miguel's demons.

Inside, in the kitchen, Miguel and his men were at the table, eating tacos from a large carton in the middle. They all ignored Antonio, except Miguel, who asked him if the truck was off the driveway like he asked.

Antonio nodded. "And I bought the ticket, like you said."

"Bueno. It's time for you to go home, Tio."

The smell of cooked meat and onions was nauseating, but it could be from nervousness. Or maybe the medicine had some kind of side effect.

Nobody followed him into the garage when Antonio went to find the box with pictures. What a relief! They suspected nothing. Time to call a taxi and leave.

Antonio went up to his room to pack everything into a suitcase. The zipper pinched his finger as he closed it. He hurried out of his bedroom but froze on the landing—the statuette of the Virgin, glued to the dashboard of the truck.

She should not stay with the truck. Can't leave her with Miguel.

He put down the suitcase and quickly descended the flight of stairs, short of breath by the time he got to the truck. What had Doctor Lee said? Make sure to rest. He stood by the cab door, waiting for the pressure in his chest to subside.

The door felt heavy; he had to lean in to open it. Another thing the doctor said: it would take time to recover his strength after the episode. Something like that. An episode. Such a calm word for what happened at the villa. The monster dog snarling and biting.

Leaning in, Antonio put his knee on the driver's seat and reached for the statuette on the dashboard with his right hand. The second his fingers touched his protector, he felt stronger. The Virgin was looking out for him. No need to think about the villa anymore.

I warned her, he thought. All that risk, but I warned Señora Dominguez in time.

He pulled on the statuette as gently as he could, yet the old glue resisted. He tugged harder, his fingers wrapped tightly around the Virgin. Not leaving her with these demons. Bringing her back to Puerto Vallarta. No place for her here.

The left side of his chest tightened with a dull ache. He sighed. The exertion hurt.

With a final tug, the statuette popped off the dash. Gracias, Dios. Antonio crawled out of the cab and slammed the door shut. One more walk through the house then off to the airport.

He looked at the statuette in his splotchy, old hand, took a step forward, and in that same instant the whole world flashed brilliant white.

Ivan flipped the switch on the controller, and from the distance of two hundred meters, the blast wave came at their car like a low-flying jet. It banged against the windows and rolled into the distance, a great wave of sound leaping over buildings and kicking off car alarms.

Foxy raised his eyebrow. "Shit, how much SEMTEX did you say it was?"

"One brick." Ivan started the car and shifted into gear.

Foxy scratched his chin. "Makes you wonder how big the bricks are in Russia."

"Russian bricks bigger. In inches, American are eight by four. Russian—ten by five, almost. Same thickness of two inches."

"You make it sound kind of kinky, Russkie Bear. Like we're measuring something other than plastic explosives."

Ivan grunted and steered the car toward the freeway. The way Foxy talked, always trying to be the funny guy, all his sexual innuendo—it was amusing once you got used to it. Back in Afghanistan, everyone in the platoon ribbed each other the same way, their jokes nastier than Foxy's. You either joked or shot heroin. Or both. And who knew smoking would be harder to quit than heroin?

Now that they were about to go into Kazbek's house to pick him up, the hungry feeling had returned to the back of Ivan's throat.

"Do you smoke?" he asked.

Foxy didn't hesitate. "No. Why, you want one? We have time to stop by the corner store."

"I want to quit."

Two police cars flew by in the opposite lane—sirens blaring—followed by a fire engine.

"I bet our Mexican friends are real busy right now," Foxy said thoughtfully. "I wonder if they'd get past the perimeter with all that rapid responding going on."

"They will separate to escape police. Maybe leave their gear behind. Takes time—to replace gear."

"We lettin' the authorities sort the competition out for us." Foxy took a sip of his coffee. He sounded like he was talking to himself, his eyes scanning the traffic in front of them. "Let's hope Eva comes through." He turned to look at Ivan. "You hungry? I know a good place. About the right distance from Eva's house. We can get to her right away if she calls early."

"I'm not hungry before the job. But they will have coffee or tea, yes?"

"Sure they will."

The drive was long enough for Ivan to consider a critical issue: Eva must provoke Kazbek enough but not too much. A delicate balance and with a lot of risk, given the unpredictable nature of violent men.

"Do you think Eva is strong enough to do it?" Ivan asked.

"She loves her Poms. Risked climbing out of a burning house for them. And then lied to the police and her husband about it."

"It's delicate. She must anger him but without too much anger. Kazbek must be upset already. Could do something . . . more than slap."

"You've seen her parties. Something tells me—even if he gets rough with her, she'll still get it done."

Ivan focused on playing an arithmetic drill with numbers on car

263

registration plates. Nothing like a bit of multiplication to distract your mind. He multiplied and divided until Foxy spoke again.

"I could use some music."

Yes, the music. "I have a question about it."

"About what?"

"In English, does 'flex nuts' mean stay brave?"

Foxy's eyebrows flew up. "What?"

"When someone says 'flex nuts' . . . it means stay brave, correct?"

"Where the hell did you get that?"

"My girlfriend—"

"Your girlfriend said that? You shitting me."

Ivan raised his palm. "I can explain. She told me I should listen to songs to learn English. Sing with the songs. But it is hard, when they sing. It is easier when they talk. So, I found songs like that. Hip-hop. Except they use American slang a lot. Sometimes, I know what they say, but I don't know meanings."

"You listen to fucking rap for English practice?"

"It's good. Old ones are clear. Here, I will play it."

Ivan skipped back to find the song and played it until the phrase came on.

"I can't believe you're listening to this shit," Foxy said with a laugh. "Flex nuts. That's hilarious."

"It means 'funny'?"

"No, no. It means you don't act tough, because you don't have to."

"I see."

"Put it back on. I like this one."

Foxy shook his head when they stepped out of the car. "Rap. You, of all people."

"I listen to folk and opera also. But it does not help with English."

"I tried singing 'Ave Maria' once. Almost tore my throat out."

"Caccini. Mezzo soprano. You need breath control. Long notes."

Foxy sighed. "I stick to pop these days."

At the cafe, Foxy ordered warmed-up apple pie, caramelized apple slices slipping from under the dough as the waitress put the plate down.

The smell of the molten apples was irresistible. "I will have one, too," Ivan said. "Please."

Foxy spooned cream from the top of his pie. "I always have a slice before tricky jobs."

"I used to smoke always."

"It's good to have a routine. Gets your mind settled."

"I check everything for routine. Go over details. But I miss smoking."

They ate their pies and drank tea and coffee, cup after cup. Eva was running late. Ivan used the data connection to download his work emails, but they only added to the tension.

"There's that Russian face again," Foxy said. "Anything I should know about?"

"It's my electronics business. In Russia, the tax office can break your business in one day. My accountant says the tax office wants to audit me."

"Oh. That sucks." Foxy left it at that and focused on his smartphone. Good partner—knew when to stop asking questions.

Ivan powered down his laptop. Bad time to deal with business problems from half the world away. He pulled a crossword puzzle book from his pocket, a wrinkled thing from the gas station. A nice distraction and would help with vocabulary.

He filled out half of it, and Eva still hadn't called.

Without lifting his gaze from his phone, Foxy said, "She's taking her sweet time, ain't she?"

"Or he beat her, and she can't call."

"You Russians are such optimists."

"We are realistic."

The puzzle had a long word across: state in which the opposing forces are balanced. Ivan nodded. How fitting.

"Foxy, how do you spell 'equilibrium'?" This pulled Foxy from his phone. He looked at the ceiling and spelled it.

"It fit." Good word. And appropriate. They both did their best to maintain this equilibrium while the phone on the table stayed silent.

Foxy pointed at a TV screen hanging from the wall. "Check this out."

A news ticker slid across the screen: Fire in East Los Angeles. Aerial footage from a helicopter showed a column of smoke rising from the skeletal remains of the Mexican's truck. No more gardening at the villa. This would distract the competition. But for how long?

Foxy went back to his phone. "Waiting sucks."

"At least we have drinks and puzzles. My last bad wait was in a snow pile."

"You should move to warmer climates."

"I was also in soggy camouflage there. Seventeen hours without moving. Target's front yard." But this mental tension was worse. Thinking of Lena made the wait unbearable. "Eh, vikurit bi sigaretu."

"What?"

Ivan pushed the puzzle aside. "Do you think they sell cigarettes here?"

Foxy kept flipping his fork between his thin fingers, from one side of his palm to the other. "Nah, man, this is California. You can't smoke indoors anywhere. Unless it's a cigar shop. Laverne got in trouble once because kids were smoking in the bathroom at the club. She got cited for that."

Ivan picked a crumb off his plate with a fork and ate it. "Laverne does not know your real job, does she?"

Foxy shrugged. "She stopped asking questions a long time ago. She knows I solve problems. How I do it—she doesn't ask."

"My girlfriend doesn't know anything. My company sells electronics and software. It's good cover. And I get good gear." Ivan patted the laptop. "You have a normal job?"

"Not really." Foxy hesitated, his eyes thoughtful. "You could say I used to do security."

"Like a bodyguard?"

"Sort of." Foxy's gaze became attentive, sharp. "What's with all the personal questions?"

"You are like me, but you are not like me." Ah. Foxy could misinterpret this. "I mean, you are not like anyone from my organization."

Foxy grinned. "I guess I'm a unique case. A shining diamond straight from the rough. Well—maybe not straight. But definitely from the rough." Foxy stared out the café window and into the street. "I guess there's no reason why I can't tell you this—I didn't actually plan to become a professional." When he turned, the few wrinkles on his face looked deeper. "You know what I mean? It was kind of an accident."

"Me too," Ivan said. "A bad accident."

"Exactly. Not really a choice. Things just kind of happened that way."

A door swung open and a bell clinked as two men in business suits came in. The hostess rushed over to them, wearing an exaggerated grin. Ivan noted their presence but kept his attention on Foxy.

"I liked it at Laverne's club," Ivan said. "You have a lot of respect there. It's nice."

Foxy yawned and stretched. "That's because of how I started. I did protection for a while. That tends to help with the reputation. They're the folks I used to protect."

When the phone in front of them buzzed, Foxy snatched it off the table like someone else was after it.

Finally, Ivan thought. Waited long enough for any news to be good news. He waved at the waitress for a check.

Foxy flipped the phone, and pulled the battery out. "She's done it. She says he hit her, but it's not bad. She told the guards the cops are coming for him."

"I'll get the car," Ivan said, rising. "You pay."

They drove around the block in their old Honda Foxy dug up from his car supplier, rolling past the police cruiser Foxy had parked earlier in the morning. Nothing looked odd or out of place. They climbed into the cruiser without taking the cover off of it and changed into the uniforms.

When they got out, the streets were quiet, most of the houses hidden behind lush but manicured vegetation. They pulled the cover off and tossed it in the trunk.

Foxy looked Ivan over. "My mom was right, you do look good in uniform."

"I had a lot of practice."

They climbed back into the cruiser, two officers in no particular hurry. Foxy took the wheel and Ivan said, "Now we check weapons."

He pulled out the Glock, this one with a larger grip and magazine but still good for the holster he'd taken from Hoffman; he chambered a round and put the Glock back in its holster on the right side of his belt. Easy access for dominant hand.

The pistol in the ankle holster—the 'P'—was the next best thing compared to the revolvers—the smallest pistol Foxy could get on a short notice.

"Heckler and Koch make good pistols," Ivan said. "And it's nice to have a second strike capability."

"You won't need it. I don't cheap out on ammo."

"It's still nice not to eject if the round doesn't fire the first time."

"Yeah, yeah. Pull the trigger till the primer fires. I told you—my ammo is good."

Ivan slid the 'P' into his ankle holster and patted it. Nice backup option for a dual-wield shooter.

Foxy took his eyes off the road to peek over. "Wait, that's weird. Are you cross-reaching for your ankle weapon?"

Ivan shrugged. "I shoot both hands."

"No, you do not. Do you? Are you serious?"

The doubt—they didn't need to doubt each other right now. "I know what you think—not accurate if with both hands."

"You bet your ass that's what I think. She said our man Kaz has a small army with him. Shit goes wrong, I don't care if you look cool—all I care about is you hitting the fucking targets."

"Don't worry, I will hit targets. Dual wield is a Russian tradition. We call it 'strelba po Makedonski'. Macedonian style, I think, in English. My left hand is not very accurate but still good aim at short range. I can't explain how. I trained it to follow my right hand aim."

"If you say so." Foxy didn't sound convinced. "We get into the heavy shit, you better hit 'em, Mister Fancy Pants. Our shotguns in the trunk could be hard to access, ya know what I'm sayin'?"

Foxy was nervous, talking so much. But talking didn't matter now. It was time to go in.

Foxy turned the lights on as soon as they reached the villa and toggled the siren. The guard opened the gate without leaving his booth and stared at the cruiser as it drove by, lights flashing.

Ivan scanned the grounds. "The guards are gone. And no dog. I don't like it. Why are the guards gone?"

Foxy shrugged. "Think like a cop: they're his clan people, right? Not private security. Our guy Kaz wouldn't want cops to spot them, the way they look. Not with the triple homicide so fresh. Plus, I bet everything they carry is unregistered. He would tell his guys to stay back."

"I don't like it."

"Duly noted." Foxy stopped in front of the main entrance. "Now let's go meet the great and powerful wizard of Kaz. Balls deep into this shit, and I still haven't even seen the fucker."

Ivan looked through the front door's glass pane. Go or not go? Foxy's logic did work; Kazbek wouldn't want the police to see his men, not when the police were coming in to respond to an emergency phone call.

They climbed out in no hurry, checking the surroundings the way cops would. No greeters this time, no outrageous costumes, no men on leashes—just a huge stretch of lawn and the smell of freshly cut grass. Towels and drinks on the chairs by the pool. Someone had been sitting there recently.

Foxy looked at the main entrance and said quietly, "Wouldn't it be funny if we took him, and he turned out to be the wrong guy?"

"No. It will not be funny."

Foxy rang the bell, and Eva opened the door wearing a bathrobe, her face streaked by tears. Her left cheekbone was bright red and swelling. Not hurt otherwise, steady on her feet—so, a good start. With what she said about the husband, she could be mending broken bones.

Foxy was already in his police officer incarnation. "Ma'am, we are responding to a report of domestic disturbance. Would you mind if we come in?"

She nodded and turned to go back inside, a towel in her hand wrapped around a bulge. A bag of ice? She left the door open, and Foxy followed her without hesitation.

Beyond the door, the atrium looked quiet, sleepy. No guards, and Eva walked steadily, unhurt.

Ivan glanced back over the grounds. No movement, and the guard back in his booth. Everything as planned, except for this heavy feeling in the legs, muscles tightening for no good reason. Must be the old injury flaring up and pinching a nerve.

He urged himself: Go. Provide cover. Nervous now, like Foxy. Too much at stake.

He stepped in but left the door open for quick exit.

Foxy and Eva were already in the atrium. Ivan willed himself to move and walked through the short corridor.

Eva stood on the carpet, holding the towel to her cheek, saying loudly to Foxy, "Oh, I wouldn't call it a fight. My husband—he has a temper. We argue sometimes. And he gets annoyed."

They were under the grand chandelier. Shafts of daylight from the windows danced on its crystals, giving the impression of the chandelier being lit.

The place resembled Laverne's club in a way: a balcony overlooked the open space. Except instead of dance floor and catwalk, here sofas and chairs took most of the space. And the bar—smaller, made of granite semicircle—was right in front, under the balcony, not to the side.

Foxy said, "Ma'am, are you feeling okay?"

Eva sat down on a square pillow of the island sofa and blew her nose into a tissue she'd picked up from a nearby box. "I'm not hurt," she said, sounding congested, "really."

Ivan stared at her feet. She wore calfskin slippers, with tufts of white fur sticking out. Why would she wear slippers this warm on such thick carpets?

"Ma'am, we still need to talk to your husband," Foxy announced loudly. "Where is he?"

"Oh, the asshole will be here. He saw you come up the driveway." She looked up and said in a weak voice, pleading, "Would you mind closing the front door for me? It's drafty."

Ivan looked around: a couple of closed doors upstairs, an empty staircase, and a wide opening to the left of the bar. Quiet enough to hear Eva's distressed breathing.

The trip to the door and back took a few seconds, his legs feeling better. When Ivan returned to the sofas, Eva coughed. In one quick movement, she rose to her feet and headed for the granite crescent of the bar. She reached for a glass from an overhead rack.

A wine glass? Nothing unnatural about the way she did it, but her movement was awkward: her fingers pinched the stem of the glass and slipped off, clumsy like you would expect from a woman in distress, but still—too clumsy.

Who used a wine glass to drink water?

She dropped the glass; it shattered on a section of the floor around the bar where the carpet didn't cover the polished marble.

She wasn't thirsty.

Ivan had his hand on his Glock and was shouting, "Foxy, take cover!" when she dove and disappeared behind the bar as if to pick up the broken glass. The doors upstairs banged open.

Ivan raised his Glock and put it down at once: rifles and shotguns, everyone in armored vests. A shooter in the hallway, aiming. Useless, the pistol. He tossed it to the floor.

Foxy sat crouched near the sofa, hand on his holster but not drawing. Good decision. Would be a bloodbath.

Someone shouted, "Show your hands or die!"

Foxy slowly raised his empty hands. His tone was playful, but with a strain. "We surrender, we surrender. Ain't no Bonny and Clyde here."

"On your knees! Put your hands over your eyes!" Amir, pointing his short AKSU rifle. Still in the track suit under a bulletproof vest. Probably wouldn't remember who gave him a flat tire and a terrible hangover.

"That's a new one," Foxy mumbled, kneeling. "A Chechen version of hide and seek."

Ivan let his knees sink into soft carpet. A prisoner for the first time, after almost two decades of war. Fooled by a woman with cute doggies. Good actress. Tears and fear and everything. Broke her glass for a signal.

Through a gap between his fingers, he glanced at Eva, who watched them from behind the bar, her mouth tight, arms crossed on her chest. She wasn't going to be kind. Time to be afraid, certainly. Nothing good would come from her Chechens. All these men wrapped around her thin fingers. She wasn't clumsy. Not at all.

Amir came down and collected their weapons. He and another one he called Murat, they hog-tied them in under a minute with well-practiced movements. Amir pulled the cell phone out of Ivan's pocket, snapped it open, and said something in Chechen. A reply came from above in a gruff, new voice, and Amir shoved the phone back in.

Not a good sign, when they put the phone back on the body this way. Even if it's a cheap burner with a single call in the log.

Ivan waited for his fear to kick in as plastic ties bit into his wrists and ankles, but the fear never arrived. Their complete and utter failure rendered everything meaningless, every worry obsolete.

A paradox. Powerless to act, but in this way unburdened, set free by captivity. At least for a few seconds.

Amir said something in Chechen again, and the same gruff voice said from the staircase, "Actually, my wife and I sometimes call ourselves Bonny and Clyde. But if you two are playing them, then which one of you is Bonny?"

"I'll take Bonny," Foxy said. "That girl could rock a beret."

The man chuckled. "Then you're the one we'll fuck first."

The voice was behind Ivan now, and he rolled over to see the man speaking. He didn't get to see anyone: as soon as he attempted a barrel roll, someone kicked him hard in the head and everything went blurry.

"You don't move," Amir said.

Ivan clenched his teeth, wishing to go back in time to that night in the Ferrari. He swallowed his anger along with a metallic taste of blood. So much for feeling elated. Get ready for an ugly interrogation. Kazbek would want answers. And Eva would want her dogs back.

Answer their questions, Ivan thought, and you'll never see Lena again.

He was still debating how long he'd last before giving them the answers when strong hands lifted and carried him deeper into the house, out of the atrium, past the bar, and then down a long staircase.

The dungeon. The same dungeon where Eva smashed the bound man's genitalia one straight jab after another.

From somewhere below, Foxy said, "Boys, you oughta look into buying a deodorant. Your armpits stink."

Nobody laughed, or sneered, or said anything.

35

East Los Angeles, California

The house heaved and shook Miguel off his chair. A thundering noise—broken dishes—everyone on the floor, coughing, dust falling on them from the ceiling.

Earthquake!

Didn't the old man say Los Angeles was overdue for a big one? No. Unlikely. Earthquakes weren't this loud. And the windows—the closed curtains caught most of the broken glass, but some of the shards in the kitchen blew in past the sink. Inward blast. And the almond smell, mixed into smoke wafting through gaping holes where the windows used to be.

Plastic explosives!

Miguel shouted, "Positiones!' and scrambled for his rifle, leaned against the wall but now on the floor.

Ears ringing: e-e-e-e.

Their training kicked in, the instinct to dominate the room: Seso by the windows, Dado to the entrance, Cho kneeling and taking aim at the garage door, everyone with their rifles raised, expecting some form of assault. Flashbangs flying in? CS gas?

Car alarms were going off all over the neighborhood—Miguel could hear them despite the ringing in his ears. He thought: at least my eardrums didn't blow out.

He moved in a crouch to a window and peeked into the yard over the sights of his rifle, ready to shoot down anyone moving through he acrid smoke.

The thought made him livid with anger: did the whore sell me out? She was clever with her games. Too clever.

But in front of the house, there wasn't any movement. He tiptoed upstairs and looked out on the backyard. Nothing. Old man's plants and the fence, intact.

Important not to make noise. Nobody rushing in didn't mean they weren't waiting for them to run. Smoke blew through the broken window, the smell of burned rubber filling Miguel's nose.

The house could be on fire: the attackers smoking out the men inside, smoke so thick it was hard not to cough.

Miguel picked up the assault map blown to the floor; crumpled, it fit into his thigh pocket. His men all made eye contact with him, except the kid. Too damn focused on his sector. Only turned when a glass shard hit him in the cheek.

Miguel signaled to everyone to exit. Glass crunched under their feet as they left the room. They came out the back in pairs, rifles sweeping every sector, Cho in the middle, Dado covering from the back. All smooth, and nobody coughing.

Still no movement in the yard. Miguel aimed around the corner of the house, at Antonio's truck, burning, along with the fence and the closest corner of the house—the explosion had blown the gate off its hinges and into the street, but no one was coming through the opening.

A car bomb? Police would never detonate a bomb like this. And the truck hadn't moved since the old man returned.

Miguel's jaw tightened. "Coño! The asshole knows we are here."

Nobody heard him, their hearing off, too.

Black smoke from the truck billowed onto the house, the red and orange flames growing taller, feeding off the shingles. Miguel signaled for them to move out, the kid doing it right—never looked away from the sights of his rifle or lowered his weapon as they headed toward the back fence, behind the garage.

Dado shouted, "Contacto!" and Miguel jerked his rifle to take aim at the sole figure in the opening where the gate used to be. The man froze with his mouth open, staring at the smoldering carcass of the truck, at the barely recognizable outline of a human body smoldering on the grass.

Miguel lowered his rifle. "Hold fire! It's Rafa. Our spotter." He waved at the man. "Go! Get out of here! The cops are coming!"

The spotter regained his senses and disappeared behind the burning fence.

At the other end of the property, Seso had already pulled the planks of the back fence aside. After a quick check, they slipped through the gap and into the backyard of the adjacent house. It was wise to move the residents out of this one. You don't pick a safe house. You pick a safe zone with an escape vehicle hidden and ready to go.

Their feet sunk into the flowerbeds as they moved along the

house's outer wall toward the pickup.

"Where's Tio?" Cho asked.

Miguel squeezed out the words: "He's dead."

Seso checked the street, on the radio with other spotters; at least he could hear them talking, even with all this ringing in the ears. In cover, they watched their sectors until Seso gestured for all-clear.

The men climbed into the truck bed and lay down, after which Miguel pulled a tarp over them; this pickup had the same long toolboxes on each side as Antonio's truck, but if the cops brought in the helicopters, they'd see the men in the bed from the air.

Miguel took the wheel and started the engine. He glanced back at the billowing smoke as he drove off. Tio, the old man. Burning next to his truck.

The vision was unnerving and brought up an odd tightness in Miguel's chest—he'd gotten used to the old fool.

"Asshole blew up my uncle," he mumbled through gritted teeth, shaking his head. "I let the old believer go back to his women, and the asshole blows him up on the way out."

He drove them out of the area, not too fast, not too slow. A few police cruisers flew by, their sirens muffled by the damage to his ears. He looked up when a helicopter roared above somewhere—good thinking on the tarp; gringos here rich enough to buy helicopters for their police departments.

The entire drive to the warehouse, he fought the urge to drive straight to the villa and kill everyone inside.

No. Reckless, without some thinking. The Chechen made his move, sure. But why now? A diversion? Yet the lookouts weren't calling in about anyone leaving the villa. And if the car bomb wasn't a diversion, then what was it?

At the corner, amidst rows of warehouses and wire fences, a bored spotter in a car nodded as they drove past—no signs of trouble here.

Miguel drove to the last warehouse at the cul-de-sac, stepped out of the truck, and rolled the warehouse door down. "We're home. Come out."

His men hopped out, stretching and patting the dust out of their clothes.

"Come here." Miguel spread their assault plan map on a table made of shipping crates in the middle of the empty floor, and they took their seats on old chairs.

"Tio was by the truck," Dado said, "wasn't he?"

"We must make them pay for it," Cho said. "He was our uncle."

Dado gave the kid a condescending look. "What do you care? You barely talked to him."

Stupid bickering. "He was nobody's uncle," Miguel said.

"But he was family, no?" Cho said. The kid learning the value of his brotherhood. Finally showing some understanding of what's important.

"True," Miguel said heavily. "That's what's making me mad." He looked at Seso, who laid out two cell phones on the table. Waiting for the lookouts to call in. "I think the truck got wired at the villa."

"It's possible." Seso scratched his chin. "Tio would park his truck inside when he went there, no?"

"So you also think the Chechen knows we're here. You have any other explanation?" Miguel turned to stare at Dado.

"No, Jefe, it's not the girls," Dado said quickly. "You know I pick them at random." Dado looked at his brother, who nodded. Dado's face showed no signs of doubt when he returned to his boss. "I'm certain it's not the girls."

"He blew up our truck but didn't hit the house," Seso said.

Dado nodded. "They blow up our vehicle in the morning when no one is supposed to be in it. To scare us off? He knows we don't scare."

"Maybe he was nearby when the truck blew up," Cho said, "watching what we'll do."

Miguel shook his head. "Our lookouts would see him."

"He could be working with the police," Seso said. "Only he figured he doesn't know where we are, so he tagged our truck. The truck goes off and cops swarm the place. The cops go after us, and while they keep us busy, he takes off to Sinaloa."

This was a reasonable thought. "You think he's gonna run?"

Seso nodded. "And it would be easier to take him off the street if he moves out in a rush. I suggest we wait and watch the villa." He waved his hand at the cell phones on the table. "Let's hear from the lookouts. I say we wait for a chance to take him on the move. And if our men say nobody's leaving, we go in."

"We should hit him now," Dado said, "while he thinks we are busy. He's not expecting anyone. Best time to come in. If he takes off, he'd be hard to catch."

Dado, itching to start shooting. They all were, except Seso. He liked thinking more than shooting.

"Seso," Miguel said. The man raised his calm, thoughtful eyes. "If we wait and your lookouts miss him, I'm gonna have to wait a long time to catch up to him. And it will be your fault."

"Let me talk to everyone, see what they see." The thinking man sticking with his judgment.

Dado shook his head. "Hermano, enough with the scouting. It's time to attack. They're not expecting us, and the second truck is ready. Tio put more steel into it last night."

Miguel stared at the map. The cops would come for the explosion at Tio's house. The Chechen using someone else again to do his work, just like in Tamaulipas when the Americans made all that fuss about their agents dying. That was bad for business and a real insult, being used like that. But Seso's argument was good, even if they were all itching to pull triggers. Picking someone up out of the car was much safer than fighting in close quarters.

Miguel flexed his fists. "Shit. Now I have to wait again."

He forced his fists open and flattened the edges of the assault plan with his palms. Tio—he was a scared old fool, but at least he provided the villa's ground-floor plan. The rest would be easy to figure out once inside.

"Let's get the kits ready. This will take time." Miguel nodded at Seso. "Call them. Ask if they saw anything new. Meanwhile, let's talk it through, street or house. Either way, we're doing it today."

Everyone nodded, no hesitation in any of them. Trusting the boss.

Cho, rising, said, "Tio was family."

Miguel nodded. "Seguro. It's past personal by now."

"Jefe, if we go in, we'd have to get in quiet. In that neighborhood, the police will come quickly." For once, the kid looked busy thinking.

"I don't care about the police. If they come, we'll take care of them. When they kill one of ours, we settle the score no matter what."

36

Los Angeles Westside, California

The basement floor felt cold against his cheek. Ivan studied the clean, concrete surface in front of his face. This explained why Eva was wearing warm slippers—she spent a lot of time in her dungeon. What a woman. A real actress, with tears and that great line: "My husband beats me."

This is what you get when you rush everything and don't trust your instincts, Ivan thought. You end up rushing into a trap.

From a room at the end of the hall came a long scream, a lungful. Foxy—still conscious. And still resisting. Good man. Keeping himself and his partner alive.

Ivan rolled over and looked into the hallway where the food trays used to be. Empty now, which explained why the sound traveled so well.

Eva's voice came from somewhere further down the hall, probably from one of the rooms at the end. "If you didn't bring my dogs, where are they?"

Foxy's scream turned into a guttural grunt. Already they were making him unintelligible, which meant they would soon switch their attention to the prisoner next door.

Ivan looked across the hall at the wardrobe he'd seen at Eva's party. What did Foxy call this? A 'grope box'. That young girl went in to be grabbed through the holes. White circles still there, painted on the exterior. Groping—seemed pretty innocent now, compared to whatever they were doing to Foxy.

He rolled over his hands to face the inside of the room. The zip-ties dug deeper into his ankle-bound wrists, his back arched backward with only his head free to move. His legs had turned numb—not enough circulation. He pulled on the restraints, fighting the searing pain in his lower back.

The Chechens sure knew how to hogtie a man—the strain made breaking the zip ties impossible.

The harness that used to suspend a woman from the ceiling was gone, the party long over. Now the platform was empty, a stage without performers. Or expecting one? In the middle of the platform, on top under a spotlight from a ceiling lamp, stood a long rectangular glass box. A short pipe stuck out from the lid. The tank walls looked like they were made of thick green glass.

A fish tank? This would explain the trickle of water going into the drain in the corner. But what kind of fish tank had a welded steel frame wrapped around glass walls? And why did the lid have latches?

Footsteps sounded from the staircase, a skipping step. Amir, coming down. Here it comes.

Ivan shuddered as a sharp pain exploded from his kidney all the way up to his neck. Amir aimed the tip of his boot real well, hooked it somehow to go around his prisoner's arms, going for a soft spot.

"I told you not to move."

One kick seemed to satisfy the bastard. The sound of Amir's footsteps receded into the hall, where a conversation in Chechen broke out. The steps returned, and Amir's voice came from behind. "Your skinny friend is not doing so good." Sounding gleeful.

When Eva giggled near his feet, Ivan glanced down on reflex. She walked in, closing the folds of the bath robe. He caught a view of her bare thigh: No underwear. Naked? What was she doing to Foxy that she had to be naked for? Wild woman. But at least she didn't go for the kidney kick—she merely stepped around and walked up to the fish tank.

Kazbek's voice sounded from behind. "Baby, you sure you want to bother with this one?"

Eva went to the tank on the platform, stuck her arm under the lid, and splashed her hand in the water. "Why not? You said we have to wait. May just as well have fun and see if he talks."

A fan hidden behind the grill in the ceiling came alive with a rattle. Ivan braced himself for the worst. Eva's idea of fun promised a deluge of blackout-level pain.

A pair of leather loafers came into view, and Kazbek leaned over in his polo shirt and slacks. "Are you worried about your partner at all?"

No point answering.

"Not talking? You're like your partner. You know—he's not telling us where you guys are from or who sent you. I know you're not working for the narcos. My wife thinks you could be Serbian. Some people in Belgrade think I owe them. Why don't you just tell us?"

"You will still kill me."

Kazbek snorted. "Well, what else am I supposed to do? You haven't left me much choice. Also, you took my wife's babies." Kazbek shook his finger like a parent scolding his child. "She was really mad when you grabbed them. Although—good idea with that film. I have to say, I almost went with her to your house. That would have been unfortunate."

"Let's see if he's more talkative after a swim," Eva said.

Kazbek turned toward the hallway. "Amir!" He added something in Chechen, and his shoes disappeared from view.

Ivan felt multiple hands grab his ankles and shoulders. They carried him high above the floor, above the platform, and into the blinding light of the lamp. There, they pushed him over. His face, arms, wrists, and knuckles scraped against the steel edge as he fell into the tank face-first.

Once he landed in the water, he wriggled to turn over for a breath, but the tank was too narrow. At least they noticed—a pair of strong hands flipped him sideways.

White steel flickered in the light. A knife! Not good, for the knife to come out this early. But Kazbek merely leaned into the tank, saying, "Lie still. I'm going to cut a few ties so you can stretch."

The release in his joints was heavenly—Ivan stretched his legs and finished the turn to face the light. Not a bad start for whatever torture they had in mind, even if the water was cold.

Kazbek's beard hovered over the tank, the man not even Chechen looking, his hair all sandy instead of black. Big nose. So that's a similarity—they all had big noses.

Kazbek leaned in, hands on the edge. "Hey. I'll tell you a secret." He glanced over his shoulder and lowered his voice. "I wish you had killed her fucking dogs. They drive me crazy. They hunt my best shoes as if they were rats. They chew them up." He sighed theatrically. "But she loves her dogs, and I love her. Bitches rule the world." He pointed with his thumb over his shoulder. "Anyway, I don't know if you could hear it, but your partner gave us a great performance. We liked that. I hope you can do the same. My wife goes wild when it's real."

Rambling? Not only perverted, but insane.

Kazbek's face disappeared. When he returned, an end of a garden hose dangled from his hand. "You know—my wife really thought we could make a quality film with you guys. She still wants the film, I tell you. But you're going to be the star this time. I'll give you directions— we like pain mixed with some good struggle. It's the best. If you mix

280

sex with good pain, it never gets old. You married?"

The Chechen all friendly. Maybe cooperate? "No, not yet."

Kazbek shook his head. "Then you don't know. I tell you—marriage is not good for desire. So you have to get creative." He grinned. "You partner really warmed her up. I was touching her, and she was moaning louder that he was. She got all horny. And with this thing—" He patted the side of the tank. "—I bet I can go a couple of times with her if her idea works."

Her idea? Horny? They were doing all this to help with sex?

Kazbek came around the tank and lifted the lid, holding it upright. His voice was full of pride. "My wife is a real artist. She designed the rack." He motioned at the room behind him with his thumb. "And this aquarium thing. I had it custom made. I mean, she wants to know where her dogs are, but I hope you can resist for a while. She's sexy when she's frustrated. Her cheeks get all rosy. She gets feisty. I love fucking her when she's like that. So, put up a struggle, okay?"

The heavy lid swung down and hit its rubber seals with a thud, and then the latches clicked. Thick glass muted Kazbek's voice, but his words came through clear enough. "Baby, come watch him when we fill it!"

Eva's white gown joined Kazbek's dark form. "Let me do it! Let me do it!" Her bright silhouette loomed over the tank, and through the opening in the lid a rubber pipe slid in.

So. That's what why the lid had the cut of pipe protruding: to fill the tank to the top with the lid closed.

When the water burst in, Ivan lifted his upper body off the bottom, keeping his head above water. Useless, though. Can't get past the lid with wrists still tied.

Eva's face came near the glass, her outline muddled. Curious? Liked to stare at her exotic fish? Crazy woman. Gone. Made Foxy look ordinary.

Ivan shivered in the cold water. No sharp edges here to break the ties against. But at least some mobility would help keep the face up and float. What did he say? Put up a struggle. They didn't want an outright drowning. Eva wanted her spectacle.

He bumped his forehead against the lid, the water high enough to float close to the top. The air from inside the tank escaped through the gap between the pipe glued into the lid and the hose. He found the gap with his lips and sucked in a breath.

Was this what they wanted? Watching a man drown? Ivan arched his back and tucked his legs under to keep his lips close to the opening. The pipe moved aside when he pushed it with his tongue.

The gurgling of water stopped, and the rubber scratched his tongue as the hose flicked out of the pipe. He wrapped his lips along the opening like some bottom-crawling fish with a sucker mouth; whenever the water splashed over his face and mouth, he swallowed it and kept breathing.

He caught sight of their outlines coming closer. Now they would start. A hand came over the opening—he smelled soap as they plugged his last breath.

Hold it. Heartbeat so loud. Ear pressure. Hold it.

His abs spasmed, and he flexed every muscle in a desperate attempt to stay at the opening. When agony reached its peak, he exhaled into the pipe, the pressure pushing the air right back. He thrashed and shivered and convulsed until a vague thought arrived: going to black out right now. But he saw the light coming through—air!

Ivan sucked in a fresh breath, pulling hard and coughing the water out. The hand came back on, and he kicked the glass in violent anger. Blyadi, playing a sick game. And she hasn't even asked about the dogs yet.

They plugged and unplugged the pipe. Eva? Kazbek? Having a good show, the bastards, judging by the giggling and thumping.

Ivan, his head in a fog, worked to keep his tongue in the opening. This time when the pipe opened, it stayed open, and he caught a few extra breaths. Along with the air came the sound of Eva's moaning. Ivan ignored it and gulped the air greedily.

Breathe. Get to Lena. Be her husband. Be a father to her child.

They closed the pipe again and the hand came off only when his face banged into the lid in a spasm. His mouth found the pipe, but his feet slipped off the tank's wall, and he sank to the bottom.

Done. Drowning.

More thoughts rushed in, sharpened by bodily panic: did they stop watching? Why aren't they asking about her Pomeranians? They must break ribs to resuscitate. Alive but half-dead all the same. Six percent of people revived keep their brain function. Six percent. Six. The lucky ones.

Die now or live as a vegetable. She'd be alone either way.

Furious, he screamed the last of his air into the water. They noticed—a beam of light shined through the opening. Up. Find it. Here. Inhale.

He was mid-breath when they poured water into the pipe. He

coughed and banged his head into the lid. Goddamn bastards—laughing. Would they pour water again? Didn't matter. Clean air this time. Just a game to them. Difficult to stay close to the pipe.

They poured water as he inhaled. Amidst the agony, the temptation of giving up grew and grew—just breathe in water and black out. No more ripping pain in the lungs. Ten minutes with lungs full of fluid, and any resuscitation would fail. Blissful oblivion.

He twisted sideways, his feet pushing against the opposite pane for leverage, shadows of Eva and Kazbek right in front of him.

He pressed his face against the glass: Come closer. I'll tell you in simple English—fuck you. Come here. Watch me pull the curtains on your freaky spectacle.

37

East Los Angeles, California

It was a long wait. When the call came in, Miguel snatched the phone off the table. "Que pasa?"

The electrician sounded flat, like when they met by the villa. "All I have is the same police car. They've been inside for a while."

"Have you seen them go in?"

"Two police, a skinny one and a fat one. No one else."

"Are you sure?" Threaten him a little. See how long he takes to respond.

"Absolutely."

"Keep watching the gate." Miguel tossed the phone on the table. All his men were looking at him. He nodded. "I'm tired of waiting. They have two local police inside. It's going to be busy in there."

"Are they black?" Cho said. "I've never killed a black one before."

Little idiot. "What does it matter? You're not choosing a whore. Black or white, he'll be shooting at you regardless." And to Seso: "How far is the ambulance?"

"Let me check."

The ambulance was worth the wait. From Irvine—where was that? But good thinking from Seso, getting the ambulance—the guard in the booth might let it in on a look if the lights were flashing. And much better for getaway.

Miguel examined the layout of the villa for the hundredth time. The bar opposite the main entrance—Tio had been sure it was there. It would be tricky, filtering in if a cop or someone else sat behind it and shot at them coming in.

Seso's phone buzzed. "Our car is here."

Miguel stood up. "Con Dios." They stood and waited for him to look them over. He gave them a nod. Weapons checked, radios, long ago.

Seso brought the ambulance in, and they got in the back. As they rode, the benches got uncomfortable after a while.

"Jefe," Cho said, "maybe we use the siren to get through this fucking city."

"Not on the way in." But tempting. They were all thinking it.

Miguel turned his mind back to the entry. Always the stickiest point, the entry.

Cho had his head between his legs, like he was about to puke. A knock on his helmet brought him up. The kid's skin was pale white.

"I told you not to drink tequila last night," Miguel said.

The kid looked miserable. "I only had one because Dado had one."

"Dado can drink like a horse—it doesn't bother him. Now, what did I tell you about movement?"

"Slow makes fast."

"Exactly. Don't go rushing ahead if I put you on point."

"Jefe?"

"What?"

"How come you don't let us use a little perico?"

"Because it makes you jump ahead like a mad goat. You can't think straight on it. Drink coffee. It'll help you think straight."

"We're getting close," Seso said from the driver's seat.

Dado moved forward with his suppressed rifle.

Miguel turned to look out of the window. Get inside the tall fences without too much fuss—from there, the hedges and the fences would block the noise, even if El Checheño's men pin them down at the entrance.

"Qué suerte," he said when the gates swung open as if the guard expected the ambulance. A bit strange, Miguel thought, but you don't question luck.

Dado's rifle snapped with a suppressed shot, and Seso went into the booth under the cover of the ambulance to close the gate.

They pulled up the driveway, past the door, and stopped right behind the police car.

Miguel took a look through the back window at two guards talking to each other near the house entrance, oblivious. Why weren't they alarmed by the ambulance? And what was that—a fucking pet lion? Sitting on its haunches like a giant statue.

"Hola," Miguel said through his teeth and pushed the ambulance doors open. Dado and Cho hopped out behind him, quick to spread out.

An upward burst at the guard, chest to head, spun the guard around. The dog! It launched into the air. Damn it—too slow with the barrel!

Miguel fired another burst and missed—Coño! The beast smashed into him and knocked him on his back. Cussing, he climbed from under it, covered in blood. From above, Dado offered a hand. "Jefe, everything good?"

The guards lay dead on the steps, Cho pulling the second one to the side by the feet. That's three assholes and one dog down, in total. Based on the headcount from Tio and the lookouts, at least four or five more men inside. So, almost even now. And still using surprise. "Seso, shotgun," he said into the mouthpiece of his radio. "Cho, on point. Dado, cover."

Cho, his rifle clipped into a sling, stood ready to go inside, white teeth showing in a crazy grin. The kid didn't need no cocaine. He'd fire full-auto at anyone inside. Fast little devil. With more training, the kid would be a good soldier.

Miguel adjusted his helmet. Still jittery from the dog. Shaken. What a start. Damn it—the beast stretched a meter and a half.

He pulled a pair of goggles over his eyes. So uncomfortable, these things. But if the raid got hot, a little discomfort would be worth it. Without these, it was impossible to see who was shooting at whom in a room full of dust. Eye protection, with nice yellow tint. Helped with aiming.

Seso, ready to breach with his shotgun, said quietly, "It's open," and moved away from the door to his spot in the middle of the stack, right behind the kid.

Miguel squeezed Cho's shoulder twice; the little devil nodded and pushed the door to open a crack.

Another lucky break: the guards had kept the door unlocked.

Seso pushed it open, and Cho slipped in quickly—they had to keep up to move in as one, with Dado left behind them to cover the grounds with his carbine.

From a half-crouch, they sprung into the hallway, bodies moving in unison.

The bar, up ahead. Keep the bead on the bar and anyone around it.

From the corridor, they split to cover the corners. Damn the kid—he never finished the sweep. Firing on his way in—at whom? Bueno. To the right, the two guards in the middle of the room—dead on the sofas. Never picked up their rifles. Good shooting from the kid. Nice to see him reload right away, his gun never coming down.

Seso already covered the left—the hall? Must be to the kitchen.

Balcony—clear. Next, take care of the rifles: Miguel had popped the top covers off the dead men's AKs to pull out the recoil springs, which he tossed behind the bar—nobody would find them. He put the covers back on so the rifles would look operable if someone wanted to grab them in a hurry.

Everyone was in position: muzzles up, far enough from the walls to avoid stray bullets flying along the surface.

Quiet so far, all the shots suppressed. But that was about to change. No time to clear every room here, not with three men total in the unit and the house so big.

Miguel pulled a semi-automatic from his hip holster. "Everyone ready?"

"Listo," Cho said, and Seso echoed the word.

Miguel covered his ear and fired a shot into one of the dead guards; he waited for the sound to spread past the doors, through the walls and halls, a chapel bell calling the congregation to worship.

They sat in a crouch, listening. Frustrating silence hung over the room, a cloud of disappointment. Room-to-room clearing would be slow. And risky. Miguel smiled when he heard the steps—always better to let the idiots come to you.

Seso moved at an oblique angle from his position half-way along the wall and fired a burst into a hallway opening near the bar and then bounced back. Good thing he did: whoever he shot had a backup; the wall behind Seso's original position exploded with fragments of concrete and paint.

Dust flew everywhere, and Miguel grabbed his nose to hold a sneeze. Good decision on the goggles.

Seso's calm voice came on the radio. "One down, one in cover. I don't hear movement, but my ears are ringing from his shots."

Miguel glanced at the slumped bodies on the sofa. How many now? The guard from the gate, two by the door, and two here, plus one by Seso. Six. How many left, scattered through the house, aware now that they have visitors? Whoever's left would regroup to protect the top guy. Wherever the shots were coming from, it could be cops or another guard—or El Checheño himself.

Miguel said into his mouth piece: "Cho, cover," and came behind Seso, now crouched by the bar, around the corner from the corridor. "Seso, hold still."

He let his rifle hang from its strap to free his hands then reached for the pouch attached to the back of Seso's tactical vest. The fragmentation grenade fit neatly into his gloved hand. A fun part—

throwing in a frag. Not like in the army, with your instructor or your commanding officer always talking about effective hostage rescue. None of that shit. No need to throw flashbangs to keep the stupid hostages unharmed. So much more fun. So much easier when it was all straight kills.

"Granada!"

Miguel pulled the pin and threw the hissing grenade into the hallway, aiming high to send it skipping off the ceiling. He covered his ears, Seso doing the same.

BOOM!

A cloud of dust and debris mixed with shrapnel tore out of the opening. Seso lurched forward as soon as he got the squeeze on his shoulder.

"Rápido! Rápido!"

Down the corridor, Seso fired into the twitching leg sticking out from behind the opening on the right. Door? Yes, another room Tio mentioned.

"Espera!" Miguel shouted.

Too late. Seso, the wise one, didn't stop, running past a room entrance without clearing it. Not so wise. Missed the door in the dark and dust.

"Pinche—"

A gun barrel emerged from the opening.

Recoil kicked into his wrist. Too late—the back of Seso's vest puffed out from the impact. And his earlobe—the silver earring flickered and disappeared as a bullet sliced through cartilage.

Miguel moved forward, shooting left to right, emptying a magazine. Past the doorway, a body on its back. Pistol. Controlled shot to the head to stop the weird arm twitch. Clear the room. Reload.

"Cho, Seso's down," Miguel said. "Cover me."

Seso lay face down on the floor to the left of a staircase leading downstairs. Miguel pulled him hard by the ankles, away from the stairs, and picked another grenades off his back.

"Granada!"

One more, off the wall, down the steps. Covered his ears.

BOOM!

More smoke and dust. Good and bad, throwing grenades in the house. The walls would contain the noise, but the blast waves were really tricky in closed space.

Seso moved, grunting into his radio, short of breath. "Estoy bien."

Gracias, Dios. Seso, the wise asshole. Impossible to replace. Years together. Couldn't just go out and buy a guy like this one. Miguel helped Seso sit up. "You're lucky."

Seso groaned. "I don't feel lucky." He reached for his missing ear. "Puta madre."

Miguel eyed thick burgundy of blood mixed with dust on the side of Seso's head. Not too bad of a bleed. "Give us cover. We're close."

He peeked around the corner—muzzle flash!—and jerked his head back. Debris bit into his cheek. Almost got his head blown off. "Shooter at the bottom!" he shouted. "Must be the basement!" That was number eight. How many men did they have in this damn house?

He fired a shot around the corner without looking, and a burst came back. Asshole. What was at the bottom of the stairs? Hard to visualize in all this shit—the steps turned left from the landing.

He pulled the pin on a third grenade and lobbed it down the stairs, aiming to bounce it off the wall. Shot from downstairs ripped through drywall.

Damn—almost caught it in the arm. Smart asshole down there. Shooting through corners and soft walls.

BOOM!

The explosion, compressed and directed by the narrow passage, pushed outward like slow ocean surf.

Everyone coughed. How were the lights still working? Find the circuit breaker and kill the power—go in monocular with night vision. No. This will delay everything and ruin their momentum.

"Cho, take point. Seso, cover. Vamonos."

Cho didn't hesitate and pushed ahead like it didn't matter. Crazy little devil.

They moved down the stairs single-file along the shredded wall to the right, their red dots dancing on the corner to the left of the landing. An arm! They fired at the same time into the opening and through the corner. A cry of pain. Finally!

They rounded the corner. A guy missing half his face slumped against the wall, good as dead. Some kind of athletic suit. Football?

Cho stepped on the last step. Miguel aimed above a string of lights on the floor. Like the landing strip at the airport. Muzzle flash!

"Retira—" He yanked the kid backward by the vest, and they fell back as a snap of bullets hit the wall behind where Cho had been. One shooter.

"Jefe, I saw him!" the kid yelled.

"Shut up. I saw him, too." Red beard. Couldn't be anyone else but

El Checheño, firing from cover.

At last, Miguel thought, licking his lips. You shit-eating coward. We are coming for you. Your best choice is to kill yourself.

He released a mostly-spent magazine and picked a fresh one off the front of his harness, saying into his mouthpiece, "Has anyone seen the fucking cops?"

38

Los Angeles Westside, California

They ignored him, staying away from the glass. Ivan returned to the pipe, found the opening with his tongue, and sealed it with his lips. His shivering had subsided, although the water didn't get much warmer. Hypothermia? He spat his exhalation into the pipe and drew a deep breath.

Anger is the best motivator. Sons of bitches. I'm not going to drown. Not yet.

This time they didn't notice he was breathing freely; he was dizzy from hyperventilation when Eva's giggling and moaning stopped.

Do your damn interrogation already, he thought. Let's play the word game. But their separate, vague outlines moved away, and their voices grew loud with urgency.

Leaving? Why?

TA-DUM. TA-DUM.

A charge of current shot through his body at the sweetest sound in the world—the crack of gunfire. A hallucination? He took a slow breath and went under the water to press his ear into the opening.

TA-DUM. TA-DUM. TA-DUM.

Single shots. The unmistakable beat of a Kalashnikov. Who was it? It didn't matter—it was a chance.

He flipped his head for a breath and put the ear back up. Between gunfire, Kazbek shouted, and Eva too, her voice a shriek over Amir barking out Chechen words. Someone crashing the sadists' party? Like that rescue by gunship. Long-awaited Krokodil helicopter roaring into the mess of scorched vehicles in Helmand. Rockets with flechette warheads. Hello and goodbye.

Ivan dove in, charged with renewed energy, and strained his eyes to see beyond the glass. Moving silhouettes. Flickers of light. Muzzle flashes?

He put his ear to the pipe and winced at the explosive sound of rapid gunfire. Real firefight! Not a hallucination! He found the pipe with his tongue to take another breath, the air now sour from burnt gunpowder.

Time to get out. Risky, but possible.

He dove in and flexed his abdomen to bring his feet against the lid, but the lame kick slipped off. Latches over glass. Solid metalwork. Not going to give.

He came up for another breath but never reached the pipe.

BOOM!

Pain in his eardrums—an invisible force lifted and tossed the tank sideways, and he spun in the water, disoriented, and banged his head on the glass as the tank crashed off the platform. All the water—gone. Easy breathing.

The thick glass and water had taken the brunt of the impact. The glass hung loose from its metal frame, a spider web of fractures across the entire sheet of the tank wall.

Glass shards. Cut the ties. Let's go.

He coughed, slid around, and brought his feet up. The sheet of fractured glass fell out after one kick; good thing they never bothered taking off his boots. He ignored the bite of glass on his ankle. Shallow cut. No time to worry about it now.

It took some rolling around, but he found the sliver of glass sticking out and worked his wrist ties with the sharp edge. His shoulders groaned with pleasure when the ties gave in. The lamp over the platform was out but the hallway remained well lit, light coming in through the entrance.

Movement. Kazbek!

Across the hall, the Chechen ran up and took cover behind the grope box, a submachine gun in his hands. Kazbek fired a few blind shots from cover. Without water suppressing the noise, the gun report was deafening; the Chechen was shooting at someone nearby, someone on the stairs.

Kazbek turned his face to the fish tank room and shouted, "Get over here! Get behind me!"

Ivan stared at him, confused until he realized Kazbek was calling for Eva.

She sat in the corner to the left of the entrance, still in her bathrobe, her hands over her ears, her face buried between her knees. Shell-shocked.

It was obvious Kazbek couldn't see inside the dark room; he couldn't see the broken fish tank. But whoever was coming, Kazbek wouldn't hold them off for long. They'd come down in an assault formation, firing at anything that moves.

Ivan hesitated. Play dead or take Eva? If it was the Mexicans, they weren't coming for Eva.

Kazbek put his gun down and reached over the grope box like he was grabbing a spare magazine from the top.

Ivan focused on Kazbek's fingers. Out of ammo?

Kazbek's hand came back empty, and he leaned into the box with his shoulder, pushing hard, his back leg slipping. The grope box rotated on its axis, and a wide, black gap opened to Kazbek's left. Fluorescent lights flickered on inside the opening.

Must be another torture chamber. Or his control room. Play room?

Kazbek stood in the full cover the box provided, holding it open with his weight. "Baby, come on! Run! Run!"

Ivan stepped to the wall near the entrance. Bullets banged against the box, but none of them hit Kazbek. Shots from the stairs sounded like sneezing, the gunfire suppressed.

Standing flush with the wall, Ivan took a careful glance into the hallway, past Kazbek. Where was Amir? He looked down at Eva, who sat with her hands covering her ears. Concussed, or her eardrums had blown out. Shivering. Her fun was over.

Ivan looked out, at the lights behind Kazbek. Hidden staircase. A clear opportunity. Nado brat. He pushed off his low crouch and slipped. Damn water. He recovered and bolted out of the platform room, crossed the hall in two steps, and smashed his left shoulder into Kazbek's chest.

The way they collided, Ivan drove right through Kazbek's body, and they fell into the opening.

Kazbek waved his arms and grabbed onto a railing or a handle on the wall as they fell, but their momentum ripped his hand right off. The floor disappeared as they stumbled forward, rolling over each other.

Tuck your head in, Ivan thought. Roll. Grab him. This is my territory now, kozel. Welcome to combat SAMBO.

Ivan pulled Kazbek closer with one arm while pushing with the other. Spin him. Lock. Head forward into a leveraged chokehold.

Kazbek clawed at Ivan's forearm as he flailed for freedom. Ivan tightened the hold to cut off the neck arteries and looked at the top of the stairs. The door. The box had closed in without a gap. No noises. Must have been a spring mechanism. It would keep the Mexicans out.

He leaned into the Chechen. Crank his neck until it snaps—so tempting. No. Not now. Operational objective was to bring him alive. Partorg wouldn't forgive if his prize enemy died.

Reluctant, Ivan loosened the hold and lowered Kazbek's unconscious, limp body to the floor. Still breathing, the son of a bitch. Still alive.

Screens and computers and stacks of papers suggested this was an office, but with an extra punch: a black-steel gun rack in the corner with submachine guns, shotguns, and rifles. Boxes of ammo. Wait—a hatch with a wheel lock?

Ivan looked around for a rope. The electric cord from a table lamp cut nicely into the Chechen's skin, the knots strong. Kazbek drooled and didn't fight the ties around his wrists and ankles.

One of the computers was on—the monitor came alive when Ivan moved the mouse across its pad, the span of the screen divided into rows of squares, timestamps running at the bottom of each.

Slavno. Live feed from every room in the house. What about Foxy?

Ivan checked the timestamps. Only two rooms recorded to the hard drive. Here—what was this? Foxy's body stretched tight over a long, wooden contraption, his ribcage pulled up. Motionless. Dead? Blyadi evo razorvali!

Ivan turned to Kazbek and grabbed him by the face, the Chechen's eyes out of focus, veins thick on his forehead. He tossed the Chechen back to the floor in disgust and returned to the screen to study the feed.

Amir, or what was left of him, lay on the floor at the bottom of the staircase leading to the hallway. Not moving. Vot oni—men in urban camouflage stepped over him, stocky, each with a headset. They moved quickly along the walls, in and out of rooms in teams of two, the lights on their guns sweeping each space on their methodical progression down the hall. Cartel men. The bombed truck didn't keep them long.

One of them dragged Eva out by the hair and dumped her in the middle of the hallway, facedown into the floor; he zip-tied her hands while others continued the sweep. This must be their team leader, Ivan thought—from the way he stayed with Eva, his foot on her back, while others finished clearing the dungeon rooms. Could be the man from the gardener's truck.

An audio feed came out of speakers next to the screen. The new arrivals spoke Spanish. The leader dragged Eva down the hallway toward the room where she killed Foxy.

On the video, the Mexican stood Eva up next to Foxy's stretched body, holding her by the arm. He yanked her down to her knees and pointed at Foxy with his silenced rifle. A mouse click brought up the audio:

"—here? Who is he? You tell me or I cut your tits."

Eva's meek reply barely came through. "What?"

The Mexican raised his voice. "Who is he?"

Eva had the tears going, the drama. "Leave me alone! I don't know anything!"

The camera was good enough to show Eva's lips moving. The Mexican slapped her hard across the face. She toppled sideways but caught herself with her hand and sat helplessly on the floor.

The Mexican pulled out a blade from a sheath and pointed it at her cheek. "Where is your husband? Talk, or I cut off your face."

"I told you I don't know! He's not here!"

Foxy moved with a groan and bent his knee. The Mexican stepped closer to lean over Foxy's head.

Ivan turned the volume knob to its maximum. Foxy—alive? What was he saying to the Mexican? Something important, but it was too quiet to pick up.

Eva must have heard it because she yelled, "He's lying! He's lying! He doesn't—"

The Mexican straightened up and caught his rifle hanging from a strap around his neck in one quick motion. Shots came through the speakers like whispers. The back of Eva's head lost its shape, and she fell to the floor.

Ivan shook his head. What did Foxy call it? You play fucked games, you win fucked prizes. Crazy woman.

He turned from the monitor and went to the gun rack. From the look of it, Kazbek lived like a man ready for a war.

39

Los Angeles Westside, California

On the radio, Seso sounded worried. "We checked all the rooms. He's not here. And we didn't find the second cop."

Miguel tossed out the used syringe through the open door of the ambulance. "The lookouts missed him. Everyone, get in the car. We've been here too long."

He looked down at the prisoner they took off the rack: arms at weird angles, both shoulder joints dislocated, burns and fresh contusions all over his dark skin. But still breathing, somehow. To put the man through so much pain and not kill him—this took skill.

Cho climbed in last and offered his profound wisdom: "Jefe, I bet he's hiding in some place so weird we need to raze the house with a bulldozer to find him."

"Shut up. I'm not in the mood for jokes right now."

Seso took the wheel. They drove through the gate and onto the street without incident. Miguel took the rifle sling off his neck. At least no confrontation with the police on the way out.

Dado stared at the thin man on the gurney. "I think El Checheño is better at hurting people than we are."

"Jefe," Cho said, "he must have something they wanted. What do you think it is?"

Useless question. "How would I know?"

"The wife was dressed like she was out for a swim," Cho said.

Dado chuckled. "That will explain all the water on the basement floor. She was taking a bath." He pulled his phone from a magazine pouch and held it out. "Hey, amigos. Take a look—I took pictures of the crazy harnesses and the chairs with spikes they had down there. It's like a museum."

Miguel pushed the phone aside. "I don't care about any of that."

The prisoner's dark skin was pockmarked by burns. Some prize. All this risk for a half-dead policeman who passed out before he could say anything useful.

296

At the warehouse, as soon as the gate closed behind the ambulance, Miguel said, "Let's roll him out. I want Seso to fix him."

Seso climbed out of the cab and came around to the gurney. He pointed at the blistering burn wound on the prisoner's belly. "That's from a torch."

"A surface wound," Miguel said. "Check him for anything serious. I don't want him to bleed out on me."

"Do you want him to last?"

"Seguro. For now."

"I'll get the kit, then." Seso climbed into the ambulance and hopped out a minute later with a bag in his hand. He put it down, unzipped it, and rummaged through it until he found a tube of cream and a bandage.

The prisoner let out a low moan when Seso touched the ripped skin that oozed clear-yellow fluid mixed with blood.

"Will he talk any time soon?" Miguel asked.

Seso spread cream and gauze over the wound. "Hard to tell. But they didn't tear up his face much. They wanted him to say things." He probed the prisoner's shoulder with his fingertips. "We must put the bone back in its socket."

"Why? I don't plan to keep him."

"He might not talk otherwise. Because of pain."

"Do we have to do it now?"

"It can wait. Where do you want him?"

Miguel waved at the body. "Put him in the office. I don't want to see him or hear him while I'm having lunch. He stinks. And let me know if we need to call in a doctor. I'm going to clean up. I've got dust in my teeth."

Afterward, when they sat down to eat, Seso joined them, ate quickly, and went back to the section of the warehouse floor behind the partition wall where he worked on the prisoner. When he returned to the table, wiping his hands with a towel, he said, "He's awake. I gave him morphine to keep him happy."

Miguel put down his soda and frowned. "Did I say I wanted him happy?"

"They dislocated his shoulder joints. He'd be screaming the whole time unless I got him high."

"I thought you were going to put his shoulders back in. Why would he be screaming?"

"Skin and tissue damage. They burned him or used pliers on him, I'm not sure. That contraption probably tore some of his muscles. I had to give him drugs—he'd be incoherent without any. You can't work him too hard when you talk to him."

"What's he doing now?"

"Resting."

Miguel wiped his mouth with his wrist. "Puta madre, we let him rest, we give him drugs—I'm not running a hotel here. How high is he?"

"He speaks funny. And he's high enough to have no fear."

Miguel threw up his hands. "Oye! How am I supposed to interrogate him if he's not afraid of anything?"

Seso shrugged. "You told me to put him together, and I put him together. If you want him to feel pain, we'll have to wait."

Rising from his chair, Miguel shook his head. "Vato, you're not helping. Come. I want to see him." He crossed the empty space of the warehouse to a supervisor's office walled off from the rest of the floor. Inside, the captive lay on an old mattress, his wrist cuffed to a pipe running along the wall. The sound of a chair pulled closer woke him up; he opened his black eyes, but only half-way.

Miguel lit a cigarette and waved the smoke away from his face. "Do you know who I am?"

"Sure." The prisoner spoke the word slowly, stretching the letters. His lips looked swollen.

Miguel frowned. "Yes? How?"

A smile crept onto the prisoner's narrow face. After all the pain, the asshole was still smiling! "You're Mister Handsome. That's your name. Cute hair. So black and curly."

Hair?

Seso chuckled and said, "I told you. He's high."

Miguel waved his cigarette impatiently at the prisoner. "You know my real name? Did he tell you I was coming?"

The man looked over to his cuffed hand and pulled. The cuffs rattled against the pipe. His goofy smile went away, and his thin eyebrows went up. "Hey, why am I cuffed?"

"Because we took you prisoner." The explanation seemed inadequate, but it was hard to explain things in English to a man blabbering nonsense.

Miguel pulled in a lungful of smoke to stifle his frustration. Spanish. This would be so much better in Spanish. The obstacle of the foreign language sure added extra annoyance to the rest of the day's setbacks.

He blew the smoke out in a long jet. "Mira. Do you know my

name or no? Miguel Alvarado."

The prisoner shrugged and winced. His free hand went to his shoulder joint to rub it. "I think I have sand in my shoulders. It feels like sand. Or electric current."

Miguel rubbed his face. This was going to be a long conversation, and the usual methods wouldn't work. This clown required patience. "Okay, puta. Start from beginning. Tell me your name."

The prisoner spoke like a child performing a rehearsed introduction in school. "My name is Foxy." His eyes darted from Miguel to an old desk in the corner where Seso left his med kit and a six-pack of beer. He switched to an adult voice and said, "Damn, I'm thirsty. Can I have a sip of that?"

"No. But tell me what I want, Foxy, and I give you a drink."

A goofy smile returned. "You're no fun. You sound like my mother."

"No matter." Miguel rubbed the back of his neck. Quite a headache here. "You were at his house. We took you from his house. You told me there—you said in my ear you know where he is. The man with the beard and tattoo."

For the first time, a flicker of clarity entered the prisoner's eyes. "Oh, that guy." He shook his head. "That guy's an asshole. Him and his wife. Jesus. I thought I knew crazy, but those two—woo-hoo, they can rewrite the fucking book on crazy. I thought they were going to cut my dick off." His eyes opened large with sudden shock. "Wait." He stuck his free hand into the sweatpants Seso had put on him, and his face wrinkled in a grimace. "Ooh. Still there." He winced. "Hurts like a mother fucker, though."

Miguel picked up a beer can, ran his finger along its dewy surface, and flicked the moisture off in view of the prisoner. "The man with a red beard. Tell me, where is he? Did your partner arrest him?"

The prisoner's gaze latched on the can and followed Miguel's finger. He pulled away from the wall, but the cuffs jerked him back. His gaze went to the pipe like he'd forgotten he'd been chained to it. He said, "Bummer," and coughed. Grimacing, he turned to face the room. His voice came out raspy. "C'mon, man. I could use a drink. My mouth is all dry." As if to prove his point, he opened his mouth, stuck out his tongue, and flexed the tip up and down.

"He's funny," Seso said from behind. "People on morphine are like children sometimes."

Like children. Children had no idea what was important. They just said things. Miguel handed the beer to the man. "Here, Foxy. Drink.

Now, your partner. Did he arrest the man with a beard?"

Foxy's Adam's apple bobbed up and down, beer spilling on his chin and chest. He finished the can and stared into its opening. "Man, where did the beer go?"

Miguel snapped his fingers in front of the prisoner's face. "Hey. Hey. Foxy. Tell me about your partner. Forget other crazy people. Your partner. Did he—"

Foxy's doleful gaze left the beer can. "Crazy ain't a good way to call them. They're fucking nuts." He tipped his head back and shook the can over his mouth. "They were getting off on my shoulders popping out. I thought they were gonna rip me in half before that Chechen fucker could blow his load." He grimaced at the memory, tossed the beer can under the table, and massaged his shoulder. "Eeeh. That woman's messed up—she likes to fuck to the wrong soundtrack. The more I screamed, the harder she fucked."

"I never heard of anything like this before," Seso said from the doorway.

Miguel reached for another beer. Foxy's gaze followed its journey from the six pack to a spot in front of his face. When Foxy reached for it, Miguel held it back. "Foxy. Your partner. Why is he not with you?"

Foxy curved his lips then said, "Shit, I don't know. Why don't you ask him yourself? I gotta warn you, though." He wagged his index finger in the air.

Miguel held back the impulse to grab the finger and snap it in half. "Warn me about what?"

"He's not much of a talker. And I don't think he likes me much."

Interesting, Miguel thought. Doesn't get along with his partner. Miguel stretched his face into a smile. "Are you not good friends?"

"Darling, that guy's nobody's friend. He doesn't like people. He likes dogs. He and I just work together. I don't know why my mother likes him. He's so stiff he should be a dildo."

This Foxy, he was like some actor, shaking his head and looking at the ceiling, rolling his eyes. A mother? Stiff? Dildo? Miguel looked back at Seso, who shrugged and said in Spanish, "Whatever this means, he's not lying."

"Hey, guys," Foxy said. "You sound real sexy when you speak Spanish."

Sound sexy? Miguel whirled and stared at Foxy's face, fighting the urge to punch the man in his stupid, puffy mouth; he drew a fresh puff from his cigarette to give himself time to calm down. "This man your mother likes," he said, keeping his voice even, "can I call him? You have his number?"

"Sure, you can call him. Gonna be a short conversation, though. He doesn't talk much. He grunts, mostly."

Miguel turned to Seso. "Didn't we find a phone on him?"

Seso pointed at the pile of clothes, at the police uniform they found in the same room where El Checheño's wife died. Miguel reached for the cell phone on top of the pile, for its battery and back cover. He pushed the battery in and powered the phone—cheap burner with an empty address book and only two calls in a call history. Odd for a police officer not to have a better phone and more calls.

He stuck the screen at the prisoner. "This is your friend's number?"

"Nah, darling, that's Nigel, my mechanic. He gets me a whip when I need one."

Miguel skipped to the next entry. "This?"

"That's him. Captain Red October hisself."

Sounding cheerful, the idiot. Miguel put the phone in his pocket. "Good. Now tell me, did your partner take the man with tattoo?"

The idiot was still smiling. "You know, I have a confession to make."

Miguel rubbed his eyes. "A confession?"

"Yes, darling. A confession. I'm in love with the curve of your ass. It's delicious. Ass like yours—you don't have to worry your pretty head about nothing."

Seso chuckled by the door. "He says he loves your ass, Jefe. I think this maricón likes to get fucked by other men. His partner and he, they probably fuck each other after work."

Hot blood ran up Miguel's neck. He swung and slapped the beer out of the prisoner's hand, the can smacking into the partition wall.

"Heeey, there is no need for—"

Miguel flicked his cigarette into the prisoner's vile face and grabbed his thin neck with both hands, squeezing and twisting, shaking the stupidity out of the bobbing head.

"Jefe, slow down," Seso said. "You can't use him if he's dead."

Miguel stared into the prisoner's black eyes veiled by drugs, at the thickening veins on his forehead, and let go. He turned away, and picked up a beer for himself.

"God. I want to kick his bullshit right back into his fucking mouth."

"He's not afraid yet, Jefe. You have to wait."

"Thanks to you and your drugs."

Miguel drank the beer in slow gulps. Patience. He turned around and stared at the bruised, pathetic shit-face chained to the wall. You laugh now, he thought. We see how you laugh when the drug wears off.

He turned back to the table, picked up the rest of the beer by the plastic string, and showed it to the prisoner. "Foxy. One more time. Your friend. Did he arrest the man of the house? Tell me, and I give you all this."

Not even a second of hesitation from the maricón. "I bet he did. He's in a hurry, you know. Wants to run home like a good dog."

"That's useful," Seso said.

Miguel threw the cans at Foxy's disgusting face and turned away, reaching in his pocket for the cop's phone. "Let's go talk at the table. I'll kill him if I look at him for one more second."

As they walked, Seso said, "I wonder if they're real cops. His name tag is for a white man."

Miguel nodded. "His phone isn't right."

"Maybe we have competition."

"Maybe. We like to play police, too."

"We did put out a contract on the Chechen. Would be funny if this maricón and his partner were working for us the whole time."

"The Chechen screwed a lot of people. Could be anyone."

"So we call."

"Exactly. We call. We call and find out. We can always make an offer if we have to."

40

Los Angeles Westside, California

Ivan picked a pistol from the gun rack. Glock 17, with a clean barrel and chamber. This would do. Largest magazine in a smallest package, already loaded. Nine millimeter. Sacrificing caliber for capacity.

A duty holster from a loose pile on the top shelf fit the Glock best. Ivan drove his waist belt through the loops and put the belt back on with the holster hanging tight from it. Even with water squeezed out, his pants were uncomfortably wet and restrained his movement. Yet it was important to look like a cop, especially on the street, moving Kazbek out of the area.

The Chechen lay tied up and motionless but already awake. So much trouble for one man. So much pain.

The lock mechanism on the hatch at the far wall looked lubricated. No rust. Ivan leaned into the wheel, careful to move it in small increments to avoid making noise.

A yellow light on the other side turned on and shone from the ceiling the moment the steel hatch opened, but the tunnel stretched beyond the reach of the weak lamp. He peered into the murky darkness—no way of telling how far the tunnel went or how it would connect to the surface streets; but a trickle of slimy water on the floor meant this was a service tunnel, possibly a storm drain, which would explain the submarine-style door.

He tossed Kazbek through the hatch legs-first, like a piece of luggage. The Chechen let out a complaint muffled by the sock in his mouth when he hit the concrete. Ivan stepped through the hatch and examined the wheel lock on the other side. The Mexicans may or may not find the hidden room. Better cut them off.

A steel clamp came down on the wheel and held it in place. It clanged as he locked it, but the sound marked a safe separation—without a welding torch, the Mexicans would have no means of coming through.

Ivan kneeled in front of the bearded face, Kazbek's eyes watchful. It was a pleasure to speak Russian again. "The Mexicans are searching your house. I'm not here to kill you. If you work with me, you will live. But if you don't, I will pay you back for everything you did to me and my partner. Understand?"

A nod.

Ivan pinched the sock and pulled it out. Kazbek turned his head and spat on the floor. "Where are you taking me?"

"Las Vegas."

"You work for the Armenians? I can pay you more than—"

Ivan grabbed Kazbek's face, beard, and cheeks, squeezing the Chechen's mouth shut. "I don't need your questions. I need answers. This tunnel—where does it go?" He let go.

Kazbek licked his lips and said, "Rain drain."

"Can we get to street level?"

"Yes."

"I will carry you on my shoulder. Don't give me problems, or I will choke you off."

Warm air filled the tunnel with a smell like rot from a kitchen sink drain. The stench and humidity thickened with every step and triggered spasms of coughing. Bluish light from Kazbek's cell phone highlighted black streaks on the tunnel walls where moisture trickled down to the floor.

"Why don't you let me walk?" Kazbek said. "There's nowhere I can run here."

"Shut up." Playing his games, Ivan thought. Look where it got you.

Ivan lumbered on as sweat burned his eyes and soaked his already wet uniform. The passageway narrowed, and the low ceiling forced him into a hunched position, the muscles in his back screaming for relief. Whenever he straightened, he scraped the ceiling with Kazbek, who stayed silent but squirmed and wiggled.

At a sharp turn, Kazbek's head hit a wall, and he let out a stifled cry. "You can't get far like this. You'll break my head open. Let me walk."

"You enjoy pain, don't you? So keep enjoying it." Ivan shifted Kazbek's body closer to his neck to keep the Chechen from slipping off his shoulder. "And stop wiggling, or I will drag you."

Kazbek hung still after that.

Puddles of foul water and mud threatened Ivan's footing with slime. Ivan shone the light along the wall. The narrow tunnel should connect to a bigger one. There.

He hopped down into a much larger space, the darkness between concave walls perforated by beams of light from above. A storm drain tunnel with grates at the top.

"Where can we exit?"

"Ladder in about fifty meters."

"Is this how you always leave the house?"

"Sure. Not that it helped any." Sounding bitter. Not liking his new reality.

A ladder leading up to the grate showed up in a column of light; occasional droplets of rain glinted in the light like specs of dust. Ivan dropped Kazbek to the ground and tried the rungs. Stainless steel. Nice upgrade to the underground infrastructure.

The knots on Kazbek's hands and feet remained solid, and the electric cord had sunk into his skin. Bastard could wriggle in the slime, but that was it. Time to get the car.

Ivan pulled the sock out of his pocket.

"Listen," Kazbek said when he saw it, "I'm not going to—"

A straight punch with the bottom of Ivan's palm to Kazbek's forehead bounced Kazbek's head into the tunnel floor. No need to break his own knuckles—a contusion would suffice. Ivan squeezed Kazbek's jaws open and shoved the sock in while the Chechen rolled his eyes.

Ivan climbed the ladder to the grate while the wet police uniform clung to his legs and flapped at his ankles. At the top, he listened for noise—sirens or conversations—and pushed the grate out after a car rolled by and the noises died down.

Outside the tunnel, the air smelled of sweet jasmine and rain, tempting his lungs to breathe more. He replaced the grate and brushed the dirt off his uniform in a slow, casual way for the chance onlooker. But nobody was there to watch him.

He walked the length of a fence facing the sidewalk. Rich people everywhere sure liked their fences.

The hills provided easy directions. He maintained an assured stride and straight posture—few people questioned confidence. They'd see a police officer at work, maybe busy with an investigation. People always trusted the uniform.

The sound of a distant siren forced him into a crouch behind a parked car. Passersby wouldn't cause problems, but police would. They'd notice the slight limp, the uniform not quite fitting. If the cops got a call about Kazbek's house, they'd be paying attention.

Ivan waited for the siren to pass and walked to a familiar corner with a long hedge covered in white flowers. He peeked ahead, to the next block. No patrol cars yet. Whatever happened at the villa, the neighbors either missed or ignored it. No sirens, no ambulances or police cruisers. Ironic—these people bought houses as big as castles, and hid inside, behind thick walls, enjoying their illusion of safety.

Safe until someone gets past the wall and makes a mess without anyone on the street hearing any of it.

The absence of cops and pedestrians quickened his pace toward the old sedan. Too much exposure here and only one exit scenario. Better hurry.

Ivan climbed into the sedan and found the keys still under the floor mat where Foxy had left them.

Foxy. Somebody always paid the price when things got rushed. Happened to be Foxy's turn this time. Still unclear if the Mexicans put him down or left him breathing. Problematic either way.

Ivan drove back to the storm drain, parked the car to shield it at least from one side, and went down into the tunnel. On the way up, his feet and hands threatened to slip off the ladder, the slime and fresh droplets making the climb treacherous. He struggled his way up one rung at a time, panting and grunting.

At the top, after a quick peek through the opening, he pushed through and almost fell back down as a passing car rolled by. The Chechen nearly slipped off his shoulder, yelping into the sock. Ivan slammed the Chechen's legs into the ladder and jammed them.

"Blyad ne ripaysya!"

Lucky that Kazbek was lightweight; if he were heavier, and with real rain instead of drizzle, this would have been impossible.

Panting, Ivan peeked out the second time, checking for onlookers. The car and fence shielded the grate on two sides, but the rest was wide open.

Taking stupid risk again. Could use a partner here. Job hard enough for two men.

Ivan pushed Kazbek through first, climbed out, and then carried the Chechen to the back of the car. Kazbek went into the trunk with scrapes on his face and head, drooling through the sock, eyes darting left and right.

Looking for opportunity, the bastard. Dreaming of real police picking him up. Ivan leaned in. "If you make any noise for attention, you die. I'd still get paid for your body. Understand?"

Kazbek nodded.

With the Chechen finally in the trunk, Ivan took Hoffman's name tag and badge off his shirt. No need for extra risk. A cop in this old car—a passing patrol might notice.

He drove off, strain in his muscles, arms and legs trembling from exhaustion, his hands shaking on the wheel. Like a drunkard or a shell-shocked soldier.

Traffic choked Sunset Boulevard and Wilshire, street names now familiar. At the light, Ivan watched a young man with Foxy's haircut cross the street.

Foxy—they stretched him like a rubber band on that thing, with his ribs sticking out. And now Laverne might have to live without her go-to person. Worse than the ambush in Helmand, this whole thing.

The realization brought bitterness into Ivan's mouth. This time, he thought, you are the one leaving a man behind.

On the freeway, the stream of cars flowed steadily past downtown skyscrapers. Ivan stared at a silver car in front as the habit of examining the operation kicked in: the snapshot of them driving up in a cruiser, Foxy ringing the bell, Eva dropping the glass and diving behind the bar.

He smarted from the images, each one deepening the disappointment. What a mess. The whole thing was rife with poor planning and preparation. The absence of the Chechen guards on the way to the door had been a clear sign for alarm, and it'd been folly to accept Foxy's explanation for it.

At the house, the Pomeranians jumped at his legs, whinnying and barking. They ignored Kazbek—flat on his back along the wall—and tore into steak leftovers from the fridge. The pooches snarled at each other from time to time; Boo-Boo poached meat from Honey, despite having meat of his own. Ivan let the dogs sort it out and opened his laptop.

Once the encryption program launched, he typed: "The negotiations were a success. The contract is ready to be signed at your earliest convenience."

Success. Right. Like Afghanistan was a success. Piles of zinc coffins loaded into the transport planes.

He sat and stared at the confirmation for the sent message. It would take twelve hours of flying and a couple of hours of driving for Partorg to get near his old foe. This, if the boss was anxious enough to leave right away.

Ivan glanced at Kazbek, whose breathing had grown loud, wide nostrils flaring with each inhalation. Ivan leaned over the man and pulled the sock out. The Chechen gasped for his first breath, grimaced, and then spat white strings on the floor.

"Can I have water?"

"I don't want you pissing all over yourself. But enjoy breathing."

Ivan went to undress and wash himself. The safe house didn't have a boiler, and the water was about as cold as the water in the fish tank. He shivered the entire time, thinking of breathing through the pipe, but the shivering went away in dry clothes.

Back in the living room with Kazbek in view, Ivan picked up a fresh phone from the gear case and called Ruslan. "I have it."

The man sounded relieved. "Thank God. They're all asleep in Russia right now, otherwise I would have called him."

Time difference. Lena asleep, too. "You are not supposed to call him."

"I know. But he called me himself."

"He called you?"

"Yesterday. I think he tried to reach the contractor first and then called me."

"What did you say?"

"I said you were getting closer."

"Did you say anything else?"

"Did I have to? I thought he would call you—"

"Do you have the storage, as I asked?"

"It's all set. I have the key."

"Don't mention the address to anyone, anywhere. Go there now. Meet me at the gate. And get me some food. A real sandwich, if you can get it. No burgers."

Ivan sat on the chair, waiting for the tightness in his chest and gut to subside. Walking on the edge of the blade here, Fedot so close to her, and now Partorg calling Ruslan—that was new. And why did he call Foxy first? Must be Fedot's doing, sowing mistrust, talking about delays. Making his papa upset.

Ivan swapped the registration plates on the Lincoln and put the dogs in the back seat. The Chechen deserved a sock back in his mouth, but the risk of him suffocating in the carpet was too great. And without the sock, Kazbek got nervous, looking at the cutout of old carpet rolled out in front of his face.

"What are you going to do?"

"I told you I wasn't going to kill you. But I am allowed to break your bones." Ivan lifted the Chechen up and dropped him down on the carpet. "Stay still."

308

The injector's gas cylinder needed replacement, and the drug vial was almost empty—the cops at the club had taken most of it. Ivan found a fresh cylinder in the gear case and screwed it into place as he stood over the Chechen.

"What's that for?"

"To make your trip go by quicker."

The Chechen tried to squirm away from the injector until a shot to his neck put a distant expression in his worried eyes; he quieted down in under a minute.

With Kazbek's body rolled up into the middle, the carpet looked like a big snake that had swallowed an animal. But in the trunk, it would look like a simple roll of carpet, should anyone pull the car over.

The drive east was quick and uneventful, the mountains left of the freeway rising taller, twice or three times the height of the hills around Hollywood. The ridge looked like the mountains around the Black Sea, the slopes marred by erosion, the brush the same dusty shade of green.

At the storage, Ruslan sat in his car by a gate that restricted access to a nondescript lineup of garage-like units surrounded by a tall fence. The buzz of speeding cars forced Ivan to raise his voice. "Which one did you rent?"

"The last one in the back, like you asked."

"Lead me to it."

With the car inside the unit, Ivan pulled down the door and unfolded the chairs that lined the wall. They sat with sandwiches in their hands, the roll of carpet on the floor between them.

"Why are you alone? Ruslan asked. "Where's the contractor?"

"We split during exit. We had problems with people from Mexico. They got close."

Ruslan stopped chewing and reached for a bottle of water on the floor. His hand shook as he held the bottle to his lips.

"Don't worry." Ivan kicked the carpet. "I left his house cleanly. The police will be looking for the Mexicans. Nobody knows about here but you and me."

Ruslan put the bottle down and wiped his hands on his dress pants, ignoring the smear of crumbs. His eyes flicked from the carpet to the gate. "I should go back to the office."

Jittery, the office rat. Rushing to go back and report. "Use the last number on the list to text me the instructions for the drop. I haven't used that phone yet."

Ruslan stood, nodding, happy to leave. He paused by the door, squirming. "If he calls again, what should I tell him about the contractor?"

"Tell him he'll be at the drop off."

With the door closed, Ivan unrolled the carpet. The Chechen, in a daze, bent his neck to look up and said in English, "What is this?" His eyes roamed, until he focused on the familiar face. "Oh, it's you. The fat fuck."

Time to put a sock back in. Ivan reached for the man's other foot and pulled the sock off, both feet now bare.

"Wait—I'll shut up, I promise. Just don't push it into my mouth."

Not so dazed now. Fully awake. May just as well have a conversation. "Tell me about the Mexicans. Your wife told us you recognized them. Why are they here?"

"What do you care? You're selling me to another buyer anyway, right?"

"My partner is either dead or they have him. I want to know if he has a chance."

Kazbek put his head back down on the carpet and closed his eyes. "They went through my men like it was nothing, and my men were good."

"I know what they can do—I've seen it. Stop praising them. How many men would they have on their team?"

Kazbek opened his eyes and stared. "Tell me what happened to my wife. I can tell you about Miguel, but I want to know what happened to her first. Did you see them take her?"

"They took her, yes," Ivan said, keeping his tone neutral. "But I don't know what happened afterward."

"Are you going after your partner?"

"If you want to save her, you must tell me more about this Miguel."

"You'll need men. A lot of men. I can get you—"

"The only thing you can get me is information. Start with Miguel."

"Information isn't going to be enough. You're talking about a man who runs security for a billion-dollar organization. He's a soldier who enjoys killing people, and he's very good at that."

"I see. Why did you fuck him over, then? We are all here because of that."

"I had no choice. The war that's going on over there? They're shooting at each other with my guns. And Miguel is going to lose because he's going against people who are going to win."

So, the Mexican was vulnerable. Ivan reached for the suitcase and pulled the laptop out, along with the card reader, and powered it. Next, he pulled the cell phone from his pocket, water still showing between the buttons. He hesitated before inserting the SIM card from the phone into the reader, but only for a second; after wiping it, he pushed it in.

"What are you doing?" Kazbek asked.

Ivan fired up the program, and it showed enough signal to relay the call. "I'm going to check if your Miguel makes the same mistake I did."

"What, you mean trusting my wife? He's not going to trust her. Or you. He's going to try and set you up."

"I'm expecting him to."

"You have no chance going against him alone. People like him don't trust anyone."

"Not true. You trusted your wife."

"I'm not like him. He's never going to trust anyone, and certainly not you."

"Everyone has one person they trust. With the right preparation, that's enough for me."

"You're crazy. Who's he going to trust?"

"Himself. If he's as good as you say he is, your Miguel is going to trust himself."

Kazbek lay silent as they waited. When the call finally came in, the application on the laptop played a few notes from Rigoletto. The voice of the opera singer startled Ivan in his seat. He wrapped duct tape over Kazbek's mouth and head, picked up the laptop, and checked the number against the list stored in the application.

Foxy's phone. Two likely possibilities: the Mexicans or the police.

Ivan stared at the screen with Foxy's number highlighted on it then put the headphones on and answered. "Who is this?"

A thick, low voice with a heavy Spanish accent said, "You took a man with a tiger on his chest, yes?"

"Why are you calling me?"

The phone moved around on the other end. Foxy's voice came in raspy. "Ivan, my man. Listen. These Mexican guys are funny. You should see them. They're all short and—"

More noise, and then the thick voice came back. "You want your friend back, no? We trade. You give me the man with tattoo, and I give your friend."

Foxy—the good partner, still alive. Good news and bad news folded into one problem. Foxy would talk to them about Partorg.

Everyone talked sooner or later. Terrible pain warped the mind terribly.

Ivan brought the microphone closer to his mouth. "And who are you?"

"Not important, who I am. I want trade. I tried to take the man you have. I still want him."

Trade. This could be done as a trade, but the whole edifice rested on the cornerstone of time. No margin for mistakes, which meant it would take time to set everything up. And the right gear was in Moscow.

The map application opened on top of the call, and Ivan scrolled through the distances. Time. Something close but far enough. "What else can you offer besides my partner?"

"You want money?"

"This contract is for quarter million. Delivery in Denver, Colorado. Where do you want him?"

"Here. We can meet at safe place here in Los Angeles."

"If you want him in Los Angeles, I can't get back until tomorrow evening."

The Mexican paused. "That's long time, no?"

"I thought my partner was dead. I am in Utah now. I can't fly back with what you want in my suitcase. I have to drive."

"No problem. You need to drive, you drive. I pay double."

"Triple. I don't come back for less. My client will be very unhappy."

A long pause. Good. But real Russian roulette. Would they believe the contractor story? Asking for money—this should convince them. Cops didn't put up demands with their operatives in danger; agencies would ask for extra time while they scrambled a team, SWAT or FBI. Show the Mexican a small operation. If Foxy talked, he'd say the truth. Contractor.

"Bueno. I pay triple. Bring him tomorrow or your partner dies in a bad way, and we look for you."

The Mexican hung up.

Ivan didn't bother saving the recording. No use saving any of this. They would call back. No other play for them. And Foxy—he sounded funny. They'd drugged him. That's why he blabbered nonsense like a drunk. At least they didn't start on him yet, and he hadn't said anything important.

Ivan closed his eyes and rubbed his face. This had to be done quickly. If Foxy talked to the Mexican about Partorg, lots of bodies would go into the ground all over the world. No more conversations at the pond, not this time. No picnics.

He bent over the Chechen and ripped the duct tape off. "How many men does he have?"

"As many as he wants. I told you. He runs a—"

Ivan grimaced. "Nonsense. A hitter like him will have only a few men he trusts. How many?"

Kazbek dropped his head back on the ground, looking up at the ceiling. He blinked until his gaze sharpened. "At least four. I know one of them is a sniper—I sold him a few Sako and McMillan rifles. You're crazy. You can't deal with them alone."

Ivan tore off a fresh cut of duct tape. "I don't plan to deal with them at all." The tape stuck to Kazbek's bearded face just fine. The Chechen's nose flared to suck in air as its owner strained for breath.

It was early morning in Moscow, which meant the call would wake Lena up. And it would worry and get her even more involved. Ivan shook his head—the worst time to worry her. This work, it was like acid: ate through every boundary. Such a careless thing to do to a wonderful woman. But too late now for regrets.

He pulled up the number and dialed. Lena sounded sleepy. "Vanya? I thought I was dreaming about the phone ringing. But then it was ringing."

"Zaichik, I didn't want to wake you up, but I need something from our garage. I have to give it to my partners here before I leave. Is Fedotov around? The bodyguard?"

She sounded confused. "No, I haven't seen him. He likes to play with Bond. He said he would check on me when he's free and walk Bond if it's cold out."

"Good. You have to get this thing for me: it's an old box on the top shelf, to the right as you go in."

"But we don't have shelves in our garage."

"Not in the city. In the country house."

"In the country house? Vanya, it's still dark here. What's going on?"

"It's an emergency. I forgot to bring it, but I had promised it as a gift. It's all my fault. I'm so sorry."

"That's nothing too bad." She sounded clearer, waking up. "I can drive over there after sunrise."

"Zaichik, you have to go now, before the traffic starts. I need it right now. It can't wait. The man I promised to give it to must have it immediately. It will all fail unless I do as I promised. I have to give the damn thing to them so I can leave." Part truth, part lie. And not a good lie.

She was fully awake. "I'll go. What will I be looking for?"

He exhaled with relief. "It's a cardboard box with six perfume bottles. Take only one bottle—they are all in original white cartons. It will say Chanel on each one."

"But how do I send it to you? Will it get there in time?"

"It will. That's why I need you to hurry. Get a pen. I'll give you my address and the number of my customs guy, Misha. He'll take care of the shipping. Just tell him you need to send it the fastest way."

He had her read the phone number back to him. She'd gotten it right at the first try.

"I didn't know you sold perfumes," she said.

"It's an extremely rare edition. They cost as much as a house."

"I can't believe you keep it in a garage."

"They don't look like much. Nobody cares about something that's not in a safe and looks cheap."

She sighed. "I better make me some coffee if I'm going to drive."

He filled his voice with urgency. "Zaichik, you must not open the bottle or damage it no matter what happens, understand? We have a roll of bubble wrap there on the shelf. Wrap the bottle like it's a champagne glass which you want to kick around the stadium."

"Don't worry, I'll wrap them."

"You are the best. Now hurry."

"When do you think you'll be back?"

"As soon as I give them the gift. I meet their boss tomorrow. I can fly the next day."

"I miss you."

"I will be there soon, Zaichik. Poka."

Tenderness squeezed his chest as he disconnected, her voice still in his ears. Lenochka. A woman like this—one in a million. Patient and kind. And she understood the urgency right away. Did what was asked, saving the explanations for later.

He stood up and looked around the garage, everything under the harsh glare of a fluorescent lamp on the ceiling. The perfume was on its way, good old Chanel No 5. But it was only a start. It would take more than a famous perfume to get this done.

He picked up his laptop and a smartphone. Time to go shopping.

41

East Los Angeles, California

Miguel took a sip from a paper cup, smacked his lips, and gave the coffee a well-deserved sigh of pleasure. A good breakfast. Sit and eat with nothing else to do but wait for the asshole to get back to town. Probably lying about Utah, but at least he wasn't a cop.

Seso folded his paper plate and tossed it into a bucket under the table. "The food is much worse in the states. But the coffee is much better."

Miguel stared at him. "Tell me, why is that? We grow our own coffee. We get fresh Guatemalan beans from across the border. Sure, some of it is coke, but most of it is coffee. Fresher than here. And somehow no one knows how to turn the beans into a good cup."

Dado sloshed his own cup of coffee around. "Here they grow nothing. But the coffee tastes much better."

Miguel reached across the table for the cardboard container the cups came with. He folded and unfolded it. "Comes with the box." He flipped the container, read the letters and grumbled. "Órale—it's made in Mexico! Can you believe it? We make the fucking containers for their coffee but can't make a decent cup for ourselves."

Noises came from the office where their prisoner had spent a quiet night, a metal-on-metal kind of noise, cuffs on the pipe. Miguel looked at Seso. "Did you give him morphine again?"

"Once."

Cho and Dado exchange glances, like they were up to something.

"What is it this time?" Miguel said.

Cho pretended he was busy eating.

Dado grinned. "He saw a video on the internet—animals solving puzzles. You know how you told us not to give water to the maricón?"

"What, you had him do tricks for you to get it?"

Cho giggled.

Dado shook his head. "No, no tricks. Well, one trick. We figured

315

he'd be thirsty as hell. So we left a can of beer overnight just out of his reach to see if he can solve how to grab it."

"He's cuffed to the pipe, you idiots. There is nothing there he can use to grab your can."

"Maybe. Cho thinks it's a good bet that he will."

Miguel shook his head. "You talked him into it, didn't you? Easy win for you."

Dado looked away. "He's the one who wanted to bet a hundred on it. I just let him."

Miguel sighed. "So who won?"

"I'm ahead. I checked on him before we sat down to eat. The beer was still there."

Seso was watching the exchange with his usual impassive expression. "I didn't give him any drugs, but he's been quiet. He must be hurting with all those burns, and I think he's trying not to draw attention to himself. Are you going to talk to him?"

Miguel gulped down the rest of his coffee. "I guess I should." He rose to his feet. This should be exciting, setting the trap for the other one. "Hey," he said to Dado before leaving the table, "you said you shot up my truck to test your rounds. Did they go through the plates?"

"Some of them. Why? You think I'll have to use them today?"

"You might." Miguel started for the office. "But don't get excited yet. The other one sounded like he didn't care about his partner much. I don't have a lot of leverage to bring him in close."

Cho said in an excited voice, "Maybe we grab them both and have them fight each other."

"Like we haven't seen enough of your gladiator shit," Dado said.

Inside the office enclosure, Seso said, "Something is bothering me." He nodded at the prisoner. "I've been thinking about his partner. He walked out of the house with the Chechen. None of us saw him. None of our lookouts either."

"So?"

"He must be good or have help."

"So we play smart. Get him out in the open and corner him."

Miguel stepped inside and stared at the prisoner who, with his head tilted back, was squishing the beer can over his mouth as if he hoped to squeeze a few extra drops from it. The cuffs were still on his wrist.

Miguel shook his head. "Looks like Dado lost money, no?" The air in the enclosure smelled of pus and rot and vomit.

Seso turned to push the door open, stuck his head out, and

shouted, "Hermano, your bet is done. You lost!"

Dado shouted from the table, "What did he do?"

Seso started with, "The beer—"

But the radio in Miguel's front pocket crackled with their lookout's voice. "Amigos, this is Rafa. I'm on the roof. Are you expecting anyone?"

Miguel picked up the radio. "What do you see?"

Seso stared and Miguel gave him a nod to send him out. Seso would get everyone moving to their weapons.

"A single car," Rafa said, "one man. Twenty meters from your door."

"Going where? Do you see anyone else inside?"

"He just stopped. Wait. He's coming out. I think he's sick or hurt. He's moving like he's in pain."

Miguel kicked the prisoner, who had his eyes closed, in the shin. "Hey. Your friend, how old is he?"

His eyelids parted slowly, like the man didn't want to see what was around him. "Who?"

"Your partner. How old?"

"Old. He so old, he dreams in black and white."

More drug nonsense. Miguel held back the urge to kick the man in the face, tip of the shoe to his teeth. He brought the radio back to his lips. "Rafa, do you see any other cars? Look as far as you can."

"Not since the workers came. And this one—he looks really sick."

"What do you mean?"

"He's barely moving. But he's definitely heading your way."

"Heading our way?" Miguel snapped. "Puta, nobody knows we are here. This can't be for us."

The warehouse floor was small enough to cross it in several quick steps. His men were ready, Cho and Dado by the entrance in their armored vests and Seso covering the side exit.

The radio crackled with Rafael's voice. "Amigos, he's near your door. He's here for you."

Miguel picked up his rifle and stopped to think. The rollup gate opened on a street lined with warehouses. With workers, at this hour. An occasional truck rolling in and out. A worker might spot the rifles and vests and call the police.

"Rafa," Miguel said into the radio. "Check the perimeter. Who else is here?"

"Nobody. No other cars."

Miguel held the radio to his lips without speaking into it. How did the old asshole find the place, and why did he come? From the roll up door came loud banging. A stick against metal? "Rafa, I need you to be sure. You hear any engines? And check in with others."

The radio crackled. "Nada. There's nobody. And I think he's knocking on your door with his cane."

"Puta, I know he's knocking. I can hear him." Miguel clicked off, shaking his head at the craziness of it. The man had taken the biggest prize like it's nothing, only to throw it away like a fool.

They all had their guns up. Cho looked like he was ready to strafe anyone coming though at the slightest opportunity.

Miguel waved at them—palm to the floor—and they all gave him a nod. No firing without command. He walked to the door and hit the button. The motor buzzed and the crack opened at the bottom, more and more sunlight pouring in, along with fresh air.

With rifle raised, Miguel stepped into the cover of the shade and activated the rifle's laser sight, ready to put a dot on the crazy fool. The door opened and rattled to a stop.

Miguel aimed out on the ramp, at a balding old man who stood bent at the waist, one hand on a walking cane, another on the handle of a small cart. The man's watery eyes, out of focus, blinked helplessly into the darker interior of the warehouse.

Miguel frowned—this feeble fool couldn't possibly have the Chechen—and hid the rifle behind his back. "What do you want?"

The old man couldn't even speak without help. Worse, he had trouble breathing, a mask on his face connected to an oxygen tanks on a cart, its hissing splitting the silence. When Miguel stepped into the light, the man squinted at him and took the mask off to rasp, "I'm here for exchange."

Interesting. Miguel motioned at him with his fingers. "Come." He stuck his head out on the street, but Rafa had been right about other visitors. Just one sedan further out, empty. Nobody else.

The geezer trudged his way up the ramp, dragging his cart with two oxygen tanks on it, the mask on his face attached to a tank's valve through yellow tubing.

Miguel punched the button, and the gate rattled down behind the geezer who shuffled his feet to the middle of the room. There, he stood and blinked at them.

Everyone was in position, shifting around to keep the old fart in the line of fire and themselves and their boss out of it. Such a strange sight, the decrepit old man coming in like this. Older than Tio, and far more feeble.

"Who are you?" Miguel asked.

Again a wrinkled hand came up to pull off the oxygen mask. "Who's in charge here?"

Miguel scratched his cheek. The old man had the voice from the phone call, so there was no mistake. "First—how did you find me?"

The geezer sucked in a breath of oxygen from the mask, the plastic foggy with moisture.

Miguel grimaced with irritation. Ridiculous. This fool could barely speak. Needed his air for every word or something.

In the light from the ceiling lamp, their visitor's watery eyes looked vague from age, bags of puffy skin under them; his gaze roamed around the empty space, ignoring the guns but stopping on the office door.

The mask came off and a delayed answer came out. "Through my partner."

Miguel exchanged a glance with Seso. It must have been something small on the maricón, hidden in his clothes.

Miguel narrowed his eyes at the visitor. "You tracked him here? Something with him?"

"Sure."

"What?"

"A chip in his phone."

Miguel nodded, his jaw tight from anger. Technology these days. You turned the damned thing off, and still it didn't die—you had to remove the battery. He glared at the visitor. "So what now? You come and scare me with your stick?"

At that, the old man stopped looking around, but his rheumy eyes betrayed no emotion. Another breath of oxygen and then, "Exchange. Do you have my money?"

"Do you have the man with tattoo?" Either crazy or stupid. Coming in like this, alone.

The old man let go of the cart. The weight of his stooped body rested on the cane as he raised his palm. "I need to take my phone out of my pocket. Do not shoot."

Miguel raised his rifle and aimed at the old man's wrinkly forehead. "Don't move." And in Spanish, he said, "Seso, clear him."

Seso came over, frowning. He went through every pocket on the old man, fingering every fold of clothes down to his socks. He pulled out a large smartphone.

Miguel took it and turned it on. It was locked. "You come here alone and bring no guns. Just a phone?"

"Just a phone."

This old man, he had balls. "You must have something. What? I know you are not police. You were in that house and left." Miguel held up the phone. "You want to negotiate? Something with this?"

"Yes. Can I?" The old man reached out with a wrinkled hand.

May just as well. Miguel handed the phone over.

The man's shaking finger went over the screen, and a video came on; he held the phone out and rasped, "Streaming video."

The length of a body stretched across the screen, a naked torso facing the camera, the tiger tattoo moving with each breath. El Checheño, tied up on the floor.

Miguel looked up from the screen. "Where is he?"

"And my partner?"

Miguel gave a nod to Seso, who walked to the office enclosure, entered, and through the glass they all saw him lean over to uncuff the prisoner. Seso lifted the prisoner by the armpits to show the old man his partner's face. The maricón, impassive, was looking down.

"Is he alive?" the old man asked.

"Go see if you want." Scowling, Miguel stepped aside and pointed toward the office. This old fart, he was something special. Running an exchange all by himself. Too old to fear anything? Some men grew fearless with time.

The visitor planted his cane and grabbed the cart handle. The tube connected to the valve on the tank snagged, or he was out of breath—he reached and adjusted the valve, and the hissing got louder as he turned toward the office.

A new smell entered Miguel's nostrils, an old woman's perfume, floral, oddly out of place. The smell brought with it a vague worry— the cart. Why did it smell?

Miguel took a step after the old man, but when his foot landed, it sunk into the concrete floor as if it were water.

Water? So strange. Feet and legs sinking. Like liquid sand. Fight— swim—hold on to—can't breathe!

Miguel fell forward, and the floor engulfed him from all sides, flowed into his lungs.

A single question bounced around his head: What is this? What is this? What is this?

His new line of sight included his rifle, his right hand only a few centimeters away from the trigger well. But it could have been Cho's hand or Dado's; the fingers lay inert, the usual connection between thought and movement completely severed.

Miguel's vision clouded from anger at the ultimate betrayal from his body. Even his eyes refused to move. His anger didn't last, soon replaced by a swelling of panic.

Air! Air! Puta madre! Inhale!

But the separation between his mind and body left his thoughts in a vacuum, his words nothing but meaningless shouting for nobody to hear.

A step further, Cho lay with his knees tucked in as if the old asshole had knocked him down with a kick to the groin. The look in the kid's eyes . . . Miguel forgot about the problem of his darkening vision and absent breath; Cho's eyes were dilated, two huge black discs of shock, like buttons. For a second, Cho wasn't Cho but a much younger kid sinking into the ground, his chest torn open by a shot from the AK.

Miguel's field of view shrunk and darkened. Images and sounds flickered in the new blackness, most of them recent memories: the flash and noise from the explosion, the rattling of the old man's cane on the gate. The memories were as clear as the real thing, past events happening anew.

When everything grew quiet, Miguel found himself in the car and heard his own words—now strangely familiar—break the eerie silence.

"It's all God's work, Tio. When God says you die, you die."

42

East Los Angeles, California

Ivan held his breath from the moment he opened the valve on the second tank. He took a few quick steps and reminded himself to slow down. With controlled movement, the seal should keep the gas out.

The thought of seal failure made him grab and press the triangular mask hard into his face. Bad time to take chances. This stuff killed one-hundred-and-seventy people. All dead inside that theatre. What did they call it in the papers? Slaughter in Moscow by SPETZNAZ. Wasn't SPETZNAZ. Different branch. Weaker version of the gas in that hostage rescue. And with bigger volume of air there. Still put everyone down flat.

He looked straight ahead, at the partition wall of the office enclosure. The Mexican who had held Foxy up, the one with the bandaged ear, was out of sight. Why?

Ivan shuffled forward, toward the office booth. The muscles between his shoulder blades stayed tight from anticipation of the possible shot from the dying Mexicans behind him.

Trust the gas. On with the rescue. What was the English saying? Do or die.

The cart wheels squeaked from behind, and the tank hissed and hissed. Not the most important sounds. Clang of the dropped rifles and the thuds of falling bodies would mean a lot more. Or a panicked shot to the back.

He relaxed when the thuds and the clanks echoed through the empty warehouse. Gas everywhere in the open space. Full saturation.

He tossed aside the cane, straightened his aching back, and glanced over his shoulder at the Mexicans, at the three bodies splayed on the floor.

Hold your breath, he told himself. Hold it. Big thanks to Kazbek for offering a practice session in his aquarium.

He set his gaze on the office enclosure with the last Mexican inside. Major risk point, this shooter. Out of view from the beginning. Could be behind the wall, hiding with his rifle. Unconscious? Sure, if the gas tank was close enough to him. But the wall could be a temporary barrier.

Get out of view. Let the gas do the work.

The possibility of the Mexican popping up from cover to fire a shot demanded quick movement, but running could compromise the mask. The seal must stay tight. A few molecules, and it would all be over. Kaput.

In a crouch, Ivan moved around the corner of the office booth and swung the cart around and kept it in front, the wheels squeaking.

Come out. Let the gas take you.

But the man didn't come out—his bullets did. A suppressor hissed louder than the tank, and shots ripped through the partition wall, left to right. Ivan jerked the cart back.

The last Mexican—the smart one. Smart enough to take cover. To set up trap. Shooting at the squeaking wheels.

Bullets banged against metal. Some ricocheted off the floor. One hit the gas tank—BAM—and the impact reverberated up into Ivan's hand. His chest and abdomen grew cold.

Rifle round. Went right through. No more clean air.

Ivan glanced at the warehouse gate. Not enough oxygen left in the lungs to make it. Screwed up everything.

Zaichik, I'm so sorry, he thought. A child without a father—it's all my fault.

The hiss of gas was gone. Ivan stared at the hole. No, it wasn't the air tank. Lucky. The nerve gas. All of it out now.

Ivan reached for the doorknob, turned it, and pulled the door open just a crack. He had jerked his hand back in time for the second volley of gunfire to blast out, much shorter this time—a tight group around the door handle. Still sharp, the Mexican. How? Holding his breath, too? But no mask.

The door creaked open, pushed out by the bullet impact.

Seconds stretched like hours until a thump came from inside, and then scraping sounds. Done. Ivan stood up slowly and looked through the window: the Mexican, draped over the table, was slipping to the floor.

Inside the enclosure, Foxy lay paralyzed on a grimy mattress, drooling out of the corner of his mouth, his hand hanging from the pipe.

They'd cuffed him to the wall.

Ivan stepped closer. Thick pipe. Impossible to yank it off. And by now at least a full minute and a half without breathing. Maybe another thirty seconds of old air left in the lungs, even with the recent practice in the fish tank. Not enough time to undo the cuffs and carry Foxy out of the building. Too much carbon dioxide in the system—the exertion would blow it out of the lungs after one or two steps.

The pulse beat in his temples: Bad news. Bad news. Bad news.

Ivan turned to look at the cart and the tanks. No choice left but to take the risk and breathe.

He pressed the mask into his face, leaned over the tank, and pushed the valve open further, flooding the mask with air. But no breathing. Not yet.

The atomizer sill hung under the cart, taped to the bottom—a thick plastic pen, like a syringe but with a triangular attachment.

He held the injector close to his face. The survivors said they felt it coming. Enough time to inject the antidote if the perfume smell showed up. Inject straight into the airways.

The urge to exhale lessened as he clenched his teeth. Slowly. Slowly. He exhaled into the mask . . . then inhaled. A smell? Inject! He almost ripped the mask off.

But—no tingling or weakness in the muscles. The seal—holding.

Breathing, Ivan let go of the mask and taped the pen to his wrist. Easy access for quick injection.

The handcuffs tying Foxy to the pipe broke with one rifle shot. Ivan slung the rifle over the tanks in the cart and squatted, holding the mask with one hand, to pick up Foxy's limp body.

Lighter than Kazbek. Blistered skin. Hang in there. The gas will either kill you or help with the pain.

The cart took some maneuvering to walk out of the enclosure, an awkward walk. Foxy's arms and legs dangled and threatened to catch and rip out the tubing.

The gate rattled up after one push of a button, and Ivan scanned the street from the shade behind the wall the Mexican had used for cover earlier. Empty street. No need for the rifle yet.

He kept the mask on until a gust of wind threw dust into his eyes. The mask popped off with a sucking sound. Good seal. Thank the clean shave for that, and the grease. The air smelled of truck exhaust. Best smell in the world.

He picked up the rifle then craned and twisted his neck to study the roof edges. No sign of the lookout—either he was on the other side of the roof or climbing down.

Traversing the pavement between the warehouse and the car took a few seconds, and still nobody showed up on the roofs. Foxy, shoved into the passenger seat, fell over the console; Ivan closed the door and crossed over to the driver's side, keeping his gaze on the car.

Watch the windows. Watch them.

He snapped the handle twice to make a loud clank then pulled the door open.

The man's reflection popped into the passenger window, only his head and the white collar of a t-shirt visible over the edge of the roof.

Ivan let go of the door and leaned into the car as if he was reaching for something, the rifle hidden under his chest. Slow movements. A man without hurry.

With a sudden twist of his body, he flipped over and faced up, rifle raised, the bead on the curious, bald head. A single burst caught the man pulling back; red mist puffed out, followed by a thud as the lookout disappeared from view.

Ivan leaned in again, pushed Foxy back onto the seat, and then fixed him with the seatbelt. Inject him here? No, too exposed. Too much reliance on luck already. A sure way to end up in some fish tank again, taking all these chances.

Ivan drove off, glancing at Foxy from time to time. Plohi dela. Eyes getting dimmer. Slow suffocation, just like those hostages in the theatre. The black October of 2002—the victims died from the lung paralysis.

The pen came off his wrist with one pull. He held the antidote between his teeth and pushed his right hand into Foxy's chest, punch after punch, to keep air flowing. Foxy's head flopped around like a ball on a string. Hard task—resuscitating a man with one hand while driving with the other. And useless, without an antidote injection.

At the stop sign, the rearview mirror showed an empty road lined with chain-link fences on both sides. No pursuit. Ivan put the car in park, pushed the triangular attachment on the pen into Foxy's left nostril, and injected half of the contents. The right nostril took the other half. Now it was just a matter of waiting.

After a few intersections, the warehouses gave way to homes and strip malls. On the freeway, Ivan listened for Foxy's breath. There. A bubble of saliva. The opioid blocker from the atomizer would do that. Laverne's weird son coming back from the dead.

Within ten minutes, Foxy's eyelids began to flutter and his mouth moved as he wheezed and rasped in short breaths.

A joke for the joker: "You are back. I hope you enjoyed the trip."

Foxy shuddered as his diaphragm contracted to pull air in. He sat slumped back in his seat, staring at the ceiling. By the time they reached the storage unit, Foxy's breath had normalized, and his gaze gained some focus.

Inside the storage, Kazbek stared at Ivan from the floor and mumbled something into the tape on his mouth.

"That's right," Ivan said. "I can't believe it either." He lowered Foxy down by the wall, only a step away from The Chechen.

On his laptop, two messages showed up from Ruslan, the last one confirming the drop-off location. The big boss, coming for his prize. In transit already. On a plane as soon as he got the news.

Foxy's first coherent statement came out in slurred pieces. "Why. Why the fuck—do you smell like Chanel? You into—perfumes now?"

Always a joker. Would joke in hell, the dancer. "I have my female side. Isn't it what you call it? Soft side." Ivan shook a water bottle in front of him.

Foxy winced and grimaced, but his hand came up, and his grip was firm enough to hold the bottle. "Who did your makeup?"

"Laverne."

Foxy nodded. "Ma is the best." Taking small sips, he watched the makeup removal.

Ivan wiped his face with a towel. "Finish the water. You will feel better."

Foxy had a new expression in his eyes. "You came back for me like a mother fucker."

"I had no choice."

"Ah-huh." Foxy pointed with his bottle at the Chechen. "You caught the big fish. And you still came for me."

"It was not good to leave you behind. I knew I could do it if you and they were together."

Foxy's broken lip twitched into a smile. "You talking sweet talk." He looked around. "I'm high as fuck. Everything's unreal."

"It's because of gas. It's a narcotic. They say you enjoy it before you die."

"I can't say I did. I didn't like the part where I couldn't breathe. Are the Mexicans gonna make it?"

"The lungs stop. You suffocate from paralysis."

Foxy nodded. "Serves them right. The angry one wanted to cut my fingers off." He shifted his gaze to Kazbek, who'd been watching them from the floor. In a lazy movement, Foxy poked him with the tip of his foot. "What up, asshole? Still trying to get off on pain and shit?"

With a grimace, Foxy leaned forward and said in a flat voice, "I don't know who the fuck you are or why Partorg wants you alive, but after all this shit, I sure can't wait to find out."

Foxy leaned back on the wall, his face pale and drawn.

Ivan handed him a shirt. "He didn't need to know about Partorg."

Foxy grimaced. "What's he gonna do, chew his way through the trunk of our car and run south? At this point, ain't nobody taking him from us until we deliver."

Kazbek fought the tape on his arms and legs until the veins on his forehead bulged out and his cheeks turned purple. The tape smothered his shouting. Foxy reached over and patted the Chechen on the cheek, each pat more like a slap.

"That's it, let it all out. Don't swallow your anger, boyo—you'll get indigestion."

Ivan pulled out his smartphone to check the map. Kazbek must have known this day would come, his past catching up to him, and still he did his thing. Everyone was an optimist in this business; you couldn't do it otherwise. The Mexicans. The Chechens. Everyone thought they'd stay ahead of their past.

"Hey," Foxy said, "What happened to the Pomeranians?"

"I gave them to Ruslan for now. But I think Laverne should keep them."

"She'd be good to them." Foxy wriggled his feet. "You got any shoes for me?"

"Runners in the trunk."

"I'll take 'em." Foxy pushed off the wall to stand, and he gasped. "Shit. They messed me up something fierce on that rack."

"When gas wears off, you will feel worse."

Foxy straightened. "You're always so sweet. You got anything in your kit I can take?"

"Yes."

"Good. I could use something to tie me over till we drop him off. I think they tore something in my back, and my shoulders rotate all wrong."

With the gear case in his hands, Ivan walked past Kazbek to the car. The man stunk with fresh urine. Not that the boss would care any. This whole operation stunk.

Kazbek let out a sustained cry into the tape, a long "M-M-G-G-H-H", a loud effort that made his eyes bulge.

"I think he wants to communicate," Foxy said. "Like, say things and shit."

"Cut the tape if you want to hear it. I don't. I'm going to the restroom on the corner."

When Ivan came back in, Foxy was drinking water by the wall, a roll of tape in his hand and Kazbek's mouth free to flap. Foxy said with a scowl, "Hey, Russki Bear. You want an island?"

"Island is boring. And I get sunburn."

Foxy kicked Kazbek with the tip of his sneaker. "You hear that? He doesn't want your fucking island either."

Kazbek strained to twist his neck and look up. He sounded hoarse. "Listen. I'm the biggest arms dealer in this hemisphere. Understand who you're dealing with—it doesn't matter what Partorg is paying for me. My people will not let you enjoy any of it if you trade me in."

Foxy tightened his lips. "Hmm." He cocked his head to the side, to align it with Kazbek's. "I like a man with confidence. But how do you know Partorg isn't gonna drown your ass in a septic tank? You can't ruin our lives after that now, can you?"

"If I die," Kazbek said, "my family will look for you till you are dead. Your best option is to take my money and tell your client I went to Sinaloa. You will have good proof you had trouble getting to me. And I can pay you cash or bonds, anything you want. In bonds and property, up to a billion."

Foxy whistled and looked at Ivan. "What do you think of that?"

Ivan's cell phone beeped a note of complaint, and he checked the screen. "My battery is low." He looked up. "We must go. The boss hates waiting."

Foxy groaned with pain as he stood up. He stepped toward Kazbek, ripped off a length of tape, and slapped it on the Chechen's mouth. Kazbek tried to shake it off, but Foxy had deftly run the roll around his head.

Foxy's voice seemed full of genuine sadness as he looked Kazbek in the face. "Ozzy, my man. I'd love to earn a billion, but my partner has principles and whatnot. So no deal." He let go with a quick push and Kazbek's head thunked against the floor.

Foxy straightened up gingerly, palms pushing off his knees, strain in his back like an old man's. It was going to be a long recovery.

Foxy groaned, "Fuck, I've seen better days."

"I will load him."

Huffing, Foxy moved to the gate. Ivan rolled Kazbek into the section of old carpet from the safe house, the Chechen protesting and wriggling like a worm.

"As they say here," Ivan said, "too little and already late."

He lifted the thick roll and lowered it into the trunk. "Con te partirò." The Italian line from the opera seemed more fitting.

The end of things. Not even curious, like Foxy, why Partorg wanted his Chechen so much. Didn't matter why. Only the child mattered.

43

East Los Angeles, California

Ivan took the 210 freeway, heading east. The mountains to the left loomed larger with every mile, smooth ridges underlining the sky. On the right, track houses stretched into the dull horizon layered with haze.

"A family road trip," Foxy said and tossed another pill into his mouth. He washed the painkiller down with a sip of water.

"But we're not relatives," Ivan said. "What do you call a trip together when you are not relatives?"

"I call it 'a date with Mr. Sexy'." Foxy chuckled and winced, holding his stomach. "Shit. Can't even laugh."

"Your jokes are back. The drugs must be working."

"Yeah, aren't they a blessing?" Foxy leaned back and looked down at his crotch. "My bandage is leaking blood and pus, and here I am, chirpin' like a bird."

Ivan frowned. Always like this, in a squad, wondering who gets the shrapnel, who gets a stray bullet to the hip. Foxy—he'd gotten the worst of it. Torn up, inside and outside. Fit for the trauma unit, but in good spirits. Not his first time with injury.

Foxy smoothed the bandage on his belly, under his shirt. "Good thing I was the only one they worked over. Did the Mexicans come in before Eva could start on you?"

"She had me in the aquarium."

"The fish tank? Why, they had sharks in it or something?"

"They kept closing the pipe so I couldn't breathe."

"I see." Foxy nodded glumly. "They water-boarded your ass. I'm surprised they didn't put both of us in that tank to watch us fight for air. Those two had ideas."

"It was only big enough for one person."

Foxy gave it a crooked smile. "Yeah, otherwise it would be like that joke about the fish."

"A joke?"

"It's a pun. Two fish get in the tank and one says to another, 'Do you know how to drive this thing?'"

"It's a joke?"

"It's funny 'cause the word tank can also mean army tank, you know, the one with a cannon."

"I see. Play on words."

"You need to work on your English jokes, Russki Bear."

"Humor is hard when things are not funny."

Foxy nodded. "You could say that again." He stared out of the window. "You know what's really funny, though? They were ripping off my arms and legs, and all I could think of was my junk."

"Junk?"

"My dick and balls. I kept thinking—I can live without legs and arms, but if they cut off my junk? I'm done living."

"It's like in the army," Ivan said, nodding. "If you step on the mine, you don't care about legs—you want to know if your dick is still working. Your woman back home will stay with you if you have your dick. You die alone if you don't have one."

"I didn't worry about no woman, but I couldn't see myself living without a dick." Foxy rubbed his temple. "So weird. When you picked me up, my head hit the door, but I felt nothing."

Ivan chuckled. "That's good. So I don't have to apologize."

"No shit. You don't owe me nothing. I sure as hell didn't expect you to bust in there."

"I had to come for you. Many reasons."

Foxy sat quiet for a while, until he said, "How did you find me, anyway?"

"Remember the porn shoot?"

"Yeah?"

"I didn't trust you then. I installed a tracking chip in your phone. The Mexicans kept your phone."

"I see." Foxy stared out of the window. "Funny, how it goes. You not trusting me helped you saved my ass."

Ivan rubbed his neck. "What are you doing next? Another contract?"

Foxy stared forward at the empty stretch of the freeway up ahead, as if his future were a road sign he needed to read. "I guess I'm gonna have to lie low for a while." He spoke slowly, as if distracted by his vision of the future. "Lick my wounds. You?"

"I want to sell electronics through my company. We sell a lot. Partorg likes money. I think he will let me make money and train the younger guys. No more killing." From the corner of his eye, Ivan caught Foxy staring at him. "What?"

Foxy shook his head. "I just don't see you selling stuff. It's like . . ." Foxy stared out of the window. "It's like asking a wolf to do gardening."

"I want a garden, yes. And a country house. It's my dream. I grew up on a farm in Ukraine."

Foxy smiled. "You never cease to surprise me. Never met a man like you before."

"The same for me. But it was good. It worked."

After they joined Interstate 5, the endless sea of housing on the right gave way to a canyon cutting through the mountains. On the other side, the desert opened up, a high plateau interrupted by islands of rock eroding under the crisp blue sky. Sand, loose dirt, and broken shrubbery flew across the freeway. The air turned much drier.

Foxy pinched his nose. "Jesus. I can't afford to sneeze, man. I'm gonna fall apart." He pointed at the dirt road leading off into the brown landscape. "I come out here for target practice sometimes."

"Long range?"

"Yeah. My guy in Barstow has a rifle collection. Last time I shot a beer can at two thousand yards with his fifty cal."

"I like three-thirty-eight cartridges better. They don't kick as hard."

Foxy sighed. "The way my shoulders hurt, I won't be shooting anything larger than a twenty-two for a long while. I'm stuck with tiny guns, Russki Bear. The kind I can hide between my butt cheeks."

Ivan nodded. "Funny. A gun between the butt cheeks."

Foxy reached for his bottle of pills. "Well, look at you. Digging my homo humor." He shook the bottle. "Shit. I think I'm low."

They drove in silence, until Foxy turned the radio on and flipped through a few local stations.

"Try the CD," Ivan said.

"Whatcha got there? You opera shit?"

"Rap."

"Oh, yeah. I forgot. Your favorite English lessons."

Angry voices burst from the speakers, shouting angry words that accompanied them to Barstow. Ivan glanced out at the bleak houses emerging on the side of the freeway. Everything tan—a desert town. A lot like Israel, the way the desert seeped into the streets with sand and debris, the wind pushing eddies of dust around.

The navigation system put them on Interstate 40, and the houses disappeared. Foxy dozed off despite the music, until the car rolled side-to-side at the end of an exit ramp and his head banged against the window.

They drove onto the sun-bleached belt of an empty highway slicing the desert into two halves. The coordinates brought them to a secluded spot within view of low, weathered rock formations, clumps of shrubs, and small bushes sticking out of brown dirt everywhere. The winter sun had already dropped behind the hills; a gust of wind pushed sand around, the air pungent with lemony smell of plants.

Foxy climbed out with a grunt and leaned against the side of the car, like he had to gather himself. Quiet for a while now, the joker. In pain. You know it was a bad operation when it silenced a talkative man.

Ivan breathed in the fresh air. "I like this desert smell. Like tree sap. A little sour."

Foxy nodded at a big shrub. "Creosote. Smells even better after it rains." He perked up. "Hey, speaking of smell . . . Seriously, why the fuck did I smell Chanel in that warehouse? I didn't see no old ladies there anywhere."

"The perfume is mixed with the gas for detection."

"Oh, yeah. If you smell it, you're fucked."

"I was thinking the whole time, 'if I smell it, it's too late.' That gas—it's military grade. Works quickly."

"I fucking noticed. One second I'm flexing my legs to kick the Mexican in the knees, next I'm on the floor, unable to breathe."

"It's an improved version. 'Kolokol' is the original name. Means 'The Bell'. FSB used it when the Chechens took hostages in the theatre in Moscow. It didn't work well for them. Too many civilian casualties."

"I'd say it worked just fine here. I made it."

"I gave you a blocker. In Moscow, they disabled the Chechens, but the hostages died too because the FSB didn't give them the blocker for the gas. People suffocated."

"Why the fuck didn't they give it to them?"

Explain a country no one understands. "Russia is a mess. FSB didn't want anyone to know they used the secret gas. They wanted the gas to stay secret. So they never told the ambulance doctors what they used. They let the people die to keep the secret."

The low rumbling of a helicopter sounded from behind the hills, and Foxy pushed off the car. "Here comes the Party Man."

The helicopter made a series of narrowing circles, hovering and kicking up a storm with its rotor blades. They stepped behind the car to hide from the wrath of dust mixed with branches biting into their faces. The wind from the helicopter shook a tall cactus nearby, its long stems waving like arms of a strange scarecrow.

Ivan zipped up his jacket. The air lost all warmth as soon as the sun dropped out of view, like the heater turned off. Always like this in the desert.

When the bird landed, two bodyguards hopped out, and then Partorg himself, dressed in a white suit. The guards never left his side, everyone bending forward, away from the rotor blast. One of the guards carried a chair—the other a huge plastic cooler with holes drilled into the sides.

Holes. The plastic prison, without agony of suffocation.

The helicopter took off into the darkening sky; once its roar receded in the distance, a hush fell on everything, interrupted only by the crunch of stones and sand under everyone's feet. The two guards, dressed in suits, carefully placed the chair and the cooler by the car and walked off without a word, heading toward the red rock outcroppings that interrupted the flatland a few hundred meters away.

Partorg pushed the chair deeper into the dirt to keep it stable, sat down, and slapped his thighs with his palms. Without greeting, he waved his hand impatiently and said in Russian, "Bring him out."

Ivan pulled Kazbek out of the trunk, dropped him on the ground, and unrolled the carpet all the way to Partorg's feet. Kazbek didn't care to look at Partorg at all, staring at the sky instead.

Partorg, sitting with his arms crossed, looked down at his prize and then at Foxy. "Did he have family?" he asked in English.

Foxy, leaning against the side of the truck, said, "His wife didn't make it. Cartel guys got to her first."

Ivan shook his head when Kazbek convulsed at the words like an animal zapped with a cattle prod. Smotrika—tears in his eyes. Strange relationship. Loved his woman, to cry about her like this, at the worst time.

With his thick fingers, Partorg worked patiently to rip the duct tape off Kazbek's mouth, piece by piece, without hurry. He collected the tape into a ball and tossed it aside then leaned forward, his gaze going over the Chechen from head to feet.

"Here you are," Partorg said in Russian. "We both knew this day would come."

Kazbek had gathered himself quickly; he sounded indifferent, no signs of grief over Eva in his voice. "At your age, you still can't let go."

"You betrayed me. I don't forget such things."

334

"You know I had no choice."

Partorg grunted. "Now you say it. You didn't say it back then."

Kazbek turned his head. "You wouldn't listen anyway."

Partorg reached inside the cooler and pulled out a plastic box but didn't open it. "I pulled you up as if you were my son. All you had to do was come and ask me to forgive you."

Kazbek jerked his head up, the muscles on the front of his neck like a thick 'V'. "You never forgive anybody."

Ivan caught the look in the black eyes: Lifeless now. No hope. Really loved his woman. Hoping to get shot.

The Chechen dropped his head back on the sand. "If I came to you back then, you would have torn me apart with your bare hands."

Partorg sounded disgusted. "You deserve it. I near lost everything because of your stupidity." He motioned to Ivan and Foxy and said in English, "Make him stand up."

Ivan turned to Foxy. "I will do it. You rest." No use, lifting anything with torn shoulders, drugs or no drugs. He walked over, grabbed Kazbek by the armpits, and lifted him to his feet.

With hands tied behind his back and feet taped together, Kazbek had a hard time standing straight. He swayed, despite being propped.

Partorg sprung from the chair like those passengers on a plane who think they can walk off as soon as it lands. He said, "You're not going to remember this, but I will," and punched the Chechen straight in the mouth. Ivan caught Kazbek falling backward, the boss already waving his hand. "Up. Keep him up."

The punches landed with a squishy sound. Kazbek's head tilted this way and that as his knees buckled. Red dots and smudges speckled Partorg's white jacket and shirt.

"I said keep him up."

Ivan held the Chechen by the sides of his body. Like in a dojo, holding the training bag for a partner to punch. Distasteful. Beating up on a dead man. Old anger. Should tire soon.

Partorg's breath grew labored after a few punches, his neck and face red, the skin on his knuckles torn and bloodied.

After Kazbek swayed back the last time, with his head tilted and blood dripping from his mouth, Ivan said, "Victor Vasilievich, you have blood on your cheek."

The remark shook the boss out of his concentration, out of his grim delight. Partorg stared at Ivan with an empty look while the words sunk in—he wiped his face with a sleeve and stared at it. "Always wanted to do this myself." He looked at Kazbek. "I've had enough. Lay him down."

Not the time yet for Kazbek to go into the cooler? After lowering Kazbek to the ground, Ivan straightened up and looked to his boss for instructions.

Breathing heavily, Partorg studied his knuckles, wincing at a flap of skin hanging loose. His gaze went to the plastic box he'd left on the chair. He picked it up and pulled out a syringe.

"Put it into his vein. Make sure it's in a blood vessel. They tell me it should be a vein or artery. It doesn't matter which."

Ivan took the syringe. The last rays of sunlight turned the fluid golden. A tranquilizer?

The vein on the Chechen's neck stood out thick against his musculature. Ivan drove the needle in. Hard to push the liquid through. Really thick.

Kazbek didn't fight the injection, but his breath grew shallow and fast, and his body began to shake.

Partorg barked, "Hold him. It's takes two injections."

Ivan pressed Kazbek's body down with both hands. The Chechen was hot to the touch, his eyes rolling up in a strange reaction. "Victor Vasilievich, I'll miss the vein with the second one if he shakes like that."

"I know." Partorg was already holding the second syringe in his hand. He turned to Foxy and said in English with mild irritation, "I didn't pay you to watch. I paid you to work. Finish it."

When Foxy walked over, he said, "Hold him down, Russki Bear. Lean in."

"I can hold down his head and chest and give you a few seconds." Kazbek's forehead was burning.

A gunshot and immense pain came together—a punch between the shoulder blades—and Ivan fell forward.

The impact of the gunshot fragmented his thoughts: Can't breathe. Face in the sand. Brown granules. Flint. Grass. Grass in the desert. Foxy shot me. Ears ringing. Pain like a nail— hammered into my spine. Foxy. This whole time . . . Lena. Zaichik. I can't—

The second blow shook and spun everything around, the desert and the sky. Dark blue and brown. Wet feeling. Hot and wet. Everything distant. Spinning black.

A familiar voice said from far away, "Do you want me to bury him here?"

44

Barstow, California

Neat squares of farm fields spun far down below. Roads and tiny ranch houses and a coppice went round and round in a nauseating twirl.

The slider—it must be stuck on the suspension lines. And now the wing would stay lopsided and spinning. Twisted lines. The slider wouldn't come down like this. Shit. Untangle it. Look up. Look up!

Ivan strained his neck to see the crumpled wing of the parachute. But the pressure on the back of his head kept him immobile, forcing him to stare down at the vertigo-inducing scene.

He flexed all the muscles from his neck down to his shoulders and let go—the headache split his mind into a thousand pieces, an explosion of pain piercing his eyeballs.

The roaring in his ears meant he was falling fast, the parachute in full failure.

Fix it. Untwist the lines or cut the damn thing free and pop the reserve.

Through the roar, a voice said into his ear, "Easy now, Russki Bear. Easy." A heavy hand on his shoulder pushed him into—a bed? Impossible. The landscape. I'm looking down, Ivan thought. A thousand meters at least.

He closed his eyes, and the spinning slowed, everything now a field of darkness in slow rotation, white dots popping in and out of it. The noise died down.

Ivan focused on the soft pressure around his face. A weird—pillow? With a hole in the middle? He slowly parted his eyelids, and the farm fields with roads changed into floor tiles, their elaborate pattern easy to mistake for a bird's eye view of the earth. As further proof of the illusion, the top of a sneaker intruded into view.

A familiar voice said, "How you feeling, big guy?"

Ivan tried to open his eyes wider, but the dizziness came back, so he spoke with his eyes closed. "Everything spins."

"You have a concussion. I shot you in the back of your head."

The statement took some thinking to process. Shot. Back of your head. Explained the headache and dizziness. Why?

Thoughts spun and swirled and refused to link up: The desert. Partorg. Rough sand.

Ivan flexed his arms and wiggled his fingers. Arms tied to something soft. Wrists cuffed tight to it but without cutting off the circulation.

A spot of dull pressure inside his elbow was mildly painful; he pulled on the restraint, and a hand pressed down on his shoulder.

"Easy. You'll rip the needle out. You need to rest. Here." Sneakers squeaked on the tiles and came around his bed. "This'll help."

A softness spread through Ivan's body, tiring softness that swallowed the vertigo, the discomfort in his hand, and at last, the headache.

The second time he woke up, the gray floor tiles weren't spinning. He turned his head slowly. A pair of white sneakers. Ankles crossed. Someone snoring.

The restraints—Ivan flexed his arms and legs to rise off the soft bed, but the attachments held back the movement, the rattle of metal parts ringing out the alarm.

"Whoa, whoa, hold on. Let me unbuckle it. You're tied to a massage table."

Foxy's voice. Ivan relaxed his arms, and the pressure around his wrists went away.

"Take it slow, man," Foxy said. "You got hit with a rubberized round straight in the back of your noggin'. I fixed you to the bed to protect the stitches."

"You shot me," Ivan wheezed out.

"I sure did." Foxy sounded mildly apologetic. "I pretty much had to, man."

Hard to concentrate. "If you shot me, why am I alive?"

Foxy let out a heavy sigh. "Well, it's kinda simple. The Party Man paid me to put you into the ground. Then some shit happened, if you recall. Eva and the dogs and whatnot."

"The water. Aquarium."

"Yeah, and the aquarium. And then the Mexican fucker wanted to slice me up, like I wasn't sliced up enough already. I was thinking, that's it, that's where I get off the ride. And then you, of all the fucking people, rolled in to save my ass. I couldn't shoot you for real after that."

"Laverne will not like it."

"Laverne? Yeah. I can't look her in the eye and tell her you're doing fine when your fat ass is rotting in the desert 'cause I put you in there."

"You shot me with—"

"A dummy round."

"My head." Ivan flexed his neck, careful this time. "Feels strange."

"I stitched the flaps of your skin together. No damage to the bone, just bruising. You lucky I know how to sew. They're nice stitches."

The conversation helped sharpen Ivan's thoughts. "I am not lucky. What day is it?"

"Tuesday. The day after. Hang on, let me get these off."

The restraints came off his ankles. "Where are we?"

"Barstow. About an hour away from where I shot you."

Ivan flexed his legs, bent and unbent his knees. He brought his hands to a pushup position and pushed off the bed, eyes closed the entire way up. His spine hurt as much as his head, a stabbing pain that made breathing difficult. But the pain was more manageable than the thirst. Lips, mouth, and throat—sheets of sandpaper, rubbing against each other.

"I need water."

Foxy pushed a bottle into his hand, fresh out of the fridge. The bottle spread coldness into his fingers, his throat begging for the same. Without opening his eyes, Ivan unscrewed the top and emptied the whole thing in greedy gulps.

"Give me another one." The room didn't spin when he opened his eyes. Foxy. In blue jeans and a pink shirt that said 'SASSY' on the chest. Worried expression in his dark eyes. "The dummy round. Was it wax or plastic?"

"Rubber composite. Family recipe. Real low velocity. But you gonna have ugly scars."

Ivan ran his fingers gently over the bandage taped to his scalp. "Was I in your contract from the beginning?"

"Yes."

"Did he tell you why?"

"His son."

"Fedot."

"Yeah. Dimitri. You Russians have difficult names. Anyway, he hates your guts. You must have done something to him. I think his papa wasn't entirely sold on the idea of offing you, but Dimitri convinced him somehow that you were a liability."

"I need to go back to Moscow." Ivan stood up, swayed, and plopped back down. Lightheaded.

Foxy grabbed a flashlight from a surgical tray sitting nearby. "Let's check your concussion first. Keep your eyes open." He shone the light into each pupil. "Looks fine. You dilate like nothing happened. How do you feel?"

The light didn't add anything to the headache. The same dull pressure remained in the back of the skull. "The light doesn't hurt. So it's not bad."

"Keep your eye on the stick." Foxy moved the flashlight side-to-side. "Eye movement looks good. I don't think I fried your brain." He went back to his chair. "You've got a thick skull. Spared you the heavy damage. Do you feel sick?"

"No. All I have is pain."

"That makes two of us."

Foxy tossed the flashlight back on the tray. "You should go someplace warm and easy. Like Belize. Or something even further where they don't have a lot of Russians. I can recommend an island in Panama. Lay low for a good stretch."

"I have to get Lena out of Moscow." Ivan grabbed the side of the bed to prop himself as he stood, unsteady with weakness in his legs. Could've been worse.

Foxy shook his head. "You can barely walk. She can wait. With you officially dead, they wouldn't care about your woman."

"Fedot will care. He's worse than Kazbek. I need to get her out of there before he gets to her."

"Why would he give a shit? I met him. I'm telling you, he's not into women."

"He has a favorite thing for setup. He always makes it look like the boyfriend went crazy."

Ivan's legs felt wobbly—he leaned against some bookshelves, bending forward. Lower. Lower. His hand reached a pack of water bottles. He grabbed one and straightened up.

Foxy's look of concern had changed to a hard stare. "You can't go to Russia, man. You're supposed to be in the grave I dug up. Your boss gets wind of your being alive, and we're all as good as dead. In case you didn't notice, he's not a forgiving type."

"Don't worry. I will make a good plan." Ivan looked down on his pants, studied the pattern of small elephants on them, the same pattern that continued to his sky-blue shirt. "What is this I am wearing?"

"My pajamas. I had to throw your clothes away. Listen, I understand you're a stubborn asshole, but if you didn't decide to come back and rescue my ass, you'd be dead by now. You're good, Ivan. But you're not that good. Lay low. Let the dust settle."

"I can't. I have to reach her first."

Foxy threw his arms up. "Jesus, man, what is so fucking special about her that makes her worth all our lives?"

Ivan leaned back against the bed. Tired. No energy. Feeling sick now. "She is pregnant with my child."

Foxy groaned and rolled his eyes. "Oh, you've got to be kidding me." He threw his arms up. "What, you never heard of birth control? I mean, seriously—we're executioners. We can't play house."

"I made a mistake and thought they take me out that day. So I made love to my woman. The last time in my life." The words came out flat, like someone else talking.

Foxy slapped his knees and stood up. "Well, we're fucked." He sighed, his hands on his hips. "Okay." He pointed at the shelf. "I got you some clothes. I'll be in the kitchen. I feel better when I cook."

A pile of clothes. A few steps away. Ivan finished the water, aimed the bottle at a garbage bin in the corner, and threw it. The bottle went in clean, without bouncing off the edge. No damage to his motor skills. Just weak.

The edge of the bed gave enough support to reach the IV rack, and from there it was only three steps to the clothes. They were the right size, jeans and a t-shirt, socks and a hoody. Foxy didn't have doubts. If he'd had doubts, there wouldn't have been clothes.

A wave of vertigo pushed Ivan off-balance while he buttoned his shirt. He held onto the shelf and the wall to cross the room and reach the hall. Cold tiles on the restroom floor felt strangely invigorating. No blood in urine—good sign.

He slid his hand along the wall on his way to the kitchen, guided by the sounds of a knife tapping on a chopping board. When he entered, Foxy, standing next to white-tiled counter, turned and said, "You like boiled eggs?"

"Anything is fine." The sight of an open plastic package with meat next to a loaf of bread pushed saliva into Ivan's mouth. Hungry—good sign.

A chair by the wooden table creaked under his weight, and for a second it threatened to sink into the worn-out linoleum covering the floor. Falling. Spinning. Ivan gripped the seat and closed his eyes.

"You look whiter than a white person with their skin bleached," Foxy said.

The smell of meat helped restore balance. Ivan opened his eyes at the bang of a plate against the table. A sandwich. He took a bite and chewed carefully before swallowing, expecting sickness. "My gear case. I had papers in it."

Foxy picked up his bottle of beer and took a sip. "I have it. They didn't care what I took."

"When did you decide to break contract?"

"After you got me high on the gas that killed the Mexicans." Foxy's lips curved, but his eyes didn't match the smile. "I blame the gas. I wouldn't have cheated on your boss if I were thinking straight."

Ivan nodded, and the headache burst from the top of his head down to his stomach. Oof—he dropped the sandwich to the table.

"Give it a minute," Foxy said.

Ivan opened his eyes once the spinning stopped. He finished the sandwich, down to the last crumb. The food sent fresh warmth through his limbs and pushed back the nausea. "Do you have shoes?"

Foxy left and came back with a pair of brown construction boots. "Here. To complete your redneck outfit."

"Do you have a car for me?"

"Yeah. It will take you as far as the city, but you don't want to take it to the airport. Park and take the taxi."

There wasn't much to pack. The jacket, papers, and a makeup kit fit into a backpack he threw into the passenger seat. Foxy stood watching from the porch, frowning.

Time for honesty. "I promise I will have a good plan. I will call right away with result."

Foxy sighed. "Yeah. Right. Have you ever mentioned Laverne or the club to anyone?"

"No."

"Use the number at Laverne's club. Ask for me." Foxy's face wrinkled into a grimace, his eyes narrow. "Just do me a favor—keep your face out of the picture. Seriously. I really don't want to take the Chechen's place."

"If you don't want me to go, you should have shot me with real round."

"Believe me, the thought crossed my mind."

Foxy turned away and reached for the door, shaking his head.

Driving off, Ivan glanced into the rearview mirror. Foxy—

unhappy about his decision, the good man. And rightfully so.

45

Kaluga Oblast, Russia

It's a long drive, from Ukraine to Russia. Longer, in the winter. Ivan kept the heater running the entire time, straining it to its limits.

So much snow. Snowed nonstop from Kiev international to Kaluga—eight hours of speeding through white murk. Flying into Kiev had cut down on the risk of showing up on the Organization's radar, but the drive—it was taking too long.

Wipers pushed snow aside, right to left, left to right, like a pendulum measuring time. With two hours' worth of travel left before Moscow, each hour stretched into the distance, long as a month.

Ivan's hand slipped into his front pocket again, his palm wrapped around a cell phone.

Call her now and tell her to run. Run, Zaichik. Get on the plane. Fly anywhere. Run.

He let go of the phone. You can't call her, he thought. It would only be a short-lived relief. And Fedot would find out, if they had tapped her phone line. And she wouldn't understand anyway, wouldn't act quickly enough. All the lies—she knew nothing. A phone conversation wouldn't work. She'd need a face-to-face explanation.

Ivan groaned and kicked the gas pedal to speed around a caravan of trailers pulling past Obninsk. Here, the clouds thinned over snowy fields and the sun broke out for the first time, its blinding beams bouncing off brilliant snow.

Too bright—he rummaged through the glove compartment for sunglasses. The headache never went away. At least not as dizzy in the blinding light.

Unlike in California, the sunlight here failed to warm the car. Cold flowed from the frozen blue sky onto the icy highway. Gaps in the frame of the old Ziguli leaked heat like a sieve leaking water.

He shivered. The heater in the old clunker on maximum, and it was still too cold to take off his parka.

Road markers went by, most of them buried under piles of snow. Another measure of time: One. Two. Three. Not fast enough. Going to be too late.

His anxious mind offered a terrifying image: Lena, with her mouth open. Fedot, his hands choking a silent scream out of her.

Ivan gunned the engine until the old rattler reached its limit, groaning and complaining, shaking and creaking.

At the sight of the speed limit, his foot came off the gas, and he scolded himself: You can't afford a delay. This isn't America. The police here always look for a handout, for a speeding car. Everyone crooked, top to bottom. They'll make you wait to solicit a bigger bribe. Is there something I can do officer? Sure, just park over there. I will be right back. Crooked filth. Lying and thieving.

Lying, Ivan thought, just like you. Liar. Lied to her for years.

Ivan kicked the accelerator, and the car lurched forward, begging him to slow down. He thought: Always a good choice, an old car. Police wouldn't look twice at it. But they are not the problem. How to get her out of Moscow without Fedot sounding the alarm—that's the problem. She would have to move but stay in the city. Can't just pick her up and take off. Partorg would know. No future that way. First, she has to go looking for her missing boyfriend.

Ivan winced. Fedot would be too close to her if she stayed in Moscow, but she couldn't just leave. A paradox. Stay but not stay. How do you do that?

The mind-wrecking search for a fix sharpened his dull headache, noise from the road splitting his brain into aching pieces.

The solution came while he was fueling his car at a station, and once he knew the answer, his headache lessened. He got in and drove off, thinking it was like the English proverb: mind over matter. Once you know what to do, the pain doesn't matter.

Moscow greeted him with honking of frustrated drivers, their cars packed into thick veins of long boulevards heading toward the center. Banks of fresh snow, pushed aside by snowplows, narrowed the roads and further slowed the traffic. But with snow, the sidewalks and drab apartment blocks looked cleaner. Where the sun shone through the openings between high-rises, its yellow beams sparked glitter on snow and ice.

Nothing like California. What would Los Angeles look like if it ever snowed there? A palm tree with a thick hat of snow perched on top?

A block away, Ivan parked the car on the street and walked—a shopping bag stuffed with clothing in his right hand, a walking stick in his left—to the door, which opened on a hallway of the apartment building opposite his. A standard design: a row of mailboxes on the wall in front of the elevator. A urine stain in the corner, next to the stairs. The elevator smelled of urine, too. Welcome to Russia. The smell of home.

Elevator doors rumbled open at the top floor, and another flight of stairs brought him to a narrow landing with a ladder on the wall. Ivan carried the shopping bag up to the roof with him as he climbed.

Here, you couldn't leave anything unattended. Not like Hollywood. Might get away with leaving a bag of old clothing in a park in Hollywood for ten minutes, but here in Moscow they'd pick up anything not nailed to the wall.

On the roof, he dropped the bag and walked to the edge to check the yard for anything suspicious. But his gaze went straight to the familiar curtains. Through the powered scope, the kitchen and living room windows looked huge. And dark. Gut-wrenching anxiety shortened his breath.

They took her. She's gone. It's too late.

He searched the darkness behind each curtain, his fingers shaking the scope.

Light!

The kitchen light came on. The sight of her silhouette dropped him to his knees the same time the stress burst out of his body in a long exhalation. His strength escaped along with the air.

She's alive. Unhurt. And so close.

In the span of several heart beats, he stayed slumped until a sobering thought brought his scope back up and down on the yard. No reason for them to post a lookout, but it didn't take much to check for one.

The cold made it easy to spot the problem car. Only one vehicle with steam rising from the exhaust pipe—a boxy patrol car parked close to the door. Strange. A transport vehicle from the local station. Obychni voronok. Lots of patrolmen on the Organization's payroll. But why post them right outside the door?

He climbed down from the roof, through the same hatch. A lattice of frost covered a window on the landing overlooking the yard. His teeth chattered from cold as he pulled on a worn-out pair of baggy trousers, a thick sweater, and a parka with goose down feathers sticking out of the holes in the cloth.

A shapeless fur hat with bald patches completed his ensemble. He wrapped a scarf around his face and checked himself in a mirror from the makeup kit. The cold would explain the scarf to the patrolmen. Good enough to go and panhandle in the Red Square. The kind of look that would make Foxy proud.

He put away the mirror and picked up a cane. Old beggar, bent by age and illness, propping himself.

Out in the frozen yard, the cane helped with balance, as the worn rubber soles of his cheap boots easily slipped on the ice or even packed snow. He leaned hard on the cane, like an old man would, moving in slow, pained steps.

With his dirty shopping bag clutched to his chest, his back hunched, and his steps uncertain, he shuffled past the patrol car and over to the trash dump. There, he picked bottles and cans out of the dumpster and stashed them in his bag, all the while keeping an eye on residents coming home, the cars coming and going. The scarf, now up to his nose, kept his face protected from the biting cold.

A few people hurried into their hallways, none of them giving him as much as a look. He picked through trash, waiting until the door to the hallway swung open and Lena stepped out in her long coat with Bond by her side, off-leash. The dog, excited from being outdoors, lurched off the steps and went sniffing, dashing from the bench to the light pole, stopping only to pee on the trash bin.

Ivan gripped the cane harder. Dangerous, to count on this garbage stink to keep Bond from smelling his owner. Would be a disaster if he started barking. He'd bark and hop all over the place. Too much exuberance, and with the patrol right there.

Empty bottles clanked in Ivan's bag as he walked in labored steps toward the arch under the building that led out of the yard and to the main street. Far enough from the patrolmen. Dark here. Nighttime. Perfect cover. She always walks him in a circle around the building. Everyone follows their routine. In this cold, she'd come along soon.

Lena stepped under the arch, wrapped in her fur coat and her hat low on her forehead. She turned and called, "Bond! Let's go! It's cold out here!"

The dog ran after her and ahead. Then he yelped and sprinted toward Ivan, jumping around him and barking while Lena stood and stared.

Bond reared up, his feet on Ivan's shoulders, and licked Ivan's face. Ivan hugged him and let go, saying crisply, "Bond. Quiet. Sit." Bond plopped on his ass, whipping his tail side to side.

Ivan looked at Lena's frozen outline. The darkness should ease the shock. She'd be processing the new sensory input. "Zaichik, it's me. I'm wearing strange clothes—don't be afraid, it's just a disguise."

Lena raised her hands, covered by mittens, to her face. "God— Vanya?" Her voice faltered.

He hugged her, filling his nostrils with her sweet smell. "I'm home, Zaichik. I'm home."

She pressed into him, sobbing, her body in a shiver. He caught her face and pressed his lips into hers, feeling her warmth, only her nose still cold. The kiss—long enough for both of them to run out of breath.

Her gloved fingers caressed his cheeks. "Vanya, I was so worried. First that bodyguard you sent, and then the perfume. Then I don't hear from you. I was sick with worry. I'm so glad you're back—" She felt the hat on his head with both hands. "In God's name, what are you wearing?"

Bond whimpered from below.

Ivan kept his hands wrapped around her waist. She's in my arms, he thought. The illusion of safety. Safe until the patrolmen decide she'd been gone too long and come looking into the archway.

He pulled her closer. Time to speak of urgency. But not too much. Bad time for panic.

"Zaichik, we're in danger. My trip—it all fell apart. I crossed some bad people. Bandits from Solzevskaya. They're after me. And you. Us. They're after everything. My company. All the property. Remember the customs problems? It was all them. I need to hide you until we can leave Moscow."

Another lie mixed with truth. Just to save her. Everything coming to an end.

"Bandits?" She sounded incredulous. "What did you do?"

He pulled away to look left and right, to the exits. Yellow streetlights over the building entrances and the light from the apartment windows lit the yard just enough. Nobody coming yet.

He faced her. "It's about my business. Years ago, I borrowed money from them to start it. I paid it back, but they wanted more, so I made an arrangement with someone else to help me. I shouldn't have. We're in great danger now. We need to hide for a while."

"But you have your guards—the guy you send to guard me. He called me earlier today—"

Like falling into freezing water. "What did he say?"

"He said he'd come by tonight, after work."

Frenzied words gushed out of him: "No. No. No. You can't see him. He's dangerous. He kills people. Women . . . Children. You can't—"

She covered her face and started to shake. "Oh God. Oh God." About to cry.

"Zaichik, breathe. Breathe."

She looked up. "I told you to stop. I told you we don't need all that money. I told you. I told you!" She pushed her fists into his chest with every word.

The guilt. Hot, and it burned right through his gut. All your fault, he thought. But not the time for this.

"Zaichik, walk with me." He pulled her by the hand toward the other side of the arch. Shake her out of her immobility. Best thing when in shock. Give her something to do. Her mind would have to snap out of shock and catch up with her body.

Guiding her, he said, "I have a house for us, in a village close to Kiev. I brought two passports, and we—"

"You're crazy. I can't—we can't just leave. Maybe we go to the police—"

Make it real to her. He said in a grim voice, "They bought everyone in the police."

"I have to tell my sister," she said weakly. "She'll go crazy if I just leave and—"

"Zaichik, you were right. We can't just leave." They were at the exit, out of time. Pulling her by the arm, he turned her so she could face him. "Here is what we must do."

Beams from a turning car swept over them. She said, "My God. Vanya, you look like an old man!"

"This way nobody can recognize me." He held her by the shoulders. "Listen. They think I'm dead. And that's what we need to do: we need to make them think you're dead, too."

Another car's beams highlighted the tears in her eyes. "But how can I be dead when I'm not?"

He watched the car go down the street. Still no one at either exit. But for how long?

"I know a surgeon. He's indebted to me. His hospital is near the University. I wrote it all down for you." He pressed a slip of paper into her hand. "Keep this in your pocket. He'll take you in. You're pregnant, and he'll take you in and put down in your history that you had a bleed. He'll make it look like you died from bleeding."

Two bright, bluish beams from a turning luxury car slid over the snow, soon to highlight them.

No! Fedot, already here? The patrol must have called him. No, a Korean car. The neighbor upstairs. Avoiding a frozen bump of ice at the turnoff. But time to let her go.

"Zaichik, you must return to the apartment now. Pack a bag and throw it from the balcony. Don't carry it. I'll pick it up. Then walk Bond out again, like the first time. Don't tell anyone anything. I'll pick you up here—" He waved to the street. "—in my car. It's an old, white Ziguli. Now go. Quick."

In one motion, he put her hand on Bond's collar and closed her fingers around it. Another car showed up—everyone coming home from work. He turned her toward the beams. A second before the lights hit them, he stepped away, hunched over the cane.

Walking toward the exit, he glanced back at her pulling Bond away. Molodez Zaichik. The poor dog fussed and struggled to go back under the arch but followed Lena around the corner.

Ivan leaned on the cane and ambled out of the archway, going the other way, back into the yard. The wind picked up, and his cheeks ached from cold by the time he reached the parked Ziguli. He looked up—no cloud cover. Without the clouds, the last of the heat evaporated into open skies, freezing air taking its place.

The starter turned the engine, but it refused to start. Blyad. Hadn't been an hour and already frozen. New spark plugs and synthetic oil helped nothing. Turn the key and pray. Stupid Russian cars. Built for California climate.

At the third turn, the engine sputtered and caught, and Ivan pulled into the street, his breath fogging up the windshield. Pulling alongside the building, he rolled down the window to check the snow underneath the row of balconies, but the white blanket looked pristine.

She hasn't dropped the bag yet. Probably deciding what to take.

Just in case the snow hid the bag, he walked over to the wall of the high-rise, and stomped about in the vague light from the lit windows a few floors above.

Nothing.

The sweep of the beams from an approaching car forced him to pretend he was a bum pissing on the wall. Worked fine this way. Some relief. Body expelling water in the cold.

After the beams swept over, he turned to watch the car swing toward the archway.

Mercedes. Shit. The twerp—it was him!

Ivan's gloved hand dropped into his pocket, fingers around a pistol handle. Had to be Fedot—two other cars like this in the building, but none with a police blinker on the roof. A rare privilege. Emergency vehicles and government officials only.

A swoosh and a loud thump turned Ivan around. A black bundle against the white snow—he snatched it and took off running. A short sprint got him through the archway, to the other side, and into the yard.

There, he folded into a stoop, his cane picking at the icy ground: Fedot stood near his car, talking with two patrolmen who'd come out of their vehicle to meet him.

Bastard. Came out for report? Why not on the phone?

Ivan studied the patrolmen, taking in the AKSU submachine guns on their slings, hanging from their necks. The men looked too casual to be quick. But they wore armor vests over their coats.

Get closer for head shots, and they wouldn't have time to fire.

Ivan ambled forward, flexing his fingers numb from cold. Scarce light from streetlamp demanded minimal distance for accuracy.

Closer—a single miss would give them a chance. Then everyone would die. Lena, Foxy. Everyone.

The thought stopped him in his tracks: Foxy. Promised him a better plan. A shootout here would break his cover.

He looked at the entrance. If she came out now, she'd be safe—they wouldn't bother grabbing her with witnesses around. Fedot would ask his questions. She'd say she's walking the dog. Back in a minute. Except she wouldn't come back. Straight to the hospital with a good explanation: I was walking, and I fell, and someone called the ambulance. Plausible, and much better scenario than three men shot in the yard.

Glancing at the hallway door, Ivan tottered toward the garbage dump, still ignored. Back to sorting through garbage.

The door banged behind him. Ivan turned and saw the patrolmen climb back into their car. Where did Fedot go? That was the hallway door—

Suka—he went inside!

No running. They'd see it. Walk. Lean on the cane. Slow walk, like with the Mexicans.

He crossed in front of the patrol car, watching the men inside from the corner of his eye. One of the cops gave him a disinterested look and went back to talking. Nobody cared about filthy old beggars.

Seven seconds from the sidewalk to the steps. The worst torture. He wanted to run but had to stay bent and feeble in front of the patrol car. Fedot probably in the elevator now. Each second like an hour.

Frantic, he entered the door code wrong—another agonizing delay. The door banged behind him, and he ran up a flight of stairs. The elevator light was still on. Run up? No, too many flights. Quicker to wait.

He shivered through the wait and the elevator ride upstairs, whispering, "Zaichik, bolt the door. Please, bolt the door!"

He slipped out of the elevator, pistol in hand, and swept the empty landing. A dash forward brought him to his apartment door. The key went in without noise, and the lock turned with a soft click. He held his breath as he pulled on the handle, hoping for the hinges to stay quiet. But the door didn't budge.

Bolted from the inside!

In a panicked frenzy, he yanked the handle, abandoned it, and ran up the stairs, toward the roof. He was up a flight when he heard Bond's barking followed by Lena's soul-scorching scream.

46

Moscow, Russia

Ivan lowered himself from the parapet to the balcony railing. Frozen metal threatened his footing, and he tightened his grip on the edge. The cars on the street below looked like toys, their headlights slicing the dusk with beams of light.

Twelve floors to the ground. Fall here, and there would be multiple bodies. Partorg doesn't forgive.

He climbed down past top-floor apartments, moving from railing to railing, slipping and catching himself.

Here—her favorite chair. TV light in the living room. Bond not barking. Why not?

Ivan broke the glass with his pistol and turned the handle. In the bedroom, his heart clenched at the sight of the door: long scratches from Bond's paws covered the entire length of the white surface—Bond must have been locked inside and tried to scratch his way out.

Ivan took two quick steps out of the room and into the hall, looking over the gun's sights, everything eerily quiet. What happened to Bond?

If Fedot had used the key and fooled Bond somehow, Lena would retreat and run further in.

Ivan turned right and pushed his way through swinging double-doors into the gloomy, silent living room, a kitchen area on his left. The beat of his pulse thundered in his ears.

Where were they?

Ahead and to his right, the TV set lay flat on the floor, glowing with gray static. Kicked? Or pulled off the stand—the cable ripped out, but not the cord.

He pivoted toward the coffee table between the TV and the corner sofa. When he saw her, words died in his throat.

"Zaichik—"

Her skin glowed in the TV's sickly glare. She lay across the coffee table, naked from the waist down, her hands zip-tied behind her back, her knitted dress bunched up around her shoulders. The top of her head rested on the floor, next to a lamp shaped like the Eiffel tower—her souvenir from their first trip to Paris.

His knees buckled, and he stumbled forward, his eyes on the dark stain spreading outward from under her hair.

Net. Net. Zaichik!

Kneeling in front of her, he dropped the pistol and slipped his fingers along her warm neck, under her jaw, looking for the artery.

No pulse.

He closed his eyes and pushed his fingers deeper into her skin. Please, he prayed. I'm begging you. God, please.

A long, bellowing cry came from someplace else, an animal cry so visceral he didn't recognize himself when it reverberated off the walls.

Shaking and wheezing, he pulled her dress down and covered the bloody smear on her buttock. He took her ravaged body in his arms and pressed it against his. So warm. Asleep.

Fooled by the hope, he glanced at her lolled head, at her half-opened mouth. No. Oh, God. He pressed his face into her dress. Such terrible silence. Her breath had always been so quick and loud when she slept. Heavier now. The weight of death.

The room walls closed in, folding inward, a mountain of guilt crushing his shoulders. He shuddered into a cry, his face pressed into her chest, the world collapsing.

A cold, judging voice in his head said, "You killed her with your lies. With your fool's hope. A child dead inside. Your child."

He sobbed and groaned, clenching her harder and harder, as if his life and warmth could revive hers.

A muted sound of the elevator doors burst into his mind, and he looked up, compelled by the old instinct.

Hard to focus on anything. Tears made everything blurry.

He wiped his eyes against his sleeve and listened. Two men were talking, stomping around the landing. A change—their voices went from muffled to loud.

They were coming in. Fedot had left the door unlocked. The bastard—he left the door unlocked for *them*.

Rage flooded Ivan's body, charging his muscles for movement. He lowered Lena gently to the sofa and stood up.

Thin voice, like a falsetto, sounded worried in the hall. "—he said wait at least an hour. I'm telling you, his father is a real big shot in the government. If we ruin it, we lose the job or worse."

A thicker voice said, "Stop whining. He's gone, and I'm tired of sitting in the damn car. A few minutes won't change anything."

"He said wait an hour then call it in. It's been less than twenty minutes. He said he'd rip our heads off if we interrupt things."

"You want to sit in the car, go sit in the car. I say we look in the kitchen and eat something. I'm hungry."

Ivan stood in front of the double doors, listening to their steps.

They'd be through the door any second. Here to eat, with her body still warm. Come, he thought. Come here, you hungry bitches. I will feed you.

When the door swung open, a short, thick patrolman stepped in first, his young counterpart on his heels. The thick one saw trouble and twitched, his stubby arms jerking upward as if a current of electricity went through them.

Startled. Pushing back and bumping into his partner still moving forward.

Ivan stood and waited for the stout man to find his wits. Davai. Davai. Go for the weapon.

Finally, the man got over the shock and came to life. His right hand went up and around his bomber jacket, looking for the gun on its sling under his arm. The conical flash hider of his AKS-74U pushed forward.

Ivan lowered his forehead and charged.

Rotate body. Forehead to the face. Shoulder to the chest. Down to the floor.

The man snorted like a pig as his head jerked back and his body toppled backward, thrown to the ground.

Stay on top. The rifle. Finish the rotation. Rifle forward. Safety lever. Cocking handle. Click. Click—Click.

Ivan, now flat on top of the thick man, dug his heels into the floor and arched his back to aim upside down at the younger patrolman, who'd stumbled down the corridor and was still gathering thoughts. The bullets tore up the man's jacket and skin on his throat and face.

Finger out of the trigger guard.

Ivan relaxed his back and dropped back down on the body underneath, swung his legs up, and rolled backward to land on both feet.

Slack in the belt. Trigger.

A shot split the hungry patrolman's meaty face, his right eye intact and still wide with fear and shock. Ivan stood up and looked at the dead bodies, at their gray jackets black with blood, at the bluish fragments of bone sticking out.

Two patrolmen. Multiple shots. Someone in the building would make the call.

Thick cotton in his ears from the gun report kept the silence absolute, only his thoughts loud now. Three bodies in the apartment. Blood and signs of struggle. No time to clean up or hide anything. And no reason to hide. Like Fedot wanted—the boyfriend did it. Fedot—came to kill her. Would sound the alarm with his patrol dead like this. He'd call his papa, and they'd send the dogs after Foxy.

Judgment pounded Ivan's brain with headache and his gut with punches of sickening, guilty thoughts.

It's all your fault. Never had the right to hope. Promised her a family. Foxy was shaking his head for a good reason. You ruined everything.

He took the rifle from the younger cop, the belt sliding easily off the synthetic jacket.

Fix this. You must fix this for those still alive.

An image of Fedot's ugly grimace—what had the twerp said on the phone? 'I walk your dog?'

Ivan swung on his heels and stepped back toward the body to go through the patrolman's pockets. Fingers—something was wrong. Ivan flipped his palms up and stared at pink flesh. The frozen metal sheet on the roof parapet had torn off a lot of skin, his palms burning like he'd touched a hot pan.

You deserve it.

He went man-to-man, pocket-to-pocket and found car keys on the thick one. At the door, he stopped and hesitated.

Don't look back, he thought. Close the door, and don't look back. This is a graveyard now.

The police car sat right outside the main entrance, the patrolmen saving themselves the trouble of taking an extra step in the cold.

Nobody saw him run to the car and climb in. He drove off, lights flashing, and headed for Solntsevo. With every light and every intersection, the exposed flesh on his palms and fingers burned hotter, despite the gloves. He gripped the wheel harder at the image of Lena's body flung over the coffee table.

"Zaichik, I'm so sorry," he whispered. "I had not right to fall in love with you. I'm so sorry."

Tears welled up in his eyes; he brushed them off and revved the engine, accelerating through congested traffic. The siren and lights scared cars out of his way. On Koltsevaya, he went faster, and with increased speed the icy road demanded more of his attention.

The mind-numbing bliss of speed.

On the exit ramp to Borovskoe shosse, he whipped the car to the shoulder to pass a delivery truck. The patrol car fishtailed in the turn but straightened up once he fed the engine more gas.

Wrong time for suicide. Still one more job left to do. Still a chance for Foxy and Laverne.

Off the freeway, he swerved into the opposite lane to pass every slow car and blow past every point of congestion. Panicked honks and beeps sounded from everywhere, oncoming cars swerving left, flashing lights. He kept his foot on the accelerator.

Faster. Faster. Only one chance to finish the bastard clean.

He almost missed Fedot's Mercedes. The twerp was shifting into the right lane to make a turn, still a few blocks away from the restaurant.

Not using the emergency light. Good. Pulling over to give way. We'll meet soon enough, Ivan thought. You'll get yours, you filth.

Ivan flew by, passing a line of cars stuck at the light. Coming around the side street, he pulled into the parking lot and went to the far end to hide the patrol car out of view.

The moment he turned the engine off, the heat leaked out as if sucked through all the small openings by the frozen vacuum outside. Another Russian-made car built for the wrong climate.

Ivan stepped out and traversed the lot toward the usual line of European luxury sedans. He was careful to hide behind the hoods when Fedot's Mercedes pulled in and crept along in search of an empty spot.

Catch him coming out. No gun for this one. Something more appropriate.

In a low stoop, Ivan took soft steps to avoid the crunch of ice and hid in between Fedot's Mercedes and a Lexus next to it. Fedot cracked the door open but didn't come out.

Ivan popped his head up once for a glance inside. The ceiling light lit enough of the interior, a shadow in the passenger seat.

Yes. Here you are, he thought. My best weapon.

He waited, scrunched down. When Fedot opened the door and put out his foot, the warm air escaped in a cloud smelling of booze.

Had his party. Here was more fun. Body forward. Slam the door into his leg. Good connect—anguished cry. Broken leg. Door almost closed.

Ivan swung the door open, leaned in, and said, "Bond. Bond!

Take!" And closed the door.

The gray and black shadow uncoiled from the passenger seat, Fedot's hand flailing for his pistol. Snarling and biting. Ripping and crushing. Clothes and flesh.

Ivan checked the parking lot while Bond doled out the punishment. The car shook and vibrated, but no one noticed the scuffle or heard the muffled cries of agony. When the floundering stopped, Ivan opened the door, glanced inside, and said, "Bond! Stop!" The dog let go of the string of skin in his jaw and retreated back into the passenger seat.

Blood-spray covered the car's beige ceiling and door panels. Fedot, thrown on the wheel, was still alive, gurgling—Bond had torn out his throat. Ivan pulled the twerp back—not much left of his hideous face. Still twitching, though. Dead soon from blood loss alone.

Several cars away, the door of the restaurant squealed open. Ivan flicked off the ceiling light switch and closed the door. A couple dressed in fur coats came out, laughing and speaking in loud voices. They headed straight toward Fedot's car.

Would they notice?

Ivan went back to hide behind the grill of the Mercedes. Visible through the clearance under the car, the woman's fashionable red pumps ground snow with her quick steps.

"It's freezing out here," she said. "Hurry up and open the damn door." Her date mumbled something in response. A jingle of keys came, and then the click of the door locks.

Squeezed under the bumper, Ivan breathed into his jacket to hide the steam. He held his breath when the woman's pumps approached the passenger door of the Lexus parked alongside Fedot's car. She climbed in, and the beams of their headlights turned the snow blue. The car pulled out and drove off.

Ivan came around on bent legs and opened the door. Fedot's hand fell out, a weak pulse still in his wrist.

"Bond. Take," Ivan said, and closed the door again.

The dog, energized by the new command, pulled Fedot's body this way and that, digging into flesh, the car vibrating anew from the bumps and movement.

Next time the door opened, Fedot's head fell out, hanging from a loose thread of spine, barely attached. Bond had eaten the skin and muscle off his face and was still gnawing at tissue.

"Bond. Heel."

The dog lost interest in feeding upon hearing the command and scrambled over the body and into the door opening. Ivan took off Bond's bloodied collar and tossed it inside.

The console screen was blinking with a notification icon—fresh voicemail. Ivan picked up Fedot's bloodied hand and pressed the icon using Fedot's finger.

Partorg's business-like tone came through clear enough.

"Dima, once you are done with your games at his apartment, I want you to stop by the north district tax office. It's the 13th, on Dimintrovskoye. Ask for Zharov—he runs it. He'll help you take over the company. And don't even think about sending one of your boys to do it. I let you play your stupid games with his woman. Now go and make sure we get whatever money he was making there."

The boss, calling the shots from beginning till end.

Before climbing back into the patrol car, Ivan wiped the blood off the dog using a rag from the back seat. They drove off, seated side-by-side, the dog and his master, reunited.

When Bond tried to lick Ivan's cheek, Ivan pushed the snout away and said grimly, "They'll blame you for murder, you know. They'll put the patrol on the boyfriend, but the twerp is your responsibility. You'll have to leave the country for a while."

The dog yelped and went in for another attempt at licking his master. As they returned to Koltsevaya, Bond stared through the windshield at the moving lights, panting with his tongue hanging out. His breath carried a metallic smell of blood.

Time to make the call.

Foxy sounded serene. "What's up?"

"It's me."

A pause. "I can't say I expected you to get back to me so soon. Hang on."

In the background, a familiar voice shouted something over the yapping of the little dogs. Foxy shouted away from the phone, "Mother, don't feed them together. They always fight over it." He came back on. "These Pomeranians are a menace. She loves them and hates them at the same time."

"They need more training. It's easier to love them if they are trained."

"Say, how's Mother Russia treating you?"

The words refused to come out, his throat in a spasm, tears flooding his eyes. Ivan pulled over and forced out a sentence. "She's dead. I—I couldn't save them."

Foxy's voice turned softer. "You hang in there, bud. Go put some of that famous Russian vodka into your system."

Ivan sucked in a long, deep breath. "You should know—I took out Fedot. He hurt her. But it's clean—I didn't kill him. So you are not involved."

"How so?"

"He made a mistake and took my dog. The dog killed him."

"I see." After another pause, Foxy said, "So, what are you going to do next?"

Ivan wiped the tears off with his sleeve and ran his hand through the wet fur on Bond's neck. This time the words came out easily.

"I'm going to do what I know how to do. I have nothing else left."

To learn more about Ivan, Foxy, and Bond, please send an email to the publisher at <u>switchmanpress@gmail.com</u>

Proof

Made in the USA
Charleston, SC
01 December 2015